Kay Adams and Nancy Markey

A Harbor of Deceit:

A Gilded Age Tale of Money, Murder, and Madness

Born and raised in Fayetteville, Arkansas, Kay Adams and Nancy Markey are lifelong friends who teamed up in their sixties to collaborate on a series of nonfiction stories set in the Gilded Age.

This novel is based on the their previously published long-form narrative, "A Gilded Age Tale of Murder and Madness," which can be found at narratively.com and smithsonianmag.com. They enjoy presenting their stories to audiences interested in the Gilded Age era.

Kay is a retired banking executive and an avid bookworm. She makes her home in Fayetteville, Arkansas, and is the mother of two daughters, Laura and Gracie.

Nancy is a labor attorney and historian who resides in Middletown, Rhode Island, with her husband, Joseph, and is the mother of two sons, Jackson and Jonnie.

This is their debut novel.

gildedageauthors.com

ALSO BY KAY ADAMS AND NANCY MARKEY

"A Gilded Age Tale of Murder and Madness"
Narratively.com, November 22, 2022
https://www.narratively.com/p/a-gilded-age-tale-of-murder-and-madness

"A Gilded Age Tale of Murder and Money"
Smithsonianmag.com, November 30, 2022
https://www.smithsonianmag.com/history/a-gilded-age-tale-of-murder-and-money-180981192/

"I Could Have Killed Him Twice"
A Gilded Age Tale of Seduction, Betrayal, and Revenge
Narratively.com, April 28, 2023
https://www.narratively.com/p/i-could-have-killed-him-twice

A Harbor of Deceit

A Gilded Age Tale of Money, Murder, and Madness

Based on a true story

A Harbor of Deceit:

A Gilded Age Tale of Money, Murder, and Madness

Kay Adams and Nancy Markey

Ochre Point Press First Edition 2026

The Library of Congress has catalogued the Ochre Point Press Edition as follows:
Name: Adams, Kay, and Markey, Nancy
Title: A Harbor of Deceit: A Gilded Age Tale of Money, Murder, and Madness/Kay Adams and Nancy Markey.
Library of Congress Control Number: 2025950116
LC record available at http:/lccn.loc.gov/
LC ebook record available at http://lccn.loc.gov/

Cover design assisted by Google Gemini

ochrepointpress.com

Printed in the United States of America

Newport Transfer Company; "1875-Anniversary Parade", VM013_GF4035, ProvLibDigital, accessed 2025/12/14, https://provlibdigital.org/islandora/object/vm013gf4035

We dedicate this book to the memory of Benjamin J. Burton (1826-1885), a visionary whose remarkable perseverance stands as a testament to the power of resilience that resides within the human spirit.

CHAPTER 1
Tuesday, October 6, 1885
Newport, Rhode Island

Mary Stoddard, the self-proclaimed neighborhood watchdog, lived in a tiny cottage on Thomas Street. A squat middle-aged woman with graying auburn curls, piercing hazel eyes, and a ruddy complexion, there was no denying Mary's Irish heritage.

On this rainy morning, she sat perched in a sturdy ladder-back chair that she had scooted as close to her front-facing window as possible. Though her yellowed dimity curtains were drawn back as far as they could go, Mary's field of vision was limited to Thomas Street, a small section of Levin Street, and the rear and backyard of Benjamin J. Burton's property.

Burton's two-and-a-half-story residence loomed impressively over the Levin and Thomas Street intersection. It was one of the largest structures in the neighborhood, dwarfing Mary's humble dwelling. The shake-shingle style building contained the Burton family's living quarters and an adjoining four-family tenement that boasted fashionable two-story bay windows and gabled dormers.

A widower and successful Black entrepreneur, Ben occupied the home with his two daughters: 17-year-old Dora and 25-year-old newlywed Maria Burton Dorsey. Maria's dashing new husband, Allen Waldorf Dorsey, who was enrolled in his final year at the prestigious

University of Pennsylvania medical school, moved in with the family immediately following their June wedding.

The neighborhood was a vibrant and densely populated enclave where a racially diverse community occupied quaint, clapboard-sided houses, some so tightly wedged together that scarcely a few feet of space separated them. Saloons, liveries, grocers, and other family-owned businesses were interspersed among the homes.

Ordinarily, Mary would be out making her rounds, walking the Levin Street beat up and down the narrow, sloping artery that stretched between swanky Bellevue Avenue to the east and Thames Street, the commercial heart of Newport, to the west. But the weather today was preventing her from doing so.

Mary became listless on mornings like these when she was confined to her house with little to hold her interest or keep her occupied. But she perked up when she spotted Idella Traeger, one of Burton's tenants, descending the back stairs of the tenement carrying a wicker laundry basket.

She watched in amusement as Idella—a wisp of a girl at barely 17—began to hang linens in the pouring rain on a wire clothesline that spanned the width of the narrow lot. Idella balanced on the tips of her toes and tossed a bed sheet over the line, almost falling before securing it with pins at either end.

A few minutes later, Maria Dorsey appeared from the kitchen door at the back of the Burton house and strode purposefully toward Idella. She wore a simple calico house dress, the bodice partially hidden by a thin gossamer wrap thrown over her shoulders.

Mary had always thought Maria favored her father with her round face and stocky build, but her lighter complexion and comportment were inherited from her mother. Maria's hair was carefully pinned up in a stylish bun, unprotected from the rain dripping down her face.

Her attention remained fixed on the girls as the two chatted animatedly for a moment before Idella picked up her basket and followed Maria up the staircase, where they disappeared inside the Traegers' second-floor apartment. As there was nothing more to hold Mary's attention, she became drowsy, and her head began to bob.

A loud pop startled Mary awake, causing her to leap up from her chair, sending it sailing to the floor behind her. Although it was not uncommon to hear loud noises above the din of the daily hustle and bustle of the neighborhood—the crack of a wheel breaking away from a carriage or a mischievous child setting off a firecracker—today, the streets were unusually quiet.

Another bang rang out. This time, Mary recognized it as the unmistakable sound of a gunshot. Her eyes widened in alarm. *That's coming from somewhere close.*

Mary hurried out the door onto Thomas Street, paused, and scanned the surrounding area, wondering if anyone else had heard the shots. A bloodcurdling scream pierced the air and echoed throughout the streets, sending chills up Mary's spine.

Before she could react, she heard a woman shriek, "Help, help! My father has shot himself!"

Mary's heart jumped to her throat. *Dear God, that sounds like Maria.*

Making a beeline for the Burton house, she threw open the kitchen door and froze in her tracks. Her hand flew to her mouth to stifle a scream.

On the floor, legs sprawled under the breakfast table lay the thickset body of Ben Burton. His upper torso was slumped against the wall, and his head was tilted slightly downward, chin and cheek resting on his right shoulder. A pistol lay on the floor next to his right hand. Mary rushed to Ben's side and dropped to her knees. Lifting his right hand, she began rubbing it vigorously.

"Mr. Burton, are you hurt?"

She heard Ben gasp once and then fall silent.

Mary closely examined Ben's face. His eyes were open and fixed, void of any sign of life. She gently placed his right hand back on the floor and reached for the upturned teacup that lay next to him. Dipping two fingers into the cup, she moistened them with the liquid still clinging to the inside. Gently, Mary raised her hand to Ben's eyes and swept her fingers softly over each of his eyelids, closing them.

She spotted a trickle of blood on his right temple, barely discernible against his ebony skin. Her attention was drawn to something white protruding from his slightly opened lips.

Good Lord, she thought. *What is in his mouth?*

Fearing it might be brain matter, she recoiled in horror. Leaping to her feet, she heard muffled sobs from the adjoining dining room.

When Mary stepped through the doorway, she found Idella and Maria's little sister, Dora, huddled together at the far end of the table. Idella wrapped her arm around Dora's tiny waist as the young girl wept.

Dora was a slight and delicate child, almost adolescent in conduct and appearance, and so timid that Mary was certain the girl wouldn't say boo to a goose. She carried her mother's Native American ancestry in her high cheekbones, almond-shaped eyes, tawny skin, and long black hair.

"Dora, where is Mr. Dorsey?" Mary demanded. "There ought to be a man down here."

"I think he's still upstairs," Dora whimpered.

Mary left the girls, hurried across the parlor, and marched up the stairs. Bursting unannounced into the first bedroom at the top of the landing, she found Allen Dorsey sitting on the edge of his bed, putting boots on his stocking feet.

"You must come downstairs this instant," Mary implored. "Mr. Burton is injured!"

Allen stood and reached for his coat. The light-skinned Black man was not much taller than Mary and had a slight, sinewy build. Sporting a fashionably trimmed mustache and short, clipped hair that was parted down the middle and slicked back with pomade into finger waves, Allen appeared calm and unflustered.

"I'm coming. I was just getting dressed."

Mary followed Allen down the stairs and watched incredulously as he stepped through the kitchen where Ben lay, glancing only briefly in passing at the body before continuing straight out the kitchen door and into the backyard. Mary hurried after him.

"Where are you going?" she called out as he rounded the corner of the house and out of sight, not bothering to answer.

Ben's stable hand was grooming a horse in the large barn directly across the street from the house on Levin when Allen threw open the door, causing him to jump in surprise.

"Go get a doctor now!" Allen shouted. "Mr. Burton is injured." Before the man could react, Allen was gone.

Allen left the stables, hurried back across Levin Street, and reentered the house through the front door. As he approached the kitchen, he caught sight of a man unknown to him leaning over Ben's body while Mary stood nearby. The stranger held Ben's arm in his hands, pressing Ben's wrist with his fingers in search of a pulse.

"Leave him be," Allen barked, prompting the delivery man—who had abandoned his wagon in the street and rushed inside in response to Maria's cries—to drop Ben's wrist and back away. "I have sent for a doctor. No one is to touch anything."

The delivery man nodded to Mary and quietly left the room. Allen circled the kitchen perimeter and positioned himself next to the back door.

***

The stable worker navigated up Levin Street, weaving his way around the neighbors who had emerged from the comfort of their homes and businesses upon hearing Maria's cries and were heading down the street to investigate. Dodging abandoned horses, empty carriages, and delivery wagons that littered the muddy street, he flailed his arms wildly to flag down a police officer already making his way to the scene.

"Officer!" he yelled out, pointing toward the Burton house. "Fetch a doctor. Boss is hurt!"

The police officer waved him off. "I've already called it in," he said without breaking his stride. Alarmed by the steady stream of gawking onlookers making their way inside the Burton house, he quickened his pace.

When he entered the house, the officer spotted a frantic Mary Stoddard standing in the kitchen doorway, blocking the entrance.

She called out to him, "Thank God you are here! I do not know who half of these people are. They have no business being here!"

"Settle down, ma'am," the officer reassured her as he peered over her shoulder at the body on the floor. "I will take charge now."

Mary remained agitated, hesitant to relinquish her post. "I asked Idella to take Dora upstairs to get her away from these hooligans. I finally convinced Mr. Dorsey to take his wife up there to join them. I have been standing guard over him, trying to keep folks away, but they keep coming," she said, her voice breaking before bursting into tears. "I want to go home," she sobbed.

The officer escorted her out the back door before returning to the kitchen to secure the scene.

Within minutes, a carriage transporting Dr. Henry Turner, Newport's long-serving medical examiner, and driven by Police Captain

Edward Hammond, rounded the corner in front of the post office and onto Levin.

Dr. Turner elbowed the captain. "Look there," he said, pointing at the people milling about in front of the Burton residence. "It didn't take long for the word to spread."

"Death attracts morbid curiosity," Hammond responded knowingly.

The coach rolled to a stop in the middle of the intersection. The spry forty-nine-year-old captain hopped out and went around to open the door for the elderly physician. Dr. Turner gripped the ivory knob of his wooden cane to steady himself as he stepped onto the street. The portly old doctor closely resembled the Thomas Nash illustrations of Jolly Old St. Nick, with his head chock-full of snow-white hair and a beard and mustache to match.

"Make way, make way," Hammond called out as he and the doctor pushed through the circus of people in the street.

They crossed the threshold into the home and found the parlor filled to capacity. A line had formed in the dining room just outside the kitchen, like patrons at the theater waiting to get their tickets for the show.

The police officer had braced himself in the doorway, his arms and legs spread wide like a fully uniformed version of Di Vinci's Vitruvian Man. He barricaded the entrance, shouting, "Get back!"

Captain Hammond stepped up to the police officer's side, putting his hand to his billy club. The lanky Civil War veteran, whose sallow, pockmarked face and dark, deep-set eyes accentuated his grim countenance, was accustomed to being in command. He was the longest-serving officer in the Newport police department, appointed to the force in 1865 upon his return from the war.

"Order, Order!" he shouted, quieting the mob. "I know you are all concerned about Mr. Burton, but we have work to do. Go on and go about your day."

Most of the crowd began to reluctantly disperse, except for close friends and family, who were allowed to remain. Those who resisted were taken out of the house by the police officer.

In the meantime, Dr. Turner entered the kitchen, propped his cane against the wall, and bent over Ben's body. He reached down and placed his fingers on Ben's neck in search of a pulse, but found no sign of life.

When Hammond and the police officer returned to the kitchen, Dr. Turner was pleased to see Coroner Francis Stanhope had joined them.

"Stanhope, I am glad you are here. I need to examine him. Let us move his body to the table."

Captain Hammond instinctively reached down to pick up the small .22 caliber revolver to secure it. He noted there were four rounds of ammunition in the chamber.

Coroner Stanhope reached into the inner pocket of his suit coat and removed a small notepad and pencil stub. He quickly sketched out a diagram of the room, scratching out a few notes regarding the position of the body and the approximate distance between the pistol and Ben's hand. He logged where each chair sat around the table, paying particular attention to the one closest to Ben that was toppled over.

The officer removed a breakfast dish containing a half-eaten sweet roll and carefully moved the table to the center of the room. It took the combined effort of all four men to lift Ben's two-hundred-and-fifty-pound body and place it on the table.

Dr. Turner began by examining Ben's head. He ran his fingers over Ben's scalp until he felt a sticky, matted area of blood near the right ear.

"There," he remarked as he leaned in closely to examine the area. He picked through the hair until he discovered a small entry wound surrounded by a scant ring of abraded skin about an inch above and a little behind his ear. He probed the rest of the scalp. "I can't find an exit wound."

"I'm not surprised," Hammond interjected, "given the small caliber of the weapon."

Turner then turned his attention to a gunpowder burn he spotted on Ben's vest. He unbuttoned the vest and discovered a fist-sized blood stain that had saturated the white shirt Ben wore underneath. He pulled the shirt open to expose his chest and found another entry wound located slightly to the right and just above the left nipple.

"This looks like the fatal shot," the doctor commented.

Coroner Stanhope turned to Captain Hammond. "What do we know so far about the circumstances of his death?"

"It was called in as a suicide," Hammond replied.

The police officer spoke up. "Yes, sir, I was the one who called it in. That is what the daughter was shouting in the streets."

"If that is the case, he must have shot himself first in the head," Turner concluded as he examined the chest wound.

Turner then looked at Ben's face and, for the first time, noticed a white object protruding from Ben's slightly opened mouth. He placed his fingers on Ben's lips and spread them apart.

"How curious, it looks to be bread," he remarked offhandedly. "Some caught up in his teeth, the rest unchewed, it seems."

Coroner Stanhope carefully recorded the odd detail in his notebook before snapping it closed.

"Looks like a clear case of suicide to me," Hammond declared.

"Not so fast, captain," Stanhope responded. "We need to speak with the family first."

"That will be a waste of your time," Hammond smugly replied. "Be my guest, but the evidence seems clear to me. We have the gun, two shots fired—"

Stanhope interrupted him, questioning, "Does it seem likely that he could shoot himself twice?"

"During the war, I witnessed soldiers get shot in the head, get right back up, and go back to fighting," Hammond responded confidently. "In my opinion, if a person is set on killing themself, they will keep trying until they get the job done. I am marking the cause of death in my report as a suicide."

The police officer bravely turned to address Coroner Stanhope. "I believe you will find the family upstairs if you still want to talk to them," he offered to Hammond's clear annoyance.

Dr. Turner washed his hands in the sink and retrieved his cane before motioning for Coroner Stanhope to follow him. The two men left the kitchen and headed upstairs while Captain Hammond stayed with the body.

Turner and Stanhope entered the front upstairs bedroom, where they found Maria, Dora, and Allen. Maria was lying in the center of the bed while her husband sat on the edge beside her, fanning her with a folded-up newspaper. Dora sat in an armchair in the corner, her head bowed as if in prayer.

"I've just come from examining your father," Dr. Turner began. "Mr. Stanhope and I would like to offer our condolences. Your father was a fine man."

Dora covered her face with her hands and began sobbing. Maria rolled over on her side, her back to Turner.

"Oh, Father!" she cried as she buried her head in a pillow.

Dr. Turner looked back at Stanhope, and the men respectfully held back for a few moments.

"I am sorry to do this, but I need to ask you some questions," Turner began. "Can someone tell me what happened?"

***

As Hammond stood vigil in the kitchen, he was startled by a commotion coming from the front of the house.

"Where is he? Where is he?" a woman shouted frantically. Mrs. Emily Burton, the widow of Ben's brother, burst in, rushing past the police officer Hammond had relegated to manning the front door. She charged into the center of the parlor, the hem of her cloak flying behind her.

"Where is my brother-in-law?" she bellowed.

Idella Traeger timidly spoke up, pointing past the dining room into the kitchen. "He's in there."

Hammond positioned himself in front of the table to shield Ben's body as the determined woman approached.

Emily stormed into the kitchen. "Is it true? What has happened here?" she demanded to know.

"It appears to be suicide," Captain Hammond responded.

Emily scowled at him disbelievingly. "Ben Burton? Kill himself? That is preposterous!" she exclaimed. "No man as singular as Ben would do such a thing! Out of my way, let me see him!"

To avoid a confrontation, Hammond stepped aside. Emily Burton was an imposing and formidable woman, both in size and temperament, one he did not wish to tangle with. He knew plenty of widows with sweet dispositions, but Emily Burton was not one of them.

Taller than most women and with stern features, she could have easily been mistaken for a man, save for her feminine attire. Emily was known for offering her opinions, often without solicitation, which led to a reputation in the community as a pot stirrer.

Emily stepped over to the table and stood next to Hammond. She was quiet, her eyebrows furrowed as she examined Ben's exposed chest before turning to face the captain.

"What makes you think it is a suicide?" she asked quizzically.

"I'm not at liberty to discuss the matter," Hammond stated matter-of-factly.

Undeterred, Emily pressed him. "Are you saying he shot himself in the chest?"

"It certainly appears that way," Hammond answered, relieved Emily hadn't asked him about the head wound.

"Where are his daughters?" asked Emily.

"The medical examiner and coroner are upstairs interviewing them."

"Are they conducting an inquest?"

Exasperated, Hammond raised his voice ever so slightly. "Mrs. Burton, these questions are better directed to the coroner. Why don't you go into the parlor and wait with the others."

Getting nowhere with the captain, Emily marched back to the parlor, ignoring the friends and family gathered there, to question the police officer stationed at the door.

"You, there! Does this appear to you to be a suicide?"

The hapless policeman naively entertained the question. "I suppose it is unusual for someone to shoot themself twice, but the captain seems pretty certain."

Emily exploded, screeching, "Two shots? He shot himself twice?" Turning on her heels, she stomped back to the kitchen to confront the captain.

"Why didn't you tell me there were two shots?" she demanded angrily. "Show me! Where is the second shot?"

Cornered, Hammond pointed at the wound above Ben's right ear. "It's right here," he said, snidely adding, "I don't know how you missed it."

Emily cut her eyes at Hammond. "So, you are telling me he shot himself twice? What kind of detective are you? Don't you think that someone else might have had a hand in this … that Ben could have been murdered?"

Hammond's face flushed with anger. "Madam, I will have you know that during my twenty years on the force, I have conducted hundreds of investigations. I don't have to answer to you."

Undaunted, Emily snapped back, "We will see about that!"

***

Coroner Stanhope moved closer to the corner where Dora sat. For forty of his sixty-plus years, Stanhope had served in a number of prominent positions in the city of Newport and was respected by all. Broad and stout in stature, he sported a balding horseshoe hairline and a closely cropped white beard. He was smartly attired in a gray wool frock suit, which added to his distinguished and confident appearance. It was vital for him to be present during the medical examiner's interview to ensure consistency in their respective reports. He positioned himself to carefully observe and easily hear the family's account of the morning.

Allen was the first to speak. "I was asleep in bed, so I cannot attest to the details."

"Did you not hear the shots?" asked Dr. Turner.

Allen shook his head. "I heard two loud bangs, but I thought it was doors slamming, so I paid them no mind."

Turner nodded, "I see. So, at what point did you realize something was amiss?"

"It wasn't until I heard Maria scream," answered Allen. "As I said, I was asleep in my bed," quickly adding, "I have been ill."

Turner turned his attention to Maria. Sympathetic to her distraught state, he gently asked, "Mrs. Dorsey, are you able to speak with me?"

Maria rolled onto her back. "I think so, if my husband will help me sit up."

Allen wedged one arm under Maria and lifted her into a sitting position while he stacked the bed pillows behind her. Maria scooted herself back and rested against the pillows.

"Mrs. Dorsey, can you tell me what you know?"

Maria dabbed at her eyes with a handkerchief. "I was down street at the post office when it happened. Father was still in the kitchen eating breakfast when I left."

"Did you have any conversation with him this morning?"

"No, I hadn't spoken to him since last night," she answered, her voice faltering.

Allen gently patted her hand. "Maria, you must tell them what your father said last night."

Maria looked to her husband for encouragement, and Allen

nodded his head.

"When Father came home, he called Dora and me downstairs and said he had something to talk to us about." Maria kept her eyes downcast. "He told us we needed to look out for ourselves. That he did not think he would be around much longer."

Stanhope interrupted, "What did you think he meant by that?"

"I thought he was referring to his health. He has not been well lately. He hasn't been the same since he fell from his wagon in May." Tears began to stream down her face. "I didn't think he meant …" Maria began before her voice trailed off.

"Take all the time you need, Mrs. Dorsey."

Allen reached for her hand and squeezed it gently. "Darling, you couldn't have known."

Maria gripped Allen's hand and continued, "He said he was not worried about me because I was married. But he regretted he had not encouraged Dora to take up a trade, like dressmaking, so that she could support herself. He said he had been too indulgent with us since mother died, but he had done his best." She added, "He was so low-spirited, more so than I have ever known him to be."

Dr. Turner turned his attention to Dora. He was struck by her fragility and softened his tone.

"Miss Burton, are you able to answer some questions?"
Dora said barely above a whisper, "I'm not sure I can help you … I don't know anything."

Dr Turner smiled sympathetically. "Why don't we start with where you were when the shots were fired?"

Dora lowered her head. "I must have been in the attic. Maria had sent me there to get some blankets to take to Father's room. I was just coming down the attic stairs when I heard Maria scream."

"When was the last time you saw your father?"

Dora welled up. "When I went to get a broom from the closet downstairs to sweep my room, I saw him sitting at the kitchen table."

"Did you speak to him?" Turner asked gently.

Dora shook her head. "No, his back was to me. If I had only known!" she wailed.

Maria leaned forward and extended her arms toward Dora, inviting her to embrace. "Come here, dear."

Dora ran to her sister's arms and buried her face on her chest.

Dr. Turner looked at Stanhope. "I think we have all we need here," he said. He bowed his head to Maria and Allen. "Again, may I offer you our most sincere condolences for your loss."

***

Muttering under her breath, *I will get to the bottom of this,* Emily Burton left the kitchen in a huff and went in search of her nieces. Climbing the stairs, she caught sight of Dora coming out of Maria's bedroom.

She rushed to her, arms outstretched. "Oh, my dear Dora! What happened?"

Dora turned and held up her hand to discourage her aunt's advance. "Don't ask me, Aunt Emily. I don't know anything about it."

"Where is your sister?"

Dora pointed to the closed bedroom door, then turned and continued down the hall to her bedroom.

Emily tried to turn the doorknob, but it was locked. She tapped lightly on the door and called out, "Maria? It's your Aunt Emily. May I come in?"

She heard the lock jiggle, and the door opened inward just enough for Allen's face to be seen through the crack.

"Mrs. Burton, Maria is resting. She is in no condition to speak with you right now. Perhaps later."

Before he could close the door, Emily thrust her foot into the doorway. "Mr. Dorsey, I need to speak to my niece."

Allen scowled. "As I said, now is not a good time."

Maria's weak voice called out from inside the room, "Howard … Howard needs to be told."

To divert Emily's attention from his wife, Allen suggested, "Mrs. Burton, would you be so kind as to go to the telegraph office and wire Howard about his father's passing? I don't believe Maria should be left alone."

Emily pulled her foot back. The thought of her dear nephew alone in New York City, not knowing his father was dead, tugged at her heartstrings.

"Of course, Howard must be told, and I am the one who should tell him," she said, as Allen nodded in agreement while closing the door.

***

As she stepped onto Levin Street, Emily turned to her left and noticed Dr. Turner and Coroner Stanhope standing under the overhang of the attached tenement entrance. They were deep in discussion with a young man she recognized as Patrick J. Galvin.

The attractive 25-year-old attorney was a popular and familiar face in the community. His magnetic charm and impeccable good manners were only surpassed by his excellent reputation as a vigorous and outspoken advocate for Newport's poor and underrepresented residents. With fair skin, a strong jaw, light eyes, and thick sandy blonde hair, the well-spoken and quick-witted lawyer was a sought-after speaker at political and civic events.

Emily pulled the hood of her cloak over her head and stood motionless to eavesdrop on their conversation.

"With all due respect, Dr. Turner," Galvin posed, "wouldn't holding an inquest be the more prudent course of action?"

Emily's ears perked up.

Turner responded, "To what end? We questioned the family. They reported their father was despondent last night, to the point of telling them he wasn't going to be around much longer. I've known this family for years. I have no reason to doubt the veracity of their statements. Why would I subject the family to the ordeal of a formal inquest?"

Galvin looked at Stanhope. "Are you in agreement?"

Stanhope acquiesced. "Ben Burton did not have an enemy on this island, or the entirety of the state for that matter, so who would have wanted to see him dead? We are all familiar with the scandalous nature of suicide. Isn't that enough for the family to bear?"

A delivery wagon driven by a young man rattled to a stop on the street right before Emily, drowning out the men's conversation. He hopped off the wagon.

Annoyed by the interruption, Emily barked, "What do you want, boy?"

The delivery boy cowered. "I have Mr. Burton's potatoes, ma'am."

"Young man, don't you know what has happened here? Mr. Burton is dead!"

The boy stepped back, shocked by the news. "I didn't know, I swear I didn't know. I was only told to deliver the potatoes. Mr. Burton said he wanted them in time for his dinner."

"Take them round back," she ordered, turning her body to point toward the Thomas Street entrance. As she did so, she saw that Turner, Stanhope, and Galvin had begun walking away.

After dismissing the delivery man, Emily walked up the street toward the telegraph office on Bellevue. She replayed what she had overheard the men say in her mind.

Despondent? Ben? Their description did not align with the jovial, good-natured man she knew. *And who, in heaven's name, would insist on potatoes being delivered in time for a meal he did not intend to eat?*

She was anxious to speak with Howard about it.

Chapter 2
Monday, October 5, 1885
The Night Before

Sitting atop the box seat of his largest transfer wagon, Ben Burton chirruped to his pair of chestnut draught horses as he tightened his grip on the reins and slowly navigated the turn from Narragansett onto Ochre Point Avenue. A low-hanging haze blanketed his surroundings. As Ben passed the entrance to Edgewater Cottage, the outline of the home's mansard roofline with ornately fashioned iron railings set against the smoky night sky reminded him of a paper-cut silhouette in a shadow box.

Ben relished the solitude on nights such as these when the crowds of the summer season had mostly departed and the streets of Newport were clear of late-night revelers. It was here where Ben often found his escape—if only for the moment—to be alone with his thoughts.

He narrowed his round, dark eyes as he peered through the mist at the imposing wooden villas that lined the narrow street like soldiers standing in formation to greet him. Ben had recently heard that Cornelius Vanderbilt II had emerged victorious in a heated bidding war over the most desirable prize of them all: a cliffside mansion at the end of Ochre Point known as The Breakers. It was no secret to him, or anyone else for that matter, that the Vanderbilts were standing toe to toe with the Astors to conquer New York society. Now, the contest was spilling over into Newport, where the Astors owned the impressive Beechwood estate on Bellevue.

Though he already enjoyed the status of being the favorite expressman among the wealthy elite who summered in his fair city, Ben was keenly aware of what adding the Vanderbilt family to his list of well-heeled clients would mean to him and the future of his business. Reeling in a big fish was better than chasing minnows if he wanted to slow down anytime soon.

Ben slowed his team as the cone-shaped turret of Vinland's large gatehouse came into view. An attendant dressed in an emerald-green livery appeared from within. Ben called his team to a halt in front of the extravagantly decorated wrought iron entrance.

"Good thing I heard you coming, Mr. Burton," the gatekeeper called out as he rushed to unlock the gate. "Mighty soupy out tonight."

"That it is," Ben chuckled, watching the young man grunt and strain under the weight as he pulled the gate open for Ben to enter.

"Your men ought to be about finished with the crates by now."

"Then I am right on time," Ben said with a smile.

"The season flew by in a blink, didn't it, sir?"

"That it did," Ben nodded in agreement. "Busy year, one of my best."

"I believe it," the gatekeeper replied, dismissing himself and walking back toward the gatehouse.

As Ben guided the wagon through the opening, he heard the familiar sound of another horse and wagon approaching. Looking over his shoulder, Ben raised a hand in recognition of the driver of the single-horse two-wheeled wagon as it passed. He recognized the small rig as belonging to a newcomer in the express business.

His mind traveled back to his early years in Newport when he had been the newcomer, and the tourist trade was still in its infancy. Ben recalled his struggles to get a foothold in a small marketplace that was already overcrowded with well-established competitors who were eager to undermine him at every turn.

He winced at the memories of his harnesses being cut, his signature green wagons being damaged or burned, and his horses being poisoned or maimed. It seemed they would stop at nothing to thwart the success of an enterprising Black man. But they had sorely underestimated his resolve.

Ben shook his head to rid himself of the unpleasant recollection. He reminded himself he had not only persevered but had flourished. For almost thirty years, Ben owned and operated one of the most respected and profitable express and transfer businesses on Aquidneck Island. And that was just the first of his many successful enterprises.

Ben guided his team under the arched red sandstone overhang of the mansion's service entrance. His two employees were stationed beside a variety of open shipping crates. As Ben crawled down from his seat, a plump middle-aged woman attired in the head housekeeper's uniform appeared at the service door. Pushing away messy curls from her face, she smiled broadly as she approached Ben.

He tipped his hat. "Good morning!"

"And the rest of the day to yourself," the housekeeper cheerfully replied in her sing-song Irish brogue. "I believe all is prepared and as it should be."

Ben laughed heartily, his broad, round shoulders bouncing. "Madam, I can always depend on you. Do you have the inventory lists?"

Together, as they did every year, they expeditiously reviewed the contents of each container before his men nailed shut and numbered the boxes as Ben instructed.

After sealing the final crate, Ben helped his men stack the load in the wagon's bed. The men secured the crates with heavy rope to prevent them from shifting en route to the docks and climbed up on the back of the wagon when they were finished. Ben added his signature attesting to the contents and count.

"There now," the housekeeper declared as she watched Ben place the papers in an oil silk pouch and tie it tight with a piece of leather string. "Safe and sound 'til you bring it all back to us next season. Now, off with the lot of you."

Ben bid the housekeeper goodbye and turned to climb up to his box seat. He glanced toward the ocean and caught a glimpse of the waning fingernail moon rising across the water's horizon. He had been too immersed in his work to notice that the wind had picked up, clearing the fog. His trip to the Long Wharf in Newport Harbor would now be easier than expected.

"Hang on tight, boys," he called out as he jiggled the reins. With a "git up," the horses jerked into action, moving the wagon forward.

Ben maneuvered the horses into a wide right turn off Narragansett and back onto Bellevue Avenue. He listened with amusement as his men argued over which of the mansions was the grandest as he traveled the short distance to his next stop at the Ocean House Hotel. They were too young to remember when there was no Bellevue Avenue lined with luxurious villas, but instead just a dirt road surrounded by windswept meadows.

Ben eased the wagon toward the loading area directly behind the Ocean House Hotel. The old yet elegant resort was once the most desirable lodging in Newport, attracting wealthy patrons in droves. Though its rooms remained at capacity every summer season, the old guard had moved on to privately owned cottages, leaving vacancies for the next generation of vacationers. Yet, the hotel remained the hub of fine dining and entertainment in Newport.

As he pulled up to the loading spot, Ben could see through the etched glass doors of the rear entrance directly into the well-appointed lobby. He was surprised to see so many employees still milling about the property. The Ocean House would soon close for the off-season, so he assumed most of the staff had already been relieved of their duties for the year.

Ben spotted a bellman pushing a gleaming brass porter trolley down the hall.

"Get moving," he instructed his men. "Go open the door and help that fellow."

"Good evening, Mr. Burton," the bellman called out as he exited the hotel.

"And to you as well," Ben politely replied, motioning for his men to hurry about their business.

After the trunks were added to the wagon load, the bellman hurried down the steps, waving an envelope.

"Sorry, Mr. Burton, I almost forgot to give this to you."

Ben took the envelope from him, tore it open, and removed a check. He returned the empty envelope to the bellman and tucked the check in his pants pocket.

"How is Dorsey doing?" the bellman inquired with a smile. "We sure could have used his help this season, but he made it clear he wasn't going to work after he got married. I sometimes catch a glimpse of him and the missus when they are out riding in one of your carriages."

Ben gritted his teeth and checked himself before he said something he might later regret. The young bellman did not deserve to be on the receiving end of his frustration.

"Tell him to drop by for a visit before we close up," the bellman continued. "That is, if he is still in town. Has he left for school yet?"

Ben frowned. While Allen may have informed his former co-workers of his intention not to work over the summer, it had come as an unwelcome surprise to Ben. Just hours earlier, he and Maria had engaged in a heated argument over the ballooning household expenses. The couple had led him to believe that by the end of September, they would be moving to Philadelphia so Allen could complete his final year of medical school. Yet, they inexplicably remained firmly entrenched in his home. Ben had made it clear to his daughter that it was time for the Dorseys to leave and make their own way.

"No, he's still here," Ben responded flatly as he tightened the reins and set off for the Long Wharf.

Ben steered the wagon a hundred yards back down Bellevue, passing his office before reaching the intersection with Levin Street, where he had made his home for the last three decades.

He slowed to make a sharp westward turn onto the narrow, downward-sloping connector. From his vantage point, the glow from the gas streetlamps bathed the neighborhood below him in an otherworldly, almost celestial hue.

To his right sat #35, the first house Ben had purchased in Newport. Though it was a rather modest, two-story timber frame dwelling, it was where he and his wife, Rosanna's, eleven children were born. It was also the place where eight of those children had died from consumption before reaching adulthood.

Just a few houses down and across the street sat the current home he had built for Rosanna. Ben's mouth curled into a smile as he pictured how her face had lit up when he surprised her with the blueprints of the house he was planning to build. His smile faded as he looked at his home's darkened windows. His wife had died before the house he had built for her was completed.

Ben pulled back on the reins to slow the team as he crossed Thomas Street. On the same side of the street, just past the intersection, sat a tiny unfinished cottage barely twenty feet in width that Ben was building for Dora and himself. Although he had intended to spend his remaining years in the big house, the fire last year had changed everything.

Ben was haunted by the fire and its aftermath, often reliving that night. His pulse raced as he recalled watching helplessly as angry flames ripped through the rafters of his massive barn. All his omnibuses, carriages, wagons, feed, hay, horses, and equipment used to operate his business ventures had been stored in the blazing structure.

Ben closed his eyes. He could almost feel the blast of heat that had knocked him to the ground when he had thrown open the stable doors. Again and again, he had run into the inferno to save his beloved horses before becoming overcome by the smoke and collapsing just outside the barn. Despite his heroic efforts, he only managed to save a few before the building collapsed, a total loss.

The fire not only destroyed the building and its contents but also took with it the decades of sacrifice, hard labor, and capital Ben had poured into creating and growing his multiple enterprises. Before the fire, people had referred to him as the wealthiest Black man in Rhode Island.

Now, he thought, *at 59 years of age, I am deep in debt and right back where I started … headed to the docks to meet the 2 o'clock steamer.*

Chapter 3
Wednesday, October 7, 1885
The Day After

Maria started down the staircase and spotted Howard asleep on the sofa in the parlor. She had heard him come in during the night, but when she sat up to get out of bed, Allen placed his hand on her arm to stop her. He told her it had been a long day for everyone, and it would be better for Maria to deal with her brother in the morning. Unable to sleep, she tossed and turned until daybreak, when she slipped out of the bedroom without disturbing Allen.

Howard was not fully asleep as his sister tiptoed through the parlor to the kitchen. He was still in a state of shock and had barely slept. He was anxious to speak with Maria. He was not ready to accept that his father had killed himself without learning more.

Maria pushed the kitchen table against the wall and arranged the chairs back to their usual places. When she looked up, she saw her brother standing in the doorway.

"Oh, Howard," she cried as she rushed to his side, "Father is dead! It was all so terrible."

Her eyes looked tired and swollen. His heart ached for his sisters. He could only imagine how devastated Dora would be. As the baby of the family, Dora and his father had always shared a special bond.

Howard motioned toward the dining room table. "Come sit with me so that we might talk."

Maria nodded and followed Howard into the dining room. He pulled two chairs out from under the table and waited patiently for Maria to take her seat before taking his own.

"I hardly know what to think," he haltingly began. "Is it true? Did Father kill himself?"

Maria looked down at her lap and fidgeted with her apron. "Yes," she said softly. "I can scarcely believe it myself."

Howard shook his head in confusion. "When I was here for your wedding in June, he seemed fine. His usual self. Did something happen?"

"The only thing I know is his health has been declining."

"What do you mean, Maria? Father was rarely ill."

"Don't you remember, Howard?" Maria prompted. "At the wedding, he was still recovering from his fall. Since then, he has been plagued with a stomach ailment. As I told the coroner, the night before Father died, he told Dora and me that he didn't expect to be around much longer. We thought he meant he was sicker than we knew."

Howard interrupted, "If he was so ill, why didn't you reach out to me?"

"We planned to write to you if his health didn't improve." She paused and drew in a deep breath. "Had we only known what he was planning …"

Howard gently placed his hand on his sister's arm. "You could not have prevented this. You should not blame yourself."

A look of relief washed over Maria's face. She reached inside the cuff of her sleeve, withdrew a handkerchief, and dabbed at her eyes.

"I know you and Father have had your differences, but he loved you and spoke of you often."

Howard choked back his tears, grateful for his sister's kind words. His thoughts turned to his youngest sister.

"And Dora? How is she faring?"

Maria looked at Howard knowingly. "Drowning in grief like the rest of us. We have been watching over her."

"Where was she when it happened?"

"I was out of the house when it happened," Maria volunteered, "but Dora was in the attic and says she didn't hear anything."

"Was Allen home?" Howard asked cautiously.

Maria nodded wearily. "Yes, but he was sick in bed. He has been ill for several days."

"Well, I am here now," he reassured her. "What can I do to help? I imagine there is much we need to accomplish today."

"Yes," Maria agreed. "We must plan for Father's homegoing. I've asked Reverend Van Horne to conduct the service."

Howard slowly rose from his chair. "When is it to take place?"

"Tomorrow morning. At Union Congregational Church."

***

Reverend Mahlon Van Horne put down his fountain pen and tried to rub the weariness from his blurry eyes. He was drafting the eulogy for Ben Burton's funeral in the morning, and the task weighed heavily on his mind. Using his thumb and forefinger, he smoothed his bushy, thick mustache and moistened his lips with his tongue. At 45, the clergyman's cropped haircut and broad forehead accentuated the premature gray that had sprung up around the temples of his coal-black hair.

Van Horne had served as a spiritual advisor to the Burton family since his arrival in Newport in 1869, when he assumed the pastorate at the Union Congregational Church. He could always count on Ben to support the church financially and by taking on an active role in the church's leadership. The two often worked side by side to bring attention to the pressing social issues adversely affecting not only their community but Newport as a whole. Their efforts to advance the rights and welfare of Black citizens and their children had resulted in Van Horne's election as the first person of color to the Newport School Committee.

He closed his eyes and pictured the day Ben spoke at a gathering last March during Van Horne's campaign for a seat in the Rhode Island State legislature … a race he won, becoming the first Black man to serve in the position. He smiled as he recalled Ben rallying the audience, his exuberance and zeal contagious to all around him. The memory created an ache in the back of the Reverend's throat as he swallowed his grief.

For the next hour, words poured effortlessly from Van Horne's pen, a bevy of emotions spilling onto the pages. His dark, expressive eyes clouded when his thoughts turned to the circumstances surrounding

Ben's death.

His mind drifted back to the events of yesterday. When he received word of Ben's death, he had rushed to the Burton house to provide spiritual comfort to the family. He was well acquainted with Ben's children—Howard, Maria, and Dora—as their clergyman and family friend.

Van Horne heard a rapping at the front door. He stood and rolled his head from shoulder to shoulder to ease the stiffness in his neck. He crossed the parlor and opened the door, surprised to find Allen Dorsey standing on the stoop.

The reverend greeted him warmly. "Good evening, Allen," he said, waving his guest inside. "Come in, come in."

Allen stepped into the parlor. "Thank you, Reverend. I am sorry to disturb you, but Maria realized earlier this evening that she had not paid your salary this month," Allen explained, awkwardly extending a handful of neatly folded bank notes toward him.

Ben was the church's treasurer and, as such, was responsible for paying Van Horne's monthly salary, a task he had recently delegated to Maria. Allen's hand remained extended for a few seconds before Van Horne hesitantly reached out to accept the money.

Van Horne had known Allen Dorsey for several years. They were both graduates of Lincoln University, a prestigious Black college in Pennsylvania founded prior to the Civil War. Although Van Horne had attended Lincoln many years before Allen's time there, he had closely followed the young man's academic achievements by reading the accolades regularly published in the Alumni Association magazine.

Allen frequently attended worship services at the church during the summer seasons while he was in Newport working as a bellman. When Allen began courting Maria, Van Horne thought they were a good match. As their courtship blossomed, he could not have been more pleased and gladly officiated at their wedding ceremony held in the parlor of Ben's home in June.

Van Horne was impressed with Allen's intellectual acumen and exceptional musical talent. He believed Allen had unlimited potential, was of solid character, and would be a good addition to the Burton Family. He prayed the young man would be successful in his relentless pursuit of becoming one of the first Black surgeons in the country.

"Thank you, Allen," Van Horne graciously replied. "But given the circumstances, you could have waited to pay me."

"To be frank, it was nice to have an excuse to get out of the house," Allen admitted sheepishly. "The constant stream of people coming by to offer their condolences has been rather overwhelming. Not to mention the abundance of funeral cakes and biscuits."

"Yes, Ben was a beloved figure in our community."

"Maria and Dora have mostly kept to their beds, leaving me to receive the visitors and respond to the newspaper reporter inquiries," Allen explained. "As I have not fully recovered from my recent illness, it has left me quite weary."

Van Horne nodded sympathetically. He could only imagine the atmosphere in the Burton home. "When I dropped by the house earlier today, Maria was in her bedroom and asked not to be disturbed. Dora was nowhere to be seen, but I was able to speak briefly with Howard. Tell me, how are the girls doing?"

Allen sighed, shrugging his shoulders slightly. "As well as can be expected, I suppose." He added, "As you know, Howard has not been home since the wedding, so he was unaware of the changes in Mr. Burton that we have witnessed over the past several months. It has made it difficult for him to come to grips with his father taking his own life."

Van Horne tilted his head, puzzled by Allen's comment. "Changes? I don't understand."

"Mr. Burton has not been well," Allen explained. "From what I have observed, he has also been depressed, even despondent at times. He was rarely at home, and when he was, he kept to himself in his room. Maria was concerned."

Van Horne considered Allen's comments. "Now that you mention it, something Ben said recently has been bothering me. When Ben and I went fishing last month, as we were watching the waves roll in, he turned to me and said he wished a wave would carry him out to sea so he could be at rest. At the time, I thought the statement was merely reflective. But now you have given me pause …"

Allen looked down at his feet as if trying to gather his thoughts. "Unfortunately, he has left us all with many questions, and we can only speculate as to what could have driven him to such a desperate act."

Van Horne agreed. "Other than his statement, I saw nothing that would lead me to believe he would do what he has done."

"Reverend, I am hesitant to mention this, but last night, I was sitting in the front parlor by an open window, going through Mr. Burton's papers. As you know, we have our share of curiosity seekers loitering around the house, some even so bold as to peek in the windows. I try not to listen to what they say, but one conversation caught my attention. I heard some men talking about Mr. Burton's gambling habits. They said he had recently lost a lot of money gambling. If they are to be believed, it was a substantial sum."

Van Horne was taken aback. "That cannot be right. Ben may have gambled many years ago, but he promised Rosanna that he would give it up. To my knowledge, he has kept that promise. Even when he had gambled, it was not his habit to wager more than a few dollars."

Allen agreed, "That is what I thought as well. But it might explain why bill collectors have been calling at the house all summer. That sort of financial distress could have been the root of Mr. Burton's despair. But I may find more clues after reviewing his papers."

Chapter 4
Thursday, October 8, 1885

The Burton family carriage traveled slowly down Bellevue, passing the Old Stone Tower of mysterious origin, which stood watch over Touro Park as it has since colonial times and perhaps for centuries more. A little further down the hill loomed the granite Egyptian revival-styled gates marking the entrance to the ancient Jewish burial grounds. Their final destination, the Union Congregational Church on Division Street, sat just past the historic Touro Synagogue.

Dora pressed her face against the carriage window. People were lined up on both sides of the narrow street, waiting to pay their respects to her father. Her pulse quickened at the sight, and a sense of trepidation washed over her.

As the carriage slowly continued, the tall Gothic-revival-style church with its pointed arched windows, white batten-wood siding, and small square cupola that sat perched on its slate roof came into view. The crowd congregating in front of the church slowly parted.

Displaying a black armband embellished with a gold star-shaped emblem, a brother in the Star of the East Beneficial Society—a fraternal organization of which Ben was a member—stepped forward to assist the family out of the carriage.

Howard was the first to step out, followed by Maria and Allen. When it was Dora's turn to get out of the carriage, Howard immediately noticed she was beginning to falter. Sidestepping around Allen and Maria, Howard rushed to Dora's side. He wrapped a protective arm around his sister's waist to keep her upright. He steered Dora away from the crowd, and the family was escorted to a private entrance at the back of the building. Once Maria had assured him that she would tend to their sister, Howard joined Reverend Van Horne at the triangular arched entrance to the church.

Maria draped her arm around Dora's shoulders as the two huddled together on a small settee in the rear of the vestibule. The sisters were similarly attired in heavy black mourning dresses and veiled bonnets constructed from layers of stiff bombazine crape, which had been tucked and tufted into stylish yet proper garments. The dresses fittingly symbolized the melancholy of grief and sorrow one would endure with the passing of a beloved father.

Allen positioned himself next to the sisters and silently observed his brother-in-law and the Reverend as they greeted each person who entered the church. Dressed in a dark wool suit with a black silk mourning ribbon pinned to the slim lapel, Allen held his hands tightly behind his back as he rocked back and forth. Maria gently placed a gloved hand on his leg to still his movement.

When it was time for the family to enter the sanctuary, Maria stood and helped Dora to her feet. Howard adjusted his black mourning armband and tugged at the stiffly starched collar of his white dress shirt to loosen his funeral tie, easing the tightness at his throat.

A flash of gold on the cuff of Allen's shirt caught Howard's eye. He froze, squinting to get a better look at the object. His face flushed with heat as he recognized the familiar oval shape with a delicate rose etched on the surface. He was certain these were the sleeve buttons his mother had given his father many years ago for his birthday. A gift that Howard knew his father had cherished. Howard clenched his jaw. He was determined to ask Maria how their father's cufflinks had come into Allen's possession.

When the family reached the front pew, Emily Burton had claimed the seat traditionally reserved for the head of the family. Howard had to nudge his aunt before she reluctantly relinquished her spot. With a dramatic wave of her Sunday best handkerchief, she shooed the more distant relatives to the far end of the pew to make room for herself.

Once the Burton family was seated, the Star of the East Beneficial Society members began their solemn march up the center aisle of the chapel. Two by two, the men slowly made their way past pews adorned with somber black festoons and toward a row of wooden chairs lined up behind Ben's casket. Their journey was accompanied by the harmonious voices of the choir, once directed by Ben himself, singing the first hymn of his homegoing.

Clutching his Bible to his chest, Rev. Van Horne stepped up to the pulpit and turned to face the audience. Black and white citizens alike filled every available space, crammed into pews and standing two people deep along the periphery of the chapel. He bowed his head and raised his hand heavenward to lead the invocation.

"O give thanks unto the Lord, for he is gracious, and his mercy endures forever. Let us pray. Heavenly Father, let us heed the example set forth by Benjamin Burton, who has left us for a better world, and emulate our lives after his, a blessing and a benefit to all around us. In thy holy name, Amen."

A chorus of Amen rumbled throughout the chapel, followed by Emily crying, "Praise the Lord!" It was now time for Rev. Van Horne to bid his dear friend farewell. Clearing his throat, he began to speak in a precise and measured tone.

"Whereas our God in his providence has taken from us our much-beloved father, friend, and advocate of justice, let it be resolved amongst all who are gathered here today that we forever cherish the rich memory and legacy of a man whose life stood testimony to the inherent worth and dignity of all men, no matter complexion, clime, or circumstance."

He turned to Howard, Dora, Maria, and Allen as he directed his words to them.

"While your father now bows at the foot of the cross, he loomed tall as a leader of men in life. In this, seek solace. Your father was an earnest and consistent servant who labored tirelessly for the sacred and worthy causes of our mission. In this, find consolation. Your father sacrificed much for the sake of his family, and his love for his children touched the deepest chords within his heart. In this, know comfort."

Rev. Van Horne paused and drew in a deep breath before addressing Ben's manner of death.

"When a man's life is filled with good works, an unimpeachable career, a loving family, and a multitude of friends, there is no reason to view him shadowed by the darkness of the circumstances of his death. Rather, let us honor him as we knew him, enveloped by the sunshine that was his good and moral life."

Howard nodded to Rev. Van Horne in agreement as his eyes filled with tears. Van Horne stepped away from the pulpit and stood next to Ben's casket. He placed his right hand on the smooth wooden surface and began the eulogy.

"Born a freeman and sired by a freeman, Ben never wavered in his battle against injustice for all. He labored earnestly every day of his life to further the noble cause of equal freedoms. He remained tireless in his efforts, from championing equal access to education to rallying the Black vote in support of leaders friendly to our cause.

"Ben's start in Newport was humble, hauling coal and goods from the docks for other business owners. But it was honest and substantial work, sufficient to support his new bride, Rosanna, and the children who were to follow.

"In the early years of operating his own express and transfer business, Ben arrived at the docks at two o'clock every morning, wagons in tow, eager to take on assignments other men rejected. Who amongst us will ever forget the pageantry of the grand procession to mark his twentieth year in the transfer business? Nine double and single teams, with Ben at the helm, paraded down Bellevue Avenue to Touro Park. Black and white, rich and poor ... we all celebrated his hard-earned success.

"But Ben was not done. He had a vision. Ben knew that the hard-working citizens of Newport had no means of public transportation. I recall when he used to say, *'Only the rich can ride.'* But Ben was determined to change that phrase to *'All can ride.'*

"He created the city's first Omnibus line and invested all of his profits from his express business into this risky venture. It began with one coach running a limited route, but quickly blossomed and expanded until citizens and visitors alike could make their way throughout the city with ease and comfort for only ten cents a ride.

"Then, in the blink of an eye, all of it was gone ... a lifetime of work stolen by fire in the early hours of that tragic September morning."

Maria lowered her head and burst into loud sobs, her breath

hitching with every cry. Dora leaned in closer and placed her head on Maria's shoulder while Allen rubbed his wife's arm and whispered in her ear.

"There are those amongst us who thought this life-altering event might have been a sign from above … that the time had come for Ben to lay down his burdens and spend his remaining years enjoying a well-deserved retirement. With Rosanna gone to her heavenly reward, Howard making his own way in New York City, Maria engaged to a promising young medical student, and Dora approaching womanhood, Ben had ample reasons to leave his life of heavy labor behind.

"Ben did not fear death, yet death shadowed him. He and Rosanna buried one child after the other until eight of their eleven children lay in the family plot. I still struggle to comprehend how these devoted parents survived such unimaginable anguish."

Emily began to wail sorrowfully, her deep and mournful cries echoing throughout the sanctuary. Rev. Van Horne continued, raising his voice to be heard over Emily's lamentations.

"Yet, through faith in God and each other, Ben and Rosanna prevailed with hope restored. Let us draw strength from the assurance that Ben has laid down his heavy burden and has now gone home. Without doubt or hesitation, I believe Rosanna and the children are now welcoming her husband and their father into the kingdom of God. Let us now bow our heads and pray for our heavenly father's blessings."

***

Following Ben's heart-rending service, Emily asked Howard to escort her home to her boarding house. Although he was reluctant to leave his sisters, particularly Dora, and possibly miss an opportunity to speak with Maria about their father's cufflinks, Emily had convinced him it might be their last chance to talk privately before he returned to New York City.

The two walked down the west side of Thames Street, deep in discussion. Emily was determined to take some type of action to force an inquest, but Howard remained skeptical. As they approached the cigar shop on the corner of Ferry Wharf, Emily stopped mid-stride and swung her umbrella in front of Howard's midsection, preventing him from taking another step.

She pointed at a rectangular sign above the door next to the shop's window. A large black image of the scales of justice had caught her attention. She recognized the symbol as one frequently used to designate the location of a law office.

Emily read the name on the sign aloud, "Patrick J. Galvin, Attorney-at-law, Second Floor." She turned to Howard excitedly, "This is the man I told you about! Maybe he can help us."

Without waiting for a response, Emily pulled the door open and followed the arrow up the stairs to Galvin's office. Realizing there was no point in resisting, Howard dutifully followed his aunt.

Galvin sat at the desk in his cramped law office, its only window overlooking a dilapidated grain storage facility. He was busily preparing a motion to submit to the judge in one of his pending criminal cases when he was interrupted by his law clerk standing in his doorway.

"I apologize, Mr. Galvin," the clerk began, "I know you said that you did not want to be disturbed, but there is a Mrs. Emily Burton and Mr. Howard Burton here to see you. They do not have an appointment, but Mrs. Burton says it is urgent."

"It's alright," Galvin replied as he gathered the papers on his desk and stacked them into a neat pile. "Send them in."

Emily appeared in the doorway, gripping an umbrella in one hand and her mourning bonnet in the other, Howard barely visible behind her.

Galvin stood and motioned for them to enter. "Come in. Please have a seat."

Galvin was curious as to why the Burtons had come to see him. He, of course, knew of Mrs. Burton by reputation, but he had never represented or had any dealings with her. He was unfamiliar with Howard, having never met him. Emily didn't keep him in suspense for long.

Without so much as a how-do-you-do, Emily marched into the room, rattling the hardwood floors with each step, and got right to the point.

"Attorney Galvin, we have just come from Ben Burton's funeral."

"Yes, of course," Galvin responded sympathetically, offering, "I know I speak for everyone when I say what a great loss his passing is to our community and—"

"Yes, yes, Mr. Galvin," Emily interrupted, waving his condolences away with her bonnet as she plopped down in a chair across from his desk and tapped the chair next to her with the handle of her umbrella, signaling Howard to take his seat.

"It is my understanding that you are a very smart young man who believes in pursuing justice for all."

Galvin took his seat. "I do believe all are entitled to their day in court."

"If that is true, then you must agree that the most prudent course of action is for the coroner to hold an inquest into Ben's death," she said, repeating word-for-word what she had overheard the attorney tell the medical examiner and coroner on the day of Ben's death.

Galvin was momentarily taken aback. How could a woman he had never met possibly know how he felt about the medical examiner's decision not to hold an inquest? He had only shared his lingering concerns with family members and close friends. Instead, he had been very careful not to publicly criticize Dr. Turner's decision because his sister was married to Dr. Turner's son. Before he could react, Emily continued explaining the reason for their unannounced visit.

"Mr. Galvin, we have come to appeal to you. To appeal for justice!" She leaned forward and lowered her voice conspiratorially. "I have good reason to believe that Ben did not kill himself."

Galvin leaned back in his chair while considering what she might be suggesting. "What makes you say this?"

"Mr. Galvin, Ben was shot twice!" she answered emphatically while holding up two fingers on her right hand. She then pointed her right index finger to her temple, "Once to the head," and then moved her finger dramatically to her breast, "And once to the heart."

She shook her head disbelievingly. "I may not be an educated woman, Mr. Galvin, but even someone like me knows that it is highly unlikely, if not impossible, for someone to shoot themself in the head and still be capable of shooting themselves a second time."

Galvin was also bothered by the two shots, but he kept this to himself. "Well, Mrs. Burton, it may be unusual, but the medical examiner believes that is exactly what happened."

Unfazed, Emily continued to make her case as Howard remained silent. "As Ben's sister-in-law and his children's beloved aunt, I am privy to particular facts. And I'm not referring to idle gossip. I do not go around spreading rumors."

"I see," said Galvin, suppressing a smile. "What facts are you referring to, Mrs. Burton?"

Emily narrowed her eyes. "Ben did not trust Allen Dorsey. Not one bit!" she emphasized, shaking her finger at Galvin. "Allen courted Maria for seven years—seven long years—without any hint of a proposal, leading some folks to fear Maria might end up a spinster."

Howard squirmed uncomfortably in his chair.

"But Ben finally got tired of Allen's dilly-dallying and confronted him, demanding to know what Allen's intentions were with his oldest daughter. Then, lo and behold, the next thing you know, their engagement was announced," Emily derisively added.

"So, you're saying Mr. Dorsey was reluctant to marry," Galvin observed. "What does that have to do with Mr. Burton's death?"

"Young man, I'm getting to that. Don't rush me!" Emily cautioned. "You see, after the wedding date was set, Maria bragged that her father had promised to give the couple a substantial sum of money as a wedding gift ... a dowry if you will."

Emily moved forward in her chair. "But, after the fire, Dora let it slip to me that their father was no longer in the position to give the couple the amount he had promised. He could still give them a wedding gift, but it would be a much smaller amount. From what Dora said, it was downright scandalous how Allen and Maria carried on in response. She said Maria turned on the waterworks whenever she saw her father, begging him for money.

"She also told me that Allen claimed he had been duped into marrying Maria. It sounds like the marriage may have been falling apart before it even got started, but they blamed Ben for all their problems. In the end, I doubt whether Ben gave them so much as a penny!"

"Mrs. Burton, all this may be true, but I have heard nothing that would suggest a motive for someone to kill Mr. Burton if that is what you are implying."

Frustrated by the attorney's interruption, Emily retorted, "But there is more, Mr. Galvin. Much more! Before their engagement, Maria had represented Allen to her father as an up-and-comer. A brilliant man of independent means, destined to become a great surgeon."

Shrugging nonchalantly, she continued, "I do not discount that Allen is a man of great intellect, schooled at the best universities, and as such, is viewed by many to be an accomplished man. But I believe Ben only supported the marriage because he thought Allen could adequately support and care for Maria. As it turns out, Allen is nothing more than a highly educated pauper. He has no money of his own. An inconvenient truth that Maria hid from her father so the marriage would go forward with his blessings."

Galvin shook his head skeptically, "I'm not sure how I can be of service to you, Mrs. Burton."

Emily responded as if it were blatantly obvious why they were there. "Young man, we need you to convince the coroner to hold an inquest, of course!"

Galvin calmly responded, "Mrs. Burton, the process in Rhode Island following any unexpected death is for the medical examiner to make the determination as to whether an inquest is appropriate."

Emily quickly interjected, "Yes, I know all that, but the medical examiner's determination is wrong. This suicide business is rubbish! There must be an inquest."

Galvin leaned forward, placing his forearms on his desk, and threaded his fingers together. "What you may not be aware of," he began patiently, "is that once the medical examiner has determined there is no need for an inquest, only the state's attorney general can overrule his decision."

Emily leaned back and defiantly crossed her arms over her chest. "Mr. Galvin, I'm sure that *you* must know the attorney general. Just tell him everything I have told you. That should be enough for him to overrule this ridiculous decision that no inquest was needed."

Galvin responded respectfully. "It won't be that easy, Mrs. Burton. The coroner also agreed with Dr. Turner's decision. As I understand it, Mr. Burton's daughters and son-in-law all agreed Mr. Burton was despondent in the days leading up to his death. I believe they told the coroner and medical examiner that on the night before his death, Mr. Burton had warned his family that he would not be around much longer."

Emily harrumphed loudly, "What utter nonsense! Would you accept, without question, the word of the very people who had the most to gain from Ben's death?"

Howard visibly winced at her words but remained quiet.

"With all due respect, Mrs. Burton …"

Emily rapped the tip of her umbrella loudly against the wooden floor. "Mr. Galvin, an inquest must be held! The sooner, the better. It is my understanding that Allen and Maria are preparing to leave town as we speak."

Emily raised her hand and dramatically circled it above her head. "Talk is all over Newport that the couple can't get out of town fast enough. What is their hurry? It's too late for Allen to join his classmates at school because the semester is already in session."

Galvin turned to Howard for confirmation, who silently tipped his head in agreement.

Emily then reached across the desk and forcefully pressed her forefinger into the stack of papers under Galvin's hands. "Write this down, Mr. Galvin! Ben Burton was murdered. Killed in cold blood."

Galvin was astonished by Emily's unabashed proclamation that Burton had not only been murdered but also by her insinuation that someone living in his own home was responsible.

"Mrs. Burton, why would anyone want Mr. Burton dead?

Emily's eyes widened incredulously. "Have you not been listening? It's obvious, Mr. Galvin … Ben was killed for his money!"

Galvin sighed in frustration. "Evidence, Mrs. Burton. What evidence do you have that would support your claim?"

Howard spoke up for the first time. "Aunt Emily, tell Mr. Galvin what Father told you about Maria and Allen."

"I was just getting to that," Emily snapped. "A week to the day before Ben died, he dropped by my house unannounced. Ben had not called on me at my home in several years, not that we were at odds, mind you."

"Of course not," Galvin offhandedly remarked.

"Ben didn't mince words. He came right out and asked me if I had seen *that fellow* who lived in his house. Couldn't even bring himself to say Allen's name, can you believe that? I told him, no, I hadn't seen hide nor hair of Allen since the wedding. I said I thought those two had already left for Philadelphia. But Ben told me, *'Well, he hasn't left,'* despite leading him to believe they would both be long gone before then."

Emily paused to take a deep breath before continuing. "Ben confided in me that he was planning to make big changes in his life. He said he had a man at the ready, eager to buy his big house at a good price. He was building a new cottage for just Dora and himself. He said he was going straight home to order Maria and *that fellow* out of his house. He complained that he had supported Maria all her life, but now that she was married, it was time for her husband to support her."

"Is that the sum of it, Mrs. Burton? Asking his daughter and her new husband to strike out on their own hardly seems like a motive for murder," Galvin gingerly suggested.

Emily raised her voice in frustration. "No! They needed money! Allen claimed he hadn't left for school because he was too sick. That's a lie. Allen wasn't sick. The real reason he didn't go back to school was that he did not have the money to pay for his tuition. When he realized his highfalutin dream of becoming a surgeon was slipping through his fingers, he was desperate to get his hands on some money."

"How would you know that?" Galvin asked.

"Allen wrote to *me* last spring asking to borrow money. He tried to sweet-talk me into sending him $125 so he could pay his tuition. When I refused to give him the money, Maria secretly borrowed the funds from her cousin in New York City. She had promised to pay her cousin back in full before the wedding. But just as I predicted, Maria never repaid her one red cent."

"How do you know the loan was unpaid?" asked Galvin.

"Because Ben showed me a letter Maria's cousin sent him complaining about Maria not repaying any portion of the loan. That was the first time he had heard of it, and he was humiliated by the news. I don't have to tell you, there was steam coming out of Ben's ears.

"But we weren't the only ones Allen and Maria begged, borrowed, or maybe even stole money from. Ben had finally wised-up to the talk around town about his daughter's shenanigans. Told me so himself. Asked me if I thought it was true."

"If what was true?" Galvin asked, having trouble following Emily's disjointed account of misdoings.

Emily sighed loudly, exasperated with Galvin's inability to follow what she considered a clear and well-reasoned chain of events leading up to Ben's death.

"Ben wanted to know if I had heard that Maria was going around town lying to people about Howard and asking them for money."

Quickly looking to Howard, Galvin noticed he appeared visibly uncomfortable now that the conversation had turned to him.

"Howard hasn't been in a lick of trouble for years," she explained, "but folks around here didn't know that, seeing how he's been living in New York City. That made it mighty easy for Maria to concoct a ridiculous story about Howard needing money to leave the country because he killed someone."

Flabbergasted by this curious twist in Emily's tale, Galvin quickly stole a glance at Howard. The poor man was bent over with his elbows planted on the arms of his chair, holding his head between his hands.

"Of course," Emily continued, oblivious to her nephews' discomfort, "Maria depicted herself as her brother's savior and went about collecting money from friends and neighbors on Howard's behalf. She must have stolen that plot from a ten-penny novel, wouldn't you say, Mr. Galvin?"

Coming to Howard's rescue, Galvin changed the subject quickly, almost afraid to ask, "Is there anything else, Mrs. Burton?"

"It seems mighty suspicious that all of these deceptions came to a head only the week before Ben's death, don't you think?"

Her question gave Galvin pause. He needed time to consider all the information she had just dumped in his lap.

"Mrs. Burton, Mr. Burton, I appreciate you both dropping by on what must be an exceedingly difficult day. Again, I extend my condolences, but I must get back to work."

Emily begrudgingly pushed back her chair and rose to her feet. Making a final appeal to Galvin's sense of justice, Emily implored, "Mr. Galvin, we need your help to expose the truth about Ben's death so we can bring his killer to justice, and Ben can rest in peace."

Galvin nodded sympathetically. "As I stated, it will be up to the attorney general to decide if anything further is to be done."

Howard offered his assistance to his aunt, and she grasped his elbow. As they turned to leave, she locked eyes with Galvin while delivering her parting words.

"Rest assured, Mr. Galvin, if the attorney general does not do something and soon, I will take my case to the governor. On this, you have my word."

***

After dismissing Howard with instructions to go home and keep his eyes and ears open, Emily continued alone up Thames Street. She replayed the conversation with Galvin in her head, debating whether he would take her concerns seriously and pass them along to the attorney general. But if he didn't, as she had told Galvin, she had no qualms about directly contacting the governor herself.

How hard could that be? she thought to herself. *After all, his family built one of the first mansions on Bellevue Avenue. I'll just knock on the door and ask to speak to the governor.*

She slowed her gait as she approached the Newport Daily News printing office. Cupping her hands around her eyes, she peered through the plate glass window and watched as the spinning cylinders of the rotary printing press pumped out the pages of its evening edition. She was struck by an idea.

Maybe I don't have to go to the governor after all, she thought as she opened the door and marched inside.

Chapter 5
October 12th -16th, 1885

Galvin left his office and headed to Francis Stanhope's novelties store. In addition to serving as the coroner, Stanhope operated a store near the City Hall and courthouses. The attorney had worked closely with Stanhope on various legal matters and considered him a friend.

After his meeting with Emily and Howard Burton and reading the most recent local newspaper coverage regarding the rumors over the cause of Ben's death, Galvin's increasing discomfort over Turner's hasty suicide ruling prompted him to pay a visit to Coroner Stanhope. He wanted to discuss the possibility of someone approaching the attorney general about holding an inquest.

When Galvin entered the store, he found Stanhope digging through mounds of packing straw in the back. He was carefully removing German Christmas ornaments and wax angel statuettes with spun glass wings from a large wooden shipping crate. Stanhope looked up from his work and smiled when he recognized Galvin approaching him. The men made small talk before Galvin broached the topic that had prompted his visit.

"It seems that in just the span of a week, the whole of Newport has formed an opinion about the cause of Ben Burton's death."

"And everyone seems more than willing to share their opinion,"

Stanhope remarked as he brushed the stray pieces of straw from his shirt sleeves.

Galvin picked up one of the ornaments and held it to the light, examining the delicate filigree pattern.

"Do you still concur with Dr. Turner's decision regarding the need for an inquest?"

"Dr. Turner doesn't need my agreement. He has the sole discretion to make the determination," Stanhope stated plainly. "My role as coroner is to oversee an inquest, not to decide if one should be held."

"But what is your honest opinion?" Galvin probed.

"Why do you ask, P.J.?" Stanhope inquired.

Galvin carefully placed the ornament back on the top of the counter. "There is talk ..."

"I know," Stanhope cut him off. "I am well aware that not everyone agrees with Dr. Turner's decision."

Galvin nodded. "The Newport Daily News is now reporting that it has a reliable source who says there was conflict in the Burton house in the days leading up to his death. Their source is also claiming that officials failed to adequately investigate the matter by not interviewing people who may have had relevant information before making the determination of suicide."

It was not lost on Stanhope that Galvin was inferring he was one of those officials.

Galvin hesitated, "Perhaps you should speak with the attorney general about holding an inquest."

Stanhope shook his head. "The man is fighting to get re-elected. He is not likely to get involved in a purely local affair like this."

"You never know. It might garner him more local votes if he displayed some interest in the matter," suggested Galvin.

Stanhope suspected Galvin may be correct, but he had no intention of approaching the attorney general.

"P.J., if you feel that strongly, why don't you voice your concerns to him? Or better yet, you could talk to your friend, the governor," he quipped before adopting a more sober tone and adding, "Of course, if either thinks an inquest is warranted, I will schedule one."

Galvin was relieved that Stanhope suggested that he should be the one to speak with the attorney general. He picked up the ornament from the counter and spun it around in his hand.

"My sister would like this one very much. Can you put it back for me?"

Stanhope's manner eased, and he smiled as Galvin handed the ornament over. "I will be happy to."

Galvin bid him goodbye, and Stanhope shook his head and chuckled as he watched the young attorney make his way out of the shop.

If he convinces the attorney general to order an inquest, thought Stanhope, *I hope this young man is appointed to represent him in the proceeding.*

***

Newport, R.I., October 13, 1885.

"On Tuesday last, Benjamin Burton, one of the foremost men of this city, was found dead in his dining room, with a pistol shot in his head and another in his breast. The circumstances all pointed to suicide as the cause of death, and the coroner declined to hold an inquest. Within the past few days, ugly reports have been in circulation to the effect that he was murdered, and it is believed the authorities will hold an official investigation."

Galvin folded the copy of Tuesday's edition of *The Boston Herald* and placed it on a growing pile of newspapers sitting on the corner of his desk. He leaned back in his chair and pinched the bridge of his nose.

As he had anticipated, the local coverage of Ben Burton's death had been plucked up by the wires, and now newspapers up and down the eastern seaboard were chiming in, laying the blame for the lack of an inquest directly at the feet of Dr. Turner and Coroner Stanhope.

As Emily Burton had predicted, Galvin's belief in equal justice compelled him to take his concerns to the attorney general. Emily was also correct in her insistence that Galvin must be acquainted with the attorney general. As a fellow Republican, he had been invited to speak at some of his official campaign events. However, rather than share Emily's laundry list of accusations, Galvin painted a vivid picture of a community besieged by a multitude of rumors and innuendos concerning the cause of the tragic death of one of its most prominent Black citizens.

He described a tempestuous atmosphere in which arguments were springing up all over town. Verbal altercations were routinely breaking out at the local grocers, saloons, downtown shops, women's sewing circles, and even creeping into Newport's most prominent gentlemen's club, The Reading Room. Not even the pulpits were above the fray.

In the end, the attorney general agreed to order an inquest and asked Galvin to represent him in the proceedings. Galvin wasn't sure if the attorney general was swayed by his dramatic depiction of the divided community or merely by his desire to win more votes in the upcoming election.

Two days later, a telegram was delivered to Galvin's office confirming his appointment as an assistant attorney general in the proceedings. The message also contained an official order requiring Coroner Stanhope to exhume the body and convene an inquest.

Galvin read the telegram with a strange mix of eagerness and trepidation. The exhumation was to occur the following day, and the inquest was to begin on Wednesday. This only gave Galvin four days to prepare. He would need to hit the ground running.

***

Stanhope walked into Galvin's law office and found him sitting behind his desk, his head buried in a stack of legal documents. The coroner quietly shut the door behind him.

"Allow me to be the first to offer my congratulations on your appointment," Stanhope grinned slyly.

"Thank you," Galvin replied sincerely. He respected and admired Stanhope. Galvin intended to get to the truth concerning Burton's death, whatever that truth might be, and he suspected Stanhope wanted the same.

Stanhope remained standing. "Have you been informed of all that is to come?"

Galvin shook his head no. "I assume I will be provided with what I need to conduct my investigation."

In his six years of law practice, Galvin worked primarily as a criminal defense attorney, often taking on clients no one else would represent. He was a good lawyer, prevailing in seemingly unwinnable cases. But now he was venturing into uncharted territory, and any help he could get from his friend was welcomed and appreciated.

Stanhope snorted and cleared his throat. "Did the attorney general mention that an exhumation has been scheduled for tomorrow?"

"Yes. What time will the body be exhumed?"

Stanhope hesitated. "As you know, Newport does not have a morgue, so the autopsy will be performed at the gravesite at one o'clock in the morning to avoid attracting a crowd."

Galvin grimaced. "That is positively morbid."

"Ahh, but you know it is true. If there is any more publicity, we will have to ask P. T. Barnum to set up his tents."

Stanhope reached into his jacket pocket, removed an envelope, and tossed it on Galvin's desk.

"What is this?" Galvin asked as he picked up the envelope and turned it over to examine it. It was addressed to Stanhope.

"Go ahead, read it."

Galvin removed a single folded paper and opened it. Neat handwriting filled the page.

Ben Burton did not kill himself.
I have heard from a reliable source that a tenant in the Burton house has heard violent quarrels between the Burtons.
The cooks on board the USS New Hampshire also have important information about Burton's death.
Signed,
A concerned citizen

"Have you shared this with the police?" Galvin asked.

"The police are not interested," Stanhope informed him. "Captain Hammond has closed the case."

"What about the mayor or the sheriff? Has anyone else seen this letter?"

Stanhope shook his head no. "They agree with Hammond. Don't expect any help from the city authorities, but you will still need to track down the pugnacious Captain Hammond to get a copy of his report."

Galvin chuckled. "I'll put that on the top of my list."

"There are only a few days before the inquest begins. I will send a request to the family asking for the names of any witnesses they would like to have testify in the proceedings. I'll forward that to you as soon as I receive it."

Stanhope opened the office door and called out as he left, "Good luck to you, P.J. Not that you'll need it."

***

Galvin stormed out of the police station, his frustration mounting. He had spent the better part of the last hour trying to track down the elusive Captain Hammond. When he phoned the police station earlier, he had been told the captain was on duty at the Newport County Jail. However, when he arrived at the jail, Hammond was already on his way back to the police station. Just now, the officer on duty at the police station laughingly informed him that Hammond had just left to return to the jail. Galvin wondered if Hammond was purposefully sending him on a wild goose chase.

As he left the police station, he spotted Captain Hammond. Determined not to let the captain slip through his fingers again, Galvin sprinted to catch up with him.

"Captain Hammond! Hold up!" he called out as Hammond looked up. "May I have a moment of your time?"

"Yes, Attorney Galvin. What can I do for you?"

"I understand that you were in charge of investigating Ben Burton's death."

"There was no investigation to be done," Hammond replied indifferently. "It was a sad case of suicide. Open and shut."

Galvin was undeterred by Hammond's apparent lack of interest. "So, you did not find it at all questionable that, after shooting himself in the head, Mr. Burton was able to shoot himself again through the heart?"

Hammond snorted dismissively. "As I already told the coroner, a suicide by two gunshots may be unusual, but it is not unheard of, especially if a person is bound and determined to kill himself."

Galvin pulled the telegram from the attorney general out of his jacket pocket and thrust it toward Hammond.

"What is that?" Hammond asked, not bothering to take the paper from Galvin's hand.

"This document explains that I have been appointed, and as of this morning, duly sworn, as acting attorney general in the Burton inquest. I will require your assistance in preparing for the proceeding."

Hammond waved him away with a flick of his wrist. "I have

legitimate cases to investigate, counselor. Why would I waste my time and the town's resources investigating a clear case of suicide?"

"Because it is your duty, as it is my duty, to present the facts in the case," Galvin stated emphatically.

Hammond's face flushed with indignation as he took a step toward Galvin. "You can present all your so-called facts, but I can assure you my position in the matter will not change."

"If the facts support suicide, so be it," Galvin conceded. "But it is my job to get to the truth of the matter. I will need copies of all the witness statements taken at the scene and a copy of your written report as well."

"Is that so?" Hammond scoffed contemptuously as he removed a small snuffbox from his waistcoat pocket. "There were no witnesses, son. The older daughter was out of the house. A neighbor confirmed that fact. The son-in-law was upstairs, sick in bed, and signed a statement to that effect. Another neighbor substantiated the fact."

Hammond took a pinch of the snuff and wiped the leftover smudge of the powdered tobacco from his upper lip. "I believe the youngest girl was upstairs in the attic or her bedroom. I don't recall which, but it is all in my report."

Galvin exhaled loudly, exasperated by the captain's lackadaisical attitude.

Hammond continued, undaunted. "Ask yourself, why would the daughters want their father dead? The youngest is a weak-minded girl of seventeen, for goodness' sake. Is that your killer?"

"You presume too much," Galvin responded firmly. "There may be others who might have had a motive."

Hammond rolled his eyes. "Ahh, yes … others. I've heard the ugly and baseless gossip about the son-in-law. He has only lived in the house for three months or so. What could have possibly occurred in that time to turn the man from a healing physician into a killer? There is no viable motive, Mr. Galvin," Hammond asserted confidently.

"By all accounts, the relations between the occupants of the home were pleasant. Plenty of folks will tell you they've heard Burton say he wished he was dead. Hell, Ben himself told me his business was so poor he didn't even know if he would be renewing his livery licenses next year. From what I gather, he had plenty of reasons to take his own life. There is no case here. Ben Burton killed himself. An inquest is nothing more than a waste of time and money."

Hammond paused, adding dismissively, "If there is nothing else, Counselor, I will resume my duties."

Galvin's face reddened with frustration. "See here, sir! While *you* might think all of this is a waste of *your* valuable time, all of it is critical information that needs to be presented at the inquest. If you will not assist me, I demand that you assign a detective to help me in the ongoing investigation."

Hammond's lips curled into a sneer. "It just so happens I'm the only detective in this town and work for the city marshal. I do *not* work for you."

"No, sir!" Galvin declared, now visibly angry, "That is *not* correct. You work for the townsfolk of Newport."

Hammond bent his head forward so closely that Galvin could feel his breath on his face.

"Listen to me, you whippersnapper," Hammond warned, teeth clenched. "I will not spend one minute nor one penny chasing my tail. And I'm certainly not taking marching orders from a young upstart who thinks he knows better than the rest of us. Do you hear me?"

Speechless, Galvin stepped back.

"That's what I thought," Hammond remarked as he turned to walk away. "My report is at the station," he called over his shoulder. "Go get it yourself."

Chapter 6
Saturday, October 17, 1885

The undertaker raised his lantern above his head as he stood on the fresh mound of dirt marking Ben Burton's grave. Dark clouds filled the night sky above the Old City Cemetery, enveloping the graveyard in shadowy darkness. The streetlights cast ghostly outlines of gnarled tree branches against the headstones that dotted the cemetery grounds.

He called out to the team of men he had hired to excavate Ben Burton's grave, "Over here, boys. This is the spot."

As he kicked away wilted remnants of floral arrangements, he crouched down to scoop up a handful of dirt. He ran the soil through his fingers. The dirt had not yet become compacted, making it easier for his men to dig. He instructed his team to place their lanterns in a circle on the ground around the gravesite to illuminate the area.

"Why does this have to be done in the dead of night?" one of his men complained.

"I reckon they don't want an audience," the undertaker replied as he nervously glanced over his shoulder down Farewell Street. Despite it being almost 1 o'clock in the morning, he spotted a group of people walking toward the cemetery.

For pity's sake, he thought.

He had cautioned his men not to tell a soul what they would be doing tonight, hoping to keep the public from showing up at the autopsy. He prayed these folks were only heading home after a night of drinking in the saloons.

"They ought to be doing this in a morgue, not out in the open," he mumbled. The mortician felt the authorities could have found a more discreet location to conduct the autopsy. In his opinion, cutting Ben's body open in a graveyard, even under the cloak of darkness, was disrespectful to his memory.

His men had removed all the dirt in the grave down to the lid of the burial vault when a carriage appeared, slowly making its way up Farewell Street.

"Bring the horses around," he called to his men as he began to uncoil the thick metal chains needed to lift the heavy iron vault from the pit.

The carriage pulled to a stop at the edge of the cemetery. Dr. Turner stepped out with his cane in hand.

The undertaker had examined Ben's bullet wounds himself when he had prepared his body for burial. Although he had seen plenty of bodies with self-inflicted wounds, he had never seen a suicide victim with a bullet hole in the head *and* one in the chest. Dr. Turner might be one of New England's most respected physicians, but he believed the doctor may have gotten it wrong in this case.

Dr. Turner pulled up his coat collar against the night's chill as he approached. "How much longer?" he asked impatiently.

"We will have him above ground shortly," the undertaker replied.

By the time the vault was unearthed and positioned on the carriage path at the foot of the grave, the mayor and the city marshal had arrived to serve as official witnesses. Turner laid out his autopsy tools on a small folding table before addressing the undertaker.

"Let's place the body on top of the coffin so I can use it as an autopsy table."

As the men lifted the coffin from the vault and lowered it to the ground, one of them lost their grip, causing the end of the coffin to hit the ground with a thud. When the lid was removed, the malodorous smell of decomposing flesh escaped from within and filled the air, causing some of the gravediggers to gag and retch. Indifferent to his workers' physical discomfort, the undertaker motioned for his men to remove the shrouded body and hold it in mid-air so he could put the lid back on the coffin for them.

"Looks like you've got company," one of the men called out as a handful of curious spectators started to gather in the cemetery. Dr. Turner suggested that the reluctant gravediggers join the witnesses to form a circle around the body.

The undertaker groaned. It was just as he feared. His eyes wandered around the cemetery until they locked on one person standing about fifty feet down the fence line. It was Howard Burton.

He shouldn't be here, he thought.

The men formed a tight circle around the body while the gravediggers held their lanterns overhead to cast light on the area. Ben's corpse was wrapped in a plain white burial shroud. The undertaker carefully loosened the fabric around Ben's head and upper torso before taking his place in the circle with his men.

Dr. Turner pulled the fabric aside to expose Ben's chest and pointed to the small entry wound in his left breast.

"I will start here," he announced.

He passed a leather-bound notebook to the mayor, asking him to record his dictation, then reached for a small measuring tape to measure the placement of the wounds.

"It appears the ball penetrated the thorax three inches to the right of the left nipple and approximately two inches to the left of the median of the chest, roughly on a level with the nipple."

He turned and picked up a scalpel from the small folding table and cut a large Y-shaped incision deep across the chest and down to the end of the sternum. He used shears to cut through the thick cartilage between the ribs and the breastbone, spreading the chest open with a loud crack. He then proceeded to remove the liver, heart, and intestines and place the spongy, jelly-like organs on the coffin lid next to the body for examination.

Dr. Turner lifted the softened heart, which had devolved into a deep eggplant color, and held it close to a lantern's light.

"It would appear the bullet passed through the heart, entering the left ventricle here at the base and exiting through the apex. Instantaneous death."

He laid the damaged heart on the table next to the other organs and used his hands to spread the chest cavity wider.

"Bring the lanterns in closer," Turner directed as he bent closer to the opening.

"The bullet hit the seventh, no, the eighth rib, and looks to me as if it might have changed course. Let's see where this bullet traveled after pinging off the rib."

Using a small surgical saw, Dr. Turner proceeded to remove the eighth rib and then cut out a large section of the surrounding tissue, laying it out next to the heart. He methodically dissected the tissue in search of the small twenty-two caliber bullet.

"There is a great deal of fat and tissue," he observed. "It may be difficult to follow the bullet's path."

Over the next hour, Dr. Turner removed layer after layer, carefully dissecting each piece until a large mass of severed soft tissue was piled next to the body. The gruesomeness of the sight was not lost on anyone. One man, and then another, became overcome by the sight and smells emanating from the doctor's work, stepping away to vomit before returning to the circle.

Sympathetic to the distress that observing the autopsy was causing the men, Dr. Turner ended his futile search for the bullet. He carefully placed the tissue and organs back into the chest cavity and folded the skin back over the chest. Motioning for the workers to hold their lanterns higher, he turned his attention to the head wound.

Placing his thumb and forefinger on either side of the wound, the doctor bent down to closely observe the hair surrounding the small, circular opening approximately an inch and a half above the right ear.

"I detect no visible signs of burning or gunpowder," he said as he removed his hand.

Dr. Turner made an incision across the head from the back of one ear to the other, careful to keep the area around the wound intact. He separated the scalp from the skull and sawed through the skull bone at the top of the head to create an opening. Some of the gravediggers, while holding their lanterns, turned their heads away from the scene in repulsion as Dr. Turner carefully removed the top section of the skull and set it aside.

"The brain is quite large and has softened considerably," he noted. "I fear any attempt to remove it for dissection will be difficult. I should be able to determine the trajectory without removing the brain. If it entered through the cranium from the right, then it is likely lodged on the left."

Gently probing the cerebrum with a pair of long-nosed tweezers, he located a small, flattened piece of metal in the posterior section of the left lobe.

"Here it is," he announced as he plucked the shrapnel out and placed it in the city marshal's outstretched hand. He leaned in for a better look. "As I thought, the bullet traveled across the cerebrum from right to left, front to back. At this angle, it could not have touched the cerebellum. He might have survived this injury. Now, I need to look inside his mouth."

After he replaced the piece of skull and smoothed the scalp back into place, Dr. Turner paused to wipe his bloody hands on a towel. He wedged his fingers between the lips and pried the mouth open with difficulty. Remnants of bread were still inside Ben's mouth and stuck between his teeth.

"This is curious, indeed," he remarked, motioning for the mayor to note it in his notebook and pushing the mouth closed.

"We are done here," Turner declared.

"Well done, men," said the undertaker, to his immense relief.

As the undertaker began instructing the men on how to reinter the body, he looked across Farewell Street, where he spotted another solitary figure standing atop a knoll in the adjacent cemetery. He squinted to get a better look. Though tall and broad in stature, there was no mistaking that it was the shape of a woman. He could hardly believe his eyes.

"This is no place for a woman this time of night," he said. "Wonder how long she's been standing there?"

"Been here all night, boss," one of his men remarked.

He thought of walking to her, perhaps offering to send one of his men to escort her home, but out of the corner of his eye, he caught sight of Howard Burton crossing Farewell Street in her direction. And it suddenly dawned on him.

Thunderation! That's no helpless lady. That's Emily Burton!

***

Emily woke with a start and glanced at the clock on the mantle in her room. It read a quarter past seven. She had arrived home from the cemetery only four hours earlier, and her body ached from exhaustion. When it was announced that an autopsy would be held, Emily had insisted that Howard not attend, hoping to spare him from the unnecessary anguish. Her heart sank when her nephew unexpectedly approached her in the graveyard.

Unlike Emily, Howard remained undecided as to whether his father had killed himself, but he shared his aunt's frustration with how quickly the authorities had dismissed any lingering questions. As Howard had walked Emily home in the early morning hours, he surprised her by announcing that he had hired a Pinkerton detective. Emily had been pleased and smiled as she pictured the smug Captain Hammond blowing a gasket over the news.

Fighting the impulse to stay in bed, Emily got up slowly and dressed. She made her way down to the kitchen to prepare breakfast.

"Morning," a hungry boarder grumbled as he waited for the coffee pot he had placed on the stove to boil.

"Breakfast will be a little late," Emily advised, grabbing a bowl, some eggs, and her biscuit tin.

After stoking the fire in the stove, she put the biscuits in the oven to bake. She then poured herself a cup of coffee and sat at the kitchen table. Someone had left the morning edition of the *Newport Daily News* on the kitchen table. As Emily took a sip, she opened the paper.

And there it was … front and center above the fold, her interview with the reporter.

Suicide or Foul Play?

Emily smiled with satisfaction as she pored over the article. The reporter had captured the salient points: that there had been trouble in the Burton house immediately before his death, and the authorities had acted too quickly when they concluded Ben's death was a suicide. Though Emily was not identified as the source, she was confident the community would figure it out.

I'm just telling the truth, she told herself … and anyone else who would listen.

Emily had received mixed reactions to her one-woman crusade for an inquest. Some people offered supportive encouragement, while others pointedly accused her of causing trouble.

Earlier in the week, she had come upon a small gathering standing on the corner, chatting with one another. One of the women took notice of her and quickly silenced the others, warning, "Here she comes."

As Emily stepped off the curb to walk around them, she sensed the hostility in their silent stares. She knew exactly what they were thinking.

How dare she, a poor, uneducated laundress from the wrong side of town, challenge the decorated police captain, the honorable mayor, the respected medical examiner, and the holy clerics who were all so insistent that the cause of Ben's death was a suicide. Half of Newport may be eager to put this unpleasantness behind them, but not those of us who seek the truth.

A few days ago, she was confronted by a woman on the street who hissed, "Shame on you, Emily Burton! Let the man rest in peace."

Holding her head high and without breaking her stride, she had retorted, "As the good Lord sayeth, the righteous care about justice, but the wicked have no such concern."

But the comment had stung Emily.

Why were some so quick to bury Ben without question? The circumstances warranted an investigation, plain and simple. When that drunkard fell down the stairs and broke his neck last month, Turner didn't hesitate to hold an inquest on the spot. And he was a nobody!

Emily tossed the newspaper on the counter and returned to preparing breakfast. She cracked the eggs in a frying pan and placed thick slices of smoked ham on a platter.

She recalled how her late husband had struggled year after year with his own fledgling transfer and express business, trying to make ends meet, while he watched his brother Ben flourish. Their fierce competition for clients had bitterly divided the once inseparable siblings. Although the brothers never reconciled, Emily was certain her husband would also have demanded an inquest.

She removed the biscuits from the oven and placed them on the table next to the platters of eggs and meat. She rang the breakfast bell after adding bowls of freshly churned butter and homemade jam. Once the boarders had taken their seats around the table, Emily took her place at the head of the table and bowed her head.

"For what we are about to receive, let us give thanks to the Lord. Amen."

Chapter 7
Sunday, October 18, 1885

At High Mass in the Holy Name of Mary, Our Lady of the Isle Catholic Church, Mary Stoddard prayed fervently to Saint Michael, the Archangel, champion of justice and healer of the sick.

The local newspapers were reporting the innuendos and rumors that were circulating town, and some of the same people who had once been certain that Ben's death had been a suicide were now not so sure. Like many in Newport, Mary had little doubt that Emily Burton had a hand in the bitter division that was developing over the authorities' handling of Ben's death.

Mary's heart ached for Maria, Dora, and Allen. Still recovering from Ben's death, they were now embroiled in a scandal not of their making.

Those poor children have been through enough, she thought, as she prayed for guidance on how she might help ease their suffering.

After a few minutes of quiet reflection, the answer came to her. She must confront Emily Burton face-to-face and try to reason with her. Mary sent up one final prayer to Saint Michael, the spiritual warrior of good versus evil, asking for his protection.

When Mass ended, Mary stepped out of the hallowed brownstone Gothic Revival church and onto the street, where she spotted Patrick J.

Galvin, his father, brothers, and sister gathered around one of the priests. The Galvin family were respected parishioners active in the church, with the youngest daughter serving as the organist.

Mary was initially disheartened to hear that the attorney general had ordered an inquest. She felt it would place an unnecessary burden on an already grieving family. However, she found comfort in the fact that the attorney general had appointed Patrick Galvin as his representative in the proceedings. She was confident that the capable young attorney would quickly put to rest any lingering doubts people may harbor concerning Ben's death.

Yesterday, she received a message from Galvin requesting that she contact his office for an interview. Now, she looked forward to helping him prove Ben's death was a suicide. Not wishing to interrupt the Galvins, Mary began making her way to Emily Burton's residence.

Shortly before noon, Mary arrived at the two-and-a-half-story gambrel-roofed home where Emily lived and operated a boarding house. She rapped on the door. Hearing no movement from inside, she knocked again, more forcefully. This time, the door was answered by a burly man Mary assumed to be one of Emily's borders.

"Is Mrs. Burton home?" asked Mary.

The man opened the door but only permitted Mary to step inside the entryway.

"She is out back doing her washing. I doubt she heard the knocking. I'll get her."

A few minutes later, Emily appeared from the back of the house, still wearing her black mourning dress, now covered by a large water-stained white bibbed apron. Her sleeves were rolled up to the elbow, and she was drying her hands on a small towel. In her haste to undertake her divinely inspired mission, Mary was still attired in her best Sunday dress and chapel veil.

"Why, Mrs. Stoddard, what brings you to this side of town?" asked Emily when she joined Mary just inside the entry.

Mary squared her shoulders and got right to the point. "Mrs. Burton, I've come to see you. I want you to know that I am fully aware of what you have been saying about Mr. Burton's death."

Emily cocked an eyebrow. "Oh? What have I been saying that has upset you?"

Mary paused, choosing her words carefully. "That Mr. Burton did not kill himself."

"That is my opinion," Emily snapped back. "I am entitled to my opinion, aren't I?"

Mary agreed, "You are, but I'm afraid that yours is not an informed opinion."

"Is that so?" Emily chuckled mockingly.

Unfazed, Mary continued, "You may not know this, Mrs. Burton, but I live directly across from the Burton home on Thomas Street. And you also may not be aware that, as their neighbor, I have come to know the Burton family fairly well."

"I know exactly where you live, Mrs. Stoddard," Emily retorted. "I also know that you are the neighborhood busybody."

Caught off guard by Emily's cutting remark, Mary took a moment to gather her thoughts. During her walk to the house, she had carefully planned precisely what she would say to Emily. She needed to stick to that plan.

"I was in the Burton house on the morning of his death," she continued.

"As was I," Emily responded, unimpressed.

"But you arrived much later," Mary quickly pointed out. "I got there right after Ben shot himself. In fact, I was the one who found him."

Emily pounced on Mary's words, "Shot himself? You don't honestly believe that Ben shot himself, do you?"

"That is exactly what I believe, Mrs. Burton," Mary declared. "I *know* that is what happened, which is why I am here. To share with you what I know to be true."

"How can you be so certain?" Emily sneered. "Were you in the kitchen when the shots were fired?"

Mary shook her head, "Of course not." She went on to explain, "But Mr. Burton told me on numerous occasions that he wished to kill himself. Indeed, only the day before he died, Mr. Burton told me that if he had a pistol, he would blow his brains out."

Instead of receiving the reaction Mary would have expected, Emily responded with a cackle.

"Mrs. Stoddard, if I had a nickel for every time I heard Ben Burton joke about killing himself, I would be living on your side of town."

Mary was dismayed at Emily's callousness. "It can't be a

coincidence that the very next day, I found Mr. Burton shot in the head with a gun by his side."

Emily stared Mary down. "If you thought that Ben was serious about killing himself, why didn't you warn his family?"

Mary fell silent. In the days following Ben's death, she had agonized over the same question. Why hadn't she told anyone about Ben's intentions? She finally had to admit to herself that she had thought he had been joking at the time. But she wasn't there to discuss her failings. She turned the conversation back to Emily.

"I've heard that you are telling anyone who will listen that someone in the house is responsible for Mr. Burton's death."

Emily quickly corrected her. "It would be more accurate to say I am telling people either Maria or her new husband was responsible for Ben's death."

Mary countered, "But I can prove that neither of them could have shot Mr. Burton. And I came here hoping to convince you of that."

Emily bowed at her waist while sweeping her hand dramatically in front of her body. "Be my guest."

Ignoring Emily's theatrics, Mary began. "I was in my house when I distinctly heard two shots, clear as day."

"Everyone knows there were two shots," Emily interrupted impatiently.

Mary stomped her foot to silence Emily before continuing.

"*Before* I heard the shots, I saw Maria come out of the house and go upstairs with Idella Traeger into the Traegers' second-floor apartment. So, Maria couldn't have been in the house when the shots were fired."

"But, what about her devoted husband?" challenged Emily. "He was in the house."

"Yes, that is true," Mary conceded. "But he was upstairs at the time of the shooting. When I found him, he was sitting on the edge of his bed, just getting dressed."

"That just proves my point … he was in the house," Emily declared. "Tell me what else you saw. Did the promising medical student rush to his father-in-law's side to render aid?"

Mary paused, remembering how Allen had walked briskly by Ben's body without stopping. At the time, she had found this behavior peculiar, but she had subsequently accepted Allen's explanation that he wanted to find a more experienced doctor to examine Ben.

"There was nothing anyone could have done for Mr. Burton," Mary argued. "As a nurse, I can attest to the fact that Mr. Burton was dead when I found him and long before Allen came downstairs. I assure you, his wife required his full attention. I watched with my own two eyes as he carried Maria upstairs. She was inconsolable.

"So, you see, Mrs. Burton, it is impossible for Maria or Allen to have played a role in Mr. Burton's death. Everything I witnessed in that house on that day points to Mr. Burton taking his own life."

When Mary finished, Emily merely scowled at her and silently shook her head in disagreement without comment.

Mary sighed in exasperation. "Mrs. Burton, even if I can't convince you, I appeal to your sense of decency. I am begging you to stop spreading these vicious rumors. You won! Your campaign for an inquest was successful. Now, allow Attorney Galvin and the coroner do their jobs.

"In the meantime, let the family grieve in peace," she pleaded. "They are trying to come to grips with the loss of their only remaining parent. Your actions are hurting them and fanning the flames of discord in Newport."

"How dare you criticize me, Mary Stoddard, when it was the medical examiner who couldn't be bothered to do his job," Emily exclaimed defiantly. "I can't spend all day arguing with you. I have work to do. I hope you don't mind showing yourself out."

With that, Emily turned on her heels, leaving Mary in her wake, and stomped to the backyard where she had left laundry soaking in a tub of soapy water. She angrily picked up a white cotton blouse from the tub and scrubbed it against the washboard, mumbling, *"Who does she think she is?"*

*****

After the close of morning Mass, P.J. Galvin joined his family and fellow parishioners as they filed out of the church at the bottom of Levin Street. Galvin lived nearby in the Fifth Ward, where a large contingent of Irish immigrants had settled. As he walked the short distance home, he thought about the work ahead of him to prepare for the inquest. He was looking forward to receiving the autopsy report from Coroner Stanhope and was hopeful he would have it in his hands before the end of the day.

As Galvin walked in the door, he found the housekeeper in the parlor serving tea to a rugged-looking man whose shoulders were so broad they strained the seams of his suit coat.

A note from Benjamin H. Richards, a New York City Pinkerton detective, had arrived at his home the night before. Galvin was intrigued as to why Richards had requested to see him.

He knew Detective Richards by reputation. A few winters ago, Richards was hired by a group of wealthy New York cottagers to investigate break-ins at their summer residences during the off-season. Not surprisingly, the local authorities had not welcomed Richards' assistance. Some police officers had complained about the outsider encroaching on their turf. However, Richards' brilliant detective work eventually enabled the local police to identify the people responsible for the rash of thefts.

"I hope I am not late," Galvin said as he made his way to the parlor.

As Richards stood to greet him, Galvin was struck by the detective's considerable height and athletic build.

"No, I was early," Richards responded, smiling broadly as he carefully balanced the teacup and saucer that looked delicate in his large hands.

Deep creases marked Richards' forehead and clean-shaven cheeks. The detective looked to be in his early thirties with a sandy-colored walrus-style mustache and fashionably styled hair parted down the middle, so the side curls turned slightly backward.

He certainly looks like a Pinkerton detective, thought Galvin as he took a seat opposite and motioned for Richards to sit back down.

"Detective Richards, it is an honor to meet you."

Richards placed the cup and saucer on the small side table beside his chair.

"Thank you for your kind words, Mr. Galvin. I must apologize for the short notice in requesting a meeting."

"I admit I am quite curious as to the purpose of your call, though I suspect it may involve the Burton inquest."

Richards smiled awkwardly. "Yes, I suppose I should get straight to the point. Mr. Howard Burton recently engaged the Pinkerton Detective Agency to investigate the circumstances surrounding his father's passing."

Galvin could scarcely contain his enthusiasm. "I'm glad to hear it. I've not had any support from the local police. The authorities have made up their minds that Burton's death was a tragic suicide. I'm sure you know from your previous experience in Newport that our esteemed officials frown on opposing opinions and outside assistance."

"Indeed," Richards agreed. "I have closely followed the newspaper accounts, and when Mr. Burton contacted the agency, I asked to be assigned to the case."

Richards reached for his tea, tossing back what was left in the cup, and cleared his throat.

"May I be blunt? Mr. Burton has paid a small retainer, but I fear he does not have the resources to keep me on the case for more than a day or two at most."

"I see," Galvin said.

"Although I assure you, I will do as much investigative work as possible in that time frame."

Galvin welcomed the help. Except for providing a copy of the police report, Captain Hammond had made it clear that Galvin would not be getting any assistance from his department. He only had a few days to conduct all the interviews with potential witnesses before the inquest began, and Galvin still had his law practice to run. Having a Pinkerton detective to assist was almost too good to be true.

Clapping his hands together, Galvin said, "Let's get started, shall we?"

He retrieved the stack of manila folders containing his notes, the witness statements, and the anonymous letter Stanhope had given him. He also grabbed the preliminary list of witnesses he planned to interview. Galvin opened the folder containing the anonymous letter he received from Coroner Stanhope.

"Take a look at this and tell me what you make of it."

Richards removed the letter from the envelope and read it carefully. He drew in a deep breath and sighed loudly. "I have never put much stock in information from anonymous sources, but I am intrigued by the references to the cooks on the USS New Hampshire."

"As am I. A tenant of Mr. Burton is employed at Coaster's Island. I understand he spends a good deal of time socializing with the cooks onboard the ship ... loose lips, I'm told. Perhaps he has revealed some particulars about the Burton family."

"I will go aboard tomorrow and question them to see what they know," Richards offered.

"As good a place to start as any. Thank you, detective. I'm afraid we have our work cut out for us. Let's see where the evidence leads us."

Richards nodded in agreement and offered his hand to Galvin. "I am pleased to be of service."

"We only have a few days to conduct the initial investigation before the inquest starts on Wednesday."

"Then we best blaze a trail," Richards smiled.

Chapter 8
Monday, October 19, 1885

Richards disembarked from the ferry onto the dock at Coaster's Island. He was there to follow up on the anonymous letter claiming that someone on board the USS New Hampshire had information about violent quarrels in the Burton home.

The detective was awed by the sight of the majestic ship anchored at the island's far end. This grand old vessel, which once served as a hospital and supply ship during the later years of the Civil War, was now the flagship for the newly formed naval apprentice training squadron. Richards could hardly wait to board the beauty.

When he reached the gangplank, he made his way up the steep steps attached to the ship's side. He looked to the stern and rendered a hand salute to the ensign as the officer on the deck approached.

"Request permission to come aboard," Richards asked as he saluted the officer.

"State your purpose," the officer replied, stone-faced.

"Detective Richards of the Pinkerton Agency here to conduct an interview with the cooks concerning possible testimony in an upcoming coroner's inquest."

"Permission granted," the officer replied, stepping aside and motioning for him to come aboard.

Below deck, Richards was met by the aroma of freshly baked bread and the sound of animated laughter coming from the midship galley. When he entered the compartment, he found three young Black men peeling potatoes at a sturdy wooden table in the center. Another man stood by one of the cooktop stoves, a large metal ladle in hand, tending the simmering pots.

The galley was smartly outfitted with gleaming white enameled counters stacked high with freshly caught fish and a variety of seasonal root vegetables in various stages of preparation. Propped against the bulkhead just below two portholes, a chalkboard contained a neatly printed menu for the week.

"Hurry along with those potatoes, men. The broth is coming to a boil," the steward called over his shoulder as he placed a lid on top of one of the pots. He looked up and spotted the detective standing inside the door. "You there, are you lost?"

"No, sir, I'm in the right place," Richards politely replied.

The steward cocked his head, looking puzzled. "What business do you have here?"

"My name is Benjamin Richards. I am a detective who has been hired to investigate the death of Ben Burton."

"What does that have to do with me? Or them?" the steward asked as he pointed toward the cooks sitting around the table.

"That's what I'm here to find out," Richards grinned. "The coroner has received a letter that alleges the cooks, or other personnel aboard this ship, may have information relevant to the case."

He put down his ladle and wiped his hands on his apron. "I'm the ship's steward."

"Glad to make your acquaintance," Richards responded with a handshake. "Did you know Mr. Burton?"

"No more so than anyone else around here, I suppose. He was always a friendly sort. I saw him about a month before he died. I sure was sorry to hear about it," the steward commented sincerely before adding, "but I'm not sure any of us on this ship can tell you anything."

He turned to address his crew, "Do any of you men know anything about Ben Burton's death?"

Richards watched as they all shook their heads no.

"We have all heard the rumors flying around out there," one of the cooks offered.

The steward returned his attention to the detective. "There you have it. Now, it's almost time for the midday meal, and we have work to do. If there is nothing more?"

Richards removed his pocket watch to check the time and presented it to the steward. "It is only 10:30 a.m. If you cooperate, I will be gone no later than 11:00."

The steward consented, not wanting to appear difficult, "All right, but make it quick."

"Is one of Burton's tenants—a fellow by the name of McGruder—employed on this ship?" enquired Richards.

"He's not employed here. McGruder works at the yard, not on the ship."

"So, you know Mr. McGruder?"

"Yes, we all do," the steward smiled slyly. "He comes by every day after his graveyard shift because he doesn't want to go home to face his missus."

"Did he ever talk about Mr. Burton or his family?"

One of the cooks chuckled and chimed in, "McGruder does like the sound of his voice, especially when he is liquored up. Might have mentioned something in passing."

Unamused, Richards continued, "What might that have been?"

"To tell you the truth, we don't pay much attention to McGruder when he is drinking," the cook snickered, causing the other cooks to burst out laughing at the comment.

Sensing the detective's increasing frustration, the steward spoke up. "Why don't you ask him yourself? He's in the enlisted quarters sleeping it off. Come on, I'll take you there."

He led Richards to the adjacent compartment where McGruder was sprawled on one of the lower bunks, snoring loudly. The room reeked of alcohol.

The steward walked over to the bunk, gave it a good kick, and hollered, "McGruder! There's a detective here who wants to speak with you." He then turned and winked at Richards before he left the room.

McGruder slowly opened his eyes to discover Richards' muscular form looming over him. He bolted upright and slurred, "I didn't do anything, I swear! I've been working all night. I was just taking a quick nap before I head home."

With an amused smile, Richards reassured the man, "Relax, Mr. McGruder. You aren't in any trouble. I'm just here to ask you some questions about Ben Burton."

"Burton? My landlord?" McGruder rubbed his head and licked his dry lips. "I paid him rent, and that's it."

"What do you know about his family?"

"I know the girl married the fellow, thinking he would make plenty of dough to pay for all her expensive do-dads. And the future doctor married the girl because he thought she was an heiress … but they both got fooled!"

McGruder threw his head back and let out a peal of laughter as if this were the funniest thing he had ever said while Richards waited patiently for McGruder's laughter to subside.

"What makes you say that, Mr. McGruder?"

McGruder grinned like the Cheshire cat. "Let's just say I hear things."

"So, what have you heard?" asked Richards, wondering if McGruder could be the person referred to in the anonymous letter.

"A few weeks ago, old man Burton was yelling. Boy, he sure was mad! Yes, siree."

"Where were you when you heard this?"

"In my apartment on the second floor, but the walls are pretty thin."

"Who was he yelling at?" asked Richards.

"It must have been that snotty daughter of his because I heard a woman crying. Sounded like he was banging his fists on the table, too."

"Could you hear what he was saying?"

"Old Burton was yelling, '*The Dorseys must leave this house!*'"

"Did he say anything else?"

"I don't recollect all of it, but there was talk about money. And there was some hollering about a letter, too. Maybe you should ask the other tenants. My place is the farthest from Burton's, so if I heard him, they must have heard it too."

"Was it common to overhear arguments in the Burton household?" Richards asked.

"Nope."

With that, McGruder lay back on the bunk and rolled away from Richards.

Recognizing that McGruder would not make a reliable or presentable witness, Richards left McGruder to sleep it off. But he wasn't ready to discredit the statements in the anonymous letter yet. The writer had been very specific that the cooks on board had relevant information concerning Burton's death. He decided to call the cooks' bluff and see if it would cause them to disclose something they knew but weren't saying.

Richards walked back into the galley and, in a stern voice, announced, "Mr. McGruder has informed me that some of you have not been forthcoming with me. Seeing how none of you are willing to talk, I will ask the coroner to issue subpoenas to each of you and will notify your commanding officer that you have not been cooperative. We will see what you have to say under oath. I'll be taking my leave now."

"What? Wait! We know nothing!" protested one of the cooks, angered by the thought of being unfairly punished by his commander.

"Watch the soup pots. I'll handle this, fellas," the steward called out as he stepped away from the stoves and strode toward Richards. "This way, detective. I will escort you above deck."

Richards followed the man back down the passageway toward the hatch until they reached the foot of the ladder, where the steward stopped him.

"Take my word for it, those men don't know anything about Burton's death. McGruder must have been trying to stir up trouble if he has said they did. I'll wager none of those men could even recognize Burton if he was staring them in the face. There's no need to bother them further. I believe it is me that you have come to see."

Richards nodded and flipped open his notebook. "So, tell me. What do you know about Burton's death?"

The steward looked embarrassed. "I didn't mention it earlier—and I should have—but I board with a family on Levin, just up the street from the Burton house."

"So, you are more familiar with Burton than you let on?"

"No, I was truthful when I said I hadn't seen him in a while," he explained. "Mr. Burton was an important man. We didn't run in the same circles, but he always greeted me kindly. It's the family I live with who knew him well. They were all pretty shaken up about Mr. Burton's death."

"Tell me about them."

"The family has three daughters who are acquainted with the Burton girls. The evening of Ben's death, when I got off the ferry, the youngest daughter was waiting at the pier, and we rode home together. She was a bundle of nerves. She was blathering on about the Burton girls and their father. That's how I found out about it ... Mr. Burton's death, I mean."

"What did she say about the Burton girls?" Richards asked.

"Mostly ladies' gossip. Gabbing on about how Burton's daughter was acting all high and mighty since her marriage, and that she wasn't taking care of her father like she should."

Richards interjected, "Are you referring to the oldest daughter? Maria?"

"Yes, that's the one. She mentioned something about Maria complaining about not having a proper wedding dress, not getting to go on a honeymoon, or some other nonsense. Brides put great stock in such things, or so they tell me."

"Did she explain why Maria went without these things?"

"She didn't come right out and say it, but she left me with the impression that Mr. Burton told his daughter he thought they were unnecessary extravagances. The man didn't get rich squandering his money on frivolities," the steward smirked.

"I remember a kerfuffle back in August when Maria was planning a party to celebrate her wedding. None of the girls in my house were invited when the invitations went out."

"Why not? Were they at odds with Maria?" Richards asked.

The steward shrugged his shoulders. "I wouldn't know, but the middle daughter complained that Maria thought she was too good for the Levin Street girls now that she was married to Dorsey. It wasn't just the girls in my house who were slighted. Some of the other girls in the neighborhood didn't get an invitation either.

"To get back at her, the girls in my house planned a party on the same day as the Dorsey party. They invited all the folks Maria hadn't included, as well as many of the same people she had. Next thing you know, the Dorseys sent out last-minute cancellation notices the morning both parties were to take place."

"Because the guests preferred to attend the competing party?"

"It could be, or maybe folks were just hesitant to go to the Burton house," the steward speculated.

"Why would that be?" questioned Richards.

"The girls say that some have discovered their money missing after visiting the Burton home."

"Are they speaking from personal experience?"

"I doubt it."

"Did they say who they suspect was taking the money?"

"They implied it was the older Burton girl."

"Did they give any reason why Maria would resort to stealing from her guests?"

"They say Maria used to whine that her father wasn't giving her enough money to buy everything she wanted or thought she needed. I didn't engage with the girls about these details, Mr. Richards. The remarks were made in passing. Who knows? It may be nothing more than gossip spread by the women in the neighborhood who don't care for the Burton girl."

"Maria may not have been well-liked in the neighborhood, but is the family saying they think she could be involved in her father's death?"

"The oldest girl has said as much. In fact, she used a profane word to describe Maria. I don't want to talk badly about anyone in my house, but I never heard a word like that come out of a lady's mouth before."

"I appreciate you telling me this," Richards said. "I don't know if the assistant attorney general will need you to testify or not."

The man's eyes widened. "I shouldn't have told you what she said. That was wrong of me. The young lady was beside herself when she said that—you shouldn't hold it against her. The family has been particularly good to me. I don't need any problems."

Richards reassured him, "I'll let Attorney Galvin know."

"I appreciate that," the steward replied as he turned and made his way back to the galley.

If he hurried, Richards could catch the next ferry back to Newport to investigate the unexpected information concerning Maria and interview the family that operated the steward's boarding house.

***

Richards stood on the doorstep of 105 Levin Street. A large hand-lettered sign hung above the door that read *Rooms Available*. A smaller sign hung to the right of the door—*Fancy Goods Sold Here*. And beneath that, a notice—*Fancy Trimmings & Ladies Hair Dressing, located next door at 103 Levin Street.*

He knocked on the door and took a step back on the stoop. He waited a few minutes before he heard footsteps from inside. Out of the corner of his eye, he noticed the curtains on the front window move aside and the profile of a woman's face peering through the window, just as a slender young Black lady answered the door.

"Good afternoon. My name is Detective Benjamin Richards."

The young lady put up her hand to stop him. "If you are here about Mr. Burton, my family has nothing to say."

"Ma'am, I have received a tip that members of this family may have relevant information."

"You have been misinformed," the young lady replied as she slammed the door shut.

"Wait!" Richards called out. He knocked forcefully on the door again and hollered, "If you don't speak with me now, I will be forced to subpoena you to the inquest."

"Go away," a voice from inside called out. "We don't want anything to do with you or your inquest."

He stood on the stoop for a few seconds before walking around the side of the house to find a rear entrance. He stopped suddenly when he heard a voice coming from an open window near the back and crouched under the window to remain unseen.

"Mother, do you think they know we wrote the note?"

"Not unless you or one of your sisters has blabbed it to someone. The detective is just fishing for information."

"But I don't want to be called to testify in the inquest!"

"You won't be if we all just remain silent. We've done enough."

***

Ting-a-ling! The shopkeeper's bell rang out as Richards pulled open the front door to the Bellevue Avenue Newport Transfer and Express Office.

"Good morning," he called out in a deep baritone voice as he entered the empty reception area.

Clarence Mason raised his hand in greeting from the back office and made his way to the counter.

"You must be Detective Richards."

He unlocked the hinged gate that separated the reception area from the offices. "Come on back," Mason motioned.

He walked to a black cast iron stove and retrieved the coffee pot from the heat plate. Returning to his desk, he poured them both a cup of steaming coffee and invited the detective to take a seat.

A native of New Hampshire and a Civil War veteran, Mason had relocated to Newport to assume the superintendent position for the New York and Boston Dispatch Company. His company shared the office space with Ben's transfer company, and over the years, Mason and Ben had developed a close relationship.

Mason was a soft-spoken, unassuming man nearly twenty years Ben's junior. He had a small, round face with heavy bags under his eyes, which made him appear much older than his years.

Richards took a long sip of coffee before putting his cup down to pull out his notebook.

"Thank you for agreeing to this meeting, Mr. Mason. Seems like very few people in this town have made themselves available, or willing, to talk with me."

Mason smiled slyly. "That's Newport folk. I find that they don't want to get involved in anything unpleasant, preferring to discuss it among themselves, if you catch my drift. But I'm more than willing to answer any questions you have."

"I appreciate that," Richards responded. "I don't think I will take up much of your time."

"Now that the season is over, I have plenty of time," Mason said with a relaxed smile.

"Thank you. Why don't we begin with how you knew Mr. Burton?"

"Let's see, I worked with Ben for about six years and saw him almost daily. That's his desk right there," Mason said, pointing to an empty desk directly across the room from where the men sat. "I'd like to believe I knew Ben as well, if not better, than most people. We talked about business, personal matters, politics, the weather … just about everything."

Mason removed his wire-rim glasses and swiped his eyes with the back of his hand. "Every success I now enjoy is in one way or another attributable to Ben's influence and generosity of friendship." His voice cracked, and he paused to regain his composure. "I'm sorry, detective. I miss my friend."

"I understand," Richards said, giving Mason a few minutes to gather himself before continuing. "Can you tell me about the last time you saw Mr. Burton?"

Mason grimaced and nodded his head. "I was with him less than an hour before he died. He was in the office that morning, came in at his usual time, and made a few entries in his ledger before he said he had to go to court."

"Court?"

"Yes, a disgruntled former employee had filed a baseless claim that Ben owed him for unpaid wages. Ben said it would be the first time he had to defend himself in court, but he wasn't worried about it. He always kept excellent records. I think he viewed it as more of an annoyance than anything. He then left to go home. He said he would change his coat and eat breakfast before heading to the courthouse."

"Do you know the fellow's name or the amount he demanded?" Richards asked.

"Ben and the boys called him 'Dink.' Not sure what his real name is, but they'll have that down at the courthouse. I think the amount in dispute was less than $50."

"Had he ever threatened Mr. Burton?"

"No, I don't think it went that far. Like I said, Ben wasn't concerned. It isn't enough money to kill a man over, or kill yourself if that's what you're suggesting."

"Still, I will follow up," Richards advised, adding, "I've investigated cases where someone has ended up dead over far less. Are you aware of any other disgruntled employees, or anyone else, who had a beef with Mr. Burton?"

"Let me think about that," Mason responded, scratching his chin. "There was a former Omnibus driver who quit on him and started a competing line. That created a rift between the two, as you might imagine. I can send him your way if you want to talk to him. Come to think of it, Dink works for him now, so you might kill two birds with one stone. But those are the only two that leap to mind."

"Did Mr. Burton ever discuss his financial affairs with you?"

"I know he had a very profitable season. He told me it had far exceeded his two previous years. It's fair to say that his revenue fluctuated like everyone else in Newport who depends on the summer season for their livelihood. Or as Ben used to say, '*We have gathered the cream, and now we will have to live on the skim of the milk until next June.'"*

Mason reached for his mug, blew a cloud of steam from the top, and slurped his coffee.

"Last week, Ben told me that he had an offer on his Levin Street property that he was ready to accept, but he wanted to keep the buyer on the hook a little while longer, hoping the man might sweeten the deal. I cautioned him about employing that strategy. I said it would be a shame if he lost the catch by giving the line too much slack."

Mason's lips curled into a sentimental smile. "But Ben just laughed and said the buyer was too hungry to let go of the worm."

Richards grinned. He tossed back the remainder of his coffee and wiped his mustache with his sleeve.

"I do know that once he sold his house, Ben planned to pay off all his debt with the proceeds. He said it would put him where he had not been for some time … debt-free."

"Did you notice any changes in his demeanor in the days leading up to or on the day of his death?" Richards asked. "Did he seem upset or despondent?"

"I saw nothing unusual," Mason responded. "I would describe his behavior as typical—laughing, joking, teasing, carrying on with his men—his regular jovial self."

Mason paused and leaned forward to place his coffee on the edge of his desk.

"I know what you're getting at, Mr. Richards, but I cannot think of any reason that would cause Ben to kill himself. As a matter of fact, I would go so far as to say Ben Burton was the last person who would be inclined to do such a thing."

"You mentioned you discussed personal matters with Mr. Burton. Did he ever talk about his home life?"

Mason furrowed his brow. "I never asked Ben about his domestic affairs, as it was none of my business, but he did talk of it occasionally. He mentioned that he was not happy with the household expenses of late because they were greater than they needed to be after his son-in-law moved in and didn't lift a finger to help."

"Had you met his son-in-law?"

"No," Mason replied, explaining, "the first time I ever saw the gentleman was on the day Ben died. He came charging into the office as if he owned the place and demanded the keys to Ben's safe. Mind you, this was only a few hours after Ben's death. I thought it was in poor taste, myself."

"Did he say why he wanted the key to the safe?" Richards asked.

"Mr. Dorsey claimed he was acting on behalf of his wife and said that the family had a legal right to Ben's keys, papers, and anything else he may have kept here. I was hesitant to give him anything without first clearing it with someone. But he insisted that he needed to go through Ben's papers right away so the family could open a probate claim."

Mason sighed heavily, "He was so persistent that I finally gave in and agreed on the condition that he would sign a document listing everything he removed from the safe."

Mason searched the detective's face for a reaction. Finding none, he asked for his opinion. "Mr. Richards, do you think I made a mistake in allowing Mr. Dorsey to take the contents of Ben's safe home with him?"

"I'm sure it's fine, Mr. Mason. Do you remember what items he removed?"

Mason slid open the top drawer of his desk and took out a key. "No, but the list is in Ben's safe.

Mason stood, crossed the short distance to the area behind Ben's desk, and unlocked the large black iron tabletop safe. He removed a single sheet of paper from within and returned to Richards, handing him the document.

"Here you go."

The detective quickly scanned the paper. The list included a ledger, invoices, bills, letters, two one-dollar banknotes, a few coins, and a check for $1.75. So far, there was nothing out of the ordinary. But when Richards reached the bottom of the page, his pulse began to quicken. The last entry on the list was a $3000 life insurance policy.

Pointing at the paper, Richards asked, "Do you know anything about this life insurance policy?"

"I think Ben purchased that life insurance policy when his wife was alive. But Mr. Dorsey didn't say anything to me about any of those items. He just took everything with him."

"Do you mind if I take this to share with Attorney Galvin?" Richards asked.

"I don't see why not," Mason shrugged nonchalantly. "The police haven't asked, and I've got no use for it."

Chapter 9
Tuesday, October 20, 1885

Mary Stoddard donned her favorite flowerpot straw hat trimmed with satin indigo blue ribbons and a lovely ostrich feather plume. With its matching velveteen upturned brim, the headpiece was a perfect complement to her new navy plaid dress. Checking her reflection in a hand mirror, Mary smiled with approval. She was ready for her interview with Attorney Galvin.

She had been looking forward to the meeting. Mary tried to anticipate his questions and even formulated some questions of her own to ask the attorney. However, when Mary arrived at the law office, she was blindsided when the clerk politely informed her that Galvin would not be conducting the interview, but Detective Richards would instead.

"Who? Why isn't Mr. Galvin here to interview me himself? We had an appointment!"

Emerging from the back office, Richards interrupted, "Good morning, Mrs. Stoddard. My name is Detective Richards, and I am working with Attorney Galvin on the Burton case. Why don't you come back and take a seat?"

Mary remained standing in place and raised her chin to get a better look at the detective.

"I don't believe I know you, Mr. Richards."

He smiled reassuringly. "I am employed by the New York City office of the Pinkerton Detective Agency, but I am occasionally assigned to work on cases here in Newport. My new bride is so taken with your fair city that she wants us to settle here."

Mary's expression softened. "Is that so? Does your wife have family in Newport? What's her name? Perhaps I know her or her family."

Richards gave her a sly smile. "I'm sure you will understand that, in my line of work, it is important to keep the details of my personal life private. Now, why don't you come back to the office and have a seat."

Why did Mr. Galvin need to hire a New York City detective? Mary wondered as she followed him into the back office. *Captain Hammond is a very competent and well-respected detective.*

"As I mentioned, I'm doing some of the legwork for Attorney Galvin in this case," Richards remarked as he sat behind the desk. "Interviewing witnesses and such."

"What do you mean by legwork? Just how many witnesses does Mr. Galvin intend to call?" she asked, thinking, *He needs only to call me and a handful of others to prove it was suicide.*

"I'm not at liberty to discuss the specifics of the investigation, Mrs. Stoddard. Please, won't you take a seat?" repeated Richards, pointing again to the empty chair.

Mary lowered herself into the chair, her head spinning.

"Mrs. Stoddard, I'd like to begin with some background information."

Mary eyed the detective suspiciously while noting, "I must say, Mr. Richards, that I find it rather peculiar that Attorney Galvin hasn't already provided you with those details."

Flashing a smile, Richards lightly tapped his pencil on his notepad. "It is my practice to get all my information directly from the person I am interviewing."

Satisfied with his response and pushing her misgivings aside, Mary answered the detective's background questions in a perfunctory manner.

"Very good, thank you," said Richards before moving on to the next topic. "Now, I'd like to ask you a series of questions concerning Mr. Burton. How well did you know him?"

"I would say that I knew Mr. Burton better than I knew the other members of his family. I am also familiar with the Burton children, but Mr. Burton and I spoke frequently," she explained.

"When did you last speak with Mr. Burton?"

"It was the day before his death. I was sweeping my front stoop when he came out of his back door. He would always cut through his backyard and walk up the side street when he went to his Bellevue Avenue office. Ben said he found Levin Street too busy and noisy. He tried to avoid it when he could."

"What did you talk about?"

"I always asked him how he was doing when I saw him. That day, when I asked, he told me that if he had a pistol, he would blow his brains out."

Nonplussed, Richards responded, "Did he say why he would want to do that?"

"Mr. Richards, did you hear what I just said?" asked Mary incredulously. "Mr. Burton told me that if he had a pistol, he would blow his brains out on the day before he did just that!"

"I'm not doubting you, Mrs. Stoddard. But I wondered if he gave you any reason why he would say that to you."

"For goodness' sake, do you need to know *why* the man killed himself?"

"Attorney Galvin needs to present evidence concerning Mr. Burton's state of mind prior to his death," Richards explained patiently. "Your considerable knowledge about Mr. Burton can assist me in gathering that information."

"Detective, wouldn't it help you more if I told you what I saw on the day of Mr. Burton's death? Once you hear that, you won't need to gather any more information."

"Very well. Then why don't you tell me what you saw," Richards conceded agreeably.

Mary painstakingly led him through her actions and observations on the morning of Ben's death, starting with her watching Idella hanging out the wash until the police officer relieved her from guarding Ben's body.

"In your opinion, could there be anyone who might have wanted Mr. Burton dead? Perhaps someone with whom he had disagreements?" asked Richards.

Mary responded hesitantly. "Well, there's his son, Howard. That boy was always getting into trouble growing up. His father had to send him to reform school to try to straighten him out. Then, as soon as he returned *re-ha-bil-itated*, he married a much older woman from the other side of town, if you know what I mean."

Mary shook her head sadly. "Mr. and Mrs. Burton—his mother was still alive then—were beside themselves when he did that. Thankfully, the marriage didn't last long, but it was quite a scandal when his former wife immediately turned around and married their next-door neighbor. I heard that Mr. Burton told Howard in no uncertain terms that he had disgraced the family for the last time and was ashamed to call him his son."

"Do you think Howard is capable of murder?"

As if she were letting Richards in on a secret, Mary leaned in and said, "You know there is talk that he killed someone in New York City."

"Do you believe the talk?"

"I don't know, I really don't know him. I'm not even sure where that rumor originated. Probably Emily Burton."

"What would be his motive if he murdered his father?"

"For heaven's sake, as I have stated repeatedly, I don't believe for one minute that Mr. Burton was murdered. You asked me if anyone would want him dead. Howard Burton is the only person I know who had any disagreements with Mr. Burton, and he had a reputation in town as a troublemaker. Certainly, neither of Mr. Burton's poor daughters nor Mr. Dorsey was involved in Mr. Burton's death. If Mr. Burton didn't kill himself—and I'm not saying that he didn't—maybe someone snuck into town, shot Mr. Burton, and then left without anyone knowing it."

"Well, that is something to consider."

***

As Richards summarized his notes from Mary Stoddard's interview, Galvin walked into the office.

"I was hoping to find you still here."

In the last 24 hours, Richards and Galvin had accomplished a great deal. In short order, the detective made progress in interviewing potential witnesses while Galvin planned their next steps in the investigation and prepared his witness examinations for the inquest.

"Are you ready to give me a rundown of your day?" Galvin asked.

Richards gave him a weary smile and stood to relinquish his seat behind Galvin's desk.

"I'm up to it if you are, counselor."

Galvin gestured for him to stay put and plopped down in a chair across the desk. "Let's hear it."

The detective opened a large folder containing all his interview notes. He began by discussing his efforts to interview the family.

"Miss Burton and Mr. and Mrs. Dorsey sent a note by messenger first thing this morning. They have respectfully declined to meet with me as they are in mourning. That means you will need to rely on the information in the police report and statements made by the family to the medical examiner on the day of Ben's death. Mr. Stanhope also sent over their list of witnesses they want you to call in the inquest."

"Any surprises?"

"Most are the same witnesses you are already planning on calling … doctors, creditors, and their tenants. But there are a couple of names that aren't on your list."

Richards slid the paper across the desk to Galvin and grinned. "I couldn't help but notice that their beloved Aunt Emily was missing from their witness list. There is also a doctor whose name I didn't recognize. A Dr. Ecroyd… do you know him? Maybe a friend or acquaintance of Dorsey's from medical school?"

"That's interesting. I don't recognize the name either. If possible, let's add him to the list of people you will interview tomorrow. I see where they've also requested John Malgan be called to the stand."

"Who is that?"

"He owns a popular saloon on Levin Street."

Richards asked, "Why do you suppose they want him to testify?"

"I've heard the family is claiming Burton was deep in debt from gambling."

"What does one have to do with the other?"

Galvin chuckled. "The dice and card games in Newport are played in saloons like Malgan's, or so I've been told by some of my clients."

Richards laughed. "I look forward to that interview. But I do have a bit of good news."

Galvin tucked the witness list in his jacket pocket to review later. "What might that be?"

"I was able to eliminate both of Burton's former employees, who

Mr. Mason identified as possible suspects. The fellow they call Dink was at the courthouse with his attorney, waiting for Burton to appear on the morning of the murder, so he has an ironclad alibi. And Dink's new boss at the competing Omnibus line doesn't appear to have a motive. After Mr. Burton lost his Omnibus vehicles in the fire, the two men no longer had competing businesses."

Richards stopped to flip through his notes.

"But the Omnibus owner did mention one curious thing. He told me that Burton had not spoken to him for more than a year and that Burton had always gone out of his way to avoid the man. But the night before his death, Burton unexpectedly crossed the street to initiate a friendly conversation with him. It is even more mysterious that Burton extended his hand in friendship before they parted."

"What do you make of that?" Galvin asked.

"It might suggest that if Burton was planning to kill himself, he wanted to reconcile with the man before his death."

"It certainly could be construed as such."

Richards then brought Galvin up to speed on his interview with Mary Stoddard.

"She is likely to be a challenging witness because she is so unwavering in her belief that Burton killed himself." Richards broke into a broad smile. "That being said, she did suggest an interesting possible suspect if Burton was murdered."

Intrigued, Galvin leaned forward in his chair. "Who might that be?"

"Mr. Howard Burton."

"The man who hired you to find his father's killer? He hired you to find himself?"

Galvin shook his head, laughing. "Wasn't Howard in New York City on the morning his father died?"

"When pressed, Mrs. Stoddard suggested it is a possibility that he or someone else might have come to Newport, shot Mr. Burton, and then snuck away without anyone seeing them."

"She's not much of a neighborhood watchdog if that is the case," Galvin wisecracked. "Assuming that is a possibility, what would be his motive?"

"The only thing suggested was a history of grievances against his father."

"That doesn't sound like much of a motive to me," said Galvin skeptically. "But aside from that, have you met Howard Burton?"

"No, I never met the man. He dealt directly with the contracting agent in our New York office. I was hoping to interview him when I return to New York."

Galvin smiled knowingly. "Now, keep in mind that I have only met him in the company of his domineering aunt, but he does not present himself as a man capable of murder. He hardly spoke a word … was very meek and unassuming."

"Those are the ones you need to look out for," laughed Richards. "But I vote to take Howard Burton off our list of possible suspects … for now."

Chapter 10
Wednesday, October 21, 1885
First Day of Inquest Proceedings

Galvin and Richards burned the midnight oil, discussing the best strategy for presenting witnesses on the first day of the inquest. In the end, they both decided it made sense to start with the testimony of the family members who were in the house at the time of Ben's death.

Galvin had read the scant police report. It only contained brief summaries of where each family member claimed to be during the shooting. This would be the attorney's first opportunity to hear directly from the family members, and he was eager to get their sworn statements on the record.

While Dora, Allen, and Maria had made it clear they had no intention of meeting with Richards before the inquest, Galvin had been inundated with daily messages from Emily Burton demanding to know when she would be interviewed. To appease her, he asked the detective to send a message assuring Emily that she would be interviewed before she testified. Based on their exhaustive prior meeting, he already had a strong notion of what she would say on the stand. He needed Richards to prioritize his time on witnesses who had yet to be interviewed.

The coroner's inquest was scheduled to begin at 1:30 p.m. in the

City Hall. Galvin had spent the morning in his office refining his questions before closing his notebook, putting on his hat, and stepping onto Thames Street. He walked purposefully down the street past the commercial wharves jutting out into Newport Harbor. As he entered the heart of the business district, he passed a hodgepodge of specialty shops, saloons, law offices, banks, and pre-revolutionary war homes.

When he reached Washington Square, the hub of colonial Newport, he paused briefly to admire the majestic Old Colony House that sat atop the gentle rise of the square's east side. Once the seat of the colonial government, it now functioned as one of the two Rhode Island state capitol buildings as well as a courthouse. The ornate brick three-story Georgian-style building was topped with an octagonal cupola. Its large turret clock that rested between two round eight-pane windows had just struck one o'clock.

Because of the overwhelming public interest in the proceedings, the inquest was being held in the city council chambers, the largest room in City Hall. Judging from the number of people milling around Washington Square, Galvin doubted any public room in Newport was large enough to hold everyone vying for a front-row seat.

City Hall was located at the foot of Washington Square in the Old Brick Market, a commodious red brick three-story colonial structure that was the perfect bookend to the Old Colony House. Galvin stopped near the entrance to survey the circus-like atmosphere that had taken over Washington Square.

A long line of people waited to enter, hoping to get a coveted seat in the chamber. A similar queue had formed in front of the hot peanut vendor's wagon parked next to the bandstand. Stationed within the bandstand, a lively street preacher took advantage of the occasion to shout his thunderous message of salvation over the din of the growing crowd.

Enterprising shop owners lined the sidewalks with wares, hoping to entice curiosity seekers into impulsively making an unnecessary purchase. A bottleneck of horses stood waiting to take their turn at the strategically located watering trough at the intersection of the three streets that funneled traffic onto Thames Street.

Galvin opened the large entry doors to City Hall and stepped inside. He could hear loud, angry voices coming from the council chambers on the second floor.

"He was murdered, I tell you!"

"You don't know what you are talking about! Everyone knows that he killed himself."

A stern warning by the sheriff followed the voices. "If you men don't settle down, I will kick you both to the curb!"

The hearing had yet to start, and already tempers were flaring. *It is going to be a long day,* Galvin thought as he rushed past the public door to the council chamber and down the hall to its rear entrance.

*****

The large wood-paneled chamber had been reconfigured specifically for the inquest proceedings. Coroner Stanhope would preside from a raised dais at the front of the room.

The spectator gallery behind the railing was filled with row after row of long wooden benches on both sides of the room, allowing just enough space to create a center aisle. The first bench on the right-hand side had been roped off and reserved for members of the press. A single witness chair was placed just to the left of the platform, and a small table and chair reserved for the court reporter sat nearby.

It would be the court reporter's duty to record the inquest proceedings and witness testimony accurately, but this hearing would differ substantially from a judicial procedure. There would be no other attorneys here to defend the rights of a potential suspect or witness, and no jury would be present. This inquest was not a trial but a publicly held inquiry.

At exactly 1:30, Coroner Stanhope entered the packed council chambers, and the spectators quieted.

As he took his seat, Galvin scanned the room. Reverend Van Horne sat next to the chairs reserved for the mayor and city marshal, who could come and go from the hearing as their duties permitted. He recognized several physicians sitting on the other side of the clergyman, some of whom he had subpoenaed as witnesses. Businessmen filled out the remaining seats in front of the bar.

The spectators in the gallery were packed shoulder-to-shoulder. Those unable to find a seat on one of the benches stood against the walls encircling the gallery.

Stanhope nodded to Sheriff Benjamin Easton, who was standing at the railing in front of the row of reporters. He was there to call and swear in the witnesses and keep order if needed.

Easton was a no-nonsense sheriff. A middle-aged man of average height, Easton was also charged with overseeing the operations of the Newport County Jail and lived in the jail's annex with his family. His muscular build came in handy when restraining prisoners, defendants, and unruly spectators when necessary. Although he could be tough when his duties required, the laugh lines around his eyes and mouth revealed his kind and congenial nature.

Galvin stacked his folders on the edge of the wooden table and began organizing his notes when Stanhope called out to him.

"Counselor, are you ready to begin?"

"Yes, sir. Ready to proceed."

Stanhope addressed the court reporter. "Do you have everything at the ready?"

The court reporter stretched out his hands and wiggled his fingers in an exaggerated manner before picking up his pen, causing a wave of laughter in the gallery.

Stanhope cleared his throat loudly, snapping the restless audience to attention. He shuffled the papers before him and skimmed through the list of witnesses a final time before turning his attention to the crowd.

"I would like to remind all in attendance today that this is a formal proceeding. I ask each of you to keep silent throughout this inquest. Sheriff Easton stands ready to remove you from this chamber at my discretion and direction if there are any outbursts or disruptions. If you are removed from the chamber, you will not be permitted to return and may be subject to a criminal charge of disturbing the peace. While this inquest is a public hearing, I will not hesitate to clear these chambers and continue the proceedings in private if proper decorum is not maintained."

Stanhope paused to adjust his glasses. "I am now going to read the charge for the proceeding. This inquest is a formal investigation to determine where, when, and the cause of Benjamin J. Burton's death, and who was responsible for the death, if it can be determined."

He cleared his throat again, then continued. "Attorney Patrick J. Galvin has been appointed to represent the state attorney general during this inquest. It is his responsibility to call forth and examine the witnesses, though I also maintain the right to ask questions of the witnesses. All witness testimony will be taken under oath; therefore, those who refuse to testify or are found untruthful will be subject to potential criminal charges."

Stanhope looked up from his papers into the eager and expectant eyes of P.J. Galvin. "Attorney Galvin, call your first witness."

Chapter 11
Wednesday, October 21, 1885
Inquest

"The state calls Maria Antoinette Burton Dorsey," Galvin announced as he pushed back his chair from the table and rose to his feet.

Sheriff Easton opened the door to the adjoining Alderman's chamber, where witnesses had been sequestered to prevent them from hearing the testimony of other witnesses. He called out loudly, "Mrs. Dorsey, please come forward."

The spectators shifted in their seats to get a better look at Maria as she stepped through the door into the chamber. Dressed in the same mourning dress, bonnet, and veil she wore to her father's funeral, she wore no jewelry except her wedding ring. Keeping her head bowed, she gracefully crossed the room to the witness chair. After Easton administered the oath, Maria pushed the veil away from her face and over her bonnet. Her face bore no visible emotion as she bent her head forward to kiss the Bible and took her seat.

Galvin picked up his notes and walked to the front of the table. He bowed his head politely.

"Good afternoon, Mrs. Dorsey. Will you begin by telling us where you live, your age, and your relationship to Benjamin J. Burton?"

Maria spoke slowly and confidently. "I reside at 63 Levin Street. I am 25 years old. Benjamin J. Burton was my father, and I lived with him. I was the housekeeper."

"Who else was living with you at 63 Levin Street at the time of Mr. Burton's death?" Galvin asked.

"In addition to my father, my younger sister Dora, and my husband, Allen Dorsey. My husband has lived with us since our marriage on June 17th of this year. I have an older brother, Howard, but he lives in New York City."

"Mrs. Dorsey, could you walk me through your actions on the morning of October 6th, starting when you first awoke?"

Maria looked away as if trying to gather her thoughts.

"I got up from bed, I believe around seven-thirty, and dressed to go downstairs. My husband was ill and still sleeping, so I left the room without disturbing him. When I got downstairs, my sister, Dora, was in the kitchen preparing a breakfast plate for Father, but he was not home."

Galvin interrupted, "Do you know where your father was?"

Maria gazed back at Galvin and firmly responded, "He was at work."

"What did you do then?"

"I went about my morning chores as usual … making Father's bed, straightening his room, and tidying up the house. That kept me busy until about 9:45."

Maria looked down and twisted the thin gold band on her left hand.

"After checking on my husband and finding him still asleep, I decided to go to the post office and maybe stop by the Boston Store afterward. Before I left, I asked my sister to go to the attic and get two blankets to put in Father's room.

"But as I was getting ready to leave, I saw Mrs. Traeger, one of our tenants, in the backyard, and I remembered that I needed to get a measurement from her. I stepped outside and asked her if we could go upstairs to her tenement so I could get the measurement."

Galvin looked puzzled. "I hate to interrupt again, Mrs. Dorsey, but can you explain why you needed a measurement from Mrs. Traeger?"

"I was making a dress for her," Maria patiently explained, "and I needed to measure her waist."

"I see," Galvin noted, asking, "Are you a dressmaker by trade?"

Appearing put off by the suggestion, Maria quickly corrected him. "No, sir, but I had an older sister who was training to be a dressmaker before she passed."

Those in the room who had known Maria's sister, whose life had been tragically cut short by consumption, bowed their heads in memory of the sweet young girl.

Maria adopted a more conciliatory tone. "I enjoyed helping my sister; she taught me how to sew. I was making a dress for Mrs. Traeger as a favor to her."

Galvin had the distinct impression that Maria Dorsey didn't want anyone in the room to think she needed to work.

"Had your father returned home by the time you left the house?"

"Yes, he was sitting at the breakfast table when I passed through the kitchen." In anticipation of what Galvin might next ask, Maria paused briefly and added, "I did not speak with him, though."

Galvin walked back and spread his notes across the table. "Please continue."

"While I was in the Traeger home, I heard two loud noises… like doors being slammed shut." Maria lowered her eyes. "I know now that they were gunshots."

"How far apart were the sounds?"

"I'm not certain. But they were close together."

Galvin looked down at his notes, then back at Maria. "Did Mrs. Traeger hear the gunshots as well?"

She nodded her head yes. "After the second bang, she asked me what I thought those noises were, and I said Dora must be slamming doors."

"So, you recognized the sounds as coming from inside your house?"

"Yes. Our home shares a wall with the Traegers' apartment."

Galvin walked toward her. "Did you do anything to investigate what might have caused the loud noises?"

"No, afterward, everything was quiet. I didn't think there was anything to investigate," Maria explained.

"What did you do then?"

"I left Mrs. Traeger's house and walked to the post office to see if we had any letters to be picked up."

"Did you pass anyone you knew, coming or going, or did you see anyone you recognized while you were in the post office?"

"Not that I recall," she admitted, "although I believe children were playing in the schoolyard at St. Mary's when I passed."

Galvin made a mental note to ask Richards to check with the postmaster to see if he or anyone on his staff could confirm Maria's testimony.

"How long did you remain at the post office?"

"Just a few minutes. There were no letters for us."

"And did you go to the Boston Store?"

"No, I changed my mind and went directly home. When I returned, I passed through the front door and went straight into the kitchen to put bread in the oven."

Maria's confident demeanor faded into a darkened expression. She lowered her head, her voice cracking, "That is when I saw my father's body lying on the floor, a gun next to his hand."

"What did you do then?"

Maria swabbed her cheeks with the back of her hand to ebb the flow of tears that had begun to stream down her face. She took a moment to gather herself before recounting her anguished screams upon the discovery of her father's body and her cries for her sister and husband to come downstairs.

"Did they respond to your calls for help?" Galvin asked solemnly, being respectful of his witness's obvious distress.

Maria squeezed her eyes shut. Her words were halting, her tone uneven. "Dora came running down the stairs … and I told her to go and get Mrs. Traeger. I ran out the front door and into the street, screaming for help. A man—I don't know who—told me he would send for a police officer, so I ran back inside my house."

Overcome with emotion, Maria fell into a grief-stricken silence.

"Take your time," Galvin offered as Coroner Stanhope leaned forward and offered her his handkerchief.

Maria dried her eyes and wiped her nose. When she found the strength to continue, the rawness in her voice was still palatable.

"When I returned home, I must have fainted and was carried upstairs because the next thing I remember was lying on my bed."

"And did your husband also come downstairs in response to your screams?"

Maria slowly regained her composure and straightened her

shoulders.

"I didn't wait for him, but I know he came down just as soon as he got dressed. But I wasn't in the house at that time."

"Do you recall how much time elapsed between the time you left Mrs. Traeger's apartment and when you returned home to find your father's body?"

"I would say fifteen to twenty minutes," Maria estimated.

Galvin walked back to the table to make a note of the timeframe.

"Mrs. Dorsey, what led you to immediately assume that your father had shot himself?"

Maria looked down at her hands, now clasped tightly in her lap.

"There was a gun on the floor next to him, and no one else was around. Father had been very despondent lately, so my first thought was that he had given up," she said wistfully.

"When you say 'lately,' what period of time are you referring to?"

She raised her head and answered earnestly, "I would say we began to notice a change in his disposition at the beginning of the summer that lasted until his death."

"Do you know what might have caused his despondency?" Galvin asked.

"It may have been because of his poor health," Maria suggested, stating her father had fallen from his wagon in May and was also bothered with a stomach ailment. She lowered her voice furtively and added, "Or maybe it was because of his financial problems. I heard my father say he was unable to meet his debts and that he had lost a good deal of money."

Galvin was momentarily caught off guard by Maria's apparent suggestion that Ben's financial condition might have led to his suicide. She had not mentioned that possibility in her prior statements. He wanted to know more.

"Did your father tell you how much debt he had accumulated or to whom he owed money?"

Maria lowered her chin and cast her eyes downward. "No, Mr. Galvin. Father would not have discussed those details with me. I can only state that bill collectors frequently knocked at our door."

"Do you recall what type of bills were being presented?"

Like reciting biblical verses from memory, Maria rattled off a long list of vendors: the laundress, the milkman, the farrier, the poultryman, the butcher, leaving the court reporter scribbling furiously to keep up.

Galvin interrupted the recitation, commenting, "Suffice it to say you are referring to the usual household expenses?"

"I would not have knowledge of any other type of bill," Maria stated flatly.

"Do you know how much money he lost or how he lost it?"

"I know that Father would often stay out late—very late—and sometimes all night," Maria responded in a sanctimonious tone, her words dripping with nefarious implications.

Side-stepping the inference, Galvin followed with a more direct approach.

"Did you ever ask your father where he had been?"

To his disappointment, she responded, "It was not my place to ask Father where he had been or what he was doing."

Maria cleared her throat and softened her tone. "My father was very irregular in his schedule, especially during the busy season. He never ate with Allen, Dora, and me. We rarely spoke in the last months of his life. The longest conversation we had during that time was on the night before he died."

"What was that conversation about?" Galvin asked.

The spectators sat motionless, no one daring to leave their seats in anticipation of hearing Ben's last words to his daughters. Maria solemnly described the conversation with her father. When she disclosed that her father had told them he did not expect to live much longer, audible gasps echoed throughout the chamber.

Maria's eyes once again brimmed with tears.

"Father was so low-spirited that night, more so than I had ever seen him."

Galvin opened the Manila folder containing the police report and thumbed through it until he removed the sheet of paper with the summary of her statement. He scanned it quickly and then looked at Maria.

"After the conversation, were you concerned that your father might harm himself?"

"No, as I said, we all thought Father was referring to the recent decline in his health. He would often say that he wished he were dead, especially after Mother's death four years ago, but we had no reason to believe that he would kill himself.

"Mr. Galvin, I swear on my saintly mother's grave that we would have done anything to stop him had we only known what he was planning," Maria wept loudly, her earnest pleas of helplessness affecting even the most skeptical listeners in the gallery.

Galvin stepped back.

"Mrs. Dorsey, do you need a moment?"

"No, I can continue," she responded, wiping her eyes.

Galvin redirected his questioning by asking, "How would you describe the relationship between you and your father?"

Maria managed a slight smile. "My father was always very kind to me, and we had a most pleasant relationship."

"What about your sister and your husband? How were their relations with your father?"

Maria met Galvin's eyes. "We all got along very well," she said with conviction, despite the now-widespread rumors to the contrary. "Father was most pleased with my marriage and was happy that I would be taken care of by my husband."

She raised her chin at the mention of Allen.

"My husband has a very bright future. He is preparing to complete his final year in medical school in Philadelphia, and I am going with him. I would say that the best of feelings existed between my father and husband."

"And your sister?"

"As the baby of the family, she shared a special relationship with my father. He was very protective of her. Allen and I had considered bringing Dora to Philadelphia with us, but Father told us he wasn't ready to let her go yet."

Adding a detail that Detective Richards had gleaned from his interview with Clarence Mason, Galvin asked, "Did your father mention to you that he was planning to sell the house you were living in?"

Maria scooted back in her chair. "No, he did not."

"Did your father ever tell you or Mr. Dorsey that you must leave his house?"

"No," she swiftly countered, "He knew we were planning to go to Philadelphia as soon as my husband was well enough to resume his studies."

"Did your husband's illness require a doctor's care?"

"Yes, Mr. Galvin. His doctor applied a mustard plaster to his chest the day before my father's death. He seemed to be improving, but my husband was still not well enough to return to school."

"Who was the doctor who treated him?"

"Dr. Ecroyd."

Galvin recognized the name from the Dorseys' witness list. He hoped Richards had contacted the doctor today as planned. He glanced back up at Maria.

"Just to confirm, the sole reason your husband had not returned to school in Philadelphia was due to his health?"

Maria nodded, "Yes, but now, with my father's death and this inquest, I don't know when we will be able to leave town."

"Do you know if your husband has paid his tuition and housing in Philadelphia for the upcoming school year?"

The question caught Maria off guard.

"Yes, Mr. Galvin," she responded defensively, "He had taken care of that during the summer."

"Did Mr. Dorsey pay the tuition from his own funds, or did he use the money from the dowry?"

She responded tersely, "I don't know what you mean by dowry."

"Isn't it true your father pledged a substantial dowry to Mr. Dorsey upon your marriage?"

Maria stiffened. "My father never gave us the wedding gift he had promised. My husband had saved enough money before we were married to pay his tuition and our room and board."

Galvin hesitated, then asked, "Did you or your husband ever ask anyone for money?"

Maria bristled at the suggestion. "No, of course not," she responded defiantly. "Neither my husband nor I asked anyone for money. We had no need to."

Galvin paused, momentarily stunned by Maria's unequivocal denials. He was suddenly struck by a sinking suspicion that Emily Burton may not have been entirely truthful with him.

Had she unfairly painted Allen as an educated pauper? His face flushed at the thought. *Could Emily be using him as a pawn in an ongoing crusade against Allen and Maria? Why would Maria subject herself to a possible charge of perjury by testifying under oath about something that could be easily refuted if not true? It didn't make sense.*

Galvin decided it was best not to question Maria any further on the issue of money until Richards had interviewed Emily again. He needed to be careful not to come across as a bully. For now, he would have to accept Maria's sworn testimony that she never asked anyone for money.

"One final question, Mrs. Dorsey. Do you know of anyone who would have any reason to want your father dead?"

Softening, Maria answered, "No. My father was loved by everyone."

Glancing up at Coroner Stanhope, who had sat in rapt attention throughout Maria's testimony, the attorney concluded his questioning.

"Thank you, Mrs. Dorsey, that will be all for now."

Galvin took his seat, his mind racing. *Someone was not telling him the truth. But who was it, Maria or Emily?* He quickly scratched a note to Richards asking him to schedule an interview with Emily Burton as soon as possible. Gesturing to Sheriff Easton, he handed him the note and asked him to dispatch the communication immediately.

Maria looked to Coroner Stanhope, who motioned for her to leave the witness chair. She gracefully rose, smoothed her skirts, and lowered her veil over her face. As she started to walk back across the council chamber, an out-of-town journalist nudged a reporter from the *Newport Mercury* and leaned closer to whisper in his ear.

"Did you notice the door to the Alderman's chamber was cracked open? I think someone was listening to her testimony from behind the door!"

***

Sheriff Easton escorted a visibly nervous and wide-eyed Dora to the witness stand as her eyes darted around the crowded room. Like her sister, Dora wore her mourning dress, but her head was uncovered, save for a translucent lace veil fastened to her braided top knot, which fell loosely about her shoulders. After being sworn in and seated, Sheriff Easton returned to his post at the railing, and Galvin began by asking Dora the same introductory questions he had asked her sister.

Dora spoke in a small, shaky voice, barely above a whisper.

"I live at 63 Levin with my sister and her husband. I am 17 years old and help my sister with the housework. Benjamin J. Burton was my father."

The court reporter leaned forward to better hear Dora's words. He looked to Coroner Stanhope, his eyes pleading for help.

"You'll have to speak up, Miss Burton," Stanhope advised. "Speak as loudly and clearly as you are able."

Galvin asked Dora to take him through her movements on the morning of her father's death. She confirmed Maria's earlier testimony about their interactions until her sister left the house.

"After Maria left, I went to the kitchen to get a broom to sweep my room. Father was sitting at the table in the kitchen, eating his breakfast."

"Did you speak with him, Miss Burton?"

Dora nervously twisted the fabric of her skirt in her hands. "No."

"Alright," Galvin said, "What did you do then?"

"I went to the attic because Maria had asked me to get blankets for Father's bed."

"Is that where you were when you heard the gunshots?" Galvin gently asked.

Dora bit her bottom lip and answered, "I heard nothing. I could have been in the attic, I don't know. I didn't hear anything until Maria was screaming that Father was hurt."

"What did you do then?"

"I ran down the stairs. I glanced into the kitchen from the dining room, and I saw my father on the floor." Dora broke down, her agonizing sobs filling the air. The young girl's anguish moved even the most hardened men in attendance.

Galvin turned to Stanhope and asked that the witness be given water. The coroner motioned to Sheriff Easton to fetch a glass. Dora took a few sips, and Galvin waited patiently until the young girl's sobs dissolved into hiccups.

"Are you able to continue, Miss Burton?"

"Yes," she whimpered, her head still bowed.

"What did you do after …" Galvin paused, cautiously avoiding any reference to the kitchen or her father before adding, "That?"

"I went to Mrs. Traeger's and brought her back to our house. While we were in the dining room, Mrs. Stoddard came out of the kitchen and asked where Allen was."

"And where was Mr. Dorsey, Miss Burton?"

"He was still upstairs, sick in bed."

"How did you know that?"

"Every time I passed his room that morning, he was in bed. He had been sick for several days and had rarely left his room."

"When did you first see Mr. Dorsey downstairs that morning?"

"It was after Mrs. Stoddard went to get him."

Galvin attempted to make eye contact, but Dora kept her chin down.

"What did you do after Mr. Dorsey came downstairs?"

Dora shook her head. "I don't know. All of it is a blur. After Maria returned, people just started coming into the house. I don't remember who came in and out. Mrs. Stoddard sent me upstairs to get away from the crowd."

Dora put her head in her hands and rocked back and forth.

"Miss Burton, can you continue?"

Dora took a few sips of water and nodded.

"I'm going to ask you a few questions about your father when you are ready."

Dora finally met Galvin's eyes. "I'm ready."

"Thank you. Miss Burton. Did you ever hear your father talk about wanting to harm himself?"

"No, but he did tell us that he didn't think he would be around much longer."

Dora then repeated Maria's testimony detailing the conversation the girls had with their father the night before his death. As she spoke, Galvin was struck by the fact that Dora's testimony was virtually identical to Maria's. Not surprisingly, Dora knew nothing about her father's debts but confirmed Maria's statement that their father had been depressed all summer.

When asked to describe her father's depression, Dora demurred, saying, "Father was rarely at home. He would often stay out late and sometimes all night."

"Do you know of anyone who would want to see your father dead?" Galvin asked.

"No."

"Miss Burton, can you describe your relationship with your father?"

Dora's eyes welled with fresh tears. "We were very close. I loved my father very much."

Galvin pressed forward, determined to finish his examination. "Did you ever quarrel with your father?"

Seemingly confused, Dora asked Galvin to repeat the question before answering, "Quarrel? No, never."

"Did you ever witness arguments between your father and your sister?"

"No."

Galvin slowly approached Dora. "Are you aware of any arguments between your father and Mr. Dorsey?"

Dora paused to take a sip of water.

"No, sir. We all got along very well. My father was pleased with their marriage."

Galvin saw no reason to belabor his examination. Dora appeared to be a delicate girl who was consumed by grief over the loss of her beloved father. Her testimony had done nothing to shed any light on the cause of Ben's death.

"Thank you, Miss Burton. I have no further questions."

***

As Allen Dorsey entered the courtroom from the Alderman's chamber, whispered murmuring filled the gallery. This was the first time many in the crowd had seen him.

"Quiet!" Coroner Stanhope called out. "Come to order."

Galvin watched with great interest as Allen strode confidently toward the witness chair, his back soldier straight, exhibiting a calm demeanor. Allen was dressed in an immaculately pressed, narrow lapel suit, accessorized with a black mourning armband on his left arm and gray pinstripe trousers, all perfectly tailored to fit his trim, small frame.

After kissing the bible, he took his seat in the witness chair. Allen spoke in a loud but calm and steady voice before Galvin could begin his questioning.

"Good morning, sir."

"And to you as well, Mr. Dorsey," Galvin replied as he stepped forward. "Why don't we begin with you telling us where you live, your age, and your relationship to Mr. Burton?"

"I have lived at 63 Levin Street since my marriage to Maria

Burton on June 17. I reside with my wife and sister-in-law. I am 25 years old and was the son-in-law of Benjamin J. Burton," Allen responded, pausing only briefly before continuing unprompted.

"I am studying to be a surgeon and have completed two years of study at the University of Pennsylvania Medical School. I am ready to complete my last year but have yet to return to Philadelphia because I have been ill with pleurisy."

Galvin ignored the gratuitously offered resume and got right to the point.

"Where were you when Mr. Burton was shot?"

"I was in bed, asleep. As I just mentioned, I was ill."

"Did you not hear the gunshots?" Galvin asked.

"I heard two loud bangs, but I assumed they were doors slamming and did not pay much attention to them." Allen went on to explain, "Living in a crowded boarding house in the bustling city of Philadelphia for the past two years has left me unaffected by loud noises. It wasn't until I heard Maria screaming that I was fully awakened."

"What was Maria screaming?"

Allen raised his voice for effect as he repeated what he heard, *"Allen, Dora! Come quick, Father is injured!"*

"What did you do then?" Galvin asked.

I immediately got out of my bed and began to dress so I could go to her. While putting on my boots, Mrs. Stoddard came rushing into my room. She told me Mr. Burton was injured, and I needed to come downstairs. I finished dressing and hurried down. When I got to the kitchen, I saw Mr. Burton lying still on the floor. I immediately thought I should get a doctor, so I ran out the back door and around the house to the stables to send someone for help."

"You did not examine Mr. Burton to determine the extent of his injuries?"

"No, Mr. Galvin. I thought Mr. Burton needed a doctor right away."

Galvin raised his eyebrows. "Did you not just testify that you have completed two years of medical school?"

Allen remained unperturbed. "I did, Mr. Galvin. However, I have yet to receive any practical training at school. Mr. Burton needed to be attended to by an experienced physician. I asked the stable man to fetch a doctor and returned to the house."

"After you returned to the house, did you attempt to comfort or aid Mr. Burton?"

"No. My immediate concern was keeping the people gathering in the house from touching Mr. Burton or disturbing the scene until the doctor arrived."

"Did you look to see where Mr. Burton was wounded?"

"No, I did not."

"And you made no effort to determine if Mr. Burton might still be alive?"

Allen slightly frowned. "No, as I have said, I was waiting for the doctor. However, Mrs. Stoddard is a nurse and was present as well. She informed me that Mr. Burton was deceased when she discovered him. Mrs. Stoddard also volunteered to stay with Mr. Burton's body until the doctor arrived so I could take my wife upstairs."

Allen locked eyes with Galvin. "I don't know if you are married, Attorney Galvin, but I'm sure you can understand that my wife was very distraught, and my priority at that time was to take care of her."

Some women in attendance smiled in quiet approval.

"There was nothing more anyone could have done for Mr. Burton," he added.

Galvin ignored Allen's comment, "Tell us about your relationship with Mr. Burton."

"To be honest, I didn't interact much with Mr. Burton," Allen claimed. "He was rarely present in the home when I was there. He came and went at irregular hours, so I didn't see much of him. Mr. Burton preferred to have his meals in the kitchen. Maria, Dora, and I usually ate in the dining room. However, on those few occasions when I did see him, our relationship was very pleasant."

"Mr. Dorsey, do you recall the last time you saw Mr. Burton alive?"

"Yes, sir, I remember it very well. It was about a week before his death. He walked past me while I was sitting at the piano. I said, '*Good morning, Mr. Burton.*' And he said, '*Good morning*' in return."

"Do you know of any reason Mr. Burton might have wanted to take his own life?"

"No, I do not," Allen answered quickly.

Galvin walked back to his table and picked up a newspaper clipping he had laid on top.

"Yet, your opinion was published in the *Providence Evening Bulletin*." Galvin paused and held the clipping closer to his face, squinting to read it. "Yes, here it is. You are quoted as saying that Mr. Burton was despondent the evening before. Is that correct?"

"Yes, but I can explain. When the reporter showed up at our door, I answered the inquiry. My wife and sister-in-law were far too distraught to speak with anyone. And yes, I am quoted in the paper."

"Did you witness Mr. Burton's despondency yourself?"

Allen smiled slyly. "That is a fair question, Mr. Galvin. No, the description of his mental state was relayed to me by my wife after she and her sister spoke with him the night before he died. Mr. Burton summoned only his daughters to come downstairs to talk to him. I was not included in that conversation."

Galvin noted, "You also mentioned in the article that Mr. Burton had not been well."

"Again," Allen reiterated, "I was relaying my wife's observations. Mr. Burton suffered from some health issues. He was also prone to what I would describe as indigestion."

Galvin turned and laid the clipping back on the table.

"I see … Did you offer to treat Mr. Burton's ailments?"

"No, Mr. Galvin, I did not. As I said, I am not a practicing physician. I believe he was seen by his personal physician."

"But surely you could have offered Mr. Burton some advice— based on your medical training—as to what could be done to soothe his indigestion?"

Allen responded agreeably, "Of course. Had Mr. Burton sought my medical advice, I would have been happy to share my opinion. However, he did not."

"Did you know anything about Mr. Burton's financial affairs?"

"Not personally, but since his death, I have heard he may have recently met with significant losses."

"What type of losses are you referring to?"

"I heard Mr. Burton may have suffered large gambling losses."

"Where did you hear that?"

"I was sitting in my house by the front window the day after Mr. Burton's death when two men walked past. I saw one of the men point to the house and overheard him telling the other man; '*This is the house where Burton lived.*' He then said, '*I heard Burton lost between five and seven hundred dollars gambling last Friday night.*"

"Did you know either of these men?"

"No, Mr. Galvin, I did not recognize them."

"Is that your only source of information regarding Mr. Burton's alleged gambling habits?"

"I have not personally witnessed him gambling if that is what you are implying."

Galvin changed the subject. "Are you employed, Mr. Dorsey?"

"Not at this time, but I have worked at hotels in Newport during previous summer seasons."

"Why didn't you work this past summer season?"

"I needed to spend the summer studying and preparing for the upcoming school term. I was advised that the final year of medical school is the most rigorous."

"Mr. Dorsey, several times now, you have referenced that you are a medical student."

"Correct. As stated, I look forward to completing my third and final year at the University of Pennsylvania medical school."

"And you stated that you could not start your final year due to illness. Is that correct?"

"It is. Initially, I was not well enough to start on October 1st, which was the first day of the term. But now, Mr. Burton's death has further delayed my studies."

"Have you paid for your final year of study in full?

Allen shook his head, smiling smugly. "That's not quite how it works, Mr. Galvin," he corrected. "You can pay a portion at the beginning of the year, and then in April, you make the last payment before you sit for the final examinations. But to answer your question, I have paid for everything that was due in order for me to start the term. I had also arranged for room and board for my wife and me during the school year."

"And where did you obtain the money to pay your tuition if you were not working?"

Allen eyed Galvin, clearly annoyed by the question.

"May I ask, sir, why are you so interested in how I paid my tuition? I don't see how that has anything to do with Mr. Burton's death." He turned to Stanhope, seeking his agreement.

"Please answer the question, Mr. Dorsey," said Stanhope.

"Well, if you must know, after I graduated from Lincoln

University, I worked as a music teacher and private tutor at an academy in North Carolina for two years. I was paid quite well and earned more than enough wages to pay for three years of medical school."

"Did you ever ask anyone for money to help pay for your tuition?"

"I did not, Mr. Galvin. As I stated, I had adequate funds of my own."

"Mr. Dorsey, before your marriage to his daughter, did you believe Mr. Burton to be a prosperous man?"

Allen broke into a broad smile. "Though my classmates teased me that I would be pretty well fixed after I married Mr. Burton's daughter, I did not need his money," he insisted as he lifted his head and spoke to the gallery. "I assure you, I married his daughter for love, not for the love of her father's money."

Galvin turned around to find the women in the audience captivated by Allen's profession of love for his wife.

"Did Mr. Burton promise you a dowry if you married his daughter?"

"A dowry?" Allen asked mockingly. "No, he mentioned he would be giving us a wedding gift of some sort. But at the time of his death, we had not received any funds from Mr. Burton."

"Mr. Dorsey, on the day of Mr. Burton's death, did you go to his office and open his safe?"

"Yes. The family needed to open a claim with probate, and my wife asked me to go through my father-in-law's papers to see if there was a will. When I did not find one amongst his belongings in the house, she suggested he might have kept one in his safe at the office."

"And you felt this must be done within a few hours of his death?"

Allen shook his head. "I was trying to appease my wife, and that was her wish. She wanted to find the will before her brother arrived so he could file the probate claim."

"And what did you discover in the safe?"

"Invoices, letters, a little money, but no will."

"Did you find a life insurance policy?"

"There was a life insurance policy, but unfortunately, Mr. Burton let it lapse. I didn't mention it because it was worthless."

"Thank you, Mr. Dorsey. That is all."

Allen turned his head and looked up at Coroner Stanhope.

"Do you have any questions, sir?"

"No," Stanhope replied. "You are dismissed."

As Allen stood up from his chair and made his way out of the council chamber, Stanhope stood and announced to those in attendance that the inquest would be adjourning for a short break but would reconvene in half an hour.

Chapter 12
Wednesday, October 21, 1885

A messenger boy in a newsie cap threw open the door to Galvin's law office. He stood in the doorway, trying to catch his breath before sputtering, "I have an urgent message for Detective Richards!"

Richards took the note from him, flipped the boy a coin, and returned to Galvin's office to read it.

Maria denies borrowing money.
Interview Emily Burton immediately.
We need proof.

Smiling, Richards crumpled the paper and tossed it in the wastebasket. *We are on the same page,* he thought. Earlier in the day, Richards sent a message requesting an interview with Emily and was awaiting her arrival.

Within an hour, the clerk appeared in the doorway with Emily standing directly behind him.

"Detective Richards, the clerk began, there is a Mrs.—"

Emily's head suddenly popped up from behind the clerk mid-sentence. Richards waved her in.

"Come right in, Mrs. Burton, and take a seat."

Emily pushed her way past the clerk and eyeballed the detective. She wasn't sure what to expect in the way of a Pinkerton detective, but if Richards' imposing appearance was any indication, Howard was on the right track. Now, it was time for her to test his mettle.

"I was beginning to think Mr. Galvin had forgotten all about me," Emily huffed. "Need I remind the both of you that there would be no inquest if not for me?"

Richards had to suppress a smile. It was already apparent that Galvin's colorful description of Emily Burton was on the money.

"Let me introduce myself. My name is Detective Richards. I've been looking forward to meeting you."

Emily sniffed at the compliment and took her seat at the front of the desk where Richards had strategically placed a list of potential inquest witnesses in plain view. As he had anticipated, she nonchalantly leaned forward in her chair to get a better look.

As a ruse, he told Emily he needed to grab a file from the law clerk. Glancing over his shoulder as he left the room, he saw Emily turn the document toward her to read it.

Good, he thought, wishing to present himself to Emily as a trusted ally.

Emily quickly scanned the names on the witness list, nodding in approval. It appeared that in the few days Richards had been on the case, he had already done more work than the medical examiner, Captain Hammond, and all the other authorities combined. She was eager to tell Howard it was a sound decision to hire a Pinkerton.

When he stepped back through the doorway, Richards cleared his throat to announce his return. Emily quickly pushed the paper away from her and sat back in her chair. Richards took his seat and jumped right in.

"Attorney Galvin has filled me in on your prior conversation with him. I must say that I am very impressed with the amount of invaluable background material you provided. I don't have any questions about that, but I would like to follow up on the information you gave him regarding Mr. and Mrs. Dorsey's attempts to obtain money."

"That's as good a place to start as any," Emily replied, pleased that the detective had already homed in on the couple.

"According to his notes, you indicated Mr. Dorsey wrote to you asking for money. Is that correct?"

"Yes, that is true. Last March, he requested I send him $125 to help pay his tuition. He must have confused me with The Mrs. Astor," she sniped.

"That is a great deal of money, isn't it?" Richards empathized before asking hopefully, "Did you keep that letter?"

"No, I didn't. I wrote N-O at the top of the letter and mailed it back to Mr. Dorsey. Why do you need it?" Emily asked, somewhat perplexed. "I am prepared to testify as to what he wrote."

Richards reassured her, "Your testimony is critical, but it would be nice to have the letter to corroborate that Mr. Dorsey asked you for money."

Emily flashed a confident smile. "Oh, if that's all you are worried about, I may not have the letter, but I have a witness who can corroborate what the letter said."

Richards' face lit up with surprise. "You do?"

"I read it to one of my boarders," she announced proudly.

He hesitated, "But did your boarder read the letter himself?"

"No, Mr. Richards, he did not. Unfortunately, he cannot read or write. But I read it to him, just like I read the letters he receives from his family in Ireland."

Richards shook his head disappointedly. "It would have been better if he had read it himself. Otherwise, he is just repeating what you told him was in the letter."

Emily frowned. "Why wouldn't the coroner believe me? He knows me."

Not wanting to offend Emily, Richards demurred, "Let's wait and see if Mr. Dorsey admits to asking you for the money."

Emily sighed heavily, clearly annoyed.

To regain her confidence, Richards adopted a conciliatory tone. "Mrs. Burton, let me assure you that Attorney Galvin and I both believe you received the letter. But memories often differ or fade."

"Then let me assure you, Mr. Richards. My memory hasn't faded. Allen Dorsey asked me for $125."

"Understood. Let's move on and talk about your niece. You also told Attorney Galvin that Maria was asking people for money on Allen's behalf. Do you know the names of anyone she may have approached?"

Emily perked up. "I'm sure Mr. Galvin has told you about the cousin in New York City who lent Maria $125. Oh, and I've also heard she borrowed money from Mr. Malgan."

"The saloon owner?" Richards asked.

Emily raised her chin haughtily. "Yes, but I am not intimately acquainted with him or any other saloon owners."

Richards thought it best not to let Emily know that he was planning to interview Malgan about the gambling rumor but made a mental note to question the barkeep about loaning Maria money.

Emily added, "I intend to keep asking around, but that's all I know of so far."

"Have you spoken with any of Mr. Burton's tenants since his death?"

"I haven't spoken to any of them directly. I think they are all in cahoots with Mary Stoddard. But one of the brethren from my church lives across the street from the Burton house. Last Sunday, he told me that Mrs. Keller, one of Ben's tenants, recently inquired about renting a room in his home. She will need a place to live when the Burton house is sold, and the estate is liquidated.

"Mrs. Keller told him she had overheard an argument in the Burton house, but he wouldn't tell me what it was about. He said he didn't want gossipmongers living in his house and asked if I thought she was one of those. You will need to talk to her, but don't tell her I gave you her name. If it got back to my friend, he might think I was repeating gossip."

Richards leaned forward as if to bring Emily into his confidence.

"I have spoken with one of the tenants, Mr. McGruder. Do you know him?"

Emily scowled. "Oh, that horrible creature! I wouldn't want to be seen associating with that man. You should avoid being seen with him too unless you want people to think you're a lazy, good-for-nothing drunkard too."

"I'll keep that in mind," Richards grinned. "Can you think of anything else we should know?"

"I read that article in *The Daily News*, and this despondency business is nonsense. Ben Burton wasn't sad or gloomy a day in his life."

"Do you have any suggestions about other people we should interview as potential witnesses?"

Emily mentally ticked through the names she had seen on the

witness list and was satisfied.

"Not at this time, but I'm sure I will."

Richards rose from his chair to escort Emily to the door. He reminded her, "You are scheduled to testify tomorrow morning. You are not to sit in the gallery. Instead, report to the sheriff when you arrive at City Hall, and he will take you to the Alderman's chamber until you are called. Until then, don't discuss your testimony with anyone. And Mrs. Burton, for pity's sake, please stop talking to the newspaper reporters!"

***

"You ruffians need to come with me," Sheriff Easton spat through gritted teeth. The sheriff had a firm grip on the collars of two troublemakers who had come to blows over a recently vacated seat in the gallery.

"But I ain't done nothing wrong," one of the men loudly protested. "I was just stretching my legs! I had to stand in line for hours this morning to get that seat."

The other man, who had been relegated to standing against the wall, wasn't leaving the room without a fight either.

"He got up. That spot was fair game."

"That's enough out of the both of you," Easton barked, struggling to subdue the men.

A police officer who had dropped by the proceedings rushed to Easton's aid, grabbed one of the men, and pushed him out the door. "You heard the sheriff, let's go."

At the dais, Coroner Stanhope patiently waited for the sheriff to return to his post and call the next witness.

Still huffing and puffing, Easton called out, "Mrs. Idella Traeger, please come forward."

Idella timidly peaked out from behind the door to the aldermen's chamber before venturing out. Smaller in stature than Dora, she could easily pass for an adolescent playing dress-up in her mother's clothes. When she took the witness chair, her feet barely touched the ground. Idella lowered her head and kept her eyes fixed on her lap.

Galvin stayed seated as he began the questioning.

"Good afternoon, Mrs. Traeger," he began kindly. "Can you tell me your age and where you live?"

"I am 17 years old, and I live with my husband in one of the Burton tenements at 65 Levin Street," Idella answered softly.

Galvin smiled. His sisters spoke with the same lilting cadence. He and his siblings were also first-generation Americans and the children of Irish immigrants.

"Where is your tenement located in proximity to the Burton house?"

Idella cast a glance at Galvin, then lowered her head again.

"We live upstairs in the apartment right next to their house."

"Mrs. Traeger, how would you describe your relationship with the Burton family?"

"I am friendly with Maria and Dora, but I didn't know Mr. Burton very well," she replied. "I don't think I ever had a conversation with him."

"I want to talk about the day of Mr. Burton's death. Can you take me through your actions that morning?"

Idella scrunched up her face and closed her eyes.

"I was hanging the laundry on the line in the backyard. Maria came outside and called out me, *'Della, I need to speak to you.'* She was making a dress for me and said she needed to take a measurement. We went upstairs to my apartment so she could do that."

"Did Mrs. Dorsey suggest that the two of you go inside to your apartment?"

"I think so."

"I must confess that I am not well versed in the art of dressmaking," Galvin remarked with a mischievous grin. "Can you explain what type of measurement Mrs. Dorsey needed?"

Idella appeared to be caught off-guard by the question. "Ummm … she measured me … for the length. Yes … she said she was all but finished with the dress except for the hem," she stammered.

A round of whispering broke out in the gallery.

"So, the only unfinished part of the dress was the hem?" Galvin asked. "She took no other measurements?"

"Not that I recall," Idella answered as she nervously tugged at the collar of her dress.

"Where in the apartment were you when Mrs. Dorsey took your measurements?"

"In a bedroom that we use as a sitting room. It's at the front of our house."

"Where is that room located in relation to the Burton kitchen?"

"The Burton's kitchen is at the back of their house."

Galvin tilted his head slightly as he asked, "Did Maria lead you to the front of the house?"

Idella's cheeks began to redden. "I followed her down the hall to the room."

"What happened next?"

"I had just handed Maria my measuring tape when I heard a loud bang and then another loud bang. I asked her what the noise was because they sounded like they were coming from inside her house. Maria said Dora must be slamming doors. I opened our door to the front stairway to listen but didn't hear any more noises. Then I closed the door and returned to our sitting room with Maria."

Galvin rose slowly from his chair.

"What did you do then?"

"Maria left. She told me she was going to the post office and the Boston Store."

"When did you see Mrs. Dorsey again?"

"A little later. Dora came running up the front stairs, screaming that Mr. Burton was shot."

"How long was it after Maria left your tenement before Dora came to get you?"

"A good amount of time."

Galvin inched closer to the witness chair.

"Can you be more specific?"

"Fifteen to twenty minutes?" Idella guessed. "I had time to empty two wash buckets and had gone on to blacking the stove by the time I heard her coming up the stairs."

"What did you do then, Mrs. Traeger?"

"I followed Dora downstairs to her house. I saw Mr. Burton..." Her voice breaking, Idella paused for a moment to collect herself. "Mr. Burton was lying on the floor in the kitchen. I did not want to go in there, so I stayed in the dining room with Dora."

Galvin stepped forward and offered his handkerchief to Idella, but she shook her head no. He put it back in his pocket and stepped back.

"Mrs. Traeger, can you describe the scene in the house when you arrived?"

"Dora and I were in the dining room. Mrs. Stoddard came in

from the kitchen and asked us where Mr. Dorsey was. Dora told her he was upstairs, and she went up to get Mr. Dorsey. Then, people just started streaming in, trying to get to the kitchen. Mrs. Stoddard told me to take Dora upstairs to get her away from everything happening. So, I took Dora up there and stayed with her."

"Did you see Mr. Dorsey?"

"Yes, he came downstairs right after Mrs. Stoddard went to get him. He looked like he had just gotten out of bed," she added, unprompted. "He went with her to the kitchen, and that was the last time I saw him that morning."

"Mrs. Traeger, have you ever heard, or do you know of anyone else who has heard quarrels in the Burton house?"

Idella kept her head lowered. "No," she whispered.

Galvin leaned in toward Idella and clasped his hands behind his back. "Are you certain?"

"Not that I recall," Idella replied, turning her head away from Galvin.

"Are you telling the truth, Mrs. Traeger? You can get in trouble if you lie under oath."

Idella jerked her head up, her eyes wide with fright.

"I would never lie, Mr. Galvin! I am a good, God-fearing Christian woman!"

"I'm glad to hear it," Galvin responded. "Have you spoken to Mrs. Dorsey or Miss Burton since that morning?"

"Only to offer my condolences," Idella said apprehensively. "I promise, Mr. Galvin, I'm telling you everything I know."

***

Mary Stoddard strode confidently out of the Alderman's chamber, the ostrich plume atop her hat bouncing with each step. She answered Galvin's preliminary questions concerning her age, where she lived, and the location of her cottage in proximity to the Burton residence.

"When was the last time you saw Mr. Burton alive?" Galvin inquired.

"It was the day before his death. He was leaving his house and stopped to speak with me. I asked him how he was doing, and he told me, '*If I had a gun, I would blow my brains out.*'"

Loud gasps and cries sprang from the audience.

Mary watched in smug satisfaction as Stanhope pounded his fist on the table to call the room to order. She had finally gotten the reaction she had always thought Ben's statement deserved.

"Settle down and be quiet," Stanhope shouted. "Sheriff Easton, please move to the front of the gallery and be ready to remove anyone who cannot maintain the proper decorum."

When the room quieted, Galvin proceeded.

"Did Mr. Burton tell you why he wanted to shoot himself?"

Mary shook her head, responding, "No, but it wasn't the first or only time Mr. Burton has made that type of statement to me."

Another commotion arose from the boisterous spectators, threatening to disrupt the proceedings again before Easton marched into the aisle and silenced them with a threatening, "Knock it off!"

"Mrs. Stoddard, do you recall the occasions when Mr. Burton made these statements to you?"

"I don't recall the specific dates, but he once told me he would crawl in a hole and die if he could find one big enough. But I do remember many times when he said that he would shoot himself."

Easton stared down the gallery, daring anyone to utter a word or make a sound.

Mary lowered her chin. "It is difficult to admit that, on each occasion, I thought he was joking. But obviously, I was wrong." She then raised her head to meet Galvin's eyes. "I will have to live with that, Mr. Galvin, but that's the truth."

Galvin moved forward, questioning Mary about her actions on the day of Burton's death, which she enumerated in painstaking detail to a captivated audience before he dismissed her.

After Mary Stoddard left the stand, Coroner Stanhope took a moment to address the audience in the gallery.

"Ladies and Gentlemen, Attorney Galvin will now call the medical examiner. The details of his testimony may not be suitable for everyone. I strongly suggest those faint of heart or with tender sensibilities exit from the chamber at this time."

No one moved from their seat. Stanhope motioned to Sheriff Easton to call the medical examiner as a witness.

"Dr. Henry E. Turner, please step forward."

Dr. Turner slowly rose from his seat in the row of reserved chairs in front of the bar railing. The doctor had his autopsy notes tucked in a bundle under his arm and leaned heavily on the knob of his wooden cane as he came forward. After he had taken the oath and kissed the Bible, he propped the cane up against the small table in front of Coroner Stanhope and eased himself into the witness chair.

After a brief introduction, during which Dr. Turner explained his responsibilities as the medical examiner, Galvin began his examination in earnest.

"Dr. Turner, were you called to the Burton house on the morning of October 6?"

Dr. Turner nodded, "In my capacity as the medical examiner, yes."

"Can you describe what you found when you arrived?"

"Many people were already in the house when I arrived on the scene with Captain Hammond. Coroner Stanhope arrived shortly after that. We cleared the house, and I had the body moved from the floor and to the kitchen table so I could examine him."

"What did your examination disclose regarding Mr. Burton's injuries?"

Dr. Turner removed the bundle from under his arm, unfolded the papers on his lap, and smoothed them flat.

"I quickly determined that Mr. Burton had expired. He had a small circular head wound and a similarly shaped chest wound."

"To be clear, you observed two separate bullet wounds?"

"Correct."

"Were you able to determine which of the two injuries was the fatal blow?"

"Not at that time."

"Did you conduct an autopsy?"

"Yes, on Saturday morning, October 17," he confirmed.

"Were you able to determine the cause of death after the autopsy?"

Dr. Turner scanned through several pages of his notes before speaking.

"I was able to trace the trajectory of the head wound and discovered that the bullet did not breach the cerebellum. This meant that this shot was not necessarily fatal. The wound in the chest, however, was likely immediately fatal."

"So, in your opinion, which shot came first?" Galvin asked.

"I do not know that I can conclusively testify to that, but I would think the shot to the head," Dr. Turner speculated. "There is abundant evidence that a man can carry a ball in the head if it only traverses the cerebrum, but the wound to the chest penetrated the heart in such a manner that it would have caused almost instantaneous death."

"Assuming the head wound occurred first, do you believe it is possible for a person to have the capacity or wherewithal to have fired a second shot?"

"I do," Dr. Turner said. "If the head wound was not fatal, a person may very well be able to fire the gun again. Keep in mind that the gun used was a very small caliber, a twenty-two."

"Did you observe powder burns around either of the entrance wounds?"

"There were visible powder burns on the exterior of Mr. Burton's vest as if the gun had been held directly against the chest. I did not observe any power burns on the head."

With his thumb up and forefinger extended, Galvin awkwardly attempted to position his arm so that the tip of his finger touched his chest perpendicularly, as suggested by the powder burns described by Dr. Turner.

"Would Mr. Burton's arms have been long enough to hold the gun directly against his chest?" asked Galvin as he struggled to recreate the motion.

Unfazed by this demonstration, Turner answered matter-of-factly, "Yes, I believe so."

Galvin then shifted his arm upward and placed his finger gun against his head just above his right ear.

"Wouldn't there be powder burns on his scalp if the wound was self-inflicted?"

"Not necessarily. It was a small caliber weapon. If the gun were held at arm's length when fired, the force would not be great enough to cause powder burns."

Galvin slowly began to move his hand away from his head while keeping his index finger pointed at the same spot where the bullet had entered Ben's head. When the tip of his finger was about 12 inches from his head, he could not extend his arm any farther and dropped it by his side.

"How did Mr. Burton manage to hold the gun at arm's length at this angle? I can't quite seem to do it."

Nonplussed, Turner responded, "My role as medical examiner is to determine the cause of death, not how the person carried out the method of death."

Galvin moved on. "Did you find anything in Mr. Burton's mouth?"

"Yes, a piece of unchewed bread was between his teeth."

"And did you find this unusual?"

"Yes," Turner acquiesced. "It suggested to me that Mr. Burton must have acted impulsively."

"Are you suggesting that he shot himself while in the act of chewing?"

"Correct."

Galvin considered his next question carefully.

"As the medical examiner, you are tasked with gathering all the necessary evidence and making a determination as to whether an inquest is warranted. Is that correct?"

Dr. Turner nodded, "Yes. That is my charge."

"What evidence did you gather before determining an inquest was unnecessary?"

"After I examined the body, I went upstairs and interviewed the members of the family. They all agreed that Mr. Burton was despondent and that the night before his death, he had stated that he would not live much longer."

"And this led you to conclude the cause of death as being suicide?"

"This, and the fact that the manner of death was consistent with suicide. There were no suspicious circumstances to suggest otherwise. The family's observations that Mr. Burton was low-spirited only served to confirm the conclusion. Therefore, I determined no further inquiry was necessary."

"Did you speak with any neighbors or question other family members who arrived at the scene before making this determination?"

"I did not. I have known the Burton family for many years. Based on my knowledge of the family and their reputation in the community, I found nothing suspect in their statements."

"What about Allen Dorsey? Did you know him?"

Dr. Turner frowned. "No, I had not met Mr. Dorsey before that day."

Changing course, Galvin asked, "Now that the autopsy has been completed, have you had the opportunity to consult with any other physicians concerning their opinion as to the cause of death?"

"Yes, I did consult with some of my colleagues."

"And after such consultation, is it still your opinion that Mr. Burton's cause of death was suicide?"

A hush fell over the spectators in the gallery, and the reporters ceased their mad pace of scribbling to listen carefully.

Dr. Turner took a lengthy pause before answering.

"Yes, I think the shots may have been self-inflicted. I think that is among the possibilities."

Chapter 13
Wednesday, October 21, 1885

It was late evening when P.J. Galvin trudged past Newport Harbor, where the waxing gibbous moon's reflection shimmered on the water's calm surface. The first day of the inquest had been arduous, but he still faced a long night of work preparing for tomorrow's hearing before he could rest. Carefully balancing the heavy folders and files he carried in his arms, Galvin slowly climbed the stairs to his office. To his surprise, Richards met him at the open doorway with a comforting smile and a steaming cup of coffee.

He took one look at Galvin and asked, "Rough day?"

"Let's just say it is always preferable to know what your witnesses are going to say before you ask questions," Galvin quipped as he plopped the documents on his clerk's desk and reached for the cup.

"Maria Dorsey denies ever asking for or receiving money from anyone. Mr. Dorsey claims he is flush with cash," Galvin remarked as he made his way to his office with Richards in tow. "Were you able to speak with Emily Burton?"

Richards gave Galvin a knowing wink. "I did, and she tells a much different story."

"Does she seem credible?"

Richards pulled up a chair and took a seat.

"I found Mrs. Burton convincing, but I'm unsure how she will come across on the stand. If possible, I suggest you don't let her stray off-topic. I'd also recommend carefully crafting your questions to avoid her appearing biased. In any event, she was able to provide me with the names of people who can corroborate her statements."

Galvin ran a hand through his thick blonde hair. This news came with the stark realization that Maria, and perhaps Allen, had perjured themselves on the stand. It just didn't make sense to him.

"Mrs. Burton tells me a cousin in New York City sent Maria $125 earlier this year."

"Yes, she told me that as well."

"Her name is Sarah Babcock. Apparently, she's been employed at Governor Cornell's home for several decades. I've sent a wire to schedule an interview with her when I return to the city tomorrow. I'll also attempt to meet with Howard Burton while I'm there. I'm assuming you will need both to testify?"

"Yes," Galvin concurred. "I will ask Stanhope to issue the subpoenas before you leave."

Richards' expression turned solemn.

"There is a rather urgent matter I need to discuss with you. I have exhausted the retainer that Howard Burton paid my agency, and I doubt he has the money to continue to fund my assignment. The agency isn't likely to send me back without some guarantee of payment."

Careful to keep a straight face, Galvin leaned back in his chair and wrapped his hands around the coffee cup to warm them. The day before, he had approached the attorney general and received his approval to cover the costs with the Pinkerton Agency … at least for the time being. But Galvin decided to have a little fun at the detective's expense before sharing the good news.

"I see," Galvin remarked as seriously as he could muster. "That is disappointing. If I had a wealthier pool of clients, I'd pay you myself."

Richards surveyed the sparsely appointed office, where portraits of Presidents George Washington and Abraham Lincoln hung on its otherwise bare walls. Besides the large desk and wooden chairs, the only other furniture in the room was cabinets filled with legal books.

"Maybe I could engage the services of Emily Burton," Galvin

teased as he took another sip of coffee. "I wager she is one tough interrogator."

Embarrassed by Galvin's awkward attempt to make light of the situation, the detective responded apologetically. "As I stated from the start, I didn't expect to be of service to you for more than a couple of days, but I believe we have accomplished a great deal in the short amount of time I've been on the case. Of course, I would be willing to volunteer my services when possible."

Galvin carefully placed his cup on the desk and began to laugh.

Richards stared at Galvin with a mixture of confusion and hurt. He didn't find the situation humorous.

Galvin stopped laughing but remained smiling as he walked over to Richards and slapped him on the back.

"Don't worry, ole boy, I assumed as much. I didn't want to mention it until I received confirmation, but I have persuaded the attorney general to cover the expense of your services if you are willing to stay on the case. I already sent a telegram to your office asking if you can continue working under my direction, courtesy of the state of Rhode Island."

Richards clapped his hands together in relief.

"You sly dog, that is good news! I have been dreading this conversation all day," he confessed as his baritone laughter filled the room.

Galvin laughed along with Richards and then extended his hand. "In all seriousness, I don't know what I would have done without your help, my friend."

In the short time the two men had been acquainted, they had quickly built a productive working relationship as well as a budding friendship.

"I agree we are making progress, but all we have so far is that both Maria and Allen may have lied about their need for money. Not being willing to publicly admit they have money problems doesn't make them murderers," the attorney remarked.

Ultimately, Galvin believed it would be the medical testimony that could decide the case. But Galvin was frustrated by Dr. Turner, who seemed more interested in justifying his hasty ruling of suicide than in seeking the truth. If the medical testimony determined that it could not be suicide, then the Dorseys were the only viable suspects … so far.

His thoughts turned from Turner to Dr. Ecroyd. "Any luck finding Allen Dorsey's doctor?"

Richards nodded. "It appears the mysterious Dr. Ecroyd has recently moved to Newport and opened his medical office on October 1. I met with him this morning. He said Mrs. Dorsey called on him a few days before Burton's death. She told the doctor that her husband had recognized Ecroyd's name in the newspaper advertisement announcing the opening of his medical practice. She was looking for a doctor to treat Dorsey's cough. Ecroyd agreed to see him and confirmed to me that Dorsey was suffering from pleurisy and that he treated him."

"How well do the two know each other?" Galvin asked.

"Ecroyd graduated from the medical school at the University of Pennsylvania in May of 1883, but Allen didn't start his first year until that fall, so they did not attend at the same time. However, the doctor tells me they have mutual acquaintances. Based on what Ecroyd has heard from the people who knew him at school, Dorsey had a reputation as a brilliant student and was respected by his peers. He is on the witness list because the Dorseys have asked him to review the medical reports and to testify in the inquest."

Richards grinned slyly. "Ecroyd is 27 years old and has no real practical medical experience. The doctor told me he spent his summers between school terms working at insane asylums and that he worked for a hospital in Philadelphia for a year after graduation. He also worked in Barnegat, New Jersey, last summer."

Galvin cocked an eyebrow. "The Jersey shore?"

"Yes."

"As an attending physician at a hospital?"

"No, he was the physician on call at a seaside resort."

Galvin burst out laughing. "So, I take it he is an expert in sunburns, skinned knees, and splinters? Or was there a spate of gunshot wounds at the beaches?"

Richards laughed at Galvin's depiction of Ecroyd's limited medical experience before turning his attention back to his interview notes.

"The doctor is of the opinion that the facts support suicide and is looking forward to testifying."

"Did he share the medical basis for his conclusion?"

"The good doctor struggled to provide specific medical analysis to support his opinion but was quick to infer his University of

Pennsylvania pedigree more than qualified him to render an expert opinion."

Galvin rolled his eyes. "Who else did you interview today?"

"I paid a visit to Mr. Malgan," Richards replied.

"Be careful, detective," Galvin quipped. "People may think you have a drinking problem or, worse yet, a gambling problem."

"Yes, that seems to be a recurring theme here in Newport," Richards retorted. "Turns out, Malgan had a wealth of information to share. It seems Burton frequented his establishment almost nightly. And as is often the case, Burton took the barkeep into his confidence. Based on what I heard today, Malgan may very well be the witness you've been seeking who can give you the most honest and unbiased perspective as to the atmosphere in Burton's home in the weeks leading to his death."

Galvin was intrigued yet wary.

"It is rarely a good idea to put too much stock in discussions that take place while under the influence of spirits. Was Burton a drinker?"

Richards shook his head. "He wasn't. Malgan insists it was Burton's habit to order a tall ginger ale with ice. He tells me he never witnessed Burton drinking excessively, play cards, or throw dice. I told him he would need to testify under oath about his conversations with Burton. He was hesitant at first to disclose their conversations, but I think I was able to convince him that his testimony is of vital importance."

"Then I'm anxious to hear it," Galvin responded enthusiastically. "I'll review your notes. He is scheduled to testify tomorrow."

"You won't be disappointed," assured Richards. "Malgan also confirmed Emily Burton's claim that he was one of the locals who lent Maria money."

"Interesting."

The men were interrupted by a knock at the outer office door.

"Who could that be at this hour?" Galvin wondered aloud.

Patting the revolver concealed under his jacket, Richards made his way to the entrance.

"Who's there?" he called out as he leaned against the closed door.

A muffled voice could be heard from the other side.

"I apologize for the late hour, but I noticed the light in the window and hoped I might find Mr. Galvin."

Richards unlocked the door and cautiously opened it to find a tall, odd-looking man wrapped in a dark green military cape and wearing a small-billed army cap. The man adjusted the wire-rim Windsor glasses on the bridge of his nose before extending a bony hand.

"Good evening, my name is Dr. William Thornton Parker, and I believe I can be of help in the Burton inquest."

***

Galvin recognized Parker after seeing him during the inquest earlier in the day, sitting in front of the bar. He had been drawn to his unique appearance and wondered who he might be. He had assumed the man to be one of the out-of-town businessmen, politicians, or physicians who had filled the seats reserved for dignitaries.

The men introduced themselves and invited Dr. Parker into the office. Galvin and Richards had barely taken their seats before Parker began speaking.

"I realize you both must be wondering what prompted an uninvited visit from a stranger this time of night. If I were in your shoes, I would think the same. But I shall cut to the chase."

Galvin and Richards exchanged a swift and befuddled glance.

"I recently moved to Newport and have closely followed the Burton case in the papers. Today, I attended the inquest to hear Dr. Turner's testimony in person. To be frank, I vehemently disagree with his determination of suicide as the cause of death."

Galvin was skeptical.

"Sir, I don't want to seem impolite, but could you state your credentials?" he asked, silently praying they didn't include a stint at a seaside resort or psychiatric hospital.

Dr. Parker remained unaffected.

"I graduated from Dartmouth College and then Harvard Medical School. I spent several years in Europe, practicing medicine in Vienna, Paris, and London hospitals."

Richards flipped open his notepad and began furiously taking notes as Galvin stared slack-jawed at the peculiar-looking man with a flinty voice.

"I was appointed a U.S. Army surgeon and assigned to the western frontier for over a decade. During that time, I was able to extensively study the effects of gunshot wounds and arrows on the human body. My most recent appointment was that of acting assistant surgeon to the United States Army."

Galvin had to resist the urge to pinch himself to ensure he wasn't dreaming.

"I assume then it is fair to say that you are familiar with gunshot wounds?"

"Yes, quite familiar," Parker responded flatly as if it were an everyday occurrence for a physician of his caliber to offer unprompted assistance in such a proceeding.

"I take issue with Dr. Turner's conclusions because of my extensive medical knowledge."

Richards smiled inwardly as Galvin pressed for more details.

"Can you be more specific about your concerns?"

"If it were a suicide, I would agree with Dr. Turner that the shot in the head would have come first. And I readily concede that the shot may not have been immediately fatal. But I disagree with Dr. Turner's testimony that Mr. Burton would have had the wherewithal to fire a second shot to his chest. I believe the headshot would have rendered Mr. Burton unconscious, or at the very least, significantly impaired his ability to think or act."

Galvin nodded in understanding as Dr. Parker continued.

"It's not just my opinion. I have taken the liberty of writing to some of my esteemed medical colleagues in Boston. In my communications, I presented the facts in the case and asked for their opinion as to the most likely cause of death. Every one of the physicians who have responded has been of the opinion that it was unlikely Mr. Burton's death was a suicide."

Galvin sat momentarily speechless before asking, "Would you be willing to testify and enter the letters you've received into evidence?"

Dr. Parker stood. "Yes, of course. I believe it is my duty."

After the doctor had taken his leave, Galvin turned to Richards and remarked, "I think we might have just discovered the unbiased medical expert we have been lacking."

Chapter 14
Thursday, October 22, 1885
Second Day of Inquest

After Dr. Parker's surprise visit, Galvin slept soundly for the first time since his appointment in the case. He awoke with a renewed sense of purpose, re-energized and ready to face the unpredictable and unfiltered Emily Burton. He had diligently prepared his questions in hopes of minimizing any opportunity for extemporaneous commentary.

Upon his arrival at the courthouse, he was pleased to find she had complied with Detective Richards' directive to report to the Alderman's chamber. He was hopeful it was a good sign of things to come.

"Mrs. Charles Howard Burton, please come forward."

Emily nudged the Sheriff aside as she forced her way past him and into the council chamber. She was dressed in her mourning frock with a bonnet securely tied under her chin. She cocked back her head and thrust her chin in the air as she walked purposefully across the room, her footsteps echoing loudly. As she neared the witness chair, she stopped and, with a flick of her wrist, tossed her handbag on top of the table in front of Coroner Stanhope. She then turned to look at Galvin, whose initial sense of optimism was quickly fading.

Emily cleared her throat loudly and straightened her back.

"Shall I begin?" she asked as she settled comfortably into the witness chair, not waiting for a response. "I am the sister-in-law to Benjamin Burton and the widow of his brother, Charles Howard Burton. I knew Ben Burton for twenty-two years," she began as Sheriff Eason rushed across the room, Bible in hand.

"No, no, Mrs. Burton!" Galvin exclaimed, approaching the witness chair and shaking his head. "The sheriff must first swear you in, and I will ask the questions."

Emily stood up, placed her hand on the Bible, her other hand in the air, and repeated the oath. She bent to kiss the Bible, then returned to her seat.

"Now then, ask away," she announced, giving permission for Galvin to begin his questioning.

Galvin stepped away from the witness chair, cautiously putting some distance between himself and Emily.

"When was the last time you saw Benjamin Burton alive?"

"The Tuesday before his death, exactly one week to the day before he was murdered."

Galvin flinched. "Mrs. Burton, it has not been established that Mr. Burton was murdered," he cautioned.

Stanhope frowned but remained quiet.

Emily shrugged, unconcerned. "Ben called at my house about half past ten in the morning and stayed about an hour."

"What did the two of you discuss?"

Galvin was relieved when Emily detailed the information she had shared during their first meeting in his office. She reiterated every pertinent fact she initially disclosed concerning Maria and Allen's efforts to obtain money from various sources and Ben's desire to remove them from the house, not once deviating from her original story.

However, Galvin became alarmed when Emily paused to take a deep breath and continued unprompted, "I set Ben straight, I did. I told him exactly what his daughter had been up to. Of course, I took no pleasure in it."

Laughter erupted throughout the gallery. Emily jerked her head up and narrowed her eyes toward the spectators as if daring them to laugh again before she continued.

Stanhope ordered, "Quiet in the courtroom."

Emily sat up on the edge of the witness chair as if suddenly remembering a critical detail.

"Ben told me that Allen Dorsey hadn't worked all summer and was just living off him. That he was either lying around the house all day or riding around town in one of Ben's carriages like a peacock. Ben complained that the couple was racking up household expenses. The laundry bill alone was over $50!"

The news of this extravagance created murmurs from the women in the gallery who were familiar with much lower household laundry expenditures.

As Galvin waited for the spectators to quiet before asking his next question, Emily forged ahead.

"When Ben left my house, he said he was going straight home to confront his daughter and order the Dorseys out of the house. But he was killed, so they got to stay and do as they please."

The gallery broke out in chaos in response to Emily's statement and Stanhope immediately took control of the proceeding.

"Order, order!" he shouted before turning to the court reporter and directing, "Strike that portion of Mrs. Burton's testimony from the record."

Red-faced, he then turned to Emily and angrily addressed her. "Mrs. Burton, I must warn you. If you give your opinion as to the cause of Mr. Burton's death again, I will strike your entire testimony from the record!"

Emily looked to Galvin for support as she opened her mouth to speak, but Galvin shot her a withering look, so she thought the better of it. As she sat quietly seething, she wondered what she had said that so angered the coroner. *I am only speaking the truth*, she thought.

Stanhope looked sternly at Galvin, warning, "Counselor, control your witness."

Galvin nodded in embarrassment. He realized he needed to get Emily off the stand immediately.

"I have no further questions for this witness."

"Then you are dismissed, Mrs. Burton," Stanhope concluded, his voice still quivering in anger.

Galvin turned and walked back to his table. Although Emily's testimony had not ended well, if he had to be honest, it went better than he expected.

"Let's take a fifteen-minute recess," Stanhope announced as he stood and abruptly left the room.

***

Over an hour had passed since the start of the hearing by the time Clarence Mason was called to the witness chair. He had sat quietly waiting in the Alderman's chamber, where he could hear the commotion and angry voices stemming from Emily Burton's testimony but could not make out what was being said.

As Mason took his seat, his sense of moral obligation weighed heavily upon him. Mason believed it was his responsibility to help find justice for his dear friend.

Galvin approached Mason and, with a slight smile, tipped his head.

"Good afternoon, Mr. Mason. Would you mind telling us how you became acquainted with Benjamin Burton?"

Mason painstakingly detailed the history of his association with Ben and their interactions on the morning of his death. Throughout his testimony, Mason repeatedly described Ben as cheerful and optimistic.

Galvin asked, "Was Mr. Burton experiencing financial difficulties of late?"

Mason was frank. "Ben was always in debt," he explained. "At the time of his death, he was not in any more financial stress than usual. Ben could raise money quicker than any man I ever met. I know he cleared over four hundred and fifty dollars this season and still had accounts receivable outstanding when he died."

Mason let out a deep breath and spoke at length about Ben's future plans, concluding, "Just the day before he died, Ben said he had an offer on his house for $6500 and that he would clear more than $1000 after paying off the mortgage and all of his debt."

Galvin questioned Mason about his unpleasant encounter with Allen the afternoon of Ben's death that Mason had described to Detective Richards.

"Did you find it unusual that Mr. Dorsey insisted on opening Mr. Burton's office safe and taking the contents?"

"Given the fact that Mr. Burton had only been dead a few hours, it seemed to me that the respectable thing to do would have been to wait until Mr. Burton's son, Howard, arrived."

Galvin finished his questioning by gently asking, "Mr. Mason, can you think of any reason why Ben Burton would want to kill himself?"

Mason's emotions came flooding to the surface, and he held back tears as he answered.

"Mr. Galvin, I know of absolutely no reason Ben would have taken his life. Ben Burton was the last man in the world that would commit suicide."

"Thank you, Mr. Mason. I have no further questions."

***

John Malgan was a man who had lived a rough and tumble life serving drinks to the underbelly of Newport, but whose appearance seemed none the worse for the wear. As the middle-aged saloon owner strutted across the room to the witness chair, he displayed the jauntiness of a teenage bantamweight boxer entering the ring.

His flaming red hair swirled in youthful curls at his ears and fell in uncontrolled locks on his brow, masking his age. He was quick to lend a sympathetic ear and known to be friendly to a fault. The rowdies and revelers who frequented the Newport saloons stayed clear of his establishment as it was well known that Malgan did not put up with shenanigans in his bar. Galvin could hardly wait to question the man.

Malgan began his testimony by explaining that he had spent most of his adult life as a bartender, saving his meager earnings until he could open his own small saloon in the lower level of his home at 110 Levin Street. Malgan proudly boasted that his humble establishment had become one of the most popular saloons that dotted the busy street.

Galvin then asked Malgan about his relationship with Ben.

"Ah, Ben came to my pub often. It was unusual if I didn't see him before he headed down to the docks. We spent many an hour together."

"So, he was a regular customer?"

"Ben wasn't just a customer. He was my neighbor and Mo Chara … a dear friend. There is nothing I wouldn't have done for Ben … God rest his soul."

Galvin smiled, then asked, "What did Mr. Burton like to drink?"

"He would always order a glass of ginger ale with ice. I never knew him to be a drinker and never saw him drunk." Malgan added, "He didn't come to drink. He came to talk."

"What did Ben talk about?"

Malgan scratched his ruddy cheek. "Ah, where do I begin? Some nights, he reminisced about his time as a teamster and prospector in California during the gold rush. Other times, he talked about his family … especially little Dora. She was the apple of his eye, the spitting image of his wife, Rosanna. He never stopped fretting over her fragile nature," he commented before pausing and adding, "You know, he lost most of his children to consumption.

"And Ben surely liked to talk about politics. He had a mighty strong opinion and didn't mind sharing it. Of course, there were his businesses. He talked about them, too. Yes, sir, we talked about everything under the sun."

"Did he ever share with you any of the problems he had in his home?" Galvin asked.

"Ben wasn't one to complain, but I know there was some tension in his home after his older daughter married. His new son-in-law was causing him some problems, and he talked about that. He was upset that the man wasn't working or contributing to the household."

Malgan paused and chuckled. "I'd say his visits to my place came earlier and lasted longer after Dorsey moved in. He was looking forward to his son-in-law returning to Philadelphia."

"So, is it fair to say Mr. Burton disliked his son-in-law?"

"In the beginning, he was happy with the marriage. He was pleased that his oldest daughter had a husband he believed would be able to take care of her financially, and that he would only have Dora left in the home. He was building a little cottage down the street for the two of them to live in once he sold the big house."

"Did he say anything specifically about Mr. Dorsey?" asked Galvin, gently steering him back on course.

Malgan frowned. He believed those conversations were shared in confidence, and he was hesitant to disclose them. Ben had spoken harshly about Dorsey, but that was uncharacteristic of Ben, and he didn't want to portray his friend as unkind. After some internal struggle, Malgan proceeded.

"He ordered the man out of his house," Malgan stated bluntly, causing a round of whispers amongst the spectators.

"Quiet," Easton shouted.

"When did he order Mr. Dorsey out of the house?"

"I don't recall the precise date, but it was shortly before he died. Ben said that he had confronted Dorsey, and the two exchanged harsh words about Maria constantly begging Ben to fund her husband's education. Ben had come to the realization that his daughter had lied to him concerning her husband's financial status, and he was beginning to suspect Dorsey may have married his daughter just to get his hands on Ben's money."

"Did Mr. Burton share the harsh words exchanged between him and Mr. Dorsey?"

"When Ben told Dorsey to leave his house, he said Dorsey's response almost made him drop in his tracks. He said Dorsey threatened that he would be the new boss of the house, and he would be the one to put Ben out of the house and not the other way around."

Easton's earlier admonition to the crowd went unheeded as the spectators erupted into mayhem. Stanhope cried out above the din, threatening to clear the room and close the proceedings if there were any further outbursts, adding there would be no further warnings.

Galvin's heart was pounding. Malgan had just confirmed Emily Burton's testimony and provided even more robust evidence of discourse in the Burton home. After quiet was restored in the courtroom, Galvin calmly continued his questioning.

"Did Mr. Burton tell you of any other disputes in the household?"

"Yes, Ben told me that he had just discovered that his daughter was asking people for money, and he was furious with her. I understand he also confronted her, which resulted in an ugly argument. It pained me to admit to him that Maria had also asked me for money."

"When did that happen?"

"At the end of August. She showed up unannounced at my home and told me that her father had told her that she should come to me if she ever needed a friend. She wanted me to loan her $20 and begged me not to tell her father."

"Did you give her the money?"

"Yes, I gave her $20 with the understanding that she would repay it within 30 days."

"Did she repay you?"

"No, she never did."

"Did she tell you why she needed the money?"

"No, and I didn't ask her."

"What was Mr. Burton's response when you told him you lent his daughter the money?"

"He was shocked. It was an embarrassing conversation for us both. I was sorry I had told him. He offered to repay me the money, but I told him not to fret over it."

Galvin then moved on to the thorny issue of gambling.

"Did you ever see Mr. Burton gamble?"

Malgan visibly flinched.

"Gambling is an illegal activity, Mr. Galvin. I don't allow it in my establishment. I have never seen Ben or any of my patrons," he emphasized, "engage in gambling … no dice or cards. Ben never spoke of it. If he did partake in that activity, it was not in my establishment."

***

Based on Detective Richards' colorful description of his brief interview aboard the USS New Hampshire with Ben's drunken tenant, McGruder, Galvin opted not to call him to the stand. Emily Burton had represented to Richards that another tenant had admitted to hearing an argument, so Galvin had made a strategic decision to subpoena Mrs. Georgia Keller instead.

Though Emily Burton had made several outlandish claims, when push came to shove, there was underlying truth in the information she had provided. He was disappointed but not surprised when Mrs. Keller declined to be interviewed by Richards in advance of her testimony, so he was cautiously optimistic her testimony would be consistent with Emily's characterization.

Georgia Keller, a sturdy Black woman in her early twenties, smiled as she took her seat. Dressed head-to-toe in indigo blue, her dress and matching bonnet were fashionably adorned with an assortment of fabric flowers in varying shades of pastel blue. Though her hair was tucked under her bonnet, two ringlets had sprung free and bounced across her brow when she moved her head.

Galvin began questioning Mrs. Keller by asking her to confirm that she was one of Ben's tenants. He established that she was not at home on the morning of October 6.

"What can you tell us about the relations within the Burton family?"

"I would say that their relations appeared to be pleasant, except on one particular occasion."

"And when was that?" Galvin asked.

"It was on a Tuesday night, the week before Mr. Burton's death. I was in my sink room directly on the other side of the wall from Mr. Burton's kitchen when I heard a quarrel between Mr. Burton and his daughter, Maria. I didn't hear the whole of it. I had just returned home from work."

"Can you tell me exactly what you heard?"

Mrs. Keller nodded energetically. "Mr. Burton was speaking in a loud, angry voice, and it sounded like he was pounding his fist on a table. I heard him say, '*There is great talk about this money north, south, east, and west. It is a terrible disgrace on me, and you will have to get it off.*'"

"What did you hear next?"

"I heard Maria tell Mr. Burton that she knew nothing about it. Mr. Burton responded it was queer that people were stopping him on the street and telling him about it."

"Go on," Galvin encouraged.

"Well," Mrs. Keller paused momentarily and then continued, "Mr. Burton said something about a letter he received from someone claiming Maria owed them money. I remember him asking her whether it was a gift or a loan."

"And how did she respond?"

"She told him it was neither, and that she could prove it with another letter she had received from that person. Mr. Burton asked to look at the letter, but Maria told him she had returned it. Mr. Burton asked her why she wouldn't keep the only evidence she had that would clear her name."

"Do you have any idea what letter they were talking about?" asked Galvin.

"They were talking about a letter Mr. Burton received from a relative saying Maria borrowed some money and had not paid it back."

"Did Mr. Burton mention the name of the relative who had sent the letter?"

"I believe he said it was Miss Sarah Babcock, the cousin who stayed nearly all spring at the house with them."

"Did you hear anything else?"

"Yes," Mrs. Keller answered. "Mr. Burton asked Maria if she told her husband she was borrowing the money. She said there was nothing for him to know. Maria said, *'Father, I haven't done it, and I think you would believe me.'* She said she always tried to do what he would approve."

"How did Mr. Burton respond?"

"He was angry. He said, *'Do you think I would approve of this?'* He told her he planned to break up housekeeping, and she was to look out for that time."

"Was that the end of it?" Galvin asked.

"No!" Mrs. Keller exclaimed. "Mr. Burton started talking about their laundry bill and the household expenses being too high. He asked Maria why her husband wasn't working. *'Is he too high-toned?'* That's what he said. He said he didn't plan on supporting an educated pauper any longer."

Mrs. Keller paused and put her hand on her chest.

"The last thing I heard Mr. Burton say was that Maria must tell her husband they had to leave. He said he was ready to throw him out if Mr. Dorsey got high and mighty with him."

"Did Maria have anything to say in response?"

"At that point, she didn't seem to be talking. It sounded to me as if she was crying."

"Mrs. Keller, have you ever heard quarrels between Mr. Burton and Mr. Dorsey?"

"I only heard the one quarrel between Mr. Burton and his daughter."

***

Although the Dorseys had provided a long list of creditors they requested be called as witnesses, Galvin determined that the administrator of Burton's estate could more succinctly supply the same testimony. The court-appointed administrator had submitted a full accounting of Ben's assets and debts, which Galvin had carefully reviewed before calling him to the stand.

"Sir, can you briefly summarize the condition of Benjamin J. Burton's estate?"

"Based on the claims presented by his creditors and the inventory of assets on hand, Mr. Burton's state is insolvent. Of course, this only reflects the condition of his estate at the time of his death and does not take into consideration his financial condition had he lived."

"Just to clarify, are you saying Mr. Burton's debts outweighed his assets?"

"Yes, there are many unpaid creditors who have presented their claims, and there are insufficient assets to pay all the claims."

"Did you consider the market value of Mr. Burton's real estate holdings in making this determination?"

"Yes, although the real estate cannot be sold until the estate is settled, I don't expect the sale will significantly alter the estate's status."

After the administrator was dismissed, Stanhope stood and announced, "This will conclude the testimony today. These proceedings will resume on Thursday, October 29 at 10 o'clock in the morning."

Chapter 15
Saturday, October 24, 1885

Galvin's heart raced with excitement as he stood on the forward deck of the Fall River steamer as New York Harbor came into view. As the ship passed Bedloe's Island, he watched in fascination as workers scaled up and down the wooden scaffolding that framed a massive granite pedestal that would hold the Libertas statue.

The statue, a gift from France, had arrived with great fanfare only a few months before. Having seen the sketches that Pulitzer published in the *New York World,* Galvin could only imagine how magnificent the gleaming copper monument would be once it was completed.

Galvin always felt drawn to the vitality of the city—the lights, the elevated train rails, the hustle and bustle of the crowded city streets—all of it, the antithesis of tranquil Newport.

After the second day of the inquest, Richards had sent a telegram informing him that he had met with Sarah Babcock and Howard Burton but had been unavoidably delayed in returning to Newport.

Galvin immediately responded, informing the detective that he had been invited to attend a fundraiser for a local Republican candidate in the city and would like to meet with Richards while he was there. He missed conferring with his friend and was eager to fill him in on

Mason's and Malgan's testimonies.

As he disembarked from the steamer, he soon spotted Richards' imposing form and unmistakable smile in the waiting crowd. The men shook hands in a warm greeting.

"Welcome to New York, my friend," Richards hailed as he steered Galvin through the shoulder-to-shoulder congestion on the dock and onto Battery Place in the direction of Bowling Green. "I have much to share with you."

Galvin flashed a cheerful smile.

"I was going to say the same thing. But before we get down to business, I hope you'll indulge me. One of my favorite things to do in the city is to walk the promenade across Brooklyn Bridge. It's a beautiful day, and I thought we could drop my overnighter at the hotel and catch up while we go for a stroll."

Richards couldn't help but laugh at his friend's childlike exuberance. Accustomed to day-to-day life in the city, he took for granted the extraordinary environment surrounding him.

"It would be my pleasure."

The men wove in and out of a crush of pedestrians as they headed up Broadway toward the bridge. Galvin was nearly knocked into the street by a pushcart, causing Richards to quip, "Eyes straight ahead, my friend, or I'll be scraping you off the sidewalk."

When they approached the elevated boardwalk leading to the bridge, the crowds thinned, and Richards turned to Galvin, asking, "Now tell me, counselor … What did I miss?"

"I will spare you the details of Emily Burton's testimony but suffice it to say that my relationship with Mr. Stanhope may never be the same," Galvin joked with a hint of seriousness. "However, she did manage to successfully convey the most important details we had both hoped to get on the record."

As they crossed onto the promenade, Galvin slowed to peer through the intricate needlework of the suspension cabling at the cargo boats traversing the East River.

"Now that her aunt has testified, I will have quite a few follow-up questions for Mrs. Dorsey. I am still trying to decide when the best time would be to recall the Dorseys."

Changing the subject, Richards inquired, "What is the pulse in Newport after the second day of testimony? According to the New York papers, the hearing will not resume until Thursday."

"Correct. What else are the papers saying?"

"*The Herald* seems to be standing firmly by its original reporting of suicide. However, *The Sun* seems to provide a more balanced account of the proceedings."

Galvin pursed his lips. The number of journalists sitting in the council chamber to cover the proceedings had doubled between the first and second days of the hearing. East Coast papers were printing daily extras to expand their coverage of the case. And he had been told the wire services were now dispatching their articles as far west as California. However, he remained disappointed with his hometown coverage of the case.

"*The Newport Mercury* is owned by a man who is closely associated with the authorities who fiercely cling to the suicide theory and support Dr. Turner. Its reporter had a field day with Emily Burton's testimony, painting her as a troublemaker with an axe to grind against the Dorseys. Airing the Dorseys' money problems may have resonated with some residents, but the testimony about Burton's insolvency may have convinced others that there would have been no point in killing Burton for money."

Galvin shook his head and sighed. "Not surprisingly, the inquest and Ben Burton's death continue to be the talk of the town. People remain firmly divided but are lining up at the break of dawn, hoping to get into the proceedings each day. Those who originally supported the Dorseys continued to do so, while those who believed Ben was murdered hold stubbornly to their convictions."

It was not lost on Galvin that many of Ben's friends perceived the inquest to be sullying Ben's legacy.

Richards did not envy Galvin's position. The rising young attorney had been thrust into a maelstrom that was evolving into more than just a local scandal. He was impressed with Galvin's ability to maintain his affable nature while under constant scrutiny. The detective could not recall being involved in a case that generated so much interest. The stakes were high for the attorney, and Richards wanted to do everything he could to help his friend succeed.

When the men reached the Brooklyn side of the bridge, Galvin turned to look back at the long span they had just crossed.

"That took longer than I remembered," he remarked. "We'll need to ride the cable car back if I'm going to get to the banquet on time."

The men paid the conductor the five-cent fare and squeezed into one of the crowded cars, nabbing two remaining seats. As they traveled back over the bridge, Richards filled him in on his meetings with Sarah Babcock and Howard Burton.

Galvin was captivated by Richards' retelling of his interview with Sarah Babcock, in which she disclosed her suspicion that the Dorseys had stolen a valuable bond from her locked trunk during her stay at the Burton home.

"Do you mean to tell me that in addition to not repaying the loan, she believes the couple stole from her while she was a guest?"

Richards reached into his coat pocket to pull out a letter from the bond issuer Sarah Babcock had given him.

"Here. It's all in this letter. It was sent from an address in Philadelphia."

Galvin grabbed the missive from Richards' hand and read it. He looked up at the detective.

"How soon can you get to Philadelphia?"

Richards frowned. "I just received an urgent assignment requiring me to remain in New York a few days longer. However, I will travel directly to Philadelphia as soon as possible if you think we should pursue it. Do you think we will be able to tie this letter to the Dorseys?"

"It's a long shot," Galvin conceded. Richards had a point … this could be a red herring and a waste of the detective's valuable time. "Let's see how the case progresses. We don't have to make that decision right now."

Richards nodded in agreement.

"Other than that, Miss Babcock confirmed the unpaid loan she made to Dorsey and spoke of other minor items that went missing during her stay with the Burtons. A skirt, I believe, although I'm not sure why Mr. Dorsey would want an article of women's clothing," he joked. "But maybe Mrs. Dorsey had the sticky fingers in that case."

"It seems petty," remarked Galvin.

"But it goes to character," contended Richards.

Richards then moved on to his interview with Howard.

"You were right. This man does not present as a killer. Howard is still conflicted. He is desperate to know if his sister or her husband had anything to do with his father's death."

"That's understandable."

"But he believes he can identify his father's gun if it is shown to him."

"The pistol is in evidence. It will be good to have confirmation whether the gun belonged to Burton or not."

Richards paused. "Howard also brought up something I think you'll find interesting … He believes his father was left-handed."

Galvin let out a loud gasp.

"Why didn't you lead with that?" he asked incredulously. "What do you mean he *believes* he was left-handed? If that is true, it would make it almost impossible for Burton to have shot himself on the right side of his head! How did we miss that?"

"Howard wasn't certain, but he said he thought his father wrote with his left hand. Do you suppose Mason or someone else could confirm that?" Richards asked.

"I would think so. I will follow up. But proving it wasn't a suicide is only the first part of the equation. We then need to uncover who fired the shots."

Richards nodded, "True, but a strong motive is developing that points directly at the Dorseys. We continue to gather evidence that the Dorseys had money problems, and Allen was counting on Burton to bankroll his education."

Galvin added, "Yes, and now we have testimony on record about discord between Burton and Dorsey. But there is a piece of this puzzle that still doesn't fit. Burton's estate is insolvent … The Dorseys stand to inherit nothing. Burton was worth more to them alive than dead."

"Have you forgotten about the $3000 life insurance policy?" Richards reminded him. "Maria's share would have gone a long way—paying for her husband's education, setting him up in practice, establishing a marital home—"

"But it had lapsed! It was worthless," Galvin argued.

Richards gave Galvin a shrewd grin.

"Ah, but did the Dorseys know that?"

Chapter 16
Thursday, October 29, 1885
The Third Day of the Inquest

Galvin arrived at the courthouse early, hoping to avoid the crowds. However, when word got out that Howard Burton and Sarah Babcock were scheduled to testify, the demand to gain access to the proceedings had ballooned. The line to get into the building was already snaked up the eastern side of Washington Square all the way to the Old Colony House, and tempers were flaring.

Newspaper reporters milled around the square, interviewing bystanders about the case. One called out to Galvin, "Counselor, will the inquest conclude today?"

Galvin smiled in response.

"It will end when it ends," he answered noncommittally before quickly disappearing inside the building.

***

"Miss Sarah Babcock, please step forward," Sheriff Easton called out as spectators in the gallery craned their necks to get a better look at the unfamiliar figure.

A statuesque Black woman of indeterminate age entered the courtroom. Dressed in a dark gray muslin dress and a simple black straw hat that unintentionally matched her salt and pepper hair, Sarah Babcock walked from the Alderman's chamber to the witness chair with a sense of purpose.

Galvin began, "Miss Babcock, how were you related to Mr. Burton?"

"Ben Burton was my uncle. His beloved wife, Rosanna Babcock Burton, was the youngest child of my grandfather. Even though she was my aunt, we were raised as sisters due to being close in age," she explained.

"Where do you live, Miss Babcock?"

"I live in New York City and have worked in the service of the Cornell family—Governor Cornell's family, that is—for more than thirty years."

"You spent some time in Newport this Spring, did you not?"

"Yes, I came to Newport in April to help my cousin, Maria, prepare for her wedding to Allen Dorsey. My Aunt Rosanna died several years ago, and since Maria did not have a mother to help her, I stepped in."

"How would you describe your relationship with Mrs. Dorsey?"

"I love Maria … Dora and Howard as well. I was happy when I learned of her engagement and was honored that she wanted me to be a part of her wedding planning. I believed her mother would have been pleased over the engagement as Maria appeared to be marrying a man of substance with a promising future."

"Had you met Mr. Dorsey before coming to Newport?" Galvin asked.

"No, I had not met him. But of course, I heard everything about this brilliant medical student from my cousin. She was clearly smitten with him. I was eager to finally meet him."

"Did Mrs. Dorsey ever ask you for money?"

"Only once," Sarah stated. "In March of this year, Maria wrote to me that Mr. Dorsey was having trouble paying his tuition at medical school. She worried he would be unable to take his exams in April unless he made the final payment. Maria said he needed $125 but that he did not have the money."

"Did you lend her the money?"

Sarah scowled. "I wanted to help the couple out. But it meant I had to go to Governor Cornell for the funds as I did not have that kind of money on hand. He was gracious enough to advance me the amount. Once that was arranged, Maria asked that I send it directly to Mr. Dorsey in Philadelphia."

"Did Mrs. Dorsey pay you back as promised?"

"No, she did not," Sarah replied with a frown.

"Did you address the lack of repayment with Mrs. Dorsey?"

"I most certainly did. I spoke with her while I was there, but she claimed she was still waiting to receive the funds from her father."

"Did you mention the loan to your uncle while you stayed in his house?"

"I should have, but I had promised Maria not to tell him about the loan because she said it would embarrass her husband. I was sympathetic to her concern. When I left for New York, the last thing Maria told me was that she would speak to her father right away. She kissed me and told me not to worry … that she would take care of it."

Galvin asked, "And then what happened?"

"When I did not get the money by the end of July, I began to worry. As you can imagine, telling the governor I needed more time to repay him was embarrassing. So, I wrote to Maria insisting that she repay the money immediately or I would be forced to go to my uncle. When I hadn't heard from her by September, I had no choice but to write to him."

"Did you receive any response from Mr. Burton?"

Sarah shook her head sadly. "I had not received a response before his death."

Galvin took a step closer to the witness chair.

"Remind me, when did you return to New York City?"

"I left in early July."

"Miss Babcock, upon your return to New York, did you discover anything missing from your possessions?"

"Yes, sir," she replied. "At first, I noticed a skirt missing from my trunk."

"Did you keep the trunk locked during your stay in the Burton house?"

"No. I only kept a strap thrown around it." Sarah looked down and shook her head. "I never dreamed that I would have the need to lock up my belongings in my uncle's home."

Several of the spectators in the gallery shook their heads and clicked their tongues in disapproval.

Sarah then glanced up and looked sternly at Galvin.

"Then, sometime around the middle of July, an acquaintance contacted me about a $200 promissory note that I held, the balance of which he still owed to me. He asked me if I still had the note in my possession. That is when I discovered the note had gone missing from a locked tin box I kept in my trunk."

"Go on," urged Galvin.

"He told me he had received a letter, written in an educated hand. The writer stated that the note had recently come into his possession and that he had a smart business proposition. He offered to return the note to the man if he would pay the writer a discounted amount of $100."

"Did he give you the name of the person who authored the letter?"

"It was a name I did not recognize, but I am certain that either Maria or her husband wrote the letter."

"What makes you believe that, Miss Babcock?"

"The letter was from an address in Philadelphia. That's where Mr. Dorsey lived."

The gallery reacted in shock just as Galvin had anticipated, though he was relieved they had quieted in short order without Stanhope or Easton's intervention.

"But wasn't Mr. Dorsey in Newport during that time?" Galvin asked.

"No, Mr. Galvin, he was not. Around the fourth of July, Allen showed me an urgent telegraph he received from his mother saying his sister had fallen ill and that he needed to return to Philadelphia immediately. He then left Newport and did not return before I departed."

Galvin picked up the letter from his desk and showed it to the witness.

"Is this the letter you received about the note?"

"Yes."

"What is the date on the letter?"

"July 8, 1885."

Galvin handed the evidence over to Stanhope and asked for the letter to be put on record.

"That will be all, Miss Babcock. Thank you."

As Galvin turned to walk back to his table, he felt reassured that buying Richards a train ticket to Philadelphia had been a wise decision.

***

Sheriff Easton called Howard Burton to the stand.

Howard was attired in a dark sack coat with a curved front opening and a high button front. A mourning armband was wrapped tightly around his upper left arm. He bore a somber expression as he took his seat in the witness chair. Galvin began his questioning in a kind and gentle tone, asking Howard to introduce himself.

Howard held his head erect. "I live in New York City and am Benjamin J. Burton's only living son. I am 29 years old."

Galvin picked up the pistol from his table and stepped back toward Howard. He held up the gun dramatically before handing it to the witness.

"Have you seen this pistol in your father's house before?"

Howard took the pistol and turned it over several times, carefully examining its markings.

"No, Father did own a .22-caliber pistol, but the handle on this one differs from the one he owned. This one has carvings on the handle. My father's pistol did not."

"Do you recall the last time you saw your father's pistol?"

"Perhaps a year ago. I saw it lying on his secretary desk when I was home for a visit."

Galvin extended his hand to take the gun from Howard.

"Mr. Burton, have you ever heard your father talk about killing himself?"

Howard stiffened. "Certainly not."

"Have you spoken with either of your sisters about your father's death?" Galvin asked.

He clenched his hands into fists and squeezed his eyes shut. "Yes. I found their characterization of my father's mental and physical condition inconsistent with my own observations."

Galvin nodded, asking, "Have you had any discussions with Mr. Dorsey concerning your father's death?"

Howard's mood darkened. "I'm afraid that my discussions with Mr. Dorsey have been limited to my numerous attempts to reclaim my father's personal effects from him."

"What personal effects are you referring to?"

"Mr. Dorsey had the keys to my father's room, which he kept locked. He was holding all the documents he removed from my father's safe, and I saw him wearing a pair of my father's sleeve buttons."

"Have you been successful in retrieving your father's things?"

Howard nodded hesitantly. "Eventually, except for the gold sleeve buttons. He claims he does not have them."

Galvin then questioned Howard about his father's finances and gambling habits. Howard could not shed any light on either subject, stating that he had spent little time in his father's house since he had struck out on his own.

"Mr. Burton, do you recall which hand your father used to write?"

"As I recall, he favored his left hand, Mr. Galvin."

Galvin glanced up to be met by Stanhope's dumbstruck expression.

As the significance of Howard's response dawned on the reporters, several leaped from their chairs and headed for the door, hoping to be the first to get the revelation in print.

"Thank you, Mr. Burton. I have no more questions."

After Howard was dismissed, Galvin was ready to recall Allen and Maria Dorsey back to the stand.

***

"Mr. Dorsey, may I remind you that you are still under oath?"

"I understand, sir," Allen replied, smiling.

"Mr. Dorsey, we have heard sworn testimony from several witnesses that Mrs. Dorsey solicited money from several individuals to help pay for your education. I ask again … were you having financial difficulties?"

Allen didn't blink.

"No, I am quite able to return to school in my current financial situation."

"Last Spring, did Miss Sarah Babcock send you money to help pay for your tuition?"

"It is true, I did receive $125 from Miss Babcock," Allen admitted coolly, explaining, "But those funds were used to take an additional course at school, not to pay my tuition. I could have easily obtained the money from other sources."

"Such as Mrs. Emily Burton? Isn't it true you wrote to her requesting the same amount?"

"Yes, I wrote to Mrs. Burton for the money, but only because she had offered it to me first. However, I did not pursue that with her because my wife obtained the money from Miss Babcock."

"I see," Galvin remarked. "Tell me, Mr. Dorsey, what is the source of your income?"

Allen appeared visibly annoyed by the question.

"As I stated previously, Mr. Galvin, I held several jobs after graduating from Lincoln University. I also worked in the Newport hotels every summer. This enables me to pay for my medical school education."

"Why couldn't you use some of that money to pay for the extra course?"

Allen smiled. "The class was not mandatory, so I had not factored the additional expense into my budget."

Galvin moved on.

"Are you aware that a $200 promissory note went missing from Miss Babcock's trunk during her stay?"

"No, I know nothing about it."

"Did you know that a letter demanding payment was mailed to the borrower in July originating from an address in Philadelphia?"

"No. I did not know about the note or a request for payment of said note."

Galvin raised his arm and pointed at Allen. "Didn't you travel to Philadelphia in July?"

Allen seemed unaffected by the implication. "Yes, Mr. Galvin, I did. I went to Philadelphia to make boarding arrangements for medical school. I was also invited to work at an event at a resort outside of Philadelphia."

"Didn't you show Miss Babcock a telegram stating you were summoned to Philadelphia because your sister had fallen ill?"

"No, sir, I did not," Allen answered calmly.

"Did Mr. Burton ever discuss his concerns over the increasing household expenses that resulted from your living in the home?"

Allen returned a frosty glare. "No, sir. He never complained to me about it."

"Did Mr. Burton ever order you to leave his home?"

"No, Mr. Galvin, he knew we were leaving soon."

"Did you ever tell Mr. Burton that you would have him out of the house before you would leave or that you would be the boss of the house?"

"No, sir," denied Allen. "I would never have spoken to Mr. Burton, or anyone else for that matter, in such a disrespectful manner."

"Are you aware that Mr. Burton referred to you as an '*Educated Pauper*'?"

Instead of becoming angry at the mention of the slight, Allen smirked. "No, I've not heard that, but I suppose it has a ring of truth to it … I am well educated."

Galvin ignored the scattered laughter from the gallery and pressed on.

"Is it your testimony that you never had any confrontations with Mr. Burton?"

"That is correct," Allen replied confidently. "Our relationship was most pleasant."

"Mr. Howard Burton testified earlier today that some of his father's belongings were in your possession. Is that true?"

"Yes, Mr. Galvin," Allen freely admitted. "I received the keys to the safe Mr. Burton kept at his office, which I opened to retrieve his papers. Mr. Burton made it clear to his daughters that if anything was to happen to him, my wife was to retrieve his important documents. I was simply assisting my wife in this matter. I have since given all his papers to my brother-in-law. And it is true I am in possession of the keys to Mr. Burton's bedroom. I am not in possession of any other items belonging to Mr. Burton."

"What about a pair of sleeve buttons?"

Allen leaned forward slightly and flashed a contemptuous smile.

"Thank you, Mr. Galvin. I appreciate the opportunity to clear up the matter regarding the elusive sleeve buttons. Last night, my brother-in-law barged into our bedroom long after my wife and I had retired for the evening. He demanded his father's sleeve buttons, acting in such an ungentlemanly manner that I thought it best not to engage in conversation with him at the time. I told him I would tell all that needed to be known about the sleeve buttons to the coroner."

Allen shifted in his chair, turning to face Coroner Stanhope directly.

"Sir, I came into possession of the sleeve buttons on the day of Mr. Burton's death. My wife and I were searching for appropriate burial clothing for Mr. Burton, but I could not find a pair of clean cuffs to put on his wrists. We decided to use a pair of my cuffs, and my wife asked me to put the sleeve buttons on them. When it was later decided to enshroud Mr. Burton's body, I left the cuffs with the sleeve buttons still attached in Mr. Burton's bedroom. To the best of my knowledge, they are still locked away exactly where I left them."

Allen turned his head back toward Galvin, who was hunched over his table, hurriedly writing a note. Allen watched quizzically as Galvin folded the paper and walked it over to the city marshal sitting in the dignitaries' section in front of the bar. He bent forward, whispering instructions as he handed off the note. Galvin then turned and walked casually back, picking up the pistol from his table. He stepped toward Allen.

"Have you ever owned a gun, Mr. Dorsey?"

"No. I have never owned a gun."

Galvin looped his finger through the trigger guard and dangled the gun in front of Allen's face.

"Do you recognize this pistol, Mr. Dorsey?"

"I can't say for certain."

Galvin lowered his hand and pushed the pistol toward Allen, signaling him to take the gun.

"Take a closer look."

Allen grabbed the gun by the barrel and held it awkwardly.

"I don't know if I have seen this pistol before or not."

"Do the markings indicate where this gun was made?"

Allen held the gun close to his eyes and squinted to read the engraving.

"Go ahead, read it out loud," Galvin suggested.

"This gun was manufactured in Philadelphia, Pennsylvania."

Galvin held his hand out, palm up, signaling Allen to return the gun. He stepped back and laid the firearm on the table behind him, his eyes not leaving Allen.

"Mr. Dorsey, where are you from?"

"I was born in Athens, Pennsylvania," Allen responded.

"And where do you attend medical school?"

"Philadelphia, Pennsylvania."

This exchange elicited hisses and jeers from the gallery, which subsided on their own when Galvin dismissed Allen from the witness stand.

As he returned to his chair behind his cluttered table, Galvin inhaled deeply to clear his mind while Sheriff Easton escorted Maria from the Alderman's chamber.

As he stood, Galvin cautioned, "Mrs. Dorsey. Please be mindful that you are still under oath."

Maria nodded silently and rested her hands in her lap.

"Mrs. Dorsey, since you last testified, we have heard testimony from several witnesses that differs substantially from yours, specifically concerning your solicitations for money. Let's begin with your cousin, Sarah Babcock. Did you borrow $125 from her?"

Maria lowered her head and looked down at the floor. After a few seconds of silence, she answered. "Yes, Mr. Galvin, she sent the funds to my husband."

"So, your testimony last week that you did not borrow money from anyone was untrue?"

"Yes, Mr. Galvin, I did tell an untruth about that," Maria admitted.

"Mrs. Dorsey, why were you untruthful?"

Maria shook her head, refusing to meet Galvin's gaze. "I don't know Mr. Galvin. I should not have been."

"Why did your husband need the $125? That's a large sum."

"I can't recall, other than it was to pay for some school-related expenses."

"For tuition, perhaps?" Galvin suggested.

"I don't remember."

"Did you tell your father you borrowed money from your cousin?"

"No," Maria replied softly.

"Did your father ever question you about borrowing money from your cousin?"

Maria raised her head slightly. "He told me he received a letter from my cousin that disclosed I had borrowed the money."

"When did that conversation take place?" Galvin asked.

"The Tuesday before his death."

"What else did he say?"

"He said he had also heard that I was going around town asking for money."

"Did he say who had told him that?"

Maria glanced up at Galvin and shook her head. "I have no idea, Mr. Galvin. That sounds like the type of gossip my Aunt Emily spreads."

A loud harrumph sprang from the back of the gallery, which Galvin had no doubt came from Emily Burton.

He continued, "Was it an angry conversation?"

"Father was angry at first, but he did not stay angry. After that night, he said no more about it."

"Did you ever pay Miss Babcock back?"

"I intended to pay her out of the funds my father promised to my husband and me. At the time of his death, he had not given us the money, so I could not repay her."

"Did you borrow money from Mr. Malgan as well?"

Maria lowered her head once again. "Yes, Mr. Galvin, I did."

"So, you were untruthful about that too."

"Yes, I was ashamed to talk about that."

"Why did you need to borrow money from Mr. Malgan?"

Maria sat quietly for a moment. "I needed additional money for household expenses. My father did not provide me with sufficient funds to run the household."

Galvin continued to pressure his witness.

"Isn't it also true, Mrs. Dorsey, that you told several people your brother murdered someone, and you wanted to send him money so he could leave the country? Was this also an attempt to obtain money for the household expenses?"

"No, Mr. Galvin, I needed that money to help my brother because I had been told he was in trouble," Maria insisted.

"Who told you that?"

"I received several letters from a woman in New York City who wrote that my brother Howard had killed someone and was in hiding. I wanted to help my brother, Mr. Galvin."

"What was the name of this woman … the one who wrote the letters?"

"I prefer not to say."

"Why not?"

"It turned out to be untrue, and she asked me not to disclose her name."

"When did you find out the story was a falsehood?" Galvin asked.

"Several weeks later."

"Mrs. Dorsey, I must remind you that you are under oath. You have an obligation to answer all questions posed to you truthfully and honestly," Galvin stressed. "Now, what was the name of the person who wrote you the letters about your brother?"

Maria raised her chin defiantly, her eyes flashing.

"I won't tell you."

Galvin paused, unsure how to proceed. Coroner Stanhope took over and addressed Maria in a commanding voice.

"Mrs. Dorsey, you must disclose the name of the woman who wrote these letters. You have no option. I am ordering you to reveal her name now."

Maria buried her face in her hands while Galvin and Stanhope waited impatiently for her response. One minute, and then another, ticked by before Maria lowered her hands and raised her head.

"Her name is Lizzie Smith. She lives on West 29th Street in New York City."

"Smith," Galvin murmured to himself, shaking his head. "Mrs. Dorsey, did you tell your father about these letters you received from this woman?"

"No, I did not want to upset my father. My brother had caused my father enough suffering."

An anguished, strangled cry suddenly echoed throughout the chamber, causing Galvin to spin around. Coroner Stanhope rose from his chair, his eyes darting around the gallery to see who had caused the disturbance.

Howard Burton, who had taken a seat next to his aunt, rocked back and forth, sobbing uncontrollably, as Emily futilely attempted to console him. He stood and walked toward the section of the bar railing closest to Maria, crying out as he approached, "Maria, do you know me?"

Maria dispassionately locked eyes with her brother.

As Howard reached the railing, he extended his hands in desperation, as if reaching out for Maria, and continued crying, "Do you know me, Maria? Do you know me?"

A great commotion broke out in the gallery as Sheriff Easton ran to Howard's side, grabbing his arm and pulling him away from the rail.

Over the growing noise of the spectators, Coroner Stanhope shouted, "Mr. Burton! Please do not speak to the witness."

Wiping tears, Howard turned and allowed Sheriff Easton to assist him down the center aisle and out of the council chamber.

Galvin was spent. It was almost six o'clock in the evening.

"This might be a good time to call an end to the day," Stanhope suggested, as Galvin nodded in agreement.

"Very well, then. This hearing is adjourned, and we will reconvene on Thursday, November 5, at 10 in the morning."

Chapter 17
Thursday, October 29, 1885

Around 8 o'clock in the evening, Captain Hammond pounded on the front door of the Burton house. Allen answered and greeted him cordially.

"Good evening, sir. To what do we owe the honor of your visit?"

"The city marshal has asked me to look for the sleeve buttons you mentioned in your testimony today."

Allen was surprised. "Did Howard Burton file a police complaint?"

"No, no, certainly not," Hammond reassured him. "The city marshal just wants us to follow up on your inquest testimony."

Allen opened the door wide, motioning him inside. "I understand. Right this way, captain."

He followed as Allen led him through the parlor to the door to Ben's room.

"	It has been locked tight since the day of the funeral," Allen remarked, "and I do not have the key. Howard does."

Hammond pulled out a key from his trouser pocket and dangled it in front of Allen.

"I have it now."

Allen stepped aside as the captain unlocked the door and entered the bedroom. Allen followed closely behind.

"Now, where did you put the cuffs?"

Allen pointed toward a stack of neatly folded clothing that lay on the bed. Hammond walked over and began rustling through the items until he uncovered the cuffs with the sleeve buttons still secured in the buttonholes.

"As I said," Dorsey commented, "just as I left them after the funeral. As you can see for yourself, I didn't take them."

Hammond picked up the cuffs and closely examined them before replacing them on the bed. He quickly sketched a drawing and jotted down a few notes in his notebook.

"I don't believe I need to confiscate them," he said, "as I have noted the location and can confirm it matches your testimony."

Hammond's eyes scanned the room. "I'll just look around a bit more while I'm here."

Allen nodded, "Certainly, captain. As I said, no one has been in this room since the funeral."

Hammond turned to face the bureau opposite the bed and began sliding open the drawers to rummage through them. When he reached the bottom drawer, he pushed aside some shirts and found a darkly varnished wooden box underneath. He quickly recognized it was a pistol case and turned it over to read a handwritten label adhered to the underside.

Pistol and ammunition for Benjamin J. Burton, $8.00

Hammond opened the lid. It was empty.

He placed the box atop the bureau and dug further. The captain found a few stray unspent bullet cartridges in the front left-hand corner and, alongside them, three white paper pouches. He picked up one of the slender packets and held it up to the gaslight. Printed in a small typeface on the front of the package was the word *POISON*.

"What is this?" asked Hammond as he turned to show it to Allen. Allen reached for the packet.

"Let me see. I believe this is used as a tonic for horses. My father owned a livery stable in Pennsylvania. I remember he kept a supply of arsenic."

"Interesting," Hammond remarked as he placed the packages of arsenic inside the pistol case. "I'll need to take all of this back to the station."

"Yes, yes, of course. Whatever you need."

The captain smiled and thanked Allen for his cooperation. He now had proof the gun used in Ben Burton's death clearly belonged to Ben, not Allen Dorsey. Allen had not taken the sleeve buttons, but instead, they were found precisely where Allen testified that he had placed them.

Now, Galvin will have to admit that he is wasting his time on a fool's errand, he thought. *I've been right all along.*

Yet, as he walked back to the police station, Hammond couldn't shake the nagging suspicion that Allen was not surprised by his unannounced visit.

Chapter 18
Thursday morning, November 5, 1885
The Fourth Day of the Inquest

SUICIDE, NOT MURDER
Newport, R.I., Nov. 2, 1885. -- The Herald correspondent is authorized to state that the adjourned session of inquiry ordered by the State to ascertain the cause of the death of Benjamin J. Burton will on Thursday render a verdict of suicide. This will officially confirm the Herald's statement made on the day of Burton's death. It will be remembered that the local authorities originally rendered a verdict of suicide in the case.

Galvin folded the *New York Herald* newspaper and shoved it in his bulging valise, which was already filled with copies of the *Boston Herald,* the *New York Tribune,* the *Evening Bulletin of Providence,* and others. Once *The Herald* broke their exclusive report, they quickly syndicated the dispatch to virtually every major publication along the Northeastern seaboard.

Galvin's frustration was palatable. Captain Hammond must have run to the reporters with his discoveries after his search of the Burton house. By week's end, articles were popping up everywhere declaring the evidence collected *"removed all doubt as to the cause of Benjamin Burton's death."*

Galvin put on his coat and hat and grabbed his valise before striking out on his walk from his Thames Street office to City Hall. It was almost ten o'clock, and though he might have been late, he did not hasten his stride. Instead, he spent the walk considering the possibilities.

If the papers were correct, Stanhope could issue his finding prior to the start of today's testimony or immediately after. Galvin wondered if he should even bother to proceed with testimony if Stanhope had already made his decision.

Once at City Hall, Galvin weaved his way through the thick crowd packed in the hallway waiting for the hearing to start before reaching the council chambers. When he entered, he saw Coroner Stanhope and the court reporter already in their seats.

"Mr. Galvin, you are late," Coroner Stanhope called out gruffly. "Are you prepared to proceed?"

Galvin glanced at the wall clock hanging behind the two rows of newspaper reporters. It was just a few minutes after ten. He lifted his valise and began to empty its contents, carefully laying his folders and notes on the table before stacking the newspapers one by one in a stack at the center.

"I apologize for my lateness, sir," Galvin said as he stood behind the table, looking at Stanhope.

"Are you ready to proceed, Counselor?" Stanhope repeated impatiently.

"Mr. Coroner," Galvin began, "before we proceed, I believe it is prudent to ask if you have further interest in hearing any additional testimony."

Galvin reached over, picked up the stack of newspapers, and held them up for the coroner to see.

"I have read numerous reports indicating you will be issuing a ruling of death by suicide today."

Coroner Stanhope was struck momentarily speechless as his cheeks flushed red in anger.

"I have made no such statement," he declared loudly, glaring at the reporters. "This inquest will proceed. Now, call your first witness, Mr. Galvin."

Galvin called Captain Hammond to the stand. He wanted

Hammond in and out of the witness chair as quickly as possible.

Through a series of rapid-fire questions, Hammond confirmed for the record he discovered the empty gun box and cartridges that he characterized as belonging to the gun used to kill Burton, as well as the existence of the packets of arsenic and the sleeve buttons in Burton's bedroom.

"Was the bedroom locked when you arrived?" Galvin asked.

"Yes," Hammond responded. "But not the drawers containing the objects."

"Was the bedroom window locked?"

"I beg your pardon?" Hammond asked.

Galvin clarified, "Could someone have accessed Mr. Burton's bedroom by crawling through the window?"

"Possibly," Hammond admitted grudgingly. "I do not recall if the window was locked."

"So, you did not check the window?"

"No."

"I've no further questions," Galvin announced as he returned to his table.

***

Ultimately, Galvin was convinced the medical testimony would determine whether Burton's death was a suicide or murder. It was time to call Allen Dorsey's physician, Dr. Henry Ecroyd, to the stand.

"Can you state your name and your credentials for the court?"

"Gladly," the dapper young man responded enthusiastically. "My name is Dr. Henry Ecroyd. I am a graduate of the University of Pennsylvania Medical School. I have been a practicing physician in Philadelphia," he announced before quickly adding, "and throughout the country."

"Have you had the opportunity to review the autopsy report, the accompanying medical evidence, and the previous inquest testimony in this case?"

Ecroyd opened the folder he carried with him, nodded, and closed it shut again.

"Yes, I have carefully reviewed the entirety of the evidence, and the medical opinions provided me."

"Do you have an opinion with regard to the manner by which Benjamin J. Burton died?"

The doctor's expression grew quite serious. "Yes. It is my expert opinion that the shot to Mr. Burton's head as well as the one to his heart were both self-inflicted."

Galvin asked, "And how did you arrive at this conclusion?"

Dr. Ecroyd answered proudly. "I was educated at the finest medical school in the country and have extensive experience as a practicing physician. It was not difficult to arrive at this determination."

"Dr. Ecroyd, how many gunshot wounds have you seen in your five years of practice?"

"I couldn't say," he responded with a scowl.

"Can you make a guess?"

"I really couldn't say," he repeated. "But I have had occasion to treat them."

"And based on this limited experience, you can confidently state that Mr. Burton shot himself? Twice?"

Ecroyd glanced at Galvin, his face beginning to redden. "Based on my studies in anatomy and wound treatment as well, yes."

"While you were a student?"

"Yes."

Galvin continued. "Now, Dr. Ecroyd, would you agree that if Mr. Burton was shot in the head while his mouth was full of food, it is less likely to be a suicide?"

Silence hung over the courtroom as Ecroyd shifted in his chair.

"Could you repeat the question, Counselor?"

"Of course. If a man is shot in the head while he is chewing his food, is it more likely to be murder or a suicide?"

Ecroyd's face was now scarlet. He haltingly replied, "I would have to say … if a man is shot while eating, it is less likely to be suicide."

"Thank you, Doctor. I have no further questions."

***

"I call Dr. William Thornton Parker to the stand."

Dr. Parker strode briskly toward the witness chair. He stood pin straight as Sheriff Easton administered the oath before kissing the Bible and taking his seat.

"Dr. Parker," Galvin began, "can you describe your medical qualifications?"

Galvin couldn't mask his smile as Dr. Parker spent several minutes ticking off the highlights of his impressive resume.

"Dr. Parker, have you familiarized yourself with the facts surrounding Mr. Burton's death?"

Parker cleared his throat. "Yes. I have read the police reports and diligently examined all the medical documentation made available to me."

"And do you have an opinion concerning the cause of Mr. Burton's death?"

"I do indeed. It is my opinion that Mr. Burton died by a hand other than his own."

Those in the gallery who had become restless during the tedious character testimony now sat in rapt attention, eager to hear more from the peculiar-looking physician.

"And how did you come to this conclusion?"

"When reviewing the police file, I was particularly drawn to a rudimentary sketch of Mr. Burton's body and the surrounding area. The accompanying notes troubled me a great deal."

"Why was that?" Galvin asked.

"The description of the position of the body seemed unnatural. I thought that the position of the body sounded as if it had been placed in that position. It was not a natural position for someone to fall in after being shot … with his legs straight out and threaded between the legs of a table. I could not reconcile how someone who had shot himself while either sitting or standing could fall into that position. In addition, if the wounds were self-inflicted, the pistol would likely be jerked away and not found lying in such close proximity to the body."

Parker adjusted his glasses and continued unprompted.

"We must also consider that the hair was not singed or burned in the area surrounding the head wound. This would also suggest that the wound was not self-inflicted. While the medical examiner suggests this absence of burns is due to the small caliber of the gun, I disagree. My experience in treating gunshot wounds would indicate that the caliber of the gun has little bearing on the matter. I further contend it would have been physically impossible for Mr. Burton to have held the gun at such a distance as not to have left even the slightest amount of singeing."

"Is it possible that Mr. Burton could have shot himself twice?"

"I don't believe so. The fact remains that if the head wound had been self-inflicted, and the one first inflicted, a loss of consciousness would have followed at once, rendering a second shot to the heart impossible. I also believe that the heart wound was almost, if not instantly, fatal."

"Is there anything else that would cause you to reject suicide as the manner of death?" Galvin asked.

"There is. Finding food in the mouth would make the theory of suicide extremely improbable. Suicide at the time of eating would seem inconsistent."

Dr. Parker continued, "Secondly, the locations of where the shots entered the body and the trajectory of the bullets internally would add to the suspicion caused by the presence of food in the mouth. A suspicion so strong that only a remarkable exception could account for the theory of suicide."

Galvin opened his mouth to speak, but Parker wasn't done.

"The point of entry for both shots is, in my analysis, foreign to the view of suicide. The wound in the head directed by suicide is more likely to be upward than downward, and the heart wound backward."

"Have you had an opportunity to consult with any of your colleagues about the case?" asked Galvin.

"Yes, I took the liberty of dispatching inquiries to many of my medical colleagues in Boston and Cambridge, and I detailed the facts of this case as they were presented. I solicited their opinions on the most possible cause of death. Those who have responded to date, I believe it was 20 in total, are all in agreement it is far more likely Mr. Burton was shot as opposed to killing himself."

"Do you have those responses available?"

"Yes, I brought them with me today," Parker replied as he removed a package from his suit coat and handed it to Galvin.

Galvin took the bundle of letters and gave them to Stanhope to include in the record.

Following Captain Hammond's discovery of the arsenic in Ben's belongings, Galvin had been increasingly haunted by the notion that the Dorseys may have been poisoning Ben.

Allen had testified that Ben suffered from indigestion, while both Maria and Dora had referred to Ben as having a stomach ailment. It was a long shot, but Galvin decided to question Dr. Parker about the possibility of arsenic poisoning.

"Dr. Parker, are you familiar with the physical effects caused by ingesting arsenic?"

Stanhope looked at Galvin and raised an eyebrow.

Dr. Parker cocked his head curiously. "Why, yes, Mr. Galvin, I am indeed."

"What would those symptoms be?"

"Ingesting arsenic would cause nausea, vomiting, and diarrhea," Dr. Parker stated matter-of-factly.

"Could a person who has ingested arsenic be misdiagnosed as suffering from indigestion or another routine stomach ailment?"

"Yes, Counselor. The symptoms of arsenic poisoning mimic many various stomach ailments. It would be quite possible if the person were unaware they had ingested the arsenic."

Galvin nodded in understanding. He couldn't shake his sickening suspicion that the Dorseys had been slowly poisoning Ben, but had become impatient, causing them to resort to shooting him.

"Thank you, Doctor. I have one final question. If a man is left-handed, could he inflict a gunshot wound to the right side of his head?"

"It would be highly unlikely."

Galvin paused to let Dr. Parker's words sink in. The gallery was deathly silent, the only sound being the furious scribbling of the reporters putting pen to paper to capture Parker's testimony.

"Thank you, Dr. Parker. That will be all."

***

After dismissing Dr. Parker, Galvin recalled Clarence Mason to the witness stand.

"Mr. Mason, you previously testified that you worked with Ben Burton for over six years and spent time with him on a daily basis. Is that correct?"

Mason concurred, "Yes, it is."

"What hand did he use to write with?"

Mason's eyes crinkled as his lips curled into a smile.

"As I recall, Ben wrote with his left hand."

***

After Mason had been dismissed from the stand, Galvin scanned the council chamber looking for Richards. Given his absence, Galvin would be forced to close the inquest without knowing what the detective had uncovered in Philadelphia.

"On behalf of the state, I have no further evidence or testimony to offer in these proceedings."

Stanhope picked up a stack of envelopes sitting on the table before him. He held them in the air as he began to speak.

"These contain letters from various members of the faculty and several students at the University of Pennsylvania Medical School, where Mr. Dorsey is a student. Each recommends Mr. Dorsey's character and, as such, will be entered into testimony."

Stanhope put the letters back on the table and continued. "I have also received correspondence from two principals and several teachers attesting Mr. Dorsey is an honorable and well-behaved gentleman. These, too, will be entered into evidence. I will consider the content of these letters when reviewing the case."

Stanhope glanced up at the wall clock.

"Ladies and Gentlemen, the formal inquest is now at an end. I want to thank the court reporter, as well as Sheriff Easton, for their assistance."

He paused briefly to remove his glasses.

"The testimony given during these four days of hearings is voluminous. I will require several days to review the transcripts before rendering my decision. We are now adjourned."

With that, Stanhope stood, gathered all his paperwork, and stepped down from the dais.

Chapter 19
Thursday, November 12, 1885

In the days immediately following the close of the inquest, Galvin repeatedly sought refuge in his father's gardens. The fall foliage had passed its peak; the autumnal shades of yellow, orange, and red now gave way to falling brown leaves and bare branches.

As Galvin walked the mulched paths that snaked through the gardens surrounding his family home on Spring Street, he couldn't help but marvel at their beauty. A host of chrysanthemums, asters, and sedums lined the path, their colorful blooms thriving in the cool autumn air. He stopped to peer through the nursery greenhouse windows where his father's seasonal plants and flowers were carefully being cultivated in anticipation of the winter to come.

Galvin never moved out of the family home, even though he owned several properties in Newport. He couldn't bring himself to leave the comfort and sense of belonging the house and gardens provided. His walks through the gardens and around the grounds soothed him when worries threatened his peace of mind.

He was one of eight children born to Irish immigrants, and his father was a fifth-generation landscaper who rapidly became a favorite of the wealthy Newport summer residents. His father created many of the magnificent gardens surrounding the villas on Bellevue Avenue and Ochre Point using the plants, shrubbery, and trees he grew and nurtured at the nurseries surrounding the family home. Though his father was initially disappointed that his son did not wish to join him in the landscape business, he eventually embraced his son's desire to study law.

Galvin wondered if he had succeeded in convincing Coroner Stanhope that Ben's death was not a suicide.

Should I have presented more testimony? Different testimony? Should I have requested a delay until Detective Richards returned from Philadelphia?

Between the end of the inquest and the announcement of Stanhope's verdict, Galvin's days were filled with endless questions and self-doubt.

Galvin considered all the evidence he had presented. Dr. Turner was a problem.

Why had the old doctor stuck so doggedly to the suicide theory? Was it a matter of pride or a dereliction of duty?

Galvin knew he would have to tighten up the medical testimony if the case against the Dorseys went forward. Thankfully, he had Dr. Parker's expertise solidly behind him. Still, he would need to gather additional testimony and evidence to counter Dr. Turner's testimony and any uncertainty it created as to the cause of death.

He picked up a stray rock from the path and tossed it aside. *I could also press for perjury charges against Maria*, he thought.

As he rounded the corner to the front of the house, Galvin spied Detective Richards walking briskly down Spring Street. Richards had finally returned to Newport after investigating Sarah Babcock's missing promissory note. Galvin waved and watched as Richards crossed the nursery grounds. He could hardly wait to find out what his friend had uncovered.

As he approached, Richards greeted Galvin with a big grin. "Good morning, counselor!"

I hope that smile is a good sign, Galvin thought as he reached his house and opened the door wide.

"Welcome back, detective. Please, come in … we have much to discuss."

Once inside, the men settled into two chairs facing one another in the parlor. Before Galvin could speak, his sister came in from the kitchen, happily humming an old Irish tune and carrying a large serving tray.

Galvin cleared the side table and pushed it between Richards and himself as she placed the tray of tea cakes, finger sandwiches, and two cups of freshly brewed tea on the table.

Galvin reached for a triangle of white bread mounded with fresh lobster salad.

"Now," Galvin said, mouth half-full, "What did you learn?"

Detective Richards settled back in his chair and smiled broadly. "I went to the address shown in the letter and was met by a gentleman by the name of Dr. James T. Potter."

Galvin interrupted Richards. "James Potter? Why does that name sound familiar?"

"You've heard it before?"

Galvin rose from his chair and retrieved his valise. Richards waited patiently until Galvin returned to his seat. He pulled out his notes from the inquest file and quickly scanned them. He could not recall any reference to Dr. Potter during the testimony, but Stanhope had provided him with a handwritten list of the character reference letters that were submitted on behalf of Allen. And there it was.

"Yes! See here?" Galvin said excitedly, pointing to Dr. James T. Potter's name and the paragraph Stanhope had penned. "Looks like Dr. Potter wrote a statement on Dorsey's behalf."

Richards leaned in to see for himself. "Then you will be quite interested to hear what I discovered."

Galvin jerked his head up and grinned slyly. "Do tell."

"During my conversation with Dr. Potter, I learned he and Allen Dorsey are intimate friends and have known each other for years, dating back to their college days at Lincoln University," Richards explained. "Dr. Potter was a year ahead of Dorsey at Lincoln but two years ahead of him in medical school."

"Did the author of the letter written to the man who owed Sarah Babcock money live there as well?"

"No, but the name belongs to a real person," Richards confirmed. "Turns out he was a medical student at Penn as well. He hails from Cuba, and according to Dr. Potter, the man returned to his homeland over a year ago."

Galvin sat momentarily stunned, shaking his head in disbelief.

"Was it difficult to get Dr. Potter to talk to you? I can't imagine he is happy to be drawn into all of this."

"I brought along one of my buddies from the Philadelphia police force just in case he was not inclined to cooperate," Richards grinned. "Dr. Potter freely acknowledged his friendship with Dorsey, but when it came to the letter and the promissory note, he feigned ignorance."

"Is that so?"

"Indeed. Remarkably, the good doctor claimed to know very little about 'The Newport Affair,' as he called it. He said all he knew was what he read in the papers. He failed to mention that he had submitted a character reference on Dorsey's behalf."

"Did he have any reasonable explanation for why his address was used in the letter?" Galvin asked.

"Not one. He insisted he was at a loss in that regard."

Galvin looked to Richards hopefully.

"Did you get a handwriting sample from him?"

"We did. Dr. Potter agreed to copy the letter in his handwriting, and we had a handwriting expert with the Philadelphia police department compare the two."

"Did they match?"

"The expert agreed Potter's handwriting was similar, but he did not believe it would be sufficient evidence to prosecute Potter for conspiracy. The best I could do was to convince the police detective to keep the pressure on Potter by issuing a statement to the papers concerning the investigation."

Galvin nodded in agreement. "I am certain Miss Babcock would be willing to press charges if the Philadelphia police decide to pursue the matter."

"P.J., I'm willing to bet dollars to donuts that the Philadelphia police department have already closed their file on the matter if they bothered to open one."

"You are probably correct in your assessment," Galvin said just before his face broke into a wide smile. "But you have given me a singular idea, detective. Perhaps it is time I invite a reporter from *The Providence Journal* to come to my office for an exclusive interview."

***

Galvin's interview appeared on the front page of *The Providence Journal* on Friday morning, November 13, and in *The Evening Bulletin* the same night. The article detailed Detective Richard's trip to Philadelphia and Galvin's continued belief that Idella Traeger—referred to anonymously as a *'key witness'* in the article—was not telling all she knew. His criticism of the city authorities' lack of support during the investigation was quoted, as well as his disappointment with Dr. Turner's testimony.

Meanwhile, Coroner Stanhope was preparing his final report for the attorney general. Stanhope was meticulous in his review of the inquest record before rendering his decision. He spent days pouring over the testimony until he was satisfied nothing more could be gleaned from the pages.

Stanhope had actually reached his final decision relatively early in his deliberation process. But recognizing the fate of at least two individuals was at stake, he continued to diligently scour the transcripts to ensure he had not missed anything.

Galvin and Richards were drinking at the White Horse Tavern when they heard a disturbance coming from the street. The men left their pints to investigate and were met at the door by a disheveled drunkard stumbling in from the darkness.

The man was flailing a torn news sheet high in the air and hollering, "Tis official! 'Ole man Burton was murdered!"

Richards recognized the man immediately. It was McGruder, Ben's former tenant. He wrestled away what was left of the tattered paper from the boozer's unsteady hand. Together, the men read Stanhope's findings.

Benjamin J. Burton came to his death on the morning
of the sixth of October
at his residence on Levin Street from the effect of two pistol shots,
one in the head and the other in the breast, fired by a person unknown.

A sense of relief began to wash over Galvin as the weeks of built up tension slowly released. As he turned to look at his friend, he was met by the detective's broad, satisfied smile and a hearty slap on the back.

"Good job, 'ole boy! I've got the next round."

***

Stanhope's decision was met with overall disappointment by the citizens of Newport. Some said—much like King Solomon—Stanhope had split the baby. Those who supported the Dorseys felt the verdict continued to cast an unfair shadow over them. Those who believed the Dorseys had a hand in Burton's death worried they had gotten away with the crime. While relieved Stanhope had found Burton's death was not a suicide, Galvin was discouraged by his refusal to name the Dorseys as the shooters.

As he had hoped, the *Associated Press* picked up the verdict, and over the weekend, newspapers nationwide were reporting Ben Burton's cause of death being officially ruled a murder.

However, the *New York Herald* focused on Stanhope's phrasing, *"fired by a person unknown,"* and reported that Allen and Maria Dorsey were now *"relieved from suspicion."*

The paper continued to insist that, *"The best citizens of Newport are still of the opinion Burton committed suicide, and there is no reason to believe to the contrary."*

***

Wednesday, November 18, 1885.

Now that the verdict had been rendered, Galvin wanted to talk to Coroner Stanhope. He hurried out the door in the direction of Stanhope's novelty store.

Stanhope greeted the attorney warmly as the two men settled into chairs on either side of his desk. Galvin briefed Stanhope on the results of Detective Richard's investigation in Philadelphia.

"That is intriguing, P.J., but I don't think this information would have changed my mind about naming the Dorseys as Burton's shooter."

Galvin was careful to avoid criticizing Stanhope's ruling as he needed his help.

"I still believe Idella Traeger is the key to this case. I was hoping you could persuade Captain Hammond to bring her in for additional questioning."

"Question her again?"

"Yes, I know she is not being truthful. She won't meet with me, but she can't say no to Captain Hammond if he were to summon her," Galvin proposed. "I fear that If Hammond knows I am behind the request, he will no doubt refuse."

Stanhope rose from his chair and reached for his coat and hat. "I'll pay the captain a visit now and sit in on the interview myself."

***

Captain Hammond was leery when Coroner Stanhope asked him to bring Idella Traeger into the police station for another interrogation.

"To what end?" Hammond asked, frowning.

"I believe she may have perjured herself," Stanhope explained. "I would rather not issue a warrant for her, if possible. She is young and does not understand the repercussions of what she has done and should be given the opportunity to tell us the truth."

Hammond's deep-set eyes narrowed. "Is Galvin behind this?"

"My desire to see a wrong righted is my motivation," Stanhope replied. "Send an officer to fetch her."

A half-hour later, Idella Traeger sat in the holding room across the table from Hammond. The intimidating captain removed his uniform cap and placed it on the table beside him. He opened his folder, dramatically pulled out a piece of paper, and presented Idella with her previous statement.

"Mrs. Traeger, is this your sworn statement? Is that your mark under the oath?"

"Yes," Idella whispered.

Captain Hammond pulled the paper back and exhaled loudly. "Mrs. Traeger, are you aware of the penalty for lying under oath in Rhode Island?"

Idella did not respond and continued to stare down at her feet.

"Lying under oath is a crime, Mrs. Traeger," he warned in a threatening tone. "You could be locked up in jail for a long time. Do you understand what I am saying?"

Hammond pointed at the coroner, who sat in a chair in the corner of the room.

"Mr. Stanhope thinks your statement is a lie. I think your statement is a lie. Why would you lie, Mrs. Traeger?"

Idella glanced up briefly at Stanhope and then shifted her gaze back to Hammond, her expression thick with fear.

"Are you protecting Mrs. Dorsey?" Hammond probed. "I understand you and Mrs. Dorsey are friends, are you not?"

Idella bit her lip and nodded almost imperceptibly but remained silent.

"Did Mr. or Mrs. Dorsey tell you what to say at the inquest? Did they pay you to lie?" his voice rising.

Stanhope watched as Idella placed her hands on her knees to keep them from bobbing up and down. The captain bowed his head and wrapped his hand around the back of his neck. He turned to Stanhope, signaling him to break the silence in the room.

Stanhope leaned forward in his chair and addressed Idella directly. "Mrs. Traeger, do you understand the seriousness of what has occurred? A man has lost his life. Does that not weigh upon your conscience?"

Idella's lower lip quivered.

Hammond picked back up with his questioning. "Why are you protecting Mr. and Mrs. Dorsey? I thought you referred to yourself as a God-fearing Christian woman," he scoffed.

Idella burst into tears.

"You don't understand!" she wailed.

Hammond's tone softened. "What don't I understand, Mrs. Traeger? Please explain it to us."

Idella wiped her nose with the back of her hand and shook her head no.

Hammond tried a different tact.

"Do you know what I think? I think you, Mrs. Traeger, believe you are doing what is right. As a good Christian woman, you have an admirable desire to do right by those you care about. But lying is never right, no matter how honorable your intentions may be."

Idella covered her face with her hands and stammered in a shuddering breath, "I'm not supposed to tell."

Coroner Stanhope lifted an eyebrow in concern. "Have you been threatened, Mrs. Traeger?"

She removed her hands from her face and shook her head no.

"What is it then?" Stanhope asked. "What is it you are not telling us?"

"Mrs. Dorsey is with child!" she blurted out, then quickly clasped both hands over her mouth and squeezed her eyes shut.

Both men sat in stunned silence as they digested the news. Stanhope was the first to speak.

"Did Mr. Burton know?"

Idella shook her head and let her hands drop from her face. "No, I don't think so. Maria said she hadn't told her father. She said it was our secret."

Hammond grabbed hold of the table's edge and scooted his chair back.

"I see. So, you wanted to protect Mrs. Dorsey. That is perfectly understandable."

Idella looked at the captain in confusion. "I suppose."

"But now it is time to protect yourself," Hammond announced, not mincing his words. "You need to tell us what actually happened that morning. If you tell us the truth, Mr. Stanhope has promised he will not press charges against you for lying in the inquest. But if you persist with this fiction, I promise I will personally see that you are prosecuted to the fullest extent of the law," he warned.

Idella nodded resignedly and sighed, her shoulders curling in.

"I was hanging out laundry. That is true," she began hesitantly. "Maria came outside and said she had some gossip about one of the neighborhood girls she wanted to tell me and that we should go up to my house. Maria led me to the bedroom at the front of the house, just as Mr. Galvin suggested.

"And Maria wasn't making me a dress … that was Maria's idea for me to say that. While we were talking, we heard a loud bang. Then we heard a thump, like something heavy fell and shook the floor. Then, another loud bang. I asked Maria what the sounds were, and she said it must be Dora slamming the doors."

"What happened then?" Hammond asked.

She took a deep breath and crossed her arms around her middle as if holding herself together.

"After that, Maria got up and went down the front stairway. I was getting ready to blacken the stove when Dora came running through the back door, screaming. She told me that Mr. Burton shot himself, and I ran downstairs with her," she wailed, breaking into sobs.

"How long do you think Mrs. Dorsey was gone before her sister came to your house?" Hammond pressed.

Idella's crying subsided as she furrowed her brow and thought for a moment. "It couldn't have been more than five minutes, probably less." Hammond shook his head. "Why then did you testify that it was twenty minutes?"

Idella frowned. "Maria told me I had to say it was longer because she didn't want the authorities to think she was involved. She said she was already sickly due to her condition, and the strain from being under suspicion would surely cause harm to the baby. I didn't want to hurt the baby … don't you understand?"

"Of course," Hammond replied, his tone uncharacteristically sympathetic. "Did you ever overhear any quarrels coming from the Burton house?"

"Yes," she answered. "About a week before Mr. Burton's death, my husband and I overheard Mr. Burton arguing with Maria. His voice was raised, and I clearly heard him say that Maria and Allen must leave the house."

"And you didn't tell us this because you were protecting Mrs. Dorsey?" asked the captain.

"I didn't want to get Maria in trouble," she explained. "I know she had nothing to do with her father's death, and I didn't want anyone to think she did. There are so many hateful people around who are jealous of the Burtons. They love to gossip about them. I didn't want to do anything that might cause her to lose the baby."

Hammond rose to his feet and picked up his folder.

"Mrs. Traeger, come with me. I'm going to draft a new witness statement for you to sign," he said tersely. Now that the captain had obtained the information he wanted, he quickly abandoned his sympathetic demeanor.

Stanhope stood and assisted Idella to her feet. She hooked her hand around his offered arm and looked at him with pleading eyes.

"Please, sir, don't tell Maria I've told you about her condition. I beg of you … she will be so angry with me!"

Stanhope nodded and patted her hand. "It is not my story to tell," he responded reassuringly as he led Idella to Captain Hammond's desk.

***

The coroner left the police station and went straight to Galvin's law office.

"How did it go?"

Stanhope settled into a chair and stretched his legs, crossing them at the ankles.

"Mrs. Dorsey is with child."

"What?" Galvin jerked up, his mouth agape as he ran his hand through his hair, unsure what to say. "Are you certain?"

Stanhope shrugged his shoulders. "I have no doubt Mrs. Traeger believes it to be true."

"Sakes alive! What else did you learn?"

"Mrs. Traeger has signed a sworn statement recanting much of her inquest testimony and stating that no more than five minutes elapsed between the time Mrs. Dorsey left her house and Dora returned to say her father had shot himself. I will be drafting the arrest warrants tonight."

Stanhope nodded his head wistfully. "I worry what will become of the youngest girl, Dora. My heart is heavy with the task that I now face, knowing that what is left of her family will soon be taken from her."

"I can call on Emily Burton this evening while you are meeting with the city marshal and the judge," Galvin offered. "She may be reluctant to take her niece in, but I believe I can convince her she is the best person to provide a home for Dora."

Stanhope nodded and rose slowly from his chair. The dark circles under his eyes made him appear drawn and weary.

"I would appreciate that, P.J. No doubt she will need a great deal of support if her fragile appearance is any indication."

As he was leaving, Stanhope turned to face Galvin and warned, "Prepare yourself, young man. News of the Dorseys' arrest is liable to throw the whole of Newport into utter chaos."

Chapter 20
Thursday, November 19, 1885

When Hammond pulled the closed carriage to the front of the police station, the whole of Ferry Wharf was bustling with people. Some in the crowd taunted the Dorseys with shouts of *'Murderers!'* and *'Shame on you!'* The captain raised his hand in an authoritative manner to quiet the throng to little effect.

He climbed down from the carriage and, out of the corner of his eye, spotted Emily Burton pushing her way through the crowd toward him. He waited until she reached his side before pulling down the folding step and opening the door to the carriage. Hammond stuck his head inside.

"Miss Burton, please stay seated while I escort Mr. and Mrs. Dorsey into the building. Your aunt will bring you inside so you may bid your sister goodbye out of the public eye."

Dora spotted her Aunt Emily standing behind him. She nodded nervously and pressed herself back against the seat cushions to hide herself from view.

"Mr. and Mrs. Dorsey, it is time," Hammond announced brusquely. "I would suggest we be quick about it."

Allen Dorsey stepped down onto the sidewalk first. Looking cool and collected, he straightened himself and smoothed the sleeves of his coat before turning back to offer a hand to Maria. As soon as his wife stepped out of the carriage, Allen released his grip and gestured for her to walk ahead of him.

Maria's eyes glistened with tears, but otherwise she displayed remarkable composure. The couple quickly made their way to the entrance as Hammond followed, serenaded by the jeers and whistles of the crowd. Distracted by the sight of the Dorseys, the crowd paid little attention to Emily as she ushered Dora inside behind them.

Hammond led the group to the holding room, where the judge, city officials, and several newspaper reporters sat waiting. As Emily and Dora started to enter, he stepped in front of them.

"Mrs. Burton, you and Miss Burton must take your leave here."

On the brink of tears, Dora's voice quivered with emotion. "But you promised. You said I could say goodbye to my sister."

He hesitated before nodding silently and stepping aside as Dora ran to Maria's open arms. The sisters embraced and held one another as their anguished cries echoed down the halls of the police station. Maria stroked her sister's cheek and whispered soothingly in her ear until the young girl's sobs subsided. Not a man in the room dared to interrupt the scene, and in the moment, even the cynical journalists found themselves moved with sympathy for the Burton sisters.

As Maria pulled away from her sister, she placed her hands on Dora's shoulders and spoke in a hushed tone.

"Do not fret. We will be back together soon."

Dora blinked away the last of her tears and whispered, "Okay."

"Very well." Maria gave Dora a final peck on the cheek and separated herself. "Go now. Aunt Emily will take good care of you."

Dora walked slowly toward her aunt, physically and emotionally drained. Emily was concerned by her niece's change in appearance. The young girl's face was gaunt and drawn, her noticeably thinner frame swallowed up by her dress.

Hammond summoned an officer to his side and asked him to accompany the women home.

Holding the indictment in hand, the judge asked, "Before I begin, do either of you wish to be represented by counsel?"

Allen responded in a clear and steady voice, "Yes, sir. My wife and I wish to be represented by the honorable Colonel William P. Sheffield, Jr."

The judge raised an eyebrow before turning to address

Hammond.

"Captain, make haste and fetch Colonel Sheffield. We will suspend the remainder of the arraignment until the prisoners have had the opportunity to speak with counsel."

***

Wiliam Paine Sheffield, Jr. was a man Galvin knew very well. Sheffield was born into a wealthy and politically prominent family headed by former United States Senator William Paine Sheffield, Sr. His father ensured that his son received the finest education available, and the junior Sheffield obtained an undergraduate degree from Brown University, followed by law degrees from the prestigious University of Paris and Harvard. Under his father's tutelage, at only twenty-seven years old, Sheffield had become one of Newport's most sought-after attorneys.

Sheffield's cultivated image had begun to pay off politically as well. In April, he was elected to the Rhode Island House of Representatives. He later received the honorary commission of Colonel due to his recent appointment to the Governor's staff. He made no secret of the fact that he hoped to follow in his father's footsteps and serve in Congress. Other than Senator Sheffield himself, Allen could not have asked for a more prominent and respected attorney.

Once Sheffield arrived, he and Allen were ushered into a smaller adjacent office so they might speak in private. Maria was left alone, waiting in the holding room. As Sheffield closed the door to the small office, Allen spoke first.

"You need to know I currently do not have the means to compensate you."

Sheffield considered Allen's statement. Like every citizen of Newport, he had read the newspaper coverage of the death of Ben Burton. He would have welcomed the appointment as assistant attorney general and was surprised when Galvin got the nod. However, he was not surprised when Galvin proved himself competent in the role. The two men had worked side-by-side in the senior Sheffield's law office for several years until Galvin struck out on his own.

Sheffield waved his hand dismissively.

"We shall worry about the money later. What I must know now is whether you are guilty of this offense."

Allen looked Sheffield directly in the eye and answered, "I swear to you, Maria and I are innocent. We did not murder Mr. Burton."

The men maintained eye contact for several seconds in silence before Sheffield responded.

"Then I will agree to represent you. Let's get to it."

A few minutes later, the two men emerged and returned to the holding room to join Maria. The judge addressed Attorney Sheffield directly.

"Colonel, are you ready to proceed?"

Standing at Allen's side, Sheffield responded, "I am."

"Then I will begin with the reading of the warrants."

Allen did not take his eyes off the judge's face as he read the lengthy warrants aloud. When he was done, the judge asked Allen and then Maria if they understood the charges. When Sheffield concurred on their behalf, the judge turned his attention back to Allen.

"In the charge of willful and premeditated murder of Benjamin J. Burton, how do you plead?"

"Not guilty, your honor," Allen responded firmly and confidently.

Turning to Maria, he asked, "Mrs. Dorsey, in the charge of aiding and abetting in the murder of Benjamin J. Burton, how do you plead?"

Maria's lips quivered as she glanced sideways at Attorney Sheffield before responding in kind, "Not guilty, your honor."

"Let it be entered into the record that both defendants have pleaded not guilty to all charges. The defendants are to be committed without bond to Newport County jail pending further proceedings. Sheriff Easton, I now remand the custody of the prisoners to your care and declare this arraignment adjourned."

The newspaper reporters leaped to their feet and scurried out of the room in a race to report the latest development in the Burton case to their respective publications. Sheffield was surprised and disappointed that none of them stopped to get a quote from him. He returned his attention to Allen and assured him he would arrange a meeting at the jail before the end of the day. He watched Sheriff Easton and Captain Hammond escort the couple from the room and down the hall.

***

From its pristine white clapboard siding and black louvered

window shutters to the traditional triangular portico overhanging the concrete steps of the Marlborough Street entrance, the Newport County jail might have been easily mistaken for one of the numerous two-story colonial-style homes that peppered the Aquidneck Island landscape. The original jailhouse was built during colonial times and was later expanded to include a housing annex with a separate entrance on the east side of the building. This annex was now occupied by Sheriff Benjamin Easton, Jr., along with his wife, Mary, and two of their daughters.

In the westernmost section of the building, both the first and second floors contained rows of individual jail cells fronted with heavy iron bars and divided by thick metal walls constructed between each enclosure. Measuring six by eight feet, each cell was furnished with a metal bunk bolted onto a side wall, a porcelain sink, a soap dish, a mirror, and a chamber pot. Nothing could be further from the privileged comforts Allen and Maria enjoyed while living under Ben's care.

Hammond stood quietly by while Sheriff Easton processed his newest prisoners. Allen would be placed in a cell on the first floor closest to the front of the building, while Maria would be housed in the last unit at the rear. Given that they were on the same floor, the couple could still communicate verbally, but not without being overheard by a jailer or the other prisoners occupying the cells in between. Easton had suffered his share of breakouts at the jail and was determined to take every precaution with the Dorseys.

Sheriff Easton's wife, Mary, accompanied the jailer as he led Maria to her cell. Maria was careful to avoid the gaze of the other prisoners as she took in her new surroundings. Mrs. Easton stepped forward, her arms filled with fresh linens and bedding.

"Here now, I'll just set these on the edge of your cot."

"Thank you," Maria whispered.

Mrs. Easton leaned forward and brushed away a stray spider web attached to the corner of the thin, ticking mattress.

"Every Friday morning, you will be provided clean linens, so you'll need to strip your bed as soon as you rise on that day. You will take all your meals and refreshments from within the confines of your cell."

Maria bowed her head but remained silent. Mrs. Easton signaled to the jailer it was time to take his leave and sat down on the edge of the cot, patting the mattress beside her.

"Come, sit with me for a moment. There are delicacies that we must discuss, woman to woman."

Sweeping her skirts aside, Maria eased down onto the far end of the mattress and folded her hands in her lap. Mrs. Easton reached into the pocket of her skirts and removed a bar of soap and a small glass jar of tooth powder.

"Here you are," she said as she handed them to Maria. "Every morning, a fresh face cloth will be on your breakfast tray for your ablutions."

Mrs. Easton then leaned closer to Maria and lowered her voice to a whisper. "When your ladies' time arrives, send word to me. I will see that you have rags available for your use."

Maria dipped her head and replied softly, "I will not need them. I am with child."

Mrs. Easton pursed her lips and studied Maria's face.

"I see," she said quietly. "I should have expected as much, newly married and all."

Mrs. Easton stood and wiped her hands down the front of her skirt before she stepped to the cell door and called out to the jailer. Maria could hear the jingling of the ring of keys as he neared.

"I'll leave you be for now," Mrs. Easton said. "I will send writing materials to you shortly so you can make a list of the things that need to be fetched from your home. I would suggest you wear your warmest nightdress and stockings, as it can get nippy being this far from the stove."

"I appreciate it," Maria replied as she watched the jailer push the cell door shut and test the lock to ensure it was secure. "Mrs. Easton? Before you leave, do you have anything I might read?"

Mrs. Easton nodded her head and smiled sadly.

"But of course, my dear. Surely, you know it was your father who organized the book drive so that we might have reading material for our prisoners. I will ask the jailer to roll the book trolley down here shortly," she said as she turned and walked away from Maria's view.

***

"I've nothing on me," Allen complained as he raised his arms while Sheriff Easton patted him down. "This is unnecessary."

"That is not for you to decide," Easton remarked as he ran his hands briskly over Allen's ribcage and back. "Turn around."

Allen spun around slowly to face the sheriff.

"When may I speak to my wife?"

"You may speak with her at any time from the confines of your cell."

Allen huffed out a sigh of exasperation and dropped his arms to his side.

"Do you know when Colonel Sheffield is scheduled to arrive?"

"I'll know when he gets here," Easton replied, his patience waning. "See here, Dorsey … let us be clear on the matter. For the immediate future, and perhaps a good while longer, you are my prisoner, not an invited guest. You will be treated respectfully and as humanely as one can be under the circumstances. But you are not the first, and you certainly won't be the last well-educated man placed under my supervision. You will be afforded the same considerations as every other prisoner, no more, no less."

"Is one of those considerations the writing and receiving of letters?" Allen asked, his tone contemptuous.

"Of course, I will ask Mrs. Easton to bring you an ample supply of stationery. Is there anything else you might require?"

"A Bible," Allen said, then quickly added, "and a novel of some kind."

Standing ready to escort Allen to his cell, the jailer spoke up. "Mrs. Easton has already instructed me to fetch the book trolley."

"Good. Show Mr. Dorsey to his cell now if you please."

The jailer scooped up a bundle of linens and took Allen by the crook of his arm. As the two approached the entrance to Allen's cell, Allen glanced down the row to see Maria peering through the bars of her cell, hands clenched tightly around the metal rails.

Allen tipped his head to her in acknowledgment and entered his cell. On the cot lay a weathered copy of <u>Washington Square</u> by Henry James. The jailer tossed the bedding on the mattress and picked up the book.

"The last feller must have left this here," he remarked indifferently as he handed it over to Allen. "Do you want it?"

Allen opened the book and glanced at the paper label adhered to the inside cover.

*This book was donated to
the Newport County Jail Library
by
Benjamin J. Burton*

Allen slammed the book shut and tossed it back at the jailer. "Get it out of here."

Chapter 21
Thursday, November 19, 1885

Galvin locked the door to his office and began his walk home. Though the Dorseys' arrest today represented the culmination of arduous work and dogged persistence, he was teeming with nervous energy and renewed determination. His friend and colleague William Sheffield, Jr.'s engagement to defend the Dorseys was unexpected, given that Sheffield traditionally catered only to Newport's wealthy elite. But Galvin knew Sheffield would be a formidable opponent.

The Sheffield law firm was located in a first-floor office on Thames Street, a block south of Galvin's office. As Galvin neared Sheffield's legal offices, he saw the lamps still burning brightly. On impulse, he stopped and knocked at the door.

Sheffield emerged from one of the rear offices and waved Galvin inside.

"Come in, P.J. … I planned to call on you tomorrow."

Galvin followed Sheffield into a spacious, well-appointed office. The wall behind the ornately carved mahogany pedestal desk was filled with a myriad of framed diplomas, commendations, and awards, some with calligraphy so elaborate that Galvin could scarcely read them.

He couldn't help but chuckle. The only thing that hung from the walls of his office was the odor of the catch of the day coming from the fishmonger shop next door.

Like Galvin, Sheffield still resided in his father's house. But the Sheffield family home was a stately Greek revival-style mansion that reeked of money and prestige and sat next to the Old Colony House at the top of Washington Square.

Galvin and Sheffield were two of Newport's most eligible bachelors, but they differed in style, appearance, and temperament. Galvin had a charmingly boyish appearance and an appealing, easy-going manner. Conversely, Sheffield, whose stylishly coiffed hair and beard gave him a more mature and polished look, was more serious and reserved.

Both men had stellar reputations in the legal community. Galvin was known for providing skillful legal defense to the disadvantaged, while Sheffield represented the well-heeled.

Sheffield gestured toward one of the Morocco leather-covered chairs carefully arranged throughout the spacious room and invited Galvin to sit.

"I have not had the opportunity to congratulate you on your recent re-election to the state legislature," Galvin said, "and on your appointment to the Governor's staff. You are a popular gentleman these days, William."

Sheffield responded with a weary grin. "If by popular, you mean I am spreading myself too thin, then I am guilty as charged."

"How is your father?" Galvin inquired. "I was sorry to hear that he did not remain in Washington. It sounded like he was doing good work in our nation's capital."

Sheffield shrugged indifferently.

"Father never intended to remain senator, though he was honored that the governor temporarily appointed him to fill the vacancy. The legislature made a smart choice in selecting the man who will replace him."

"Spoken like a loyal Republican," Galvin teased.

"Nonetheless, Father is glad to be back home. He already has his hands full with some particularly important cases."

"So I hear."

Sheffield leaned forward, removed two cigars from the mahogany humidor atop his desk, and offered one to Galvin, who declined.

"Of course, I am certain Father will make himself available to assist me in the Dorsey matter, if necessary," he casually remarked as he retrieved a double-bladed guillotine and snipped off the ends of the cheroot.

"I suppose that means I should not rely on him to be a resource for me in this case," Galvin responded, smiling. "I was wondering when we would stop dancing around the subject."

Sheffield struck a match across the sole of his shoe.

"Yes, well …" he stammered as he puffed on the cigar, exhaling a plume of smoke and watching it float toward the ceiling.

"Look on the bright side, Will. Now that you are representing the Dorseys, we will get to see each other more often."

"Joke, if you will," Sheffield responded flatly, "but I have closely followed the case in the papers."

"Do tell."

Sheffield shook his head. "Sad case. I was shocked when the Dorseys were arrested this morning. I must admit I was surprised but flattered when Mr. Dorsey requested that I represent he and his wife."

"The Dorsey's have the right to the best representation available. You are a wise choice."

"I appreciate the compliment, P.J., but you must know I would never have taken the case if I wasn't convinced they are innocent of the charges. It is no secret that Mr. Burton's financial situation and his state of mind both suggest he was intent on killing himself. Not to mention, there is simply no motive in this case."

He continued, "With all due respect, the only thing you may have proven in the inquest was that Maria Dorsey uttered a falsehood or two in order to borrow some money, and that was with your fancy New York City Pinkerton detective on the case."

Galvin ignored the slight. He reminded himself that Sheffield had been on the case for just a few hours and was only parroting what was being said in certain circles around town.

"Even if Mrs. Dorsey is a liar, that does not make her a murderer," Sheffield reasoned. "And Mr. Dorsey? You must appreciate how unusual it is for a Black man to be accepted into the top medical school in the country. I understand he excelled in his studies and was on course to graduate next Spring."

Galvin remained silent as Sheffield let out an exasperated huff.

"I don't understand you … You all but publicly shamed Dr.

Turner by inferring to the newspaper reporters that he did not do his job. Isn't your sister married to Dr. Turner's son? What did she have to say about that?"

Galvin felt the heat rising in his cheeks. Sheffield had caught him off guard by bringing his sister into the argument.

"I'll thank you to leave my sister out of this!" Galvin warned angrily. "She understands what is required of me in my capacity as assistant attorney general."

Sheffield raised his eyebrows at Galvin's rare display of temper, but he did not back down.

"It is no secret the city officials have questioned your pursuit of the Dorseys. The marshal, the mayor, police officials … they all think you have lost your mind. What happened to P.J. Galvin, patron of lost causes and champion of the downtrodden? I contend, if you had not been appointed acting attorney general, you would be the one sitting by Mr. and Mrs. Dorsey's side defending these wrongly accused people. The P.J. Galvin I know should be outraged by their arrest."

An awkward pause followed as Galvin gripped the arms of his chair. When he finally opened his mouth to speak, his words were calm and measured.

"William, you say that I am the patron of lost causes. You say I am a champion of the downtrodden. Both statements remain as true today as they have ever been."

Galvin leaned forward in his chair, locking eyes with Sheffield.

"I represent a man who cannot speak for himself. I represent Ben Burton, a man who made a name for himself through honest labor. A man who hauled the possessions of the privileged residents, such as yourself, back and forth to the docks in the middle of the night while you all slept soundly in your beds. A man blessed with God-given forward thinking, who took every hard-earned penny and invested it right back into Newport to make life better for all of us."

Sheffield started to interrupt, but Galvin ignored him.

"And just as Ben Burton was preparing for his elder years, after a life of service— yes, William, service—he was callously shot and buried by the very people he expected would love and care for him. This is who I represent, William. I see no contradiction in my actions. I remain dedicated to seeking justice."

Sheffield sat back in his chair, the expression on his face a combination of smug satisfaction and curiosity. He had succeeded in arousing Galvin's ire, but he had also underestimated the intensity of Galvin's passion in the case. He would leave well enough alone … for now.

"I will need to see all of the statements and evidence that has been collected to prepare my defense for the trial," Sheffield said.

Galvin rose from his chair.

"Of course. I will turn everything over to you that I have in my possession."

As he turned to leave, Galvin paused for a moment and then turned back to face Sheffield.

"I think you will find that my case is substantially stronger than the reports in the newspapers or idle gossip about town might have led you to believe."

Smiling, he tipped his hat to Sheffield.

"I thank you, old friend, but now I must bid you goodnight."

With that, Galvin turned and strode confidently out of William Sheffield's office.

Chapter 22
Saturday, November 21, 1885

Dora had barely spoken since joining her Aunt Emily's household. She refused to join the others at mealtime and sequestered herself in the small room she was forced to share with a middle-aged female boarder.

Balancing a tray of cod chowder and soda crackers, Emily trooped up the stairs to Dora's room. She was growing anxious by Dora's increasing frailty and had decided the girl had remained in her room long enough.

If Dora were to fall ill under my watch, she thought, *the whole of Newport would point the finger of blame directly at me.*

Without knocking, she pushed open the door to Dora's room to find the young girl curled up in a ball under the covers, sleeping.

"Wake up!" Emily bellowed. "You can't keep to your bed again today … you aren't the Queen of Sheba."

Dora rolled away from her aunt and pulled the quilt over her head.

"Here, I've brought you something to eat," she said, placing the tray on the bedside table, adding, "While I agreed to take you in, I didn't agree to be your lady's maid. Why are you carrying on so and refusing to eat? It's your sister and her no-good husband who are in jail, not you."

Uncurling herself, Dora rolled onto her back and lowered the quilt a few inches to peek out.

Exasperated, Emily propped her hands on her hips and leaned over the bed, glaring at her niece as she cowered under the quilt.

"Just look at you … you're as thin as a rail. You should thank your lucky stars that I took you in when I did."

Dora squeezed her eyes shut and covered her ears with her hands, causing Emily to lash out.

"For the love of God, why are you protecting them? What has Maria said to you? What has Allen done to twist your mind? Tell me!"

Dora began to weep silently, but her tears only served to provoke her aunt further.

"Child, it's time you faced the cold, hard facts about your dear sister and her husband. They had it all planned, don't you see? They would kill your father and make their escape south with his money. Were you foolish enough to believe they would take you to Philadelphia with them and not leave you high and dry without a penny to your name?"

With her harsh words hanging in the air, Emily stormed out of the room, slamming the door behind her.

***

As she stood at her ironing table pressing freshly laundered linens, Emily thought about her conversation with Galvin the night before the Dorseys' arrest. Initially, she flatly refused his request to take Dora in, insisting she did not have a room available. But when his appeal to her sense of moral obligation failed, his assurance that the state would pay for Dora's room and board caused her to reconsider.

Although she didn't disclose her intentions to Galvin, Emily also considered it might be an opportunity to glean information from Dora. However, she now feared that her strong rebuke damaged her ability to gain the girl's confidence.

I may never get her to open up and tell me what she knows, she worried.

Waves of guilt and shame began to wash over her. Emily reminded herself that Dora had lost everything dear to her: a home, the comfortable life she had enjoyed under her father's care, and her beloved and constant companion, Maria.

Maybe Dora just needs more time, she thought, silently vowing to be more patient and understanding toward her niece. With that in mind, she cautioned her boarders not to mention that Ben's estate sale was being held that day to avoid upsetting Dora further.

***

Emily was awakened later that evening by a loud hacking cough coming from Dora's room. Her niece had taken ill, and her condition continued to worsen steadily until the sputum gave way to a bloody discharge.

The boarder who shared the room with Dora remained steadfast by the girl's side all night as Emily ran up and down the stairs, hauling away the soiled linens, bloody rags, and stale drinking water before replacing them with a fresh supply.

As the sun rose, Emily bent over the deep aluminum tub in the sink room, scrubbing the blood stains out of the pillowcases taken from Dora's room. Her brow furrowed with worry.

Now that Dora was confined to her bed and desperately ill, Emily couldn't shake the thought that she had played a role in the girl's rapid decline. She pulled the pillowcase through the wringer a final time and stepped around the corner into the kitchen to place it on the drying rack next to the stove. She looked up to see Dora's exhausted roommate lumbering down the back staircase, holding an empty water pitcher.

"Is she sleeping now?" Emily asked.

"Yes, but we need to send for a doctor. She is weak as a kitten … so tiny and frail. A sickness such as this could very well kill her."

Emily nodded in agreement. She feared the same thing. During the night, Dora's skin had taken on a gray, almost ghostly pallor.

"I will send for Dr. Turner," she said as she removed her damp apron and tossed it on the back of a chair. "I won't be long."

Turner arrived less than an hour later and immediately went upstairs to examine Dora. Emily stayed downstairs and waited anxiously in the kitchen.

"She is in bad shape," the doctor announced when he finally reappeared. "I've given her a tincture of medicine and applied a poultice, but there is little more I can do. She will need to be watched closely for the next few hours."

Emily held vigil over Dora. When she was awake, she patiently spooned warm broth and skimmed cream into her niece's mouth to build her strength. Sometime shortly before midnight, Dora awoke and spoke for the first time since falling ill.

"Am I dying?" Dora asked, her voice raspy and weak.

"Don't be silly, child," Emily whispered as she scooped her arm under Dora's neck and raised her head forward. She held a cup of apple cider to her lips and encouraged her to drink.

"The doctor said you will get better if you start eating and drinking."

Dora sputtered as she sipped on the cider before weakly pushing the glass away from her lips.

"It hurts to drink," she murmured as she laid her head back on the pillow. She closed her eyes and spoke so softly that Emily had to lean in closely to understand what she was saying.

"There is something … I need to tell you … before … before it's too late."

Emily grasped Dora's gaunt hand and asked, "What is it, child?"

Dora opened her eyes and, in a gravelly voice, whispered, "It was Allen … Allen killed Father."

Emily's heart pounded as her suspicions were confirmed. She fought to maintain her composure.

"Quick, child, tell me everything."

"He did it … I, I … didn't think he would do it … but he did."

Emily sat back as her niece's words slowly sunk in.

Didn't think he would? Had Dora known in advance? Surely, it is the medicine talking.

"But I thought you were upstairs when the shots were fired?"

"No," she whimpered, shaking her head feebly. "Downstairs."

Emily dropped Dora's hand and sat in stunned silence.

"Please, Aunt Emily," she trembled. "Send for Mr. Stanhope … Mr. Galvin too. I … I need to confess … before it's too late."

Confess? Dear God, is she claiming she had a hand in it?

Dora collapsed back against her pillow, closing her eyes. Emily ran downstairs to scribble a message, handing it to one of her male boarders.

"Go quickly," she instructed. "Go to Mr. Galvin's house. He'll know where to find Mr. Stanhope. Don't come back without them.

Hurry, please hurry!"

Chapter 22
Monday, November 23, 1885

"P.J. … wake up, laddie!"

Galvin opened his eyes to find his father standing in his night-shirt at the foot of his bed.

He jerked awake. "What is it?"

"A fella is waiting for you in the parlor."

Galvin tossed back the sheets. Trying to orient himself, he glanced around the darkened room.

"What time is it?"

As his father turned to return to his bed, he replied, "The wee hours. Best hurry. Yer man says it is urgent."

Galvin quickly donned his shirt and pants and raced barefoot down the stairs. A bug-eyed young man stood in the middle of the room, nervously clutching a folded sheet of paper.

"What brings you here this time of night?" Galvin asked in a hushed tone.

He thrust the note at Galvin.

"Mrs. Burton sent me. Her niece … she is in a bad way, sir."

Galvin scanned the note and looked up in alarm.

"I just came from the police station," the man advised. "Captain Hammond said he and Mr. Stanhope will meet you there. I'm to bring you back with me."

Taking two stairs at a time, Galvin rushed back to his room to finish dressing.

***

Emily met Galvin at the front door in a state of panic. Stanhope and Hammond had arrived only moments earlier and were waiting just inside.

"Hurry, gentlemen. She is awake now but fading fast."

As she led the men to a tiny room at the end of the hall on the second floor, she apprised them of the developing situation. She put her hand on the doorknob and looked over her shoulder, cautioning, "She is exceedingly fragile, and I fear she has taken a turn for the worse."

The men all nodded in understanding. As he entered, Galvin was struck by the stale stench that permeated the room. Stanhope maneuvered through the cramped space and made his way to the window to let in some fresh air while Hammond found a small footstool and placed it next to the headboard of Dora's bed.

Watching from the doorway, Emily wearily announced, "I'll be just down the hall," before she closed the door.

Galvin took a seat on the footstool to face Dora. Her cheeks were sunken, and her breathing labored. Remnants of dried blood stained the corners of her mouth, and her lips were cracked and dry. But the young woman's eyes appeared clear and focused.

He tilted his head toward her, asking softly, "Miss Burton, are you able to speak with me?"

Dora responded with a slight nod and whispered, "Yes."

He smiled tenderly in response. He had witnessed the suffering caused by the seeds of consumption in his own family.

"Your aunt says that there is something you wish to tell us. What is it?"

Dora rolled her head to the side to look up at Galvin.

"A secret," she drawled breathlessly. "It is killing me by inches. I want to tell the truth before it dies with me."

As her words hung in the air, Galvin studied Dora's face as a sense of calm began to wash over her. He bent his head forward, gently asking, "What is it, Miss Burton? What is your secret?"

Unflinchingly and in a voice just above a whisper, Dora revealed her hidden truth.

"Allen murdered my father."

Galvin shot a look over his shoulder at the grimaced expression on the face of Captain Hammond, who was now staring at the floor. He turned back to face Dora.

"Did Mr. Dorsey confess this to you?"

"No," she paused before meekly admitting, "I was there."

"Yes, we know you were in the house. Is that what you mean?"

Dora struggled to form the words. "No … I was *there.*"

"In the kitchen?" Galvin asked in alarm. "Are you saying you saw Mr. Dorsey shoot your father?"

Dora squeezed her eyes shut, slowly shaking her head. "No, I was in the parlor. I heard the shots."

"Did you know Mr. Dorsey was planning to shoot your father?"

"Yes … I did," she stammered, gulping for air. "I … I was his lookout."

The room was deathly still as the three men slowly came to grips with Dora's revelation. It had come as no surprise to Galvin that she might confirm Allen's guilt once she was removed from under his influence. But her confession that she, too, had been involved was utterly unexpected.

Galvin shattered the silence in the room with one word.

"Why?"

"Because Allen told me to."

"Was your sister involved? Did she know?"

Dora nodded her head.

"Why would Mr. Dorsey kill your father?"

She coughed and took a deep breath. "Because Father had ordered him and Maria out of the house. And for money."

Galvin poured a glass of water and handed it to Dora. He helped her sit up so she could take a few sips.

"Are you able to continue?" asked Galvin cautiously.

She nodded. Despite her weakness, Dora spoke with a determined sense of purpose and without interruption for almost an hour, pausing only occasionally to catch her breath or take a few sips of water. The men sat spellbound as her tragic tale unfolded.

Galvin carefully recorded Dora's words as she described her

role in—as well as the Dorseys' planning and execution of—her father's murder. After she had unburdened herself of all she needed to say, she collapsed in exhaustion.

Galvin transcribed her confession into a sworn statement and read it back to her. With a trembling hand, Dora signed her name in agreement, and Galvin added his signature, notarizing the document.

***

Tuesday, November 24, 1885

At first light, the cries of the newspaper hawkers began echoing up and down Thames Street and could be heard for blocks around. *Read all about it! Burton's daughter confesses! Daughter says Dorsey pulled the trigger!*

People gathered on the street corners, encircling the newsstands in a frenzy to read the latest update. Anxious consumers were ripping the papers from the hands of the paperboys. The demand for the morning editions far exceeded the supply on hand, sending wholesale agents running to their telegraph offices to wire for more copies.

"Send as many as you can print … we can sell them all" was the order of the day.

Attorney William Sheffield, Jr. was caught up in the melee as he navigated his way down Thames Street en route to city hall. He dodged and weaved his way through the congestion of newsboys and growing crowds until he was spotted by a newspaper reporter waiting on the sidewalk.

"Colonel Sheffield!" the reporter cried out. "Have you heard? The young Miss Burton has confessed and signed a sworn statement saying your clients are guilty."

Sheffield cavalierly waved off the question and continued walking. "Yes, I've heard," he called over his shoulder.

"Colonel!" the reporter persisted. "Do you have a statement you wish to offer the press on the Dorseys' behalf?"

Sheffield stopped and slowly turned around.

"My clients are innocent of the charges against them. I am not going to try this case in the press, but you can quote me. My clients are innocent and will be proven so."

Sheffield turned away and ducked into city hall, leaving the reporter on the sidewalk. He quickly made his way up the stairs to the office of the clerk for the court.

"I need to see a judge," Sheffield said, getting right to the point. "I have an urgent motion." He reached into his valise, removed several pages, and handed them across the desk. "How soon can this be heard?"

The clerk shuffled through the pages slowly, scanning the document. He placed the papers on his desk and lifted his head to address an impatient Sheffield.

"I will need to send word to Attorney Galvin and ask the judge if he can hear your motion before court is called to session."

Within an hour, Sheffield stood before the judge with Galvin sitting at the prosecutor's table just behind him.

"Your honor, my clients wish to meet with Miss Dora Burton as soon as possible."

Galvin jumped to his feet.

"Your honor, in the interest of justice, you cannot grant this request."

Sheffield continued, ignoring Galvin's outburst. "There is no law against them seeing one another. They are family and have a right to be together. Miss Burton can be brought to the jailhouse."

Galvin again objected. "It is obvious that the defendants merely want to use the visit as an opportunity to convince the young girl to recant her damaging statement against them. It cannot be allowed."

"Order, order!" the judge shouted as he pounded his gavel on the stand. "Gentlemen, you know better. Sit down, both of you."

Sheffield returned to the defense table while Galvin sat down in his chair with a huff.

"Mr. Sheffield, I have reviewed your motion," he began. "I see no reason your request cannot be granted."

Galvin stood and objected once more.

"Your honor, the Dorseys hope to take advantage of Miss Burton's weakened condition to intimidate her."

"Attorney Galvin, you, or your representative can be present to ensure nothing inappropriate occurs. We are dismissed. Good day, gentlemen."

The judge stood and left the courtroom, leaving a frustrated Galvin. He approached Sheffield, who was still gathering his papers at his table.

Sheffield spoke first. "P.J., what you have done is scandalous. Her statement has all the markings of a forced confession."

Galvin raised his hand in objection.

"William, we have known each other for a very long time. I take umbrage at your suggestion of improper conduct. I had not laid eyes on the girl from the time she was taken to live with her aunt until I heard her confession. Coroner Stanhope can attest that her statement was given of her own free will. While I do not owe you an explanation, Miss Burton was gravely ill and feared she was dying. She simply wanted to clear her conscience. When I met with her to witness and notarize her statement, she made it quite clear that she is determined to tell the truth about her father's death."

Sheffield shook his head in disgust.

"P.J., you and I both know she did not confess of her own volition. We shall see if this so-called confession holds up to scrutiny."

At that, Sheffield turned and marched out of the courtroom.

***

Emily fished three cents out of the coin purse she kept hidden underneath her woolens in the bureau. She was anxious to get her hands on the evening edition of the *Daily News* so she could read Dora's confession in its entirety. In his rush to leave, Galvin had not provided her with any details except to confirm Dora's statement that Allen had been the shooter.

She threw on her cloak and made her way to Washington Square, where she spotted several newsboys in front of the Old State House shouting the headline and waving the papers in their hands. Keeping her head down to avoid notice, Emily nearly collided with a woman exiting the confectioner's shop.

"Well, as I live and breathe, if it isn't Mrs. Stoddard." Emily drawled, her words dripping with sarcasm. "What do you have to say to me now?"

Emily viewed Dora's now well-publicized admission that Allen Dorsey had pulled the trigger as a total vindication. She fully expected an apology—or at the very least, an acknowledgment—from her nemesis that she had been right all along. But to her astonishment, Mary launched into a castigating rebuke instead of an apology.

"What do I have to say to you, Emily Burton?" Mary Stoddard asked incredulously. "I say you should be ashamed of yourself! Wasn't it enough for you to publicly humiliate the Dorseys? Now, the whole town's talking about you and how you took advantage of that poor, sick girl and forced her to tell lies. You have no shame … no shame!"

Emily was dumbstruck by Mary's attack.

Forced? Is that how she sees it?

It had not occurred to her that Dora's confession would be questioned as untrue, much less coerced.

Why, in God's name, would people believe that?

As Emily struggled to make sense of the accusation, Mary hiked up her skirts, sidestepped around her, and dismissed her with a cutting tone.

"Now, if you will kindly excuse me, I'll be on my way."

After purchasing the paper, Emily skulked home, her mind swirling with all the biting retorts she wished she had heaped on Mary Stoddard. Once home, she fixed herself a cup of tea, settled into a chair at the kitchen table, and opened the paper to pour over Dora's confession.

Dora painted a disturbing picture of a cold and calculated murder. Although Emily had suspected all along that Allen Dorsey was the shooter, she was having difficulty wrapping her head around the fact that both Maria and Dora were involved in their father's death. She did not like or trust Maria and had publicly denounced her, but it still came as a shock to see the truth in black and white.

But by far, the most unexpected and heartbreaking disclosure was Dora's admission that she had known about Allen's plan to kill her father and had done nothing to prevent it. Emily could not fathom why her niece made no attempt to save the father she professed to love and who had doted on her since birth.

Engrossed in her reading, Emily did not initially hear Dora's roommate entering the kitchen. Emily was grateful to the kind-hearted widow for assuming responsibility for Dora's daily care. She was not ready to face her niece and was now giving serious thought to asking that Dora be removed from her home, even if it meant putting the sickly girl in jail.

On the other hand, though Emily was disgusted by Dora's role in Ben's death, had it not been for the girl's confession, the Dorseys might have gotten off scot-free.

As her tenant went to the pump to fill the pitcher with water, Emily took the opportunity to question her.

"Is that for Dora?" she asked.

"Yes, I am trying to encourage her to drink more."

"How is she today?"

Weary from the sleepless night of caretaking, the woman drew a deep breath. "It's hard to say. I believe she is improving, but we must be patient. It will take time for her to regain her strength."

"Is she talking?"

"A little."

"Has she said anything about her father or the Dorseys?"

"Some, but not too much"

"Allen Dorsey should hang for what he has done," spewed Emily. "The state of Rhode Island should reinstate the death penalty just for him."

Her tenant nodded in agreement, saying, "Dora told me that Mr. Dorsey doesn't fear the noose. She said that on the day of her father's funeral, her brother-in-law asked her if he would hang if caught."

Emily sat speechless as the widow explained.

"When Dora told him the most severe punishment he could receive in Rhode Island for murder was a life sentence, she said he responded by telling her he would bash his head against the wall rather than spend the rest of his life behind bars."

"He would be doing the state a favor," Emily scoffed brazenly, "but mark my words, Allen Dorsey is far too fond of himself to muss so much as one strand of that slick-backed hair of his. Dora says nothing about Maria?"

"Only that she is eager to see her sister and hopes she is well enough to go to the jail for their visit."

"If she goes, I suppose I will be expected to accompany her," Emily remarked, bitterly adding, "God help me if Maria decides to confess while I am there."

***

Wednesday, November 25, 1885

Dora and Emily arrived at the jail by carriage just before two in the afternoon. Galvin and Stanhope had arrived moments earlier and were waiting in the entrance area with Sheriff Easton.

"Where is Sheffield?" Galvin asked.

"Mrs. Dorsey was repeatedly offered the opportunity to have her attorney present, but she declined," Easton replied. "Hammond should be here shortly, though."

Galvin had no expectation that Maria would offer a confession, but all parties agreed that Captain Hammond should be present just in case. He peered through the front window to see the women attempting to disembark from the carriage. Galvin rushed out to assist Emily with bringing Dora inside.

Easton quickly ushered the party from the reception area to the drawing room in the sheriff's quarters, where his wife was waiting. Although the drawing room was considered part of Easton's living quarters, it was occasionally used as a meeting room for prisoners and their attorneys or small gatherings.

It was a comfortable, homey venue with a large front-facing window adorned by a set of faded woven jacquard curtains held back by bronzed tieback hooks. A small settee covered in soft maroon velvet was centered in front of the window, while overstuffed chairs were arranged in a circular fashion throughout the room. Matching Lincoln rockers, each with a small side table and decorative gas lamp, sat on either side of the fireplace.

Once Captain Hammond arrived, Sheriff Easton announced he would send a jailer to get Maria.

"Oh, yes, please do," Dora said, scooting slowly to the end of the settee to make space for her sister.

When Maria entered the room, she ran to her sister and scooped Dora up into her arms. For the better part of the next hour, Ben Burton's daughters sat side-by-side, holding each other in a warm embrace while exchanging loving sentiments in hushed tones.

"You look so weak and tired," Maria said with genuine concern as she stroked her sister's cheek. "Is Aunt Emily taking good care of you?"

Emily, who was carefully observing her nieces, frowned at the comment. Dora lifted her head from Maria's breast and looked lovingly at her sister.

"I feel so much better now that I have confessed. It is as if a horrible weight has been lifted from me. You must also confess and put these tribulations behind you. I worry about what this burden could do to the baby."

Maria visibly flinched at the mention of the baby but returned Dora's gaze with an equally affectionate one.

"Hush, my dear one," she whispered. "We must not speak of it. I need to know all about your sickness … when did you fall ill? Are you in pain?"

Dora did not answer her sister's questions. Instead, she returned to the subject of their father's death. She spoke in a low yet insistent tone.

"Oh Maria, I beg you to tell Captain Hammond or Mr. Galvin what Allen has done. You must do this for me. I can still see it all in my mind. I can hear the gunshots. I can smell the gunpowder … it was all so horrible."

Maria drew Dora closer and hugged her tightly. She rested her cheek on her sister's head as the young girl began to cry.

"Father was so good to both of us," Dora sputtered between sobs. "He did not deserve to die. Please, Maria, I beg of you … confess."

Maria spoke softly. "We must leave it in the hands of the court. We should not talk about these things. We have such a brief time together. Let us talk of happier times."

Dora lifted her head and weakly pushed herself away from her sister's hold.

"Maria, there cannot be happier times unless you confess," she pleaded. "I am much better now that I've told the truth, but I will never be truly happy until you do the same. Then, we can be together again, don't you see?"

Maria managed a feeble smile and pulled Dora close again to whisper in her ear.

"Not tonight, my darling. Not tonight. But all will be well in the end, I promise."

***

When the sisters' visit concluded, Galvin agreed to accompany Dora and her aunt home. The women did not speak to each other during the short ride, and Emily did nothing to comfort her niece, who quietly wept as she leaned against the carriage window.

After he had helped Dora up the stairs to her room, Galvin thought about hiring a carriage for himself but decided the walk home would do him good. As he neared the intersection of Thames Street and Ferry Wharf, he spotted a gathering of boisterous men standing in a circle around a police officer.

When he drew closer, he recognized Captain Hammond as the officer holding court in the middle of the group, puffing on a thick cigar. Hammond had a broad smile on his face and laughed heartily along with his companions. The captain was wasting no time sharing the details of the sisters' meeting with his cronies.

Galvin lowered the brim of his hat and stepped behind a carriage parked in front of the fishmonger's shop, hoping to pass unnoticed.

He heard someone standing in the circle remark, "I still can't believe it. She seemed so sweet and innocent. She sure fooled me."

"She fooled all of us," another piped up. "Except for you, Captain. She didn't fool you," he declared, slapping Hammond soundly on the back.

Galvin turned his head slightly toward the crowd and watched as Hammond removed the cigar from his mouth to speak.

"Nope. She didn't fool me. Right from the beginning, I could see clearly through the lot of 'em. I couldn't let on, you know—had to keep my cards close to the vest. No, sir, they didn't bamboozle me. Not for one minute."

Hammond took another puff of his cigar as the men laughed.

"I knew I'd get 'em. Just had to be patient and wait … criminals always trip up. You just need intuition and a keen eye," he bragged, tapping his finger on his temple and smiling smugly.

"Yes, sir," another man spoke out. "As they say, murder will out."

"I bet there will be a promotion in it for you, Captain," another said. "Maybe they will make you Chief of Police."

The last comment drew loud laughter from the group.

"Chief Hammond. Now, that has a ring to it." the man announced to peals of laughter.

Galvin had heard enough and quickened his step as he made his way down Thames Street, putting distance between himself and the group of men.

He has no qualms about taking credit for solving the case, he thought. What about Detective Richards? From the moment he hit town, he worked diligently on the investigation. But Hammond? He didn't come around until the last minute and only after hearing Dora's confession. Ben Burton would have been buried and long forgotten if it had been up to him.

As he turned the corner onto Spring Street and passed St. Mary's Church, he recalled the parable of the eleventh hour as told in Matthew. He took a deep breath and exhaled slowly to quell his simmering indignation. He was eager to get home and put his thoughts on paper.

The Newport Mercury
Saturday, November 28, 1885

To the editor of the Mercury:
"When, therefore, there were some that came about the eleventh hour, they received every man a penny. So shall the last be first, and the first last, for many are called, but few are chosen."
The persons who have "borne the burden of the day and the heat" in their efforts to establish the cause of the late Benjamin Burton's death should not be discouraged, even if those who came in just in time to congratulate the workers on their success now receive the same need of praise and endorsement for the accomplishment of the end in view. The recognition which should have been generously extended to Mr. Benjamin H. Richards for his fidelity and perseverance, I fear has been withheld. If it is not too late, let me say that he has acted well his part and should receive the acknowledgment for it that is justly his.
Patrick J. Galvin

Chapter 23
Sunday, December 6, 1885

As the Dorseys' days in confinement dragged on, Sheriff Easton noticed a shift in the couple's interactions. Since the sisters' meeting, Allen had begun displaying a cool indifference to his wife. Maria, too, had all but stopped attempting to communicate with her husband.

Upon hearing Easton's reports of growing discord between the couple, Galvin suspected Maria's resolve might be waning. After Sunday Mass, he headed to the Newport jail.

Sheriff Easton opened the door to his drawing room and motioned for Galvin to enter.

"Welcome, Counselor. Come on in."

Galvin smiled and thanked the sheriff as he sat in one of the Lincoln rockers beside the fireplace.

"I am sorry to bother you on the Sabbath, but I wanted to speak with you about Mrs. Dorsey."

Easton lowered himself into the matching rocker on the other side.

"It is no trouble, P.J."

"I'll get right to the point. Are relations between the Dorseys still deteriorating?"

"Yes, I believe so," Easton confirmed. "Mr. Dorsey has shown little to no concern over his wife's condition or well-being. My wife tells me Mrs. Dorsey often cries in her cell—which he must hear—but he makes no attempt to comfort her. I've never seen a man so utterly apathetic to his wife's delicate condition. My wife tries to comfort Mrs. Dorsey and encourages her to keep her spirits up. She reminds her daily that it is important to eat with a child on the way."

"I'm sorry to hear it," Galvin replied sincerely.

Easton leaned in towards Galvin and lowered his voice.

"There is something else I should tell you. I heard some ugly gossip when I was in town earlier this morning."

"I have no doubt you did, "Galvin remarked. "The people in this town—"

Easton quickly interrupted, "No, P.J., this rumor may explain why the Dorseys are not speaking to one another and could be why the younger sister confessed."

"Oh? Let's hear it, then."

Easton adjusted himself in his chair, obviously uncomfortable with what he was about to say.

"It has been suggested that Mr. Dorsey's relationship with his sister-in-law was highly improper. More than just friendly, if you know what I mean."

"Is this rumor courtesy of Emily Burton?" Galvin asked, hoping that wasn't the case.

"I honestly don't know the source, but I don't dare tell Mrs. Easton what I heard. It is far too scandalous."

Easton considered his own daughter, who was the same age as Maria and had also recently married. He also had a younger daughter who was about Dora's age. The idea of the youngest Burton girl having relations with her brother-in-law was too much for him to bear. He shook his head to clear his mind of the thought.

"Of course, It's probably just nonsense and idle gossip. But I do believe Miss Burton's words weigh heavily on Mrs. Dorsey's mind." He added, "My wife suspects Mrs. Dorsey may be displaying symptoms of quick consumption. She languishes in her bed and eats very little. I'm concerned that if something doesn't change, she or the child she is carrying may not make it."

"There may be a solution," Galvin suggested. "I would like you to petition the court to move Mrs. Dorsey."

"Move her? Where?" asked Easton.

"Under Rhode Island law, if a prisoner cannot be adequately cared for in the local jail, the sheriff can petition the court to move her to the state prison. This will not only force a separation of the Dorseys, but I believe it would be in the best interest of Mrs. Dorsey. I mean no offense, Sheriff, but the Newport jail does not have the facilities nor the medical staff to care for prisoners in Mrs. Dorsey's condition. While Mrs. Easton should be admired for her work here, the state prison has a nurse, a round-the-clock matron, and a doctor on staff."

Easton considered Galvin's proposal.

"I am not opposed to filing the petition, but I bet the Dorseys and their attorney will object," he speculated. "The couple may not be on speaking terms now, but I doubt they'll want to be separated from one another. All they have is each other. The only person who visits with any regularity is Reverend Van Horne, and only Maria will agree to see him."

Easton stood and joined Galvin as they walked to the front door. He extended his hand.

"I will do as you suggest, counselor."

✳✳✳

Monday, December 7, 1885

When he opened the door to the jailhouse, Easton was greeted by his wife, who was sweeping the floor of the reception area.

"You've been gone a long time," she said.

"Yes, my dear. I've come straight from the courthouse."

"Did the judge approve the transfer?"

"It is done," Easton replied. "Mrs. Dorsey is to be transferred on the twenty-first of the month. Will you accompany me while I inform Mrs. Dorsey? I am worried what her reaction might be."

"Of course, dear," Mrs. Easton agreed. She leaned the broom against the wall and reached around her back to loosen her apron strings.

Easton glanced lovingly at his wife as they walked to Maria's cell. She was fond of Maria, and he knew it would be difficult for her to witness Maria's reaction to the news of her transfer. When they reached Maria's cell, they found her lying in the cot, facing the wall.

"Mrs. Dorsey," Mrs. Easton called out, jingling the keys to the cell.

"May we come in and visit with you for a moment?"

Maria slowly rolled over to her other side and tucked her pillow under her chin.

"Yes."

Mrs. Easton handed the keys to her husband. He pulled the door open, and they stepped inside. He helped his wife lift Maria into a sitting position. She took Maria's hand and closely examined Maria's gaunt and lined face.

"Mrs. Dorsey," Easton began, his voice lowered so as not to be overheard. "The court has ordered you to be transferred to the state women's prison in Howard."

Maria pulled her hand back in a sudden movement. "What do you mean? I haven't been convicted of anything. Why would the judge send me to Howard?"

Sheriff Easton said calmly, "This is not a punishment, Mrs. Dorsey. The transfer was arranged so you might receive better medical care. Mrs. Easton and I have done our best for you, but you need to be under closer medical supervision given your …"

Easton faltered as his wife spoke up in her husband's stead, "Given your delicate condition."

He interjected, "At the state prison, matrons, nurses, and doctors will be available to care for you. They have a fully equipped infirmary with soft beds where you will be under a doctor's care. It will be far more comfortable than what we can offer here."

Mrs. Easton rubbed Maria's shoulder reassuringly. "It is for your own good and well-being, Mrs. Dorsey."

Maria glanced up at the sheriff, her eyes questioning. "Will Mr. Dorsey be going to Howard with me?"

Easton shook his head, "No, Mrs. Dorsey, he will not. He will stay here until the trial."

"Oh," Maria remarked, her tone flat. "Does he know?"

"No, not yet," answered Mrs. Easton. "Mr. Easton will tell him."

Suddenly, Maria's thoughts turned to Dora. "Will I be allowed to see my sister before I leave?"

Mrs. Easton smiled encouragingly. "I will send her a message straight away and tell her you have asked to see her. If she agrees, of course, we will arrange it."

Maria closed her eyes and squeezed Mary Easton's hand.

"Thank you," she whispered gratefully before asking if she might lay back down again.

The couple helped Maria get situated on her cot before Mrs. Easton covered her with a quilt.

"Let me know if there is anything you need," she whispered in Maria's ear before joining her husband outside of the cell. It had gone much better than she expected.

As the couple walked toward Allen's cell, she stopped suddenly and turned to her husband.

"Do you want me to be with you when you tell Mr. Dorsey?"

"No," Easton said. "I will take care of it."

***

Monday, December 21, 1885

The boat that Maria Dorsey would take from Newport to Providence was scheduled to depart at eleven o'clock. Mrs. Easton was busy ensuring all of Maria's belongings were clean and packed for the move. When she delivered the last of Maria's freshly laundered clothing to the cell, she took the opportunity to bid her goodbye.

She hugged Maria and said, "I'm sorry I could not convince your sister to come see you."

Maria responded cryptically, "If you see Dora, tell her—that for her sake—I will tell all."

When it was time to depart, Maria was led to the front of Allen's cell. Allen was sitting on the edge of his cot, his hands on his knees. The jailer called out to him, "Aren't you going to say goodbye to your Missus?"

Allen slowly rose and stepped to the front of his cell as Maria stood motionless. He lifted his hand and pointed a finger through the metal bars.

"You must not talk as much," he warned, "as it makes it harder for you and me. Maria, I want you to remember all that I have told you. Impress it firmly on your mind and keep still."

Allen stepped back and returned to his seat on the cot as Maria was led from the corridor.

***

Though the job of cleaning the empty cells should have fallen to the jailers, Mrs. Easton took it upon herself to give them a good going-over after a prisoner was released from their custody.

As she once told her husband, "I know it is a jail, but we are housing human beings, not animals. They deserve decent meals and clean surroundings."

When she entered Maria's former cell, she began pulling and tugging at the mattress to remove it from the metal cot for cleaning. As she extricated the mattress from the frame, she discovered an envelope hidden underneath.

Did Maria mean to leave this behind? she wondered.

Mrs. Easton turned the envelope over in her hands. The script on the outside was neatly written, but it did not contain a return address, so she assumed they must have been delivered by messenger. With a slight twinge of guilt, she opened it and read the letter inside.

Oh, my sister,
I have just received your note. For my sake,
if not for your own, will you not confess?
My sister, it would not be so hard to bear
if you would only tell what you know.
I would try then to be contented.
You say you love me. Oh, then, for my sake,
for your little sister's sake, grant this one wish, for I may never see you.
Sometimes, I feel as if I would go crazy,
but I pray to God to forgive me.
Oh, then, if you do love me, please do as I wish.
Oh, for my sake, please do.
I shall take my medicine so that my body may be strengthened,
that I may be able to testify against both you and Allen,
who are guilty of the murder.
For myself, I prefer to be arrested and deserve to be.
I do not want to go for a less term than my life,
for I am as guilty as you both.
I could have prevented it had I wished to do so.
Dora

Mrs. Easton rushed from the cell to find her husband.

***

December 23, 1885

Nursing a snifter of brandy, William Sheffield, Jr. warmed himself in front of the enormous fireplace that dominated the front parlor of his family's Washington Square mansion. He was eagerly waiting for his father to join him. The senator had been traveling since his son had agreed to represent the Dorseys, and this would be their first chance to discuss the case in person.

Sheffield hoped to convince his father to join him as co-counsel in the Dorseys' defense. In addition to his expertise as an attorney, he thought the addition of the respected and revered senator would carry significant weight with a jury.

When he finally heard his father's footsteps coming down the stairs, he called out, "In here," and got up to pour his father a brandy.

At sixty-five, the elder Sheffield's thinning gray hair was the only observable evidence of his age, as his clean-shaven and smooth, unlined face gave him the appearance of a younger man. The senator carried himself in a formal and dignified manner and, like his son, had a penchant for fashionable clothing.

After the men settled in with their drinks, the senator spoke first. "What is it, Will?" he asked. "I sense something is weighing on your mind."

"I want to discuss the Dorsey case with you."

"Have they paid you a retainer yet?" the senator inquired.

"No, and I don't expect one," the younger Sheffield answered defensively. "I doubt they will be able to pay anything until he is acquitted and can resume his studies."

"Will, you cannot let your preoccupation with this case affect your other work. You have paying clients that you cannot neglect."

"Father, you have often said that performing pro bono work is not only an admirable pursuit but is also required by our profession. I would think that you would approve of my efforts to defend a man falsely accused of a heinous crime."

The senator responded with skepticism. "What makes you so

confident the Dorseys are innocent of these charges?"

"Because Allen Dorsey told me they were."

The young attorney realized how ridiculous his response sounded as soon as the words left his mouth, but his father's hearty guffaw still stung him.

"Father, I can't explain it, but I believe him. Mr. Dorsey looked me directly in the eye and swore to their innocence. At that moment, I knew without hesitation that he was speaking the truth."

"Proclamations of innocence spring forward effortlessly from the mouths of the accused, even from those still holding the bloody knife," the senator countered.

"True … I have had clients who claimed to be innocent and were not, but Dorsey is different. You haven't met him, but when you do, you will understand. There is something special and unique about this man, and I believe him," the young Sheffield reiterated firmly.

"Think about it, Father. Why would Dorsey—an intelligent man on the precipice of becoming a physician after overcoming obstacles you and I could not fathom—throw it all away? And for what? A few dollars?

"I have been meeting with Dorsey at the jail frequently. Since his arrest, he has taken the initiative and obtained statements from Penn Medical School showing he was current in his tuition payments. He also has communications from his previous employers supporting his claim that he had earned enough to pay for his medical schooling."

The senator considered his son's argument before addressing his primary concern.

"Son, are you sure you are not being driven by your desire to best P.J. Galvin?"

When the two young attorneys were employed in his office, their fierce competition—arguing over the law, debating courtroom strategies, and vying for clients—had been a source of amusement to him. But he knew his son had been disappointed when he was passed over, and Galvin was asked to lead the inquest.

The junior Sheffield's face flushed with resentment at the suggestion.

"No, of course not, Father. That is ridiculous. You know that I respect P.J., but I think he has been wrong about this case from the beginning. He was singularly focused on the Dorseys right from the start and barely put on any medical evidence during the inquest that would support an obvious suicide."

"Be fair, Will," his father cautioned. "As I understand it, P.J. put on a balanced case. Dr. Turner and Dr. Ecroyd both testified in support of suicide. While Dr. Turner is certainly a respected medical examiner, I suspect there are other medical experts who can bolster Turner's opinion more effectively than Dr. Ecroyd. I can make some inquiries on your behalf."

"Thank you. I would welcome your assistance with the case. Would you consider joining me as co-counsel? Your presence in the courtroom would be invaluable. I would do all the preparation work for the trial, and you could question the physicians and make the closing argument."

Sheffield believed his father's ability to speak eloquently was unmatched. Whenever his schedule permitted, he liked to sit in the courtroom and watch his father give closing statements. He was in awe of his father's ability to effortlessly break down even the most complex facts of a case for the jurors.

The senator considered his son's request. He had doubts as to whether he wanted his name attached to this case. His limited knowledge of the case had not convinced him that the Dorseys were innocent. And it had been years since the elder attorney had been involved in a criminal case, preferring to represent the New York elite in contract and other civil disputes.

"I'm not sure I would be much help to you," he replied with a grin. "But I would like to look at what you have prepared so far."

The men then sat together and reviewed the proposed witness list.

"There certainly is no shortage of people willing to provide character references for Dorsey," the senator commented. "But what about the young Burton girl's confession? If the jury does not believe Burton killed himself, then I see that as your Achilles heel."

His son's face brightened.

"Ah, that's because you aren't as familiar with her aunt, Emily Burton, as I am. I believe that she is the perfect foil to the confession. Mrs. Burton is a biased, conniving troublemaker. I will prove she extracted a forced confession from her niece when the girl thought she was dying. When I finish my cross-examination, the jury will not believe Mrs. Burton or her niece."

The senator smiled. He admired his son's confidence.

"Will, I want to caution you about questioning the delicate Burton girl on the stand. Reserve your aggressive questioning for Emily Burton, whom the jury will be less sympathetic toward."

"Duly noted."

"I look forward to seeing you in action," his father said, smiling with pride and patting his son on the back. "I will be honored to join you at your defense table."

Chapter 24
January - May 1886

In the months following Maria's transfer, the rabid interest in the Burton case began to ease. Life in Newport resumed its typically slow, off-season pace.

Early reports from the women's prison indicated Maria now spent her time sewing and was allowed to write to her husband once a month. Allen, now assuming the role of a model prisoner, remained in the Newport Jail. Dora continued to suffer a miserable existence at her aunt's house, wishing instead to be sentenced for her role in her father's death.

The Sheffields spent the winter months redoubling their efforts to prove the Dorseys innocent. The younger Sheffield was thrilled to learn his father had used his influence to engage Dr. David Hayes Agnew to testify for the defense.

The nationally renowned chief surgeon to the late President Garfield was also a prestigious faculty member at the University of Pennsylvania Medical School. Agnew was prepared to present similar cases he had uncovered that supported suicide as the cause of Ben's death. The doctor had also convinced another of his esteemed medical colleagues from Pennsylvania to testify for the defense.

While his father was busy rounding up medical experts, Sheffield interviewed a number of local merchants and businessmen who were willing to testify as to Burton's precarious financial woes. His search for individuals who could attest to Burton's gambling habits had proved more elusive. Still, Sheffield was confident that he would eventually find a saloon owner or patron who could be persuaded to testify, given the right enticement.

The Sheffields' law practice was absorbing significant travel and accommodation expenses for the expert witnesses and the out-of-town character witnesses, but the men viewed these expenses as necessary.

Richards returned to New York City and resumed his duties with the local Pinkerton office, though he and Galvin kept in constant contact. The detective was eager to assist Galvin in his preparation for the Dorseys' criminal trial.

Galvin planned to bolster the case he presented at the inquest by including additional expert medical testimony. Richards' willingness to travel to Boston to interview physicians was invaluable to Galvin, who needed the time to focus on his existing law practice.

The extensive newspaper coverage of his masterful handling of the Burton inquest had resulted in a surge of inquiries from both local and out-of-state prospective clients. However, Galvin remained committed to prioritizing his representation of the underprivileged in his community.

On April 2nd, Maria gave birth to a baby boy. She named him Eugene Waldorf Dorsey in honor of her late brother Eugene, who died from consumption when he was just a toddler. She added Allen's middle name, as it was fashionable to name the eldest son after his father.

The child was a weak, sickly baby, and the matrons at the prison were not convinced he would live. Maria remained bedridden following the birth, the seeds of consumption having taken root, further weakening her condition.

Chapter 25
May and June 1886

The native violets of Rhode Island were reaching their spring peak when the Supreme Court was scheduled to reconvene in early May. The morning before their session began, Galvin received a note from Dora asking to meet with him as soon as possible.

Shortly before noon, Dora appeared in his doorway. Galvin had not seen her in months and was alarmed by her appearance. Her dress now hung loosely over her skeletal frame. Her hair was thinning, and her face was ashen with sunken eyes and hollow cheeks. He feared that Dora would have crumpled into a heap on the floor had he not quickly pulled out a chair.

Galvin felt his face flush with anger. Emily had assured him that she could put aside her hostile feelings toward her niece and continue caring for her until she testified at the Dorseys' trial at the end of June. He was kicking himself for trusting that she would advise him of any changes in Dora's condition.

Dora collapsed into her chair, gasping for breath, which dissolved into a fit of coughing. She placed a handkerchief over her mouth until the attack subsided.

"Can I get you some water?" asked Galvin with concern.

Dora shook her head no.

"What can I do for you, Miss Burton?" Galvin asked.

Dora lowered the handkerchief and cleared her throat. She could barely manage to speak above a whisper.

"Mr. Galvin, you must help me," she pleaded. "What is to become of me?"

Galvin felt genuine sympathy for the girl.

"Miss Burton, your destiny is in the hands of the judge. I've made no promises."

Dora shook her head, "No, you do not understand. I want to be sentenced now. I should have been sentenced the moment I confessed. I want a life sentence, no less. I desire it."

"You must first be arraigned, Miss Burton," Galvin explained. "I can ask the court to schedule your arraignment for tomorrow morning."

"Then will the judge will send me to prison?"

"It is not so cut and dried. You will be given the opportunity to plead guilty or not guilty."

Galvin paused, then asked, "Miss Burton, have you spoken to an attorney? You have a right to plead not guilty and be tried by a jury of your peers," he advised. "A jury might rule in your favor or find extenuating circumstances and recommend a reduced sentence."

"No!" Dora cried out with a force that surprised Galvin. "I do not want a trial. I am ready to be sentenced and sent to prison."

Galvin shook his head in dismay. He had spent most of his career representing defendants who sought to delay or avoid incarceration. None of them, especially those charged with the most heinous crimes, voluntarily offered themselves up for the maximum sentence.

Dora sighed defeatedly.

"I don't know why this is taking so long. I don't want to stay at my aunt's house any longer. It is killing me."

She might be right, he thought, *judging from her appearance.*

"I understand, Miss Burton. I will ask the judge if he can arraign and sentence you tomorrow."

Even if the judge did not agree to sentence Dora, Galvin was confident that he could convince the judge that she would be better cared for at the prison while she awaited testifying at the Dorseys' trial.

***

On the following morning of May 6th, Dora Burton was officially arraigned on the charge of aiding and abetting the murder of her father. Dora trembled violently as she stood next to Galvin and listened to the reading of the lengthy indictment.

When the judge asked for her plea, Dora tearfully replied, "Guilty," before quickly sitting down and covering her face with her hands.

Galvin asked for her to be immediately sentenced, and the judge addressed Dora directly.

"Do you have anything to say to the court as to why the sentence should not be passed upon you?"

"No, nothing," she responded.

"You are then sentenced to imprisonment in the state prison, at hard labor, for life," the judge concluded.

Galvin whispered to Dora as the sentence was being written. He explained she would stay at the Newport jail until she could be transported by boat to the women's prison in Howard.

Once the clerk read the sentence aloud, Sheriff Easton took the young girl by the arm and led her down the center aisle. As they neared the courtroom door to make their exit, Dora locked eyes with a solitary figure who had been quietly standing in the rear of the courtroom observing the proceedings. It was her Aunt Emily.

As she passed, Dora mouthed, *"Forgive me."*

***

After Dora arrived at the state women's prison, she was immediately confined to the infirmary where Maria was kept before and after baby Eugene's birth.

Before her arrival, the doctor moved Maria to a cell so the sisters would continue to be separated until the trial. Maria spent most of her days in solitude, holding and stroking her baby between feedings and dissolving into a torrent of tears when the child was taken from her arms.

The prison matrons had grown concerned with Maria's attachment to her son. If she were to be convicted or perhaps die, the baby would have to be adopted by another family. The matrons began to have necessary but agonizing discussions with Maria concerning the baby's future.

"Mrs. Dorsey, you need to be thinking about making plans for the baby in the event that you are unable to care for him," the matron began, careful to avoid the word 'convicted' or any reference to her declining health. She had barely gotten the words out before Maria broke down, her body shaking.

But the matron pressed forward. "Have you thought of a friend or family member who might be able to care for the child? At least until …"

When she stopped crying, Maria responded, "I did write to my husband about the matter, as you suggested. But I have not heard back from him. He has a sister who may be willing to help."

But Maria did not share with the matron the fact that Allen's sister was also sick with consumption and not a likely possibility. "How about one of your relatives? Your aunt, perhaps?"

Maria shook her head emphatically, "No!"

"Are there no friends in Newport who could do it?"

The topic had become too painful for Maria, and she abruptly ended the conversation by saying, "I will think about it, I promise. I will write to my husband again."

***

A few days prior to the start of the trial, Allen Dorsey agreed to be interviewed by a correspondent from a Philadelphia newspaper, *The Times*. The interview was conducted in Allen's jail cell and appeared in the paper the following day. The reporter began the article by noting that Allen seemed in excellent health and good spirits.

"*I believe,*" Allen was quoted as saying, "*that the more intelligent portion of the community have become favorably impressed on my behalf. I have excellent counsel in the person of William Sheffield, Jr., assisted by his father, Senator William Sheffield, Sr.*"

Allen then spoke briefly of Maria and his infant son.

"*My wife is in better health than she was. It seems odd for a man never to have seen his own son, now several months old, but I hear from them every two weeks, and they are both in good health.*"

Allen became animated when turning his attention to individuals who stood ready to vouch for his character during the upcoming trial.

"*My friends are showing interest in my case. I was a student at Lincoln University, and the president of the institution will be present to testify on my behalf. The acting principal of the academy where I taught in North Carolina will also testify. As you may know, I was a University of Pennsylvania Medical College student. The renowned Dr. Agnew has sent over a communication signed by all the members of the faculty expressing a favorable view of my character."*

The reporter questioned Allen as to whether any new evidence had come to light that would favor the defense.

"New evidence has been found since the last hearing, proving that the revolver with which the deed was committed was bought by a friend of Mr. Burton's who purchased the gun in Philadelphia. It was supposed to be mine because it was a Philadelphia make."

"What about Dora Burton's confession?" the reporter asked next.

"Well, she may believe it. She is a hysterical, undeveloped girl and has been under the control of her aunt, who is a woman of great willpower and magnetism … Such as one who can set a whole congregation shouting during a meeting. Expert medical witnesses have also been summoned from Philadelphia."

Allen concluded the interview by saying, *"I am an innocent man. And I believe, in the event of a fair trial, that I shall be able to prove that fact."*

***

On the morning Allen was being interviewed, Dora and Maria boarded the boat in Providence. It was the first time since Dora was imprisoned that the sisters were permitted to see one another. Her health had greatly improved due to the efforts of the doctor and the nurses in the prison infirmary. Much of her strength had returned, though she still struggled to gain weight and suffered periodic bouts of coughing.

The other passengers showed a keen interest in the heartfelt and genuine reunion. The girls sat close, their foreheads pressed together as they cooed over the baby Maria held in her arms.

When they arrived at Newport, Sheriff Easton and his wife were waiting at the end of the gangway to meet them. Mrs. Easton was excited to see Maria's son for the first time.

"He is such a pretty baby," she exclaimed as she reached to take the child into her arms.

At three months old, baby Eugene had smooth, tawny brown

skin and silken black hair almost two inches long. Maria had dressed Eugene in a long white linen dress with pretty red bows attached to the shoulders. His hair was parted on both sides along the top and rolled into a long curl surrounded by tight ringlets on either side. Mrs. Easton noticed Eugene's large, bright brown eyes and remarked that they were quite expressive for a baby so young.

After retrieving the traveling bags the prison matron prepared for the sisters, Sheriff Easton loaded the women into the carriage and returned to the Newport Jail. Allen would soon meet his son for the very first time.

Chapter 26
Monday, June 29, 1886
The First Day of the Trial

The Supreme Court convened at ten o'clock in the morning in the Old Colony House courtroom. The three justices presiding over the trial were seated behind the bench. Galvin stood ready at the prosecution table while Richards had taken a position right behind him in the first row in the gallery.

Galvin removed his linen jacket and draped it across the back of his chair. He rolled up his shirt sleeves and loosened the tie around his neck. He glanced back at Richards for support and was met with a comforting smile.

The Sheffields entered the courtroom, and the attorneys greeted one another with respectful nods as father and son made their way to the defense table. The younger Sheffield wore a neat black suit with a stylish black cravat tied around the stiffly starched collar of his white shirt, while his father was similarly attired in gray, his cravat studded with a diamond stick pin.

Outside in Washington Square, a close carriage pulled up in front of the Old Colony House. The bystanders who had been unable to gain access to the building rushed toward the carriage as Allen and Maria attempted to disembark.

Maria moved slowly, carefully cradling baby Eugene close to her breast due to the crush of the crowd. Two police officers who held the crowd at bay assisted her out of the carriage, up the stairs, and into the building.

Because his wrists were handcuffed, Allen also required assistance stepping out of the carriage. The jailer accompanying the Dorseys from the jail escorted Allen as he ascended the steps to the doorway.

Allen and Maria maintained the same calm and collected demeanor they exhibited throughout the inquest. Maria clung to baby Eugene as she sat at the defense table while the women in the gallery strained their necks to steal a peek.

After the police officer removed the handcuffs from Allen's wrists, he took his seat next to Maria and picked up the notebook placed there for his use. The senator sat in the first seat of the defense table, quietly reviewing his notes.

Allen tilted his head slightly toward his attorney, and the two men conversed quietly for a few minutes. He then turned to Maria and chatted pleasantly while she bounced the baby in her lap. Maria chirruped at the infant, trying to get the boy to smile for his father. Allen ran his fingers over his son's tummy, playing the old game of Creep Mouse with the child to elicit a response. Baby Eugene did not disappoint, cooing and smiling to Allen's delight.

Before the trial started, the defense had successfully argued that the men in Newport and the surrounding area had already formed an opinion on the case, forcing the court to only consider potential jurors who lived off Aquidneck Island. As a result, all nineteen of the prospective jurors were white farmers or small business owners from distant rural communities who had left their homes before daybreak to travel the distance to Newport.

By eleven-thirty, twelve men were seated in the jury box. At the justices' signal, Galvin stood and walked to the area between the bench and the jurors, ready to begin his opening statement. He turned his attention to the twelve men seated in the straight-back wooden chairs they would occupy for the duration of the trial. Farmers clad in sweaty coveralls with leathery, sunbaked faces and tobacco-stained beards sat side-by-side with smartly dressed merchants sporting neat, closely cropped whiskers.

"Gentlemen, thank you for being here today and performing your civic duty. I know your presence presents a hardship for many of you, but your role in these proceedings is essential to our justice system."

Galvin then launched into his opening statement. He spent the next two hours carefully reciting the facts of the case and presented an impassioned review of the previous testimony given at the inquest.

As if he were a journalist, Allen sat at the defense table, taking copious notes. Meanwhile, Maria struggled to keep the baby quiet when the infant's cries echoed and threatened to drown out Galvin's words.

When Galvin was finished, he tipped his head respectfully and said, "I thank you," before returning to his seat.

The court recessed for the midday meal before the trial resumed at three o'clock. Maria returned without baby Eugene in her arms. Her mood changed dramatically after her child was removed. She appeared sullen and on the verge of tears.

In a strategic maneuver, Galvin had scheduled Dora as the day's first witness. He wanted her haunting confession to remain foremost in the minds of the jurors for the duration of the trial.

When the bailiff called Dora's name, she appeared in the doorway, flanked by her aunt. Maria gasped audibly at the unexpected sight of her Aunt Emily, whom she had not seen since meeting with Dora at the jailhouse in late November.

Under the table, Allen pressed his index finger hard into Maria's thigh, signaling her to remain calm.

With her aunt trailing closely behind, Dora slowly made her way down the aisle and lowered herself into the witness chair. Allen attempted to make eye contact with her, but Dora kept her eyes down.

Before taking her seat, Emily pointed to the gallery and whispered loud enough for only Dora to hear, "I will be watching from over there."

Galvin then led Dora through her confession and the events leading up to the morning of October 6th. Dora repeated the role she and her sister had played in their father's death and identified Allen as his shooter. She also confirmed that the motive for the murder had been the urgent need for money to pay for Allen's education.

When Galvin presented the pistol to Dora, she turned her head away and began to nervously rock back and forth in her chair.

"Is this the gun Mr. Dorsey was holding in his hand that

morning?" He waited patiently for Dora to steady herself, then repeated, "Miss Burton? Is this the gun?"

"I think so," Dora nodded. "It looks like the gun."

"Had you ever seen this gun before October 6th?"

"Yes. I have seen it in my father's bureau."

"Do you know how Mr. Dorsey obtained the gun?"

Dora's voice quivered, "I told Allen that Father kept it there."

Galvin proceeded gently. "When did you tell Mr. Dorsey that your father kept a gun in his chest of drawers?"

"About a week before Father died. It was after Allen first said he wanted to kill my father."

At the defendant's table, Allen hurriedly penned a note and slid it to Sheffield. The movement caught the senator's attention, and he looked at Allen with annoyance.

Galvin pressed on, asking, "When Mr. Dorsey told you that he wanted to kill your father, was your sister present?"

Dora turned toward the defense table and locked eyes with Maria. "Yes, she was there."

"Did you make any objection to Mr. Dorsey's intentions?"

Dora grimaced and slowly shook her head, "No."

"Why not?"

"I did not think he would do it," Dora whimpered as she lowered her gaze and wrapped her arms around her middle.

"Did your sister object to her husband's intentions to murder your father?"

"No," she cried, her tears beginning to spill.

Galvin repositioned himself directly in front of Dora to block the Dorseys from her view. He concluded his questioning by asking, "Did Mr. Dorsey ever express any remorse over killing your father?"

Dora sat silent momentarily with her head bowed as she mustered all her remaining strength. She slowly raised her tear-stained face to meet Galvin's gaze head-on.

"He told me his only regret was firing a second shot. He feared his lapse in judgment would be his undoing."

An outcry of gasps from the spectators echoed loudly throughout the courtroom as Galvin tipped his head and turned away to return to the prosecutor's table.

"Thank you. I have nothing further."

Colonel Sheffield slowly rose from his seat. His face was flushed with indignation as he began his questioning.

"Was it your decision to stay with your aunt after Mr. and Mrs. Dorsey's arrest?"

Dora bowed her head. "No. I had nowhere else to go."

"Did your aunt treat you well after you moved into her home?"

"I suppose."

Sheffield tilted his head questioningly.

"I'm curious, Miss Burton. What would prompt you to confess to a crime when you were not under suspicion?"

"The night I confessed, I had a lung hemorrhage and was coughing up blood. I feared I was dying, and I wanted to unburden myself."

"Is that what your aunt told you to do?" Sheffield suggested. "Did she tell you that you needed to confess before you died?"

Dora shook her head emphatically, "No, sir. I did not want people to believe my father killed himself."

"Miss Burton, when you fell ill, did your aunt withhold medical care until you agreed to confess?"

Dora cried out, "No, that is not true!"

Sheffield circled to the front of the defense table.

"Isn't it true, Miss Burton, your aunt told you that if you did not confess, she would let you die?"

Incensed by the scandalous allegation, Emily struggled to control herself. She clenched the back of the seat in front of her and began to pull herself up to a standing position to protest when she made eye contact with Galvin. He frantically motioned for her to remain seated, so she sat back down.

Dora shuddered, her face ashen.

"No, she never said such a thing."

"Wasn't it your aunt who suggested that the coroner and police captain come to the house so you could confess?"

"No, I asked her to bring them to the house," Dora insisted.

Sheffield's eyes narrowed. "Did anyone suggest that you should have an attorney present?"

"I don't recall. I did not think I needed an attorney."

"According to your testimony, you tell us Allen Dorsey killed your father. If that is true, it would seem to me you had an ample opportunity to tell someone—Dr. Turner, Coroner Stanhope, Captain Hammond—they were all there that fateful morning, were they not? Why didn't you say anything …" Sheffield paused before adding sardonically, "before *unburdening yourself* to them?"

Dora burst into tears and moaned woefully, "Because I knew I was as guilty as Allen and Maria."

Sheffield pointed toward Emily, sitting in the gallery.

"Did someone insinuate that to you?"

All eyes turned to Emily Burton, who was violently shaking her head from side to side in response.

Dora shook her head and wept, "I knew it myself."

"How would you describe your relationship with your sister, Mrs. Dorsey?"

Managing a weak smile, Dora leaned sideways in her chair to look past Sheffield and make direct eye contact with Maria.

"Since my mother's death, Maria has been very protective and nurturing toward me. I would have been lost without her."

Maria appeared to nod her head slightly while Sheffield ignored the quick connection between the sisters.

"And how would you describe your sister's relationship with your father?"

"It was also good."

"After you learned that your father ordered Mr. and Mrs. Dorsey from the home, did you notice a change in the relationship between your father and your sister?"

"No, I did not. I thought everything was fine."

"You allege that you heard Mr. Dorsey discuss his desire to kill your father but that you did not object to his intentions. Is this correct?"

"I told Maria that if Allen did that, we would get caught up in it." Sheffield smiled slyly as he stepped closer to Dora.

"To be clear, you did not object to your father being killed but instead objected to being caught up in the crime?"

Dora stiffened in her seat. "I did not wish my father dead. I didn't think Allen would do it."

"You testified that you told Mr. Dorsey where he could find a gun in the house. Is this correct?"

Dora lowered her head ashamedly. "Yes."

"That sounds to me as if you wanted him dead."

Dora gasped, "No! I did not want him dead. I loved my father."

"Then why would you tell Mr. Dorsey where he could find the gun?"

"I don't know," Dora cried. "I just don't know."

"Isn't it true that it was YOU who retrieved the gun?"

"No!"

Sheffield took another step closer to Dora and leaned forward menacingly, causing her to push back into her chair to maintain a distance.

As he hovered over her, Sheffield sneered, "And isn't it true that it was *you*—and not Mr. Dorsey—who used the gun to kill your father?" The clamor in the gallery increased as the spectators reacted to the drama playing out before their eyes.

"No! No! I could never do that!" Dora pleaded as her body shook with fear.

Sheffield straightened his back and moved back a step, his voice rising.

"Miss Burton, you have placed yourself in the house during the shooting. You previously testified under oath that Mr. Dorsey was sick in bed, and Maria was out of the house. Isn't it true that *you*, Miss Burton, were the only person downstairs and in the vicinity of your father at the time of his death? Weren't you the only person who knew where to find the gun?

"And wouldn't you, Miss Burton, do anything for Mrs. Dorsey, the sister who—how did you put it—without whom you would have been lost? Did you desire so desperately to keep your sister with you that you would kill your beloved father?"

Just as Galvin rose to object, Maria cried out, "Stop! Stop! That's not true."

As the chief justice banged his gavel and shouted for order, a heavy thud, followed by the noisy rattle of a wooden chair hitting and skidding across the marble floor, echoed throughout the room.

Maria Dorsey lay motionless on the floor. Allen was kneeling beside her while Senator Sheffield hovered above them.

Dr. Turner rushed forward from his seat in front of the gallery and pulled Allen back by the shoulder so he could crouch down by Maria's side to examine her. He smacked her cheeks in rapid succession.

"Mrs. Dorsey, can you hear me?"

When Maria did not respond immediately, he unbuttoned the top of her bodice and pulled the fabric open and away from her neck. He repeatedly called out Maria's name but received no response.

"Quickly! Someone bring me a glass of water," he shouted.

Dr. Turner splashed water on Maria's face, and she slowly began to regain consciousness. Dora put her hands to her face and wailed mournfully.

"Stand back," Dr. Turner ordered. "Give her air!"

Allen and the attorneys stepped back away from Maria as the doctor reached for her wrist to check her pulse. Maria's eyelids fluttered, yet her pulse was strong. Dr. Turner glanced over his shoulder at Allen.

"Mr. Dorsey, help me get her into a sitting position."

Dr. Turner then motioned to Senator Sheffield. "Pull her chair over here, and let's see if we can get her back in it."

Once she was lifted onto the chair, they propped her upright with a grain sack pillow offered by a woman in the gallery.

Feigning husbandly concern, Allen frantically fanned his wife with notebook paper as he leaned in and whispered through gritted teeth, "For God's sake, Maria, control yourself!"

When she seemed to have been stabilized, the chief justice questioned Maria directly.

"Mrs. Dorsey? Are you able to proceed?"

Maria nodded her head weakly.

The judge continued, instructing, "Dr. Turner, kindly move your chair to the defense table so you can monitor her condition."

Again, Maria nodded in acknowledgment. Allen reached over and smoothed his wife's hair away from her face. Dr. Turner soon joined them at the crowded table, poured a fresh glass of water, and set it in front of Maria before he took his seat.

Once everyone was settled, the judge asked Galvin, "Counselor, did you have an objection?"

Senator Sheffield stood and interrupted, "Your honor, the defense requests that you instruct the jury to disregard the comments made by the defendant and strike them from the record."

The judge turned to the jury. "Gentlemen, you must disregard the defendant's outburst."

Galvin stood and addressed the court.

"Your honor, I must protest. Counsel's brutish and threatening line of questioning is out of order. Miss Burton's confession is in the record, and she has been charged and sentenced for her role in her father's death."

Losing his composure, Sheffield angrily retorted, "Maybe she should be charged and sentenced for perjury as well," before glancing back to see his father's disapproving expression.

He quickly softened his tone, "No further questions."

The chief justice looked to Dora. "You may step down, Miss Burton."

Dora didn't move.

"Miss Burton, did you hear me? You may step down."

She raised her head, locking eyes with Maria as she extended her arms toward her, and called out, "Maria, please … Tell them the truth. Tell them."

"Miss Burton, do not speak to the defendant, or I will charge you with contempt," the judge warned angrily.

He turned to address the jury a second time.

"You are to ignore this witness' statement to the defendant," he instructed before banging his gavel again and announcing, "This court is in recess."

Keeping her eyes on Maria, Dora slowly stood, stepped down from the witness chair, and mouthed to her sister, "Please."

Allen forcefully turned his wife's face toward him to prevent her from looking at Dora.

The jury had sat riveted during the cross-examination of Dora and the ensuing chaos. Some appeared uncomfortable with Sheffield's aggressive questioning. In contrast, other jurors were beginning to question if the young girl had been the one to shoot her father, just as Sheffield had hoped.

But now, all eyes were on Maria.

Chapter 27
Monday, June 29, 1886

The Sheffields sent their private carriage to the Commercial Street Wharf to meet the steamboat that carried Dr. David Hayes Agnew and his University of Pennsylvania Medical School colleague to Newport. Following a long day of travel, the physicians arrived at the Sheffields' Washington Square mansion for a welcoming late-night dinner.

After enjoying aperitifs in the library, a servant ushered them inside the elegantly appointed dining room. At the head of the table, the senator raised his glass in a toast.

"Dr. Agnew, it is a pleasure and a privilege to welcome you and your esteemed colleague to Newport."

"Thank you, senator, though I am hopeful the next occasion will be to attend one of Newport's famed social events as opposed to testifying in a trial," the physician responded, bringing his hosts to laughter.

Although the senator and Dr. Agnew moved in some of the same social circles, it was Agnew's expertise as well as his prominence in the medical community that had prompted the senior Sheffield to pursue the physician as an expert witness.

Senator Sheffield signaled for his servant to commence the dinner service. The wine glasses were filled as the first course of raw oysters was placed on the table.

"I hope you don't mind if we mix business with pleasure," the younger Sheffield interjected, "but we should discuss your testimony."

"Of course," Agnew nodded, wiping the liquid from an oyster off his white walrus mustache with a crisp linen napkin. "What can you tell me about the prosecution's medical experts? Anything newly revealed on that front?"

Over the soup course, Senator Sheffield summarized what they expected to hear from Dr. Parker and the four Boston physicians' testimony.

Dr. Agnew looked at his colleague. "It sounds as if their opinions will rely heavily on the fall between the first and second shot, do you agree?"

"I do," he nodded, adding, "As well as the food found in the mouth of the victim."

The senator confirmed their assessments before commenting, "I must say that I was surprised by Attorney Galvin's decision to present the testimony of five physicians. In my opinion, he risks the jury becoming overwhelmed or bored by so much repetitive medical testimony."

Dr. Agnew inquired, "You did not mention it, so I assume their experts will not cite any case studies to support their arguments. Rather, it sounds as if they will discredit the possibility of suicide solely based on their knowledge and experience as physicians."

"Yes, that is what we believe. We are confident your testimony alone will be very powerful," the senator asserted before turning to his other guest. "Yet it will be beneficial to have another highly esteemed expert to validate your opinion."

Agnew's colleague agreed. "I think that the case studies we have discovered, which are very similar to your case, will leave no doubt in the minds of the jurors that a person can shoot himself again after inflicting a first shot to the head."

The younger Sheffield could barely contain his enthusiasm.

"We have also put together a solid case proving that the Dorseys had no reason to murder Mr. Burton. The state's money motive will not withstand the evidence that we have collected showing Allen Dorsey was not in need of money and had many avenues available for him to obtain funds."

"I believe the number of character witnesses who have already arrived in Newport may occupy an entire day of testimony alone,"

Senator Sheffield boasted.

He was proud of his son's work in convincing former employers, instructors, and peers to come to Newport to testify on Dorsey's behalf.

"We also have several witnesses scheduled to testify as to Burton's growing indebtedness and gambling habit," his son added.

The senator frowned at his son's mention of gambling. The witnesses he had convinced to testify were unsavory characters who could only testify to seeing Burton out late at night yet could not attest to seeing him playing cards or throwing dice. He had disagreed with his son's decision to present these witnesses.

The doctors sat quietly for a few minutes, digesting the Sheffields' assessment of their case before Agnew asked pointedly, "Colonel, are you at all concerned about the younger sister's confession implicating the Dorseys?"

Sheffield smiled confidently before responding.

"The girl testified today, and I believe that my cross-examination convinced the jury that she is either lying or responsible for her father's death."

He failed to mention the chaos that erupted during her testimony to the physician. The elder Sheffield, who had been uncomfortable with his son's aggressive questioning of Dora and was concerned over the young girl's pleas to her sister, remained silent.

"Well, senator, it sounds like you are living up to your reputation as one of the country's leading litigators. You and your son have built a defense certain to result in an acquittal," Agnew said as he eyed the platter of sea bass smothered with hollandaise sauce that had just been brought to the table.

***

Tuesday, June 30, 1886

Mrs. Easton approached Maria's cell and found her sitting on her cot, still in her nightdress, with an untouched breakfast tray by her side.

Alarmed, she remarked, "Mrs. Dorsey, are you ill?"

Maria stared blankly at her infant son as he slept soundly on a pallet at her feet.

She could not imagine the emotional torment Maria must be

enduring. Her husband had described to her Sheffield's brutal cross-examination of Dora, followed by Maria's fainting spell. Still, Mrs. Easton was under strict orders not to discuss the details of the trial with either Maria or Dora.

She unlocked the cell door and joined Maria inside. Taking a seat next to Maria on the cot, she tenderly reminded her that it was time to get dressed as she was due to be in court in just a few hours.

"Could I see my sister before we go?" Maria asked softly.

The heart-wrenching appeal touched Mrs. Easton. The sisters had been kept apart since their arrival to ensure they had no contact for the duration of the trial. She had just come from Dora's cell upstairs, where Dora was also begging to see her sister.

"No, Mrs. Dorsey. As I told your sister, we are under strict instructions to keep you two apart … for the time being. Come, let's get you dressed for court," she suggested.

"No, I don't want to go to court. I want to go back to Howard," Maria said with a hitch in her breath.

She lowered her head. "I have prayed to God, as Reverend Van Horne has encouraged me to do. I have prayed to God for an awfully long time."

The mention of Van Horne spurred Mrs. Easton into action.

"Why don't I send for the Reverend?" she suggested. "Would you like to speak with him? Let's get you dressed, and I'll send word."

***

Sheriff Easton greeted Reverend Van Horne at the front entrance to the jail.

"I am sorry to have disturbed you, but Mrs. Dorsey is not in a good state. She is in one of the upper rooms now with the baby and my wife."

This wasn't the first time Mrs. Easton had sent for Rev. Van Horne. He had visited Maria regularly at the Newport jail as well as the prison in Howard, so there was little reason for him to suspect anything out of the ordinary.

The sheriff guided him up the stairway to the room where Maria and his wife sat side-by-side on a small sofa.

Mrs. Easton rose from her seat.

"I will leave the two of you in peace. If you require my assistance, I will be in my quarters."

She averted her eyes as she passed Van Horne, which did not go unnoticed by him. This unusual behavior, combined with her quick exit, forewarned the pastor that this visit might not be entirely spiritual in nature.

Maria looked up at Van Horne, her eyes red-rimmed and moist with tears. He stepped forward and lowered himself to his knees in front of her.

"Shall we pray, Maria?" he asked gently.

"Yes," Maria whispered, offering her hands to the Reverend.

He offered a prayer, asking God for guidance and wisdom in Maria's hour of need. When the prayer ended, he released her hands and steadied himself as he rose. He sat on the sofa beside Maria and patiently waited for her to speak.

"I am so weary," she said, breaking the silence. "I don't think I can bear another day of sitting in the courtroom."

Van Horne nodded in understanding. He wasn't sure he could bear it himself.

Maria stared down at her infant son sleeping at her feet.

"Can you take me back to Howard?" she pleaded. "I want to go now."

Van Horne was confused. *Did Maria not understand she could be acquitted of the charges and going back to the prison in Howard was not a certainty?*

"Do you not expect to be cleared of these charges?"

Maria shook her head sadly, "No."

She turned to face Van Horne.

"Father was truly kind to me. I will never be able to atone for my role in his death. I deserve to go back to the prison and remain there for the remainder of my natural life."

"Maria, what are you saying?" Van Horne asked, his eyes pleading.

"God is guiding me now, Reverend, showing me the way. Everything I did, I did for my husband. I wanted to protect him, to shield him. But I know now there is no other path forward."

Van Horne slowly reached for Maria's hand.

"Then you must tell the truth. God directs us to tell the truth."

She nodded in understanding. "I want to see Mr. Galvin. It is time I confess."

"Would it not be better to speak to Senator Sheffield? He should be advised of your intentions."

Maria pulled back her hand. "No, Reverend. I do not want to see him. I fear he will try to talk me out of what I must do."

Van Horne rose from the sofa.

"I will send for Mr. Galvin and Senator Sheffield so you might speak with them both."

***

Senator Sheffield arrived at the jail before Attorney Galvin.

"Where is she?" he demanded as he slammed the door behind him. "What has happened here?"

Sheriff Easton pointed to the staircase, "She is in the upper room to the right. Reverend Van Horne is with her."

Senator Sheffield hurried up the stairs with the ease of a much younger man. Van Horne was waiting at the door to the room.

"Would you like me to join you?"

"No, thank you, Reverend. I want to speak with my client alone," he said as he entered the room and closed the door behind him.

Galvin arrived at the jail a short time later. Van Horne greeted him downstairs in the reception area.

"Senator Sheffield is upstairs speaking with Maria now," he informed him. "She told me she wants to confess."

Galvin took a deep breath to calm his nerves. He long hoped that Maria would relent, but he blamed Allen's domination for preventing her from doing so.

Still, he had to wonder … *If she truly intends to confess, why now? Was it Dora's heartfelt plea from the witness stand that had finally weakened her resolve?*

"The senator may convince her otherwise," Galvin speculated.

Van Horne shook his head, "I don't think so. She seems quite determined to clear her conscience."

To Galvin's surprise, when Senator Sheffield appeared back downstairs, he offered no objection to Galvin's presence. Instead, he merely mumbled, "We will speak later," as he walked briskly past the men and out the jailhouse door.

Van Horne accompanied Galvin to the upper room. Maria was still seated on the sofa where Van Horne had left her. She appeared exhausted but alert. Galvin pulled a chair from the opposite side of the room and, careful not to disturb the baby, placed it a few feet in front of Maria. He opened his valise and removed his notebook and pen while Van Horne took a seat beside her.

"Mr. Galvin," Maria began in a strong and confident voice, "I am ready to tell you everything."

She looked to the Reverend. "I promised Reverend Van Horne that I would tell the whole truth, and I aim to do so."

"Shall we start at the beginning?" Galvin suggested as he positioned the notebook on his lap and removed the cap to his fountain pen.

"Tell me what happened."

***

After recording Maria's statement, Galvin was eager to meet Richards at the courthouse to share the news of Maria's eleventh-hour confession. They debated how it could potentially play out in the courtroom. Both agreed that a meeting with the Sheffields before the trial continued was in order.

Galvin sat alone in a small, secluded meeting room adjoining the courtroom while Richards remained in the hall awaiting the Sheffields' arrival. Within a few minutes, the father and son appeared.

Senator Sheffield's face bore an expression of stoic resignation, while his son's countenance was one of determination. Richards directed them to the room where Galvin was waiting.

"Thank you for agreeing to meet with me before the trial resumes," Galvin began.

"As you must be aware, Mrs. Dorsey has made a full and voluntary confession implicating both herself and Allen Dorsey in the murder of her father."

He handed a document to Senator Sheffield.

"This is her signed statement for you to review. In light of her confession, I must ask if you will be changing your clients' pleas to guilty?"

The senator took charge.

"When I spoke with Mrs. Dorsey, I found her to be in a highly emotional and unstable state of mind. I am concerned that she may not have been able to comprehend the ramifications of her statements."

"Yes, first we need to determine if Mrs. Dorsey wishes to recant anything she has said," the younger Sheffield added tersely. "Certainly, it is premature to suggest that her statement changes our belief in the innocence of our clients. As you know, under Rhode Island law, Mrs. Dorsey cannot testify against her husband, and we will forcefully assert his privilege to prevent her from making any incriminating statements against him if necessary."

With that, the men abruptly left the room.

Richards, who was waiting to hear the outcome of the meeting, joined Galvin.

"The senator appears embarrassed by the situation," the detective observed. "Not that I can blame him. I can only imagine what he is saying to his son in private. He can't be happy about being associated with this case now that it is dramatically falling apart after only the first day of trial."

"They are just trying to protect their clients' interests," Galvin remarked. "Despite their bravado, I am hopeful they will no longer proceed with presenting a defense and accept that their clients are probably guilty."

"It didn't look to me like Colonel Sheffield was ready to give up the fight," Richards remarked.

Galvin reasoned, "Maybe his father more fully understands that Mrs. Dorsey has not only pulled the rug out from under their defense but has potentially damaged his son's reputation as well."

Chapter 28
Wednesday, June 30, 1886
The Second Day of the Trial

His jaw clenched, Senator Sheffield sat stewing at the defense table. His son, whose flushed cheeks and sweaty brow betrayed his internal torment, sat morosely between him and Allen Dorsey.

Casually cleaning under his fingernails with a tightly folded piece of paper, Allen sat a noticeable distance away from, and with his back to, Maria. Baby Eugene was nowhere to be seen.

The justices entered the courtroom, and the bailiff called, "All rise."

When the spectators were ordered to take their seats, Senator Sheffield remained standing. The chief justice acknowledged the senator.

"Is there something you wish to say to the court?"

"If it pleases the court," the senator began, "Something has occurred which has removed the cause that led me to enter the case. Therefore, I wish to withdraw from these proceedings."

Cries rang out in the courtroom. The chief justice pounded his gavel, calling the court to order. Once the gallery had quieted, the judge spoke.

"Senator, you are excused."

He placed his bowler on his head, patted his son on his shoulder, and made his way down the long center aisle of the courtroom to the exit. Several reporters leaped from their seats and rushed out of the courtroom, their shouted questions to the senator echoing through the corridors as they followed him out of the building.

The chief justice addressed the court.

"Is there any other business before we proceed?"

"No, your honor," Galvin replied, with Sheffield concurring.

"Very well," he said. "The state may proceed with their case."

Galvin stepped forward and announced the state was calling Reverend Mahlon Van Horne to the stand.

Sheffield shifted forward in his seat, ready to pounce. Van Horne was originally scheduled to testify for the defense concerning his observations of Ben's despondency and to vouch for Allen's good character.

After he was sworn in, Galvin stepped forward to begin his questioning.

"Reverend Van Horne, have you had any conversations with Mr. or Mrs. Dorsey this morning?"

Taking his cue, Sheffield rose quickly from his chair.

"Objection!" he shouted. "The defense objects to the inclusion of testimony regarding any conversation the Reverend may have had with Mrs. Dorsey that might incriminate her husband and in which Mr. Dorsey was not a part."

The chief justice turned his attention to Galvin, awaiting his response.

"Your honor," Galvin explained, "this witness received a full and voluntary confession from Mrs. Dorsey. There can certainly be no objection to this witness testifying to the contents of that interview."

"The objection is overruled. Proceed, Mr. Galvin."

Sheffield interrupted, calling out, "Your honor, I wish to announce to Mrs. Dorsey that I am withdrawing as her counsel. I represent Mr. Dorsey alone."

Galvin had just opened his mouth to speak when the judge responded gruffly.

"The withdrawal of counsel in the middle of a murder trial is unprecedented, counselor."

"Mrs. Dorsey indicated to me before court convened this

morning that she does not wish for counsel," Sheffield argued, "Of course, I will continue to represent her if she has changed her mind."

The chief justice turned to Maria and stated firmly, "Mrs. Dorsey, you should not go unrepresented."

Maria sat at the defense table, unmoved.

The judge scanned the gallery before spotting a familiar face.

"Perhaps Attorney Ives, who I see is present at the bar, could act as counsel for Mrs. Dorsey?"

Ives rose from his seat.

"We will adjourn to allow Mr. Ives time to consult with Mrs. Dorsey. Attorney Sheffield, I suggest you join them."

Sheffield and Maria rose from the defense table to join Attorney Ives in an adjoining room. When the parties returned to the courtroom, Ives announced to the court he would represent Maria.

Sheffield made one last ditch effort to salvage what was left of the case he spent months building in defense of his client … and perhaps the future of his legal career.

"Your honor, I move that my client be separated from Mrs. Dorsey and be tried individually at his own proceeding."

Still on his feet, Galvin objected. "The defendants stand together and should be tried together."

"I concur. Your motion, Mr. Sheffield, is denied."

Sheffield slowly lowered himself into his chair, his face flushed with exasperation. Despite being cruelly betrayed by his clients, he had done all he could for Allen Dorsey.

***

After the brief interruption to sort out Maria's counsel, Reverend Van Horne was recalled to the stand. He proceeded to detail Maria's mood during their meeting and her insistence on confessing to her role in her father's murder. He concluded by describing her request that Galvin be brought to the jail to hear her confession.

"Outside of asking Mrs. Dorsey why she chose to take the course she did, I did not ask specific questions about the murder," Van Horne stated. "I prayed with her and recommended she speak to Senator Sheffield before speaking to you, Mr. Galvin."

"Can you tell the court what Mrs. Dorsey said?"

Van Horne methodically laid out the events leading to Ben's murder, as Maria described during her confession. He reported Maria also revealed she had knowledge of, and had given her consent to, Allen Dorsey shooting her father. He testified Maria told him that the murder was in revenge for her father's refusal to provide them with money and for ordering them out of the house.

Galvin then showed him a copy of Maria's signed confession.

"Did you witness Mrs. Dorsey sign this document and my notarization of it?"

Van Horne held the document in his hand and examined it.

"Yes, this is the confession you recorded as she dictated it."

Sheffield rose from his chair.

"The defense objects to anything in that document that implicates her husband in any crime. She cannot testify against her husband. On behalf of my client, I am again asserting his privilege."

"The jury will be advised with regard to spousal immunity when the instructions are given," the judge responded.

Galvin then gave the document to the court clerk so it might be entered into evidence.

"Thank you, Reverend. I have no further questions.

"You honor, the state rests," said Galvin as he slowly walked back to the prosecution's table and took his seat.

"Attorney Sheffield, do you have any questions for the witness?"

"No," responded Sheffield flatly.

"Attorney Ives, do you have any questions for the witness?"

"No, your honor. Not at this time."

The chief justice turned his attention to Sheffield.

"Do you have an opening statement to make before presenting your case?"

Sheffield slowly stood and replied resignedly, "Your honor, the defense rests."

The judge then turned his attention to Attorney Ives and asked if he had an opening statement.

Ives rose from his chair.

"Yes, your honor, I would like to address the jury. I will also be calling Mrs. Dorsey to testify that her role in the murder was the direct result of coercion by her husband."

Ives took his place before the jury box and delivered a brief statement.

"Mrs. Dorsey will testify about the events of October 6, 1885, and the circumstances surrounding her participation in them. I ask you to give her testimony due weight. It will be up to you to decide if she was acting under the direction of her husband or if she was acting of her own free will. If you find that Mrs. Dorsey was acting under coercion by her husband, I will ask you to find her not guilty."

Ives stepped away from the jury box and called Maria Dorsey to the stand.

She began her testimony by stating she and Allen were married on June 17 of the previous year, and they were married for four months at the time of her father's death.

"Mrs. Dorsey, did you ever hear your husband say he was going to kill your father?"

"No, my husband said he would 'fix' my father. He never used the word kill."

"Did your husband give you any directives on the morning of your father's death?"

"Yes, on the morning of the murder, my husband told me to go to Mrs. Traeger's to keep her from hearing the shots. I went to the Traegers because he told me to go. I went according to his direction," she added.

"Mrs. Dorsey, does your husband have a temper?"

Maria hesitated before responding. "He was quite provoked at not getting the money Father promised us and was violent with me on one occasion."

"What happened then?" Ives probed.

"It was in late September, when I had been unable to raise enough money for him to return to school. He was desperate. I thought he was going mad.

"All summer, he was obsessed with getting money. It's all he talked about. I tried to raise money in every way. I begged and borrowed from our friends and family. I could not ask for more because I had not repaid anyone what I had already borrowed. I was at a complete loss as to where I could get more money, and time was running out."

"What do you mean by 'time was running out'?"

"The semester started on the first day of October, and my husband was adamant that he would be in attendance on that day. He said if I didn't raise the money before then, he would divorce me."

"Go on."

"On the night he struck me, he claimed he had been duped into marrying me. He said I had misled him about our financial future and broken all of my promises of living a comfortable life. He said it had been a terrible mistake to marry me."

Allen furiously scribbled a note and pushed it toward Sheffield. The attorney ignored it and kept his attention on Maria.

Assuming that Sheffield hadn't seen the paper, Allen shuffled it back and forth across the table to get the attorney's attention. Sheffield silently pushed it back toward Allen.

Undeterred, Allen leaned in to whisper to Sheffield, who raised his hand and turned his head away.

Meanwhile, Maria continued her description of Allen's violence towards her.

"He was in a rage and slapped me across my face, knocking me to the floor. I was afraid he was going to kill me. At that moment, I told him I knew where we could get the money. That I had seen a large life insurance policy in my father's office."

"Did you intend for your husband to kill your father for the life insurance settlement?"

"No, I did not. I thought I would go to my father in the morning and beg him one last time for money. I was certain he would relent and give us enough money so we could leave for Philadelphia. I did not willfully take any part in the killing of my father. As I shall have to answer for it hereafter, I never did."

"No more questions," Ives said, returning to his chair.

"Attorney Galvin, do you have any questions for the witness?"

"Yes, your honor," Galvin responded as he rose and approached the witness chair.

He smiled politely. "Good afternoon, Mrs. Dorsey."

Maria smiled shyly in return. "Good afternoon to you as well, Mr. Galvin."

"You heard Reverend Van Horne's testimony earlier today," Galvin began.

"Yes, sir, I did."

"Do you agree with everything the Reverend had to say during his testimony?"

"Yes," she nodded. "His statements were correct."

Galvin walked over to the clerk's desk and lifted the confession, holding it in his hand.

"I show you this statement that contains your signature. Do you acknowledge that this is the written statement of the confession you dictated to me?"

"Yes, Mr. Galvin."

"Thank you, Mrs. Dorsey," he said as he returned the document to the court clerk.

"Now, I would like to ask you a few questions concerning the testimony you just gave regarding your willingness to participate in your father's murder. Did you object when Mr. Dorsey told you he would 'fix' your father?"

"Yes, I did, but he called me chicken-hearted."

"You have testified that you told your husband about your father's lucrative life insurance policy. That doesn't sound like you objected to your husband 'fixing' your father, does it?"

"I only told him that because I wanted to buy myself more time. As I stated, I thought if I went to my father once more and begged him, he would give us some portion of the money he had promised.

"But on the Tuesday night before my father's death, my father made it clear that he would not be giving us a penny and wanted us out of the house. I knew then that there was no hope. Allen was infuriated when I told him we had to leave and there would be no money."

"When your husband told you to go to Mrs. Traeger's house, what was the first room you entered when you arrived in her tenement?"

"Her kitchen."

"Did your husband instruct you to take Mrs. Traeger to the farthest room away from your father's kitchen?"

"No, it was my habit to go into that room."

"So, it was of your own free will?"

"Yes," Maria nodded.

"Was it by your own free will that you closed three doors behind you as you led Mrs. Traeger to the front bedroom?"

"I don't recall closing the doors."

"Did you speak with your father after you learned that Mr. Dorsey planned to kill him?" Galvin asked.

"I don't recall, Mr. Galvin. I must have."

"Did you ever make any effort to tell your father what your

husband was planning?"

"No, Mr. Galvin, I did not. As I have stated, I did not think my husband would kill my father. I did not. My father was a powerful man. I did not think my husband would dare harm my father."

"Did you lie to protect your husband after your father's death, Mrs. Dorsey?"

Maria bowed her head.

"Yes, I am ashamed that I did. But I did it because I was afraid of my husband."

"Is it your testimony that your fear of your husband was greater than your love for your father?"

"No. I loved my father. As I stated, I did not think my husband was serious about killing my father. I thought he just said these things in anger."

Galvin let Maria's words hang in the air for effect before announcing, "No further questions."

"Mr. Sheffield, do you have any questions for the witness?"

"No, your honor."

"Mrs. Dorsey, you are dismissed," said the judge.

Attorney Ives stood and announced, "The defense rests."

***

"Colonel Sheffield, now that all parties have rested, do you wish to give a closing statement?"

Sheffield rose from his chair without looking at Allen.

"I will leave the case to the jury without argument."

"Very well, then," the chief justice responded, turning his attention to Attorney Ives. "Counselor, would you like to make a closing statement on behalf of your client?"

Ives stood to address the court.

"Yes, your honor. Gentlemen of the jury, Mrs. Dorsey's testimony today is straightforward, though it incriminates her. She denies nothing but her intent. Her body moved in obedience at the direction of her husband, but her soul is innocent."

Ives paused to study the faces of the jurors. His client's fate rested in the hands of these men. He needed to convince them that Maria acted under the coercion of her husband.

"The question you must decide," he advised the jurors, "is whether Mrs. Dorsey willfully and intentionally aided in her father's murder. This she denies and presents her innocence before God and man. As you deliberate her fate, I would ask you to consider the words of Solomon as they are written in Proverbs, chapter 28, verse 18: *He that covereth his sins shall not prosper, but who shall confesseth and forsaketh shall have mercy.*"

Ives bowed his head solemnly before turning and walking back to his seat. He had done all he could do.

The chief justice addressed the prosecution, "Attorney Galvin, do you wish to make a closing statement?"

"Yes, your honor," he replied before striding purposefully toward the jury box. He began in a measured tone.

"Benjamin J. Burton's fate was sealed on the 17th day of June, when Allen Dorsey married his daughter, Maria.

"Mr. Dorsey assumed his financial future would be secure from the marriage. That there was no need for him to work and his days as a bellman were now behind him. He fancied himself a physician, a gentleman much too educated to work a menial job.

"Conversely, Ben Burton was a man who labored his entire life and believed in the value of hard work. He was offended by Mr. Dorsey's unwillingness to earn money to support his daughter or pay for his schooling.

"While it is true Mr. Burton had promised the couple a generous amount of money at the time of their marriage, he rescinded the offer after weeks of watching Mr. Dorsey freeloading and lounging about his home at his expense. When Mr. Burton finally reached his wit's end, he ordered the Dorseys out of his house.

"The motive for his killing was simple … money. Allen Dorsey could not return to medical school because he did not have the means to pay. By October, he had become obsessed to the point of madness, believing that Ben Burton was deliberately preventing him from fulfilling his dream of becoming a surgeon."

Galvin turned and looked at Maria.

"Instead of honoring her father, Mrs. Dorsey offered him up for sacrifice. Like a lamb, she led him to the slaughter."

Maria sat numbly, staring at the floor.

"It was Maria Dorsey who, in desperation, disclosed to her

husband that her father had a large life insurance policy that would enable Mr. Dorsey to pay the remainder of his medical school expenses."

He gestured toward the defense table.

"Counsel for Mrs. Dorsey admits the state has proved its case against her. The state had no reason to anticipate any admission of guilt by Mrs. Dorsey. However, this morning, she saw fit to make a confession to her spiritual advisor. In so far as it is lawful testimony, it must be weighed.

"However, she claims her husband forced her to participate in this murder scheme. Under the law, indisputable coercion by her husband would warrant the finding of innocence for his wife. But if she was acting only on her husband's order, she is guilty of aiding and abetting in the murder of her father.

"Mrs. Dorsey readily admits nothing prevented her from telling her father, the police—or anyone else for that matter—about her husband's intent. She was not being held captive under lock and key. And yet, she told no one and instead took additional steps to cover up the crime.

"On the morning of October 6, Allen Dorsey assumed the role of puppet master ... and Mrs. Dorsey and Miss Burton became his marionettes. As the curtain rose, he began pulling their strings, sending Mrs. Dorsey to the Traeger house and stationing Dora at the window to act as the lookout. Once his puppets were in position, he was ready for the final act and headed to the kitchen with a gun in hand."
Galvin turned back to face the jury box.

"Mrs. Dorsey did not see her husband commit this crime, but Miss Dora Burton was there. She saw Mr. Dorsey—with a pistol in his hand—enter the kitchen where her father sat eating his breakfast. She heard the shots and smelled the gunpowder. Miss Burton witnessed him exiting the kitchen and heard him say, *'I've done it.'*

"I am not surprised the young woman confessed. She loved her father a great deal and has visibly suffered unimaginable guilt over her role in his death.

"My only surprise is that Dora Burton was permitted to live after the crime was committed. She was Allen Dorsey's weak link. It was Miss Burton who not only confessed to her role in the murder plot but begged her sister to unburden her conscience as well.

"If Miss Burton had remained silent, it is very possible that Mr.

and Mrs. Dorsey would have gotten away with the murder, and Ben Burton would have been buried with the word *SUICIDE* carved on his tombstone."

Galvin turned and pointed at Allen, who coldly stared down the attorney.

"Mr. Dorsey believes himself to be too shrewd for the state. It's true that he may be the smartest man in the room, but the brilliant medical student made two critical missteps. His impulsive decision to fire the second shot was his first mistake. He likely would have gotten away with murder had he just waited for Mr. Burton to die from the first shot.

"But his second and most fatal mistake was underestimating Dora Burton's love for her father."

The attorney met Allen's gaze, searching to see if his words had their intended effect. But Allen's cool and calculated demeanor remained unflinching. Galvin shook his head in disgust and spoke with a growing fervor.

"Gentlemen, this was a murder committed with malice and premeditation by the hands of an evil man who has no remorse. The only possible defense that could be expected was that Burton committed suicide, but Mr. Dorsey's attorney does not even raise it. The state has proved he has committed murder beyond the slightest doubt."

Galvin then drew his argument to a close.

"The state asks you to find Maria Dorsey guilty of aiding and abetting the murder of Benjamin J. Burton and to find Allen Dorsey guilty of his murder."

The chief justice waited until Galvin returned to his seat before announcing, "The court will recess for fifteen minutes."

***

Despite the late hour, no one left their seats in the gallery. Nine long months had passed since Ben Burton's death, and the whole of Newport was ready to put the case—and the Dorseys—behind them. At seven thirty, the chief justice began reading the charge to the jury.

"The charge by the government in regard to Mr. Dorsey is that of murder. The state must prove this beyond a reasonable doubt. Mrs. Dorsey's confession cannot be taken as evidence against her husband. A wife cannot be compelled to testify against her husband.

"With regard to Mrs. Dorsey, the charge is aiding and abetting the commission of the murder. She either knew what her husband was going to do or assisted her husband. However, the jury must consider the question of coercion as a defense."

The remainder of the charge filled the hour. When the chief justice was done, he dismissed the jury to begin deliberations. Most of the people in the courtroom expected a quick verdict.

When the jury had been out for over an hour, they sent the clerk back to the courtroom with a written message for the justices.

Is Mrs. Dorsey guilty
if she acted under the natural influence of her husband?

"Yes," the chief justice responded after hearing the clerk read the question aloud.

The clerk recorded the answer and returned to the deliberation room with the response.

Allen Dorsey sat quietly reading a New York City newspaper account of the trial, while Maria sat in a trance-like state, staring blankly into space.

Most of the spectators remained in the courtroom. Many of them were women whose constant chatter resembled the buzz of a sewing circle. Sheffield and Galvin chatted with some of the men, who praised each attorney for their respective efforts in the trial. Shortly before midnight, the jury returned.

"Have you reached a verdict with regard to both defendants?" asked the clerk.

"We have," the jurymen responded collectively.

The judge asked Allen Dorsey to rise to hear the verdict.

"In regard to the charge of murder, what is your verdict for Allen Dorsey?"

The foreman rose and announced in a firm voice, "Guilty."

The judge then asked Maria to rise and face the jury.

The clerk continued, "What is your verdict with regard to Maria Burton Dorsey?"

"Guilty," the foreman replied before quickly adding, "But with mercy."

Neither Allen nor Maria showed any visible emotion as their

verdicts were announced.

Galvin rose and made a motion for immediate sentencing.

The chief justice asked, "Do either of the defendants have anything to say about why sentencing should not be imposed?"

Allen replied first. "No, sir."

"No," Maria responded, adding, "I am guilty and willing to abide by the consequences."

"I hereby sentence you both to imprisonment, confined to hard labor, for the duration of your natural life from and after the first day of July 1886. Court is now adjourned."

As the crowd began to disperse, Galvin watched as Allen and Maria were placed in handcuffs and led out of the courtroom. He then turned and looked at Richards, who nodded solemnly. Galvin began to walk toward Sheffield to shake his hand, but the attorney quickly gathered his belongings and exited the courtroom without acknowledging his friend and colleague.

As Galvin and Richards made their way out of the courtroom, Emily Burton was waiting for them in the doorway.

"Turns out I was right from the start, Mr. Galvin. You are a very smart young man who believes in pursuing justice for all."

Chapter 29
Thursday, July 1, 1886

*"The Burton murder will go into history
as one of the most remarkable cases in the history of the city."*
The *Newport Daily News*, July 1, 1886

Allen sat on his cot in his cell, patiently waiting for his breakfast tray
to be delivered. When he spotted Mrs. Easton approaching, carefully
balancing the tray with both hands, Dorsey stood to greet her.

"Good morning," Allen called out. "I see that my looking glass
has been removed from my cell. I suppose you thought I would shatter it
and slit my wrists?"

She was caught off guard by the question and stopped mid-stride
just before she reached the cell door.

"Well, we thought it best …" she began before being interrupted
by Allen.

"I assure you that I shall never do anything of the kind," he
remarked, looking Mrs. Easton directly in the eyes.

"If I so desired, even now, it would be easy to smash the soap dish
or strip my blanket and hang myself," he said, smugly pointing out the

futility of her actions.

An uneasy silence followed as the jailer moved to unlock the door. Mrs. Easton wondered if she should hand Allen the tray and quickly retreat, but Allen continued to engage her.

"Well, it is true," he said matter-of-factly as the jailer pulled open the door. "I am guilty. It is as the girls reported."

"Oh?" she replied, unsure how to respond to Allen's spontaneous confession.

He took the tray from her hands.

"Don't worry, Mrs. Easton," he chuckled as he sat on the cot and placed the tray on his lap. "I am not the monster the press has portrayed me to be."

She stood frozen in the entrance to the cell as Dorsey continued.

"Though they were wrong about my motive. I didn't do it for money."

"No? Then why?" Mrs. Easton asked softly. "Why did you do it, Mr. Dorsey?"

Dorsey stabbed his fork into one of the sausages on his tray.

"That, Mrs. Easton, is something I shall never tell. The motive shall go with me to my grave."

Allen brought the fork to his mouth and bit off the end of the sausage, slowly savoring the bite before swallowing.

"Rest assured, Mrs. Easton," he said calmly, wiping the grease from his chin with the back of his hand, "I have suffered the torture of the damned ever since the act."

"Would you like for me to send for Reverend Van Horne?" she offered awkwardly, not knowing how else to respond.

Allen shook his head and reached for a piece of toast.

"No, I shall make no regular confession to Mr. Van Horne or any other man of the cloth. I am ready to abide by the consequences, and my atonement will be made as best I can, direct with my God."

Spooning jam onto the toast, Allen continued.

"I was within one year of a happy, brilliant future, but my one wicked, bad act crushed it all. My intellect, ability, and accomplishments will now be buried alive in the state prison," he concluded as he lifted the toast to his mouth and took a large bite.

Mrs. Easton slowly backed out of the cell while Allen continued eating breakfast, paying her no further attention. She motioned wordlessly to the jailer to come back and lock the door. When the lock clicked shut, she turned and ran to find her husband.

***

Saturday, July 3, 1886

Sheriff Easton and the city marshal were tasked with accompanying the three persons convicted of Ben's murder to prison. The city marshal assigned Captain Hammond and two veteran officers from the Newport police force to assist with the transport.

As the trio waited to be loaded into the carriage that would take them away, Mrs. Easton kissed Baby Eugene's forehead. She bid the baby and Maria a tearful goodbye before turning to give Dora a quick embrace. She gently reminded her husband that the photographer stood ready to photograph Allen and the sisters for their prison records.

When they arrived at the photographer's storefront on Thames Street, Maria and Dora eagerly disembarked from the carriage. Excited at the prospect of having their pictures taken, the girls chatted spiritedly while they waited, practicing the smiles they would share with the camera while they styled each other's hair.

Sheriff Easton watched wistfully from across the room, nostalgic for the days not so long ago when the Burton sisters were a constant fixture in the community. He remembered the girls smiling and laughing as they strolled the city streets arm-in-arm, joyfully greeting friends and strangers alike.

Maria and Dora were both so pleased with the negatives of their portraits that they requested additional copies be made and sent to them at the prison.

Allen voiced his displeasure to Sheriff Easton throughout the operation. When the time came for his picture to be taken, his eyes were squeezed shut, and his cheeks were wet with tears. As a result, his image was poor. He did not request additional copies.

The sidewheel steamer stood docked at the wharf, ready for the trip to Providence. A gathering of citizens, much smaller than those who attended any of the previous public events surrounding the Dorseys, awaited the departure of the prisoners.

The sun shone brightly as Sheriff Easton and the marshal led the group up the gangway. Allen was in leg irons and handcuffs, followed by Maria, cradling Baby Eugene in her arms. Dora was right behind, both women still wearing happy smiles.

Once the prisoners were seated in chairs on the outside deck, Maria and Dora talked incessantly, taking turns holding the baby and bouncing him on their knees. Allen sat not far from the sisters, with Hammond at his side, and showed no interest in his wife or baby.

Standing silently alone at a distance removed from the crowd, Patrick J. Galvin unobtrusively watched the scene unfold. As the steamer began to pull away from the dock, he felt a soft tap on his shoulder. He turned to discover Detective Richards standing beside him with a broad, satisfied smile.

"Well done, my friend. Well done."

"The Dorsey case is over now; let us have peace."
The *Newport Daily News*, July 2, 1886

Chapter 30
March 31, 1888
The Women's State Prison
Howard, Rhode Island

"Mrs. Dorsey, wake up … the newspaper reporter will be here soon."

Maria rolled over in bed to face the matron.

"Why is he coming here?" she asked in a weak and unsteady voice.

"Don't you remember, Mrs. Dorsey?" the matron prompted as she lifted Maria's head from the pillow to give her a sip of water. "He said he wants to ask you about your father, and you agreed to meet with him. But I can send him away if you've changed your mind."

She slowly unfastened Maria's nightgown, carefully sliding it out from underneath her emaciated frame before lowering a clean dress over her head. After gently pulling her arms through the sleeves, the matron lifted and propped Maria into a semi-sitting position, steadying her by stacking pillows behind her back. When she was done, she tucked the quilt under her legs and brushed Maria's thinning hair away from her face, fixing it into a small bun at the nape of her neck.

"There now, you are ready for the day," she said, stepping back to admire her work.

Maria managed a meek smile of gratitude for the matron, who had become her most trusted friend since her arrival at Howard more than two years earlier.

It was the matron who had initially encouraged Maria to unburden her mind and tell the truth about her role in her father's death. She had attended to Maria during the birth of Baby Eugene and had consoled her when the child was taken away and adopted by a Newport couple.

And it was the matron who had faithfully remained by her side during the dark days of overwhelming grief that consumed Maria following Dora's death in January of 1887.

When the reporter arrived, the matron pulled two chairs up at Maria's bedside. She sat beside the reporter and assumed a protective role over her charge, warning him to keep the interview short because Maria tired quickly.

"Good morning, Mrs. Dorsey," the reporter began. "Thank you for agreeing to meet with me. I won't take much of your time. I have a few questions about your father … and your husband."

Although Maria was caught off-guard by the comment about her husband, she nodded in agreement, signaling him to proceed with his questions.

"I want to ask you about the secret attached to your father's tragic death that has not yet been made public."

Maria looked at the reporter in confusion, unable to understand.

"There are no secrets," she countered. "I have confessed to everything."

"Yesterday, I met with your husband at his request. Mr. Dorsey wanted to reveal to me his true motive for killing your father."

"The true motive?" Maria stammered. "I'm sure I don't know what he means."

"Mr. Dorsey tells me that three years before you were married …" the reporter paused, lowering his eyes before continuing, "and after your mother's death, you began an intimate relationship with your father."

Maria gasped in horror and tried to bolt up in reaction but could not muster the strength and fell back against the pillows. The matron grabbed her hand in concern.

The reporter continued, "He says he did not become aware of this fact until shortly before your marriage when someone wrote to him about it."

Maria protested as forcefully as she could manage, saying, "As God as my witness, that statement is a lie. I cannot understand how my husband could say such a thing."

Maria began coughing uncontrollably, making it impossible for her to continue speaking.

"Please don't get worked up, Mrs. Dorsey," the matron cautioned as she shot the reporter a withering glance and passed a handkerchief to Maria. "We know that isn't true."

When her hacking eased, Maria continued in a raspy whisper.

"My husband shot my father for his money."

The reporter pressed, "Then why would your husband assert that you engaged in criminal intimacy with your father?"

The matron stepped in and responded on Maria's behalf.

"I will tell you why! Mr. Dorsey paid us an unexpected visit last fall. Mind you, it was the only time since he was incarcerated that he requested permission to see his wife.

"He showed up demanding that Mrs. Dorsey sign a confession he had written up. The statement had her taking all the blame and making a full admission to being the one responsible for her father's death. Of course, Mrs. Dorsey told him that she would never sign such a document. She said she had told the truth at the trial."

"How can he stoop so low?" Maria muttered under her breath, shaking her head morosely.

But how can I disprove his lies? she thought, her mind clouded as she struggled to think of any evidence she could use to refute Allen's claim other than her categorical denial.

She glanced up at the matron, who was patting her hand sympathetically. Suddenly, remembering there might be something, Maria rallied.

"Go fetch that box Mrs. Easton sent me."

The matron left, returned with a small wooden box, and placed it in Maria's lap.

"I have some items my husband left behind in his cell in Newport," Maria explained to the reporter as she carefully held the box. She removed the top and pulled out a handful of letters, slowly sorting through them until she found what she was looking for … a greeting card. She turned it over, and on the back was a note written in pencil.

"This is a communication my husband wrote to his sister the day after we were sentenced."

She passed the unmailed card to the reporter. It was addressed to Alma Dorsey, Tiago, Owego County, New York.

The note began with Allen expressing his desire for his sister to take custody of his son before turning to the topic of Maria.

He admonished his sister, writing that she was not to blame his wife for their situation, saying, *"Maria is what I made her, for when I married her, she was a pure, virtuous, noble-minded woman. I am to blame for all she ever did."*

As the reporter furiously copied down the letter's contents in his notepad, the matron spoke up.

"We are done here. Mrs. Dorsey needs her rest. I will show you out."

The reporter gathered his notes, thanked Maria for the meeting, and followed the matron to the exit, where she stopped and turned to address him.

"Mrs. Dorsey is telling you the truth. Her husband is a cold, calculating, and heartless man. I had hoped he had come to visit her because he was informed that she was dying. I hoped he wanted to make amends or to say goodbye. But Maria was heartbroken when she realized the real reason for her husband's visit.

"As I was walking him out, Mr. Dorsey told me it was downright selfish of his wife not to take the blame for her father's death, given she was likely to die soon. He said he thought that Mrs. Dorsey would want him to be pardoned so he could continue to pursue his dream of becoming a surgeon. We never heard from him again and assumed he had given up on his scheme."

The reporter promised he would visit Mr. Dorsey again before printing a follow-up story sharing Maria's denial.

When the matron returned, she was stunned to find Maria sitting upright in bed. She turned to the matron and spoke with an angry intensity that caught the matron by surprise.

"Father was a just, upright, and good man. Never did he do or say anything in my presence that was improper in any manner. I cannot go to my grave with people believing Allen's scurrilous lies. Bring me a writing box with stationery and a good pen. I have something I need to say."

Epilogue

A copy of the five-page letter Maria Burton Dorsey wrote to Allen Dorsey to refute his accusations of incest, can be found in a moldy, water-damaged book of prisoner correspondence now in the custody of the Rhode Island State Archives.

The *Newport Mercury's* condensed version of Maria's letter was published on the front page of its Saturday, April 14, 1888, edition. Below is a transcript of that article in its entirety.

ALLEN W. DORSEY'S VILLAINY:
His Plan for Obtaining Pardon for Murder—
Attempt to Blacken the Memory of His Dead Victim
and Place the Burden of His Awful Crime
on His Dying Wife—Proofs of His Guilt.

"An alleged interview with Allen W. Dorsey in State Prison, published in the Sunday papers of the first instant, revealed the dastardly plan by which that deepest dyed of villains proposed to work upon the sympathies of a people to the extent of obtaining pardon for the crime of murder. Not content with having taken in cold blood the life of his father-in-law and benefactor, and making his wife and wife's sister equal sharers in his infamy, he would gain his freedom by charging his wife, who is now dying from consumption, with incest with her father and making that appear as the reason for murdering the father.

Fortunately he reveals this plan while his wife yet lives to refute the charge and there are other proofs, even over his own signature, to show the utter falseness of his statements, thus presenting himself in his true criminal character and instead of winning sympathy he will get but the desserts which his double crime merits, so far as the law provides.

Those who knew the late Benj. J. Burton hold his memory in high esteem and any attempt on the part of his murderer to implicate him in a foul crime as a stepping stone to freedom is sure to meet the prompt action so dastardly an act merits.

The interview referred to above was shown to Maria B. Dorsey, who like her unnatural husband is serving a life sentence at the state institutions, and though so enfeebled by consumption as to be expected to die at any moment, she wrote a vigorous denial of the awful charge and sent it to her husband. The following is a verbatim copy of the letter:

Allen Dorsey:

Added to your audacious inhuman crime in which I was your co-partner and influenced victim, you have made a statement about me and my poor murdered father (who cannot now defend himself) that is as false and mean as no one but a person devoid of all principle, as you are, could make, and which even the fiends in torment would shrink from making.

But remember, I still have many friends, and, as you say you have proofs as to what you say, you will before long have a chance to present them.

I am no longer a child, remember, but a woman who, through your evil influence and baseness, has suffered, both mentally and physically, the deepest torture and wrong it is possible for mortal to suffer, and now to add still more to my torture, thinking I am almost dead, and in order to get pardoned, you make this last excuse for the cause of your act in shooting my father, thinking it will have some effect. But I thank God that I am able still to think and talk and have full presence of mind.

I have all your letters, Allen Dorsey, written to me before my marriage; I also have the letter written by you to your sister after we were sentenced, and other things that can prove that what you say is false, and also prove you are entirely unprincipled.

You thought of this as being a good reason,—not being man enough, after you had done the act, to tell the truth and say your object was money, so not daring to name any living person in your statement, you name my father, knowing he could not defend himself, and believing me to be too far gone to dispute it. But you will have a chance to present your proofs, which will be thoroughly examined.

You say you were informed of the facts before we were married— then why did you marry me? Explain that satisfactorily, if you can.

Allen Dorsey, you have not forgotten that, after hearing from another source, you told me of your baseness in relation to a certain party south. I am also in keeping with other facts, which, if told, will injure you more than you ever can me, for all the wrong I ever did is publicly known and half of your baseness is not known.

But I shall now keep nothing, and will present no false letters to prove my statements, but living witnesses.

You have done me too much wrong for me to remain quiet any longer. I am no longer your tool to use as you choose; your power over me is gone. You have long sense turned my regard for you into deep, deep scorn.

Had I known of this statement the day you were here, I should, in the presence of witnesses then and there, spoken it aloud and had you give your proofs; but no, you said nothing of it, for you dared not even allude to such a thing to me, for you know in your heart, if you have any, that it is as false and mean a statement as was ever made.

You know, Allen Dorsey, that when I married you I gave you my whole affection, all that it is possible for any woman to give the man she loves, and what did I receive in return?

If I was not virtuous when I married you there never was a virtuous person. No one living or ever lived can say different, or aught against my character before my marriage. All the wrong I did I did for you and through your influence. Nor have I shielded myself one iota. I have told all the wrong I did, deed by deed, and never have I said aught about you that was untrue. Still you make this mean, audacious statement.

What did Dr. Francis, our family physician, say to you the day you went after him when my father was ill, when you drove to the house together?—What did he say to you in my presence, while he was writing the prescription in the front parlor? There were people in the back parlor at the time who heard his remarks and afterward told me, and who are still living.

He had been our family physician since I was a child and I had been under his care continually. Did he speak aught detrimental about me?

No, Allen Dorsey, you studied and studied to find an excuse rather than tell the real cause of the act, and thought of this. But you will have a chance to prove it. I hope you have now reached the limit of your baseness.

M.A. Dorsey
Howard, RI 4-2-88

P. S.—I am prepared now for anything you will say, for you are capable of saying or doing anything, but be sure and have some foundation, for you will be called upon for proofs.

An additional proof not only of the utter falseness of Dorsey's charge but of the fact that the very idea of it has been conceived since his confinement for the murder of Mr. Burton, will be found in the following two letters which he wrote the second day after his sentence and placed in a trunk addressed to his sister.

The letters are written in pencil on the backs of two Christmas cards and apparently in considerable haste. On the face of one of the cards, along the margin, is written: "Miss Alma J. Dorsey, Oswego, Tioga Co., N. Y." And on the face of the other, "Alma Dorsey," simply. Following are verbatim copies of these letters:

Maria thinks you blame her. I have told her you do not, neither must you. I was to blame. The child I want you to take when some older. If M- gets out in a few years, she has promised me to come to where the child is, and I have promised you will gladly receive her.

Don't blame Emily (Dora) either, it is better as it is. She only did what was right and I don't blame her.

Good by, and may you, after the first blow is over, think kindly of us all. Tell Granny—if I ever come out she will be dead—I never shall forget her, though dead her memory will live with me. Emily and Maria will get out in a few years, that is certain—I am the greater criminal. I may never, still there is always a chance and they have forgiven me.

I was within one year of a happy, brilliant future; my one wicked, bad act crushed it all. My intellect, ability, accomplishments, buried alive in State prison.

If you do have the child, never tell it about the parents, only what you know good of them. I have plenty of friends away from here—same as ever—but none in Newport. Good by. After some days, write me at Howard, R. I. Write Maria, and don't forget about Emily too.

Allen

The other:

Some of the things M- sent in the trunk will do for the baby, when you have him. It will lessen the expense, as I know your circumstances. I thank you more than you know for your sisterly acts, also Mother—a man only has one mother. My fate is a poor return for your kindnesses. But when you think of your Boy—remember me as I was when I first left home.

Make my few clothes over for baby. His name is Eugene Waldorf. You will be a mother to him until M- gets out. I can write once a month; you can write me as often as you like, also to M- and her sister.

Your Bro. Allen

M- is what I made her, for when I married her, she was a pure, virtuous, noble minded girl. I am to blame for all she ever did.

At the request of the few of the late Mr. Burton's friends, desiring to have all the weapons possible with which to crush the lies of the scoundrel Dorsey, Maria has made the following affidavit:

I, Maria B. Dorsey, wife of Allen W. Dorsey, formerly of Newport in Rhode Island, both of us now serving life sentences for the murder of Benjamin J. Burton, late of said Newport, on oath depose and say that my attention has been called to an alleged interview with said Allen, which interview was published in the Boston Herald, of date Sunday, April 1st, 1888, that I deny all and every part of the alleged statements of the said

Allen wherein he charges me with having been criminally intimate with my father, the said Benjamin J. Burton; that at no time before, or after my marriage with the said Allen were my father's relations towards me other than those of the highest, noblest and most pure character; that my father by look, act or word never suggested such relations with me as stated by said Allen W. Dorsey, and I further depose and say that I am entirely innocent of having had any unchaste relations with my father, whose memory has been needlessly and unjustly assailed by said Allen without the slightest excuse or justification therefor.

    (Signed)   *Maria B. Dorsey*

Witness to signature: *James H. Eastman*
STATE OF RHODE ISLAND & c.
Providence & c.
In Cranston, on the 9th day of April, A. D. 1888, said Maria B. Dorsey personally appeared and subscribed and made oath to the truthfulness of the foregoing statement.

                        Frank C. Viall
                        Justice of the Peace

The following affidavit is from Benj. Easton, jr., who at the time of Dorsey's conviction was high sheriff of Newport County and as such in charge of the jail in which Dorsey was confined. It is made in view of the fact that Dorsey has recently denied his share in the crime, asserting that his wife, Maria, did the shooting.

I, Benjamin Easton, Junior, of Newport, in the State of Rhode Island, on oath depose and say that I conversed with Allen W. Dorsey, in the Newport County Jail, on the morning after he was sentenced by the Court for the murder of Benjamin J. Burton, and he then and there told me that he did the act of shooting that caused the death of said Burton.

                        Benj. Easton, Jr.

Subscribed and sworn to in Newport, Rhode Island, this 13th day of April, A. D. 1888,

                   Before me,
                   Patrick J. Galvin, Notary Public."

Afterword

EMILY "DORA" BURTON:

Ben's youngest and most favored child succumbed to consumption on January 16, 1887, during the seventh month of her life sentence. Her sister, Maria, was at her bedside when, as the *Newport Mercury* would later describe, *"her liberation came."*

Dora's body was temporarily entombed at the state prison to await interment in the family plot at the Old North Cemetery. However, her brother, Howard Burton, was unable to raise the necessary funds to have his sister's body transported to Newport for burial. P.J. Galvin offered to pay for the transport, but by the time the ground was thawed enough to excavate the grave, her body was too decomposed to be moved.

Dora's remains were interred in the prison cemetery until her sister's death when Reverend Mahlon Van Horne arranged for the sisters to be buried in the same plot in Newport's Common Burial Ground. Their final resting place is unknown as the grave site is unmarked.

MARIA A. BURTON DORSEY:

At one point during the deliberations in Maria's trial, the jury voted seven to five in favor of acquittal before finding her guilty.

Maria Burton Dorsey died from consumption in December 1889, three years into her life sentence. Had she lived, it would have been highly likely that the Governor would have pardoned her due to the jury's recommendation for mercy.

ALLEN WALDORF DORSEY:

During his time in prison, Allen Dorsey was considered a model prisoner and was afforded many privileges not generally granted to a 19th-century inmate. At that time in Rhode Island, it was typically assumed that prisoners completed their 'life sentence' once they had served 20 years. However, it would take Allen numerous attempts and more than twenty-five years before he finally received a pardon from the Governor in 1912.

Upon parole, he moved to New York City, where he worked as a waiter and porter, eventually remarrying. Five years later, in 1918, Allen would die at the age of 60 in a Manhattan psychiatric hospital. He is buried in an unmarked grave in a Potter's Field in Queens, NY.

CHARLES "HOWARD" BURTON:

The last surviving child of Ben Burton remained in New York City and worked as a telephone operator until his death from Bright's disease in 1907 at the age of 53.

For the remainder of his life, Howard staunchly opposed every petition made by Allen Dorsey to receive a pardon. It was only after Howard's death that Dorsey was successful in his effort.

EUGENE WALDORF DORSEY (EARNEST YOUNG):

Allen and Maria's son, Eugene Waldorf Dorsey (Baby Eugene), was adopted by a Newport couple, Essex Young, and his wife, in January 1887. The Youngs changed the baby's name to Earnest Young and relocated with the child to New York City. Earnest lived in New York until the death of both of his adoptive parents, and at the age of 20, he moved to Virginia.

Earnest never married or had children. He was employed as a farm worker for most of his adult life. His military registration describes him as a light-skinned Black man, five feet two inches tall, with a slender build.

He died in a Virginia nursing home in 1969 at 83. He was the last known direct descendant of Ben Burton.

MRS. CHARLES HOWARD "AUNT EMILY" BURTON:

Following the arrest of Allen and Maria Dorsey, the *Newport Daily News* finally credited Emily for her persistent efforts in bringing the Dorseys to justice.

On the evening of January 24, 1888, while walking home from church services in Providence, Emily suffered a heart attack. She crawled to the doorstep of a private residence, begging for help, but was denied entrance by the homeowners. Emily died on the doorstep and is buried in the Burton family plot in the Old North Cemetery in Newport, next to her husband, Charles Howard Burton.

Her final resting place is only steps from the grave of Ben Burton and his beloved wife, Rosanna.

PATRICK J. "P.J." GALVIN:

The state of Rhode Island took more than two years to compensate P.J. Galvin for his legal services in the Burton inquest and the Dorseys' criminal trial.

Galvin continued his successful legal career in Newport until he died in 1897 at the age of 40. His health had been in a state of decline for several years before he succumbed to pneumonia and sepsis after falling and breaking his leg in his fiancé's Boston townhouse.

His brilliant handling of the Dorseys' trial was highlighted in his obituary.

DETECTIVE BENJAMIN RICHARDS:

Benjamin Richards' reputation as a Pinkerton detective earned him national recognition. As a result of his involvement in the Burton case, he became enamored with Newport and eventually relocated to the City-By-The-Sea.

He began his service with the Newport Police Force as a detective in 1892 before being appointed Chief of Police in 1900. He remained in that position until he died in 1905 from sepsis caused by a burst appendix. He was approximately 50 years of age at the time of his death.

COLONEL WILLIAM P. SHEFFIELD, JR.:

After serving several terms as a representative in the Rhode Island legislature, Sheffield was elected City Solicitor in 1891 and to one term in the U.S. House of Representatives in 1909. He died in 1919 at the age of 62.

The city of Newport named a neighborhood school in his and his father's honor in recognition of their many contributions to the public educational system.

DR. W. THORNTON PARKER:

In June 1887, Dr. Parker presented a paper to the American Medical Association's annual meeting entitled *The Burton Case,* which was published in the Journal of the AMA. In it, Parker summarizes the medical details of the case and the physicians' opinions that supported his testimony that Burton could not have fired the fatal shots.

DR. DAVID HAYES AGNEW:

Although Dr. Agnew never had the opportunity to testify as an expert for the defense in the Dorseys' trial, he presented a paper entitled *Medical and Legal Aspects of Cranial and Heart Wounds* based on the research he prepared for the trial. The paper supported his theory that Ben would have been capable of shooting himself in the chest after he shot himself in the head.

The 1889 graduating class of the University of Pennsylvania Medical College commissioned famed American artist Thomas Eakins to paint Agnew's portrait. The resulting and now famous seven-by-eleven-foot painting, *The Agnew Clinic*, can be viewed at the Philadelphia Museum of Art.

1885 Newport: Then and Now

The north side of Levin Street was demolished in 1967 to widen it to accommodate the increase in traffic between Easton's Beach, Bellevue Avenue, and Thames Street. The street was renamed Memorial Boulevard.

35 LEVIN STREET:

Ben Burton's first home in Newport was demolished as part of the widening of Levin Street to create Memorial Boulevard.

63 LEVIN STREET:

Ben Burton's house and tenements at 63-67 Levin Street were eventually sold by the administrator of his estate at a steep discount to the same person who had previously agreed to purchase the home prior to Ben's death. The structure was eventually condemned and demolished by the city sometime during the 1970's.

Today, Nickolas Pizza occupies the former site of his home and is located at 38 Memorial Blvd West.

49 LEVIN STREET:

The small cottage Ben Burton was building for himself and Dora was completed after his death and is still standing as a private residence at 54 Memorial Blvd. West. It is a two-story structure, and each floor has 491 square feet. The lot size is 1625 feet.

17 THOMAS STREET:

Mary Stoddard's tiny cottage was demolished, and a small empty lot remains today.

58 THAMES STREET:

Emily Burton's boarding house was renovated by the Doris Duke's Newport Restoration Foundation in 1975 and is currently a single-family home.

41 WASHINGTON SQUARE:

The Sheffield Mansion was moved to Touro Street and currently serves as the Youth Center for the Touro Synagogue.

49 DIVISION STREET:

The historic Union Congregational Church building on Division Street still stands and has been converted to condominiums.

13 MARLBOROUGH STREET:

The Newport County Jail became the headquarters for the Newport Police Department until 1986. After the jail was moved to Washington Square, the original building was converted into a popular hotel called The Jailhouse Inn.

127 THAMES STREET:

In 1900, Newport built a new City Hall on Broadway, and the old City Hall (Brick Market)—where the Burton inquest was held—was used for various purposes until purchased by the Newport Historical Society.

Today, the building houses the Historical Society's Museum and gift shop.

OLD COLONY HOUSE:

The Old Colony House, also known as the Old State House, is owned by the State of Rhode Island but managed by the Newport Historical Society.

The colonial-era building where the Dorseys trial was held is the fourth oldest statehouse still standing in the United States. It is open only for special events or private tours. It also houses an original Gilbert Stuart portrait of George Washington.

53 DEARBORN AND CORNER OF SPRING STREET:

The house that P.J. Galvin and his family once occupied remains intact and is privately owned. However, the beautiful gardens, nurseries, and greenhouses that once surrounded it are long gone.

Authors' Note and Acknowledgements

In 2020, the world as we knew it began to change dramatically due to the onset of the Coronavirus. In May of that year, Nancy lost her father to COVID-19. With travel severely restricted, she drove from Rhode Island to Arkansas to collect his ashes and settle his estate. There, Kay welcomed Nancy into her home.

During this quarantine period, we—two lifelong friends who met in elementary school—began discussing the possibility of collaborating on this book. An idea that began on a whim quickly evolved into a 4-year adventure of research and writing.

It is our hope that sharing the story of Benjamin J. Burton's exceptional life and tragic death will help to preserve the legacy of this singular man and of those individuals who courageously fought to bring his killers to justice.

It should be noted that this novel is a fictional account based on a true story. The factual aspects include the names of the individuals, the dates and locations in which the events took place, and the outcome of the legal proceedings. It was our intention to recount the story as accurately as possible, but when records were lacking, we created or altered scenes to fill the gaps.

When feasible, we have utilized direct testimony and actual statements as they were reported in contemporary newspaper accounts. Since the trial transcripts have not survived, we have attempted to present an authentic account of the court proceedings based on our research and consistent with the era. For the reader's benefit, we condensed three separate legal proceedings into two while retaining their salient content and outcomes.

The depiction of the characters is our interpretation based on the available historical record of their lives and commentary made about those individuals by newspaper reporters, friends, or family members. We cannot vouch for the accuracy of the comments, and our portrayal of the characters should be viewed solely as our creation.

The old cliché, *we could not have written this book without the assistance of the following people,* has never been truer due to the restrictions in place during the pandemic. Initially, we relied heavily on archival newspaper accounts and other online resources to gather background information. We sought further assistance from numerous dedicated professionals who were confined to their homes or whose worksites were then closed to the public. These individuals heroically came to our rescue.

We owe a debt of gratitude to Narratively.com, which initially published our long-form narrative, *A Gilded Age Tale of Murder and Madness,* and especially to its founders, Noah Rosenberg and Brendan Spiegel.

We give special thanks to Brendan for his invaluable advice, encouragement, and mentorship, as well as the countless hours he spent patiently editing and gently guiding our storytelling.

We offer our thanks and admiration to the Newport Historical Society staff who work tirelessly to preserve Newport's renowned history, and especially Ingrid Peters and Bertram Lippincott III, for their support and assistance with researching the Burton family.

We want to acknowledge Reference Archivist Ken Carlson of the Rhode Island Department of State for fulfilling our numerous requests for Burton's family probate records and the prison records of Allen and Maria Dorsey. It was Ken who uncovered the original handwritten letters penned by the Dorseys and placed them in our eager hands.

We would also like to thank the following:

The staff of the University of Pennsylvania Medical School Archives who provided us with Allen Dorsey's student records.

Andrew Smith, Administrative Assistant for the Rhode Island Supreme Court Judicial Records Center for tracking down the surviving records regarding the Dorsey trial.

Kate Wells, the Curator of Rhode Island Collections at the Providence Public Library, who provided newspaper accounts of the Burton inquest and the Dorseys' criminal trial that were unavailable on other online sites at the time.

Joyce Tice with the History Center of Bradford County, Pennsylvania, for assisting with our research regarding the Dorsey Family history in Athens, Pennsylvania.

Gloria Miller of New Haven, Connecticut, who shared her ancestral connection to Burton family and graciously assisted us during our early days of digging into the Burton family records.

The knowledgeable and dedicated assistance of the reference staff at the Rhode Island Historical Society, the Newport Public Library, and Newport City Hall.

Cathy Markey, our first copy editor, whose editing skills and critical input were invaluable to the development of the novel.

Roy Lee Jackson, for suffering through the reading and editing of the first of many, many drafts of this book.

Finally, our families for their enduring love and unconditional support.

Joseph Markey, Jackson Markey, and Jonnie Markey
and
Laura Weiderhaft and Gracie Weiderhaft

9 781968 954000